Lizzie Harper

Maria Monk's daughter

an autobiography

Lizzie Harper

Maria Monk's daughter
an autobiography

ISBN/EAN: 9783741112249

Manufactured in Europe, USA, Canada, Australia, Japa

Cover: Foto ©Raphael Reischuk / pixelio.de

Manufactured and distributed by brebook publishing software
(www.brebook.com)

Lizzie Harper

Maria Monk's daughter

MARIA MONK'S DAUGHTER;

AN

AUTOBIOGRAPHY.

BY

MRS. L. ST. JOHN ECKEL.

LONDON:

BURNS AND OATES, 17, PORTMAN STREET, W.

1880.

PREFACE.

IN the following pages I may say many severe things about my mother. Well, I know that the world will throw the reproach in my face, that " she was your mother, and God commands us to honour our parents."

To this I must answer: It is not that I hate the memory of my father or my mother; but duty and religion alike compel me to expose the injustice and calumny that my mother heaped upon the Roman Catholic Church and her religious Orders.

The truth of my sister's statement, that she knew my mother's book to be a lie, as my mother had told her so, is fully confirmed by the statement of Colonel Stone, the Protestant editor of the *New York Commercial Advertiser*, who made a personal examination of the Hotel Dieu Convent at Montreal.

I appeal to the hearts of all Christian mothers and ask them, Who is my mother? I can already hear their reply: " that the Catholic Church is my mother:" for it was she who took me by the hand and raised me out of the abyss of spiritual misery into which the faults of my parents had helped to plunge me. It was through her that God first gave light to my soul, which she has nourished by her teachings until at last she has wedded me to my God. If the mother who bore me has claims on me, the mother who saved me has still greater; and it is to satisfy these that God in His justice and mercy inspired me to write this book.

The critics of the book will find severest things to say of the personal history of the author, and from her own showing. But they will not make me out as bad as I know myself to have been.

I would have told more of my miseries, if it could have served any good purpose; and I would not tell less, because I would encourage those who have suffered, and groped, and wandered, and sinned like me, to seek pardon and peace where I found them.

I have lived over again in these pages the follies of my life, and dwelt upon frivolities, upon which with God's grace I have turned my back for ever, to lead others through them, as I have been led myself, to the knowledge of the truth and the love of the only life that is worth living. May it please God to make such portions of my history effective warnings to those of my readers who have not yet found by their own experience the bitterness of sin and the emptiness of the world, so that of no one of them may it ever be said with truth: " It is thy own history," —*de te fabula narratur.*

London, April 23*rd,* 1880

MARIA MONK'S DAUGHTER.

CHAPTER I.

TICK.

Tick's Family—Tick's Portrait—Domestic Scenes—Tick's Companions—
Hard Knocks—A Legacy.

IN the year 1843 a family of the name of St. John occupied
the first floor and basement of a tenement-house in Goerck
Street, in the city of New York. The basement was used as a
kitchen and sleeping apartment for the servant. The first floor
consisted of two rooms; the front one of which was occupied as
a bedroom, and the back one did the double service of a dining
and sitting room. The front one was covered with a cheap,
faded, ingrain carpet, while a dirty rag carpet did a similar duty
for the other, and a few cheap articles completed the furnishing
of both. On the walls of these dingy and scantily-furnished
apartments hung five or six rare oil paintings of great value.
They were the only articles of luxury, and they formed a strange
and cheering contrast to the meanness of all else.

The family consisted of four persons—the father, mother, and
two little daughters. The father might have been forty; but
the deep furrows on his face showed premature signs of age.
He had been a wild boy; had run away from home; had been
to sea, and had travelled nearly all over the world, and would
never return to his boyhood's home, unless driven by misery, ill
health, or despair. He was his mother's favourite son, and the
pet of his aunt Huldah (his mother's sister): they both doted
upon him, and would receive the prodigal with open arms and
forgiving hearts whenever he would appeal to them for shelter
or assistance. He had four brothers then living, all of whom
had risen to wealth and position. The St. Johns were said to be
descended from one of the noblest English families. They
traced their genealogy to Henry St. John, Lord Bolingbroke.
Mr. St. John's brothers were his very opposites. They were
energetic, industrious, and ambitious. They all spurned and

shunned their erring brother, and left him to that lot which usually befalls those who prefer pleasure to labour and the gratification of their passions to the fulfilment of duty. His follies had been many, and his punishment was severe.. The hour of retribution had come, and demanded payment for a misspent life, and it found him ill prepared to acquit himself of the debt : for his mind had always been set on what the world calls pleasure—on being free and untrammelled by the restraints of the laws of God and well-regulated society. He had no religious convictions, and therefore nothing to sustain him in this combat with misfortune and misery. He stood, or rather lay, thoroughly defenceless in their iron grasp.

The woman whom he called his wife, and with whom, in an evil hour, he had linked his destiny, was the instrument Providence had chosen to bring the misguided man to repentance. She was in her twenty-sixth year, and might once have been handsome ; but a life of misery and sin had already robbed her cheeks of their roses and her form of the graces of youth. She was short in stature, thick-set, with oval features, dark-grey eyes, and long brown hair. The reader can best judge of her character and disposition from her acts.

The eldest daughter, whom I will call Georgina, must then have been in her eighth year. Her large hazel eyes lighted up a face of Grecian mould and matchless beauty. She had a quick aptitude for acquiring knowledge, and at that early age would read story-books and the newspapers aloud to her mother

The expression of her face was cold and sad, and bespoke what she really was, the offspring of misfortune. Her nature was proud and wilful. She had never been treated like a child ; she had been fed upon praise from her mother's breast, and whatever she did or said was considered perfect. Every childish wish was gratified, and her family treated her as though they were only there to do her homage. Yet, notwithstanding such a pernicious course of early training, she was superior to most children of her years, and even at that tender age her actions were guided more by reflection than by childish impulse.

The younger daughter was just the opposite of her sister in looks, in character, and in disposition. She was in her sixth year ; and as she had never been known to keep still everybody called her " Tick." She was very homely—so homely, that the boys in the streets would make fun of her, and her mother and sister would constantly tell her, that " she was the ugliest child they had ever seen." She had a round face, a bad complexion, a pug nose, and short hair, with no head at all—I mean no sense in her head,—or she had what the French would call *une tête à l'envers*.

She always acted from impulse; never from reflection. With her there was never a moment's pause between the conception of an idea and its execution, when possible; and from the rapidity of her acts and the serious consequences they would often entail, she had become the terror, the dislike, and the butt of the household. She was by no means a fool; she was always saying or doing some extraordinary thing, and her life at that age was made up of being scolded, beaten, or laughed at. Her eyes were not large and beautiful, like those of her sister, but when she was excited they would sparkle like fire. Their colour and expression always depended on Tick's emotions: they were the only redeeming feature in that little, ugly face. She was small, thin, and quick as a flash. She had long been accustomed to come head-first down the steps, and the family said that it was at the foot of a long flight of stairs that Tick got her ill-shaped nose. Tick never looked tidy; her face and hands were almost always dirty, and her hair was rarely combed. It made very little difference to her whether her hair was combed or her face washed or not, since, in any case, everybody who saw her for the first time would invariably exclaim: "What an ugly child!" while the first sight of her sister would elicit expressions of admiration for her beauty.

Georgina was Tick's half-sister; Mr. St. John was not her father. He had adopted her. She went by his name, and called him father. The lives of the two sisters seemed to be distinct. Georgina was treated like a lady, but Tick like a household drudge, who could be kicked and cuffed about at the pleasure and whim of each. Tick's father was the only one who never spoke unkindly to her; he never gave her a blow. Georgina was supposed to speak the truth always, Tick never.

The mother loved her eldest daughter, yet Georgina feared her mother's ill-temper; for, when she was angry, she would abuse this daughter with harsh words and threatening looks, yet she seldom struck her.

The mother and eldest daughter were more like friends than parent and child; for the mother would impart to her all her secrets, even the most delicate. Georgina can say with truth that she never was a child. They would sit and converse together for hours; yet they seldom spoke to Tick—the mother never, unless it was to scold her or to give her an order. But Tick was an attentive listener to what they were saying, and she would roll it over and over in her mind. The mother would ever talk against the father, and would make threats and declare that she would be revenged, and Georgina would abuse him too. Mr. St. John loved Georgina better than his own child; but she never returned his affection. It made Tick sad to hear them abuse her father, for she loved him, although she knew that she only stood second in his heart. She was only too grateful for such love as he gave her, it was the only ray of light that feebly glimmered for her in that wretched home.

Mr. St. John and his wife hated each other, and they were nearly always quarrelling. Neither ever went to church; yet the mother would frequently go out during the week—no one ever knew where, nor when she would return. It would always enrage the husband to find his wife absent. Georgina would then try to soften him, and pretend that she knew where her mother was, and would say everything she could to excuse her absence. The mother usually returned intoxicated, and a dreadful scene would ensue. The husband would load her with accusations, of which Tick did not understand the meaning. He would attempt to strike her; but Georgina would go between them to defend her mother, and her presence and tears would always calm the infuriated husband.

During those scenes Tick would get into a corner and kneel behind a chair, through the back of which she would peep, till all was over; when she would say to her sister: "Why did you not let him strike her?" Then her sister would reproach Tick for heartlessness towards her mother. But Tick could not feel the reproach; for she never loved her mother. She had always feared her. Tick cannot remember that her mother ever kissed her, and Tick can remember ever since she was three years old. But what could have been the secret of this mother's aversion for her child, which seemed to amount almost to hatred? She would beat her, as though she were gratifying some secret desire for vengeance. Was it because she was the child of her hated husband? or did the devil, without her knowing it, inspire her to pour out her wrath upon the child, who would one day try to undo her work?

Tick had a hard life of it; yet she was always gay. Five minutes after being beaten she could laugh as merrily as though she had never been struck a blow in her life. She was always happy when she was alone, either in the house or in the streets, or when her father was at home, which was very seldom. She had few companions; and those were among the worst children who ran the streets. No one liked her mother, and, consequently, the neighbours would refuse to let their children go with her.

When at home alone, she would amuse herself by talking to herself, to the chairs, the table-legs, to the pictures on the wall, to the footstool, and to the shovel and tongs—making believe that the tongs were a boy and the shovel a girl; and she would name each object after the boys or girls she liked or hated most. On the former she would bestow caresses and good marks, and the latter she would beat with the poker. The furniture was thus frightfully marred, and sometimes broken; but no one knew how it was done, and the fault was generally laid to the servant. This was one of Tick's favourite sports, and she began to form attachments for the objects in the room, as though they were living beings. They were the only companions who never gave her pain and always brought her joy. She loved dearly, too, to roam by herself through the streets, and talk aloud to herself without being noticed, or to sit on the curbstone and swim her shoes in the gutter.

Mr. St. John often threatened to abandon his wife if she would not reform, and he would have done so long before, had it not been for his attachment to her child. The mother took advantage of this; for whenever he would threaten to leave her, she would always say: " But my child remains with me ;" and the afflicted man would submit to stay for Georgina's sake. He foresaw too well the inevitable doom which awaited her if he abandoned her to the care of her mother.

Tick inherited her father's qualities and disposition. It had always been a trait of the St. Johns to have a remarkable memory. Tick had inherited that quality in an eminent degree. She resembled her father in everything but his movements ; for he was slow and languid in his gait, whereas Tick's every motion was as quick as lightning. To be put out of the way, she had been sent to a public school before she had completed her fourth year. Here nothing escaped her that she could take in with her eyes and ears ; but her restless nature would not allow her to apply herself. She could repeat the alphabet as fast as her sister, although she did not know one letter from the other.

Georgina was a beautiful reader—and Tick would tease her until she read to her all about Polly Bodine's trial. Tick had heard everyone talking about it, and she was much interested to know if she should be hanged or not. For Tick her father used to buy playthings, but books for Georgina. Their mother, too, would sometimes buy books and playthings for her elder daughter, but never anything for Tick. Finally, about this time, Tick became a sort of confirmed vagabond. When out of school she was always in the street. Her mother became every day more cruel to her, and Tick avoided her as much as she could.

The cruel treatment she received never cowed Tick's spirit. Georgina seldom dared to strike her, for Tick would make a stout defence. She neither loved, hated, envied, nor imitated her sister; and in spite of all the hard knocks she received, she always chose to be herself rather than anybody else. In spite of her mother's cruelty, Tick pitied that mother, when she saw her afflicted and wretched and in tears; she could have thrown her arms around her neck and kissed her, had she dared to.

Her mother would often send the child for beer, and it was with a heavy heart that she brought it; for she knew that it was so much fuel for the drunken wrath that was sure to burst on her own devoted head. Georgina would seldom go on this errand, but would on her knees implore her mother to do without it. The mother would sometimes yield, but would oftener become impatient and threaten. Georgina, too, dreaded her mother when intoxicated, and then she would stay near to Tick and talk with her.

When Tick was six years old, a little stranger came to gladden the father's heart, in the person of an infant son.

From Goerck Street the family moved to a house out of which they were turned by the landlord, on account of the mother's quarrels with the neighbours. Then they moved into a rear house, whose only yard was the wretched alley-way. They had not been there long, when one day the father came home jubilant, with the good news that his uncle, Samuel St. John, of New Haven, who had just died, had left him an annuity, and also a small one for each of his children when they should come of age. The next day he took Georgina, Tick, and his son, who was then over a year old, and went to an office, where a gentleman handed him a book. He placed his right hand on it, and swore that the three children were his own. His love for Georgina caused him to take a false oath, and it was that false oath that sealed his doom. His family had already shunned him for his vices, but now they shrank from him as a perjurer. His crime might have ever remained a secret, had not the woman, for whose unfortunate child he had sacrificed his conscience, spitefully betrayed him.

When Mr. St. John returned home, after taking this oath, he began to converse with his wife. The usual quarrel ensued. She rose from her seat, raised her hand, and swore, that she would be revenged. Her heart was filled with rage and hate.

She loved her elder daughter, but her hate was stronger than her love. She had long thirsted for a full revenge for all the real or imaginary wrongs she had treasured up against her weak and erring husband. At last that long-wished-for hour had come. The next day found this woman in the same office, where her husband had stood the day before. She laid her hand on that little Bible, which he had desecrated for her child, and there swore that her husband was a perjurer; that only the two younger children were his, and that her eldest child was born before she knew him who called himself its father. This voluntary declaration on the part of a woman who claimed to be his wife, cast doubts even upon his marriage to her, which his pride could not permit him to remove, and the misguided man, who but a few hours before was revelling in bright hopes of a happy future for his children, and for the child he had taken to his heart, saw those hopes for ever extinguished. He humbly acknowledged his fault, but declared that, in forswearing himself, he had only yielded to the earnest solicitations of his wife. His uncle had left a large fortune, providing annuities for the five brothers, his nephews, and their descendants, to the third generation. The estate was only finally to be divided when the youngest of the last generation should have reached his majority. All this was devised in order that the St. Johns might remain for at least four generations without wanting for bread. Mr. St. John swore that he was really married to the woman, who had so ruthlessly betrayed him. But he would not give her *maiden name*. As he had once taken a false oath, the executors refused to receive his two children as heirs, unless he should produce his marriage certificate, signed by responsible witnesses. This he refused to do; for it must bear *that woman's name*. No, never would he breathe the name of her, whom Providence, as a just punishment for his sins, had thrown across his path. And thus were his children not only deprived of future support and left to an inheritance of misery and danger, but they were branded before the public with the shameful stigma of *bastards*.

These new domestic griefs had not much power to depress the buoyant spirits of Tick. She could readily forget them all in the delight of an occasional trip with her father across the water to Williamsburg. She would stand at the back of the ferry-boat, as if riveted to the deck, watching the waves, and with no eyes for anything else. Tick was fond of building castles in the air. She would sometimes tie her mother's apron on behind her, to form a train, and would make a paper crown and put it on her head, and in that guise she would promenade up and down the room or the alley, imagining that she was in a palace, and that she was herself a queen or the lady-love of some prince ; and she would sigh to be big enough to wear long clothes, believing, that when that day came, she would be presented at court, and the courtiers would vie to do her homage. For her sister read aloud stories of kings and queens and courtiers and palaces, and her father, too, would tell what he had seen in England ; and she fancied that it must be the acme of all happiness to go to court and revel in its pleasures.

CHAPTER II.

MARIA MONK.*

Misery—A narrow Escape—Abandoned.

ONE day Tick and her mother were alone, when two rough-looking men came in.   The three entered into conversation. At last one of the men spoke out : " I know who you are, *you are Maria Monk !* " It was the first time Tick had ever heard that name. Many years have passed since then, but Tick has never forgotten the dread feeling that came over her the first time that fatal name fell upon her ears. Then both the men spoke up and said : " We know you are Maria Monk ;" but the mother denied it. Frequently, after that, people would come in and repeat those same words. After a while, Tick would hear her mother acknowledge to one woman, that she *was* Maria Monk, and deny it to another ; but at last she ceased to deny it to anyone, and would tell everybody that that was her name. There was something in that name which displeased Tick, yet she could not tell why. Although she was hardened in sin, and had not much fine feeling to boast of, and was considered the bully of the alley, yet she felt ashamed that her mother's name should be Maria Monk. She could not have felt worse if it had been Polly Bodine. The neighbours became so troublesome at last, by constantly coming in and bringing others to see Maria Monk, that the St. Johns were obliged to leave the neighbourhood.

The family had been getting more and more miserable, and their home was now so wretched, that the father dreaded to come

* Early in the year 1836 a book appeared entitled, " AWFUL DIS-CLOSURES OF MARIA MONK." The book was a tissue of calumnies against the inmates of the Hôtel Dieu, or Black Nunnery, in Montreal. Maria Monk represented herself to be an escaped nun from that convent. The reader will learn more of her book in the course of this history.

near it. Although Mr. St. John received the annuity left him by his uncle, yet it did not seem to better his condition ; for his family would live for a few days sumptuously, and like beggars the rest of the year. They had long since done without a servant. Georgina, who was in her tenth year, did all the indoor work, while Tick did all the errands. The only trouble about sending Tick on errands was, that they could never depend on her. If she met an organ-grinder, she felt as though it looked mean and poor to pass him by without giving him something, and the money that was intended to buy a loaf of bread, would oftentimes be put in the outstretched paw of a monkey. The father used sometimes to give Georgina the money to provide for the family, and she would have to conceal it from the mother, lest she should force her to give it to her for beer. Oftentimes the mother would go off ; and the father would come home late and find the three little children sitting disconsolate around the stove, the youngest crying with hunger. The girls, too, were hungry, but they were long accustomed to that.

One day the mother told Georgina to get the baby ready, and that they all should go down by the river for a walk. Georgina commenced to do as she was told ; but suddenly she stopped, and seemed buried in thought. She felt that something was wrong. It was a strange thing for her mother to do, for she seldom took any of her children out with her. Georgina refused to go, or to get the children ready. A loud altercation took place between them. The next day there was a repetition of the same thing. The next morning Tick saw her father and sister in close conversation in the little hall. She listened, and heard Georgina hint her suspicions. The father was convinced that her suspicions were too well founded, for his wife had often threatened to drown her children. Tick heard her father say that her mother intended to throw all her children into the river and then jump in herself.

Tick's heart was drawn towards her sister, as she remembered the scene of the previous day, when the mother had upbraided her, and she herself had joined in, and begged her to go and do as her mother wished. And she recalled her sister's quiet and firm attitude, and how she had said to Tick : "*And you shall not go either ;*" and Tick had felt like striking her for speaking to her with so much authority.

In spite of her reckless head, Tick appreciated and admired the wisdom and fortitude of the girl, who, in fact, was not three years older than herself. She felt that it was time for her too to be a woman, and accordingly she made up her mind to be serious,

and devote herself to her sister. The father left, and so did Tick.
She went out and played in the streets all day, and never thought
for a moment of what might be going on in the house.   That
evening she learned from the conversation of her father and sister,
that the mother had sold all their furniture for the sum of three
dollars.   She was then out; and as she had money they were
expecting, or rather fearing, that she might come in at any
moment drunk.

The furniture was all in disorder; some of it had already been
carried away, and the man was coming for the rest in the morning.   Tick's heart was desolate, because she missed the very
pieces of furniture that she most loved to talk to.   The father
was standing, his little boy was looking up into his face, and
held up his hands for his father to take him; but the father was
so intent on what he was saying to Georgina, that he did not
appear to notice either Tick or her brother.   "I shall leave her
this very night," said he; "will *you* come with me?"   At those
words Tick made a spring, and clasped her father's side, and
cried out: "O father! let us go before she comes back."
Georgina was quite as ready to go as Tick, for the last week's
experience had frightened her so, that she was only too glad to
get away from such a mother.   Mr. St. John took his family to
a neighbour's, who sympathised with him, knowing the dissolute
habits of his wife.   The next day, towards evening, he called
for them.   He took up his son on his arm, and they started out,
Georgina on one side and Tick on the other.   Tick took hold of
her father's hand and began to skip—her usual gait.   They had
hardly gone a dozen steps before they were in front of a grog-
shop.   Tick casually looked into the grog-shop as she skipped
along.   It was a hurried glance, but long enough for her to see
a woman, with drunken gestures, standing bareheaded in the
middle of the floor, her back partly turned towards the street.
It was her mother.   That was the last time I ever saw MARIA
MONK.

CHAPTER III.

TICK IN HER NEW HOME—LONGS AT LAST FOR THE OLD ONE.

Roaming.

FEELINGS of joy and sadness alternately flitted through me,
as I skipped by my father's side.   In spite of my giddiness I
inquired of myself what would become of her.   I asked my
father twice, who would take care of *her*.   He made no reply,

but continued to talk with my sister. I did not love my mother;
but at the thought that she had been abandoned without the
smallest resource, I forgot my wrongs. If my father had only
said that he would take care of her, I could have given myself
up fully to the joy of leaving her: but pity prevented my being
happy. Poor mother! If she had known my heart at that
moment, I am sure that she would have repented of all her
unkindness to me. I tried to get her out of my mind; but she
was ever before me, just as I had seen her in that hurried
glance. Yet I would not have gone back to her for worlds.

We stopped before a beautiful house near St. John's Park.
Father said to us that it was there we were to live. It was a
boarding-house kept by a lady named Beecher. She received us
kindly, but at once exclaimed: "Why, I never would have taken
them for sisters!" She kissed Georgina, took my brother on her
knee, threw a glance at me, slightly frowned, and paid me no
more attention. My father requested her not to let us go into
the street, lest we should meet our mother or some of her
acquaintances; for he was afraid that she might give him trouble
on Georgina's account, and he was determined to do everything
to save her.

I said to my sister several times: "I wonder how *she* felt when
she found herself abandoned?" (We never called her mother.)
Georgina would answer: "I don't know; it served her right;
but let us not speak of *her*." And in a few weeks all mention
of *her* ceased between us.

After a while my vagabond propensities came back in full
force, and I longed to run in the streets. At length my father
consented that I might walk up and down a few blocks near the
house. I stretched the permission by roaming about the streets
and running in the park. But there I soon began to feel lonely;
for the nice children kept to themselves, and I felt above playing
with vagrants, now that I wore fine clothes. But they must
have had an instinct which told them that I was no better than
they, for they would look at me and make faces. I therefore
soon avoided the park, and would pass my time strolling through
the streets and getting free rides on the steps of omnibuses, at
the expense of an occasional lashing from the whip of the driver.

One day I resented vigorously my sister's attempt to make me
wear her old clothes. Mrs. Beecher took sides with her, and
emphasised her view of the matter by throwing me on a bed and
giving me a good beating. She left me, and I fell asleep. When
I awoke I immediately wished myself back again in the old
wretched home with my mother: for a mother can do many

cruel things, which a child will readily forgive and forget, while the tithe of such provocation from a stranger may engender a spirit of hatred, which only a miracle of God's grace can overcome.

We were soon put to board in the country, at Flatbush, where my sister engrossed the company of girls of equal age and refinement with herself, leaving me to myself or to play with the boys. This was a new and delightful experience for the cramped spirit of a child, to whom the most familiar landscape hitherto had been the rear view of tenement-houses. I revelled day after day running in the meadows, chasing the butterflies and gathering wild flowers; and sometimes our host would take us to the seashore, where my freed soul found new delights in the shells, the sands, and the waters.

CHAPTER IV.

TICK GOES A SHOPPING—SHE ASPIRES TO BE A RAGPICKER—HER
ASPIRATIONS KNOCKED IN THE HEAD

Hopes of Fortune.—Disappointment.

SHORTLY after our return to the city the quarrels between my sister and myself became so frequent and so violent, that our father thought well to separate us, and placed me to board with a dressmaker. As the dressmaker was always busy, I was left to run the streets and do as I pleased. Sometimes I would pass days going from one shop to another, asking the prices of things, with perhaps only one cent in my pocket; and no matter what the price of an article might be, if I wanted it, I would try to coax the shopkeeper to give it to me for the amount of money I might have. At last two shopwomen took such a dislike to me, that they would lie in wait for me, and, if I attempted to pass beyond the sills of their shops, they would seize me and give me a good shaking.

One day I had only a penny, and I wanted to buy half a·yard of ribbon for my doll. I entered a fancy shop, and made a woman unroll all the narrow ribbon she had at two cents a yard. When I had made my choice, I said I would take *half* a yard, at the same time handing her the penny. She took it, threw it out on the sidewalk, and told me to go after it, and never dare to come into her shop again. The very same day I saw in a shop window a little bottle of perfumery, which I coveted very much. I eagerly inquired the price. It was twelve cents; and I had only *one*. I begged the woman to give it to me for that. She sarcastically advised me to wait till I had more to put with it. On my way home I met a ragpicker, and as I had always been told that all ragpickers were rich, I took it into my head that I should go at once to work, and make a fortune at ragpicking; and that then I could buy what I pleased.

By the time I got home I found that it was too late to begin that day, as it was nearly dusk. The next morning, after breakfast, while the dressmaker was clearing away the table, I went into the kitchen, took the market-basket and the poker, and started out. But I wandered through street after street, in the broiling sun, without finding a rag, or so much as a piece of paper. At last I was tired, for I found the basket and poker a load in themselves; and I wheeled about and started for home. I had nearly reached the house, when I met a ragpicker with a great lot of rags in a basket fastened to her back. I instantly accosted her and cried out: "Old woman, tell me where you found all those rags? I have been hunting through the streets ever since breakfast, and have not found one yet." The old woman passed on in contemptuous silence; but I ran until I got directly in front of her, and said, this time rather coaxingly: "Oh, Mrs. Ragpicker, won't you p-l-e-a-s-e tell me where you found all those rags?" At that the ragpicker assumed an infuriated mien, particularly when her eyes fell on my basket and poker; and before I had a chance to divine what was coming, she struck me a blow on the head with her hook, and then started off on a half run. As I went into the house with my hand pressed upon my smarting head, I met the dressmaker. The moment she saw me with her market-basket she flew into a rage, seized the poker, and exclaiming, "You little imp!" began to beat me over the shoulders with it, telling me at the same time, in a screaming voice, how I had made her lose all the morning hunting through the house for her market-basket and poker.

By such rude blows were dashed my first bright hopes of fortune!

My father and sister seldom came to see me; and if my sister stayed over an hour, our interview would always end in a quarrel.

My father had often spoken to us of a beautiful country,—the land where his aunt Huldah lived; and he would tell us how kind she had ever been to him, never refusing him the aid he asked of her. One day he told us that his aunt had proposed, if he would let her have his little son, to bring him up and leave to him all she had. He was ever talking of that country, and promising to take us there; and he would sometimes add that it would be a very secure place in which to hide us from our mother. Georgina and myself, who rarely agreed on any point, would beg him in unison to take us to that country. He was always shifting us about, through constant dread of our mother. In the course of these migrations we found ourselves again at Flatbush ; when our father came for us one day, and told us that he had decided to take us to Amenia, the country he loved so much, and where he had passed his happiest days.

We returned to New York, where our father bought us several handsome suits of clothes, made of the richest and finest material, so that any one who saw us as we started for Amenia might have believed that we were spoiled children of fortune. As the boat moved slowly away from the dock, I gladly bade New York good-bye, little thinking how that journey was big with my destiny. We landed at Poughkeepsie ; and early the next morning we started for Aunt Huldah's in South Amenia, Dutchess Co., N. Y., where we arrived about noon, after a drive of twenty-five miles. Our father told us never to mention our mother's name, and if anyone should ever speak to us about her, to say that she was dead, that she had died long ago, and that we had forgotten her.

CHAPTER V.

MY AUNTS—A STURDY METHODIST—THE HIGHLANDS OF DUTCHESS.

The wild Woods—A Child of Nature—My first Love.

AUNT HULDAH was near to her seventieth year. She had never been married, and had always regarded our father as her son. She received us all as affectionately as if we were her children.

Our father was noted for his fondness for children, and for making great sacrifices to aid any unfortunate child that might cross his path. Years before the time I am describing he had brought to Aunt Huldah a little orphan girl, whom he prevailed upon her to adopt.

This child had grown to be a woman, and had married, and resided about two miles from our aunt's house. My father decided to place me with her, to prevent the usual quarrels with my sister. He counted on this woman's gratitude, and thought she would be a mother to his child. But she had no sooner seen me fondling my father, and seen my trunk upacked, than she became envious and jealous, and began to complain that my father had never bought her as many nice things. We had hardly been together a day before we hated each other.

She was a spoiled child. Aunt Huldah had always indulged her, and she was the person least fitted to have the care of a wilful little creature like myself. She was poor, miserly, lazy, and cruel. She treated me as badly as my mother had done, even worse, for she used to beat me with a cane, whereas my mother used only her hands.

I went there in the autumn; and I passed the long winter, suffering with hunger and cold, and longing for my father's return. The view from the house was bleak and desolate. For hours I would sit at the window, which looked out on that dreary landscape, hoping to see my father enter the gate; and I would often ask the woman when she thought he would come. This provoked her, and she would answer, that she hoped he would come soon, that she might let him know what an imp I was.

One day I went to see my sister. Aunt Huldah ran to the gate to receive me; but before she could open it, I began to tell her how cruelly this woman treated me. Aunt Huldah, who was fond of her adopted daughter, took instantly a bitter dislike to me, for she did not believe that what I said could be true. In this opinion my sister confirmed her, by declaring that I had never been known to speak the truth.

A few days afterwards Aunt Huldah sent for my torturer, and told her what I had said. She denied it all, and Aunt Huldah's bad opinion of me was irrevocably fixed. The woman came home, and from that time her treatment of me was simply inhuman.

I would often wonder what my father had ever seen in that land to love.

At last summer came, and one bright morning brought my father. The woman complained of me, and would give me no opportunity to speak with him alone. When they had all retired, I arose and crept softly to my father's bed. He took me in his arms; I nestled in his bosom, and began to weep. He whispered to me to " hush," for fear the woman might hear me. I soon fell asleep, and in the morning I told him all. He kissed me, but made no reply.

The next day my father came with a Mr. Clark, one of his cousins, and told me that he would take me where I would have a good home. It was a beautiful day in the middle of June, 1847. I sat on my father's knee as we drove along. We passed towards the south through a beautiful fertile valley, bordered on the east and west by ranges of hills known as the " Highlands of Dutchess." At the foot of the western slope flows a narrow, limpid stream, which still retains its Indian name of the Weebatuc. We did not drive far before we made an abrupt turn to the east, and, in a few moments, we were ascending a hill. It seemed to me as if I had just seen the country for the first time. I could not help exclaiming all along the way : " How beautiful !" I had been in the country eight months, and had done nothing but weep and mourn by the side of that cruel woman. But now I was once more with my father. Every few moments I would throw my arms around his neck and make him promise me that he would never take me back to that home again. I was happy, and everything around me seemed to smile and rejoice with me.

As we ascended the hill we could see birds of nearly every note and hue fluttering along the rustic fences which lined the road ; and on either side were flocks of sheep grazing, while their lambs were skipping and playing in the noontide sun. When we reached the summit of this hill a most beautiful landscape spread itself on every side, and a delicious little vale lay at our feet, with but one solitary humble dwelling, occupied by one of my father's cousins. In passing through this charming valley we halted for a few moments at the house, and we were soon surrounded by merry children, who fairly made the hills ring with their hearty welcome. We had still another long hill to climb before we could reach my future home. The left of this steep was bordered by a long ledge of rocks, out of which sprung a lofty chestnut grove. On the right could be seen, for miles, the surrounding country ; and as we advanced, the scenery appeared ever to grow more beautiful. A little further and we came to an open level space, which was hemmed in by forests and hills. To the left stood a little white cottage, with rose-bushes at the door, and shaded by cherry-trees laden with fruit. It was there that I was to find that " good home," which my father had promised me.

I ran into the house, and was most kindly welcomed by its inmates. It was neatly furnished, and everything breathed comfort and happiness. The family consisted of Mr. Clark and his wife, and Aunt Lavinia, who was sister to my father's mother. Mr. and Mrs. Clark had passed the middle age, and were known throughout the country as uncle Horace and Aunt Mercy. They owned a large farm, and were in comfortable circumstances. They made much ado over me, fondled and caressed me, and laughed at everything I said. They examined me from head to foot, and said that I was the very image of the St. Johns : that my face was the image of my father's mother, and the expression of my countenance, my quick mode of speaking, and a nervous move-

ment of my head, when trying to bring out my thoughts, showed
a most striking family likeness. The next day my father left for
New York. He took my sister with him, but left my brother
with Aunt Huldah.

Our nearest neighbours were a poor family, whom I will designate as the Dot family. The wife was a weaver, and the husband
a mason. My Uncle Orin's house was in sight of our cottage;
he was Uncle Horace's brother.

I was sent immediately to school. The school-house was
situated down in the valley, about a mile and a quarter from my
home, and very near Aunt Huldah's.

Without any cause whatever I disliked my Aunt Mercy at first
sight; but she soon won me by her kind and tender devotion to
me. It was the first time I had ever received a mother's care,
and I at once changed and became one of the best children in
the place.

The Clarks were all high-toned and devout. Uncle Horace
was a plain, honest, blunt-spoken man. He tried hard to live
up to the golden rule, of doing unto others as he would have
them do to him. He was a firm believer in the doctrines of
Christianity as expounded by John Wesley. He was devoted to
his church, and thoroughly believed that the Methodists *alone*
possessed the perfect knowledge of the way to salvation. He
had strong prejudices against Catholics; he was always abusing
them; his house was well supplied with books breathing hostility
against them; and he believed every absurd statement he had
read concerning them. He was to be pitied for his ignorance,
but not to be despised, for he was sincere. His wife also tried to be
a good Christian. She possessed a character with many excellent
traits; but its equanimity was sometimes disturbed by a quick
temper, which she was too proud to conceal and too weak to
control. She was strictly moral, and had an instinctive hatred
of vice.

My uncle and aunt had never had any children, and it was for
this reason that my coming was hailed with so much joy. I was
sent regularly to school, to church, and to Sunday-school. I
tried to be good, and had ceased to tell falsehoods. I liked
everybody and tried hard to please everybody. I was never
punished, and seldom reproved. As my father paid for my board,
Aunt Mercy's conscientiousness would not permit me to render
her the slightest assistance in her work; and, when I offered to
do so, she would always tell me to go and play. When I would
go to romp in the woods, she would dress me up in old
clothes, so that I could soil and tear them as much as I

liked; and she never scolded me when I returned. Sometimes she would give me a lunch, and I would remain away nearly the whole day. Everything was peace and comfort in that little mountain home, and everything breathed joy and happiness for me in the woods and hills that surrounded it.

During the harvest months there was vacation, and I was left to run in the woods, and do as I pleased. One day I was roving by myself, and I sat down to rest on a ledge of rocks which overlooked a broad landscape.

I was then in my tenth year, and had never had a strong attachment for anything or anybody but my father. I remember well this day: I had been sitting for a long while, watching the shadows which one hill would cast on another; wondering at the blue haze that floated around the hilltops, enveloping them in a mysterious veil, and admiring the varied shades of green that draped the surrounding scene. A sensation of ineffable sweetness came over me, that thrilled my bosom with delight. I began to jump about, springing from rock to rock, catching hold of the drooping branches of the trees, and kissing their leaves, until I was out of breath. I then threw myself upon a rock and pressed my cheek against the moss, which I fondled with my hands. I began to weep, and then laughed merrily that I should weep, for I had never been so happy. I started up, and climbed the mountain, and, when I had reached its top, I began to sing, with all my might, an Indian song which my aunt had taught me. I soon ran down the steep again, my feet hardly touching the ground. I would try to fancy that my mother was pursuing me—a favourite sport I had invented to while the time when rambling alone. When I reached the level, I still ran with all my might, and jumped across a little brook, and began to pant for breath, as though I were really hunted down. I got so in earnest, that I felt my mother's hand seizing me. · I sprang over the fences, and kept up the flight, until I reached the house, where I met my aunt, who threw her arms about me, and I wrapt myself in her skirts. I was so out of breath that I could hardly speak. The first words I uttered were: "No one can come here and take me away, I hope?" She kissed me and said: "No, no, my child; your father said that you could always live with us; we have no little girl, and you shall be ours."

Nearly every day she would let me go. I would hardly leave the house before my bosom would begin to glow, and I would pass the livelong day climbing over the rocks, swinging in the wild grape-vines, and gathering berries or woodland flowers. At twilight, after tea, I would go down the road to the chestnut grove, among the rocks by the hill-side, to hear the katydids sing. Sometimes my aunt would have to drag me to bed, when I would have sat up all night on the sill of the door, listening to the cricket that sang under the stone step.

Far in the woods I had discovered a small stream, which rippled down a hillside; and near by was a ledge of rocks, which, when I spoke or sang, would echo back my words. There I would speak to nature, as I would have wished her to speak to me; and then I would leap about for joy, as though she had replied; never forgetting my aunt's injunction to watch the western hills, that I might hasten home when the sun touched their top. When it was time to go, I would call each tree and rock by the names which I had given to them myself, and would bid them all good-bye, with a promise to return. Sometimes I would take a book, and would teach them how to read, and would repeat to them so often old poetry and songs that I learned all the verses myself.

When I went into the woods I would take off my shoes and stockings and hide them in the fence, and I never wore my bonnet. The rocks, heated by the sun, often burnt my feet, and the sun scorched my face; but my heart was so light, that I did not mind the pain.

When the days were very hot I would undress and go into the brook, where it was shaded by a little hemlock grove. At other times I would sit close to the stones, over which the water dashed, and would reach out my hand to play with the stream, and would bow down my head to kiss it as it flowed.

A childish weakness comes over me, and my tears begin to flow, as I try to write the tale of those once happy days. For that wild and savage woodland was my *first love!* I lose myself among those scenes as I did years ago, and it pains me now to leave them, as it did when, as a child, I looked over at the mountain whose top the sun had touched—the sign which told me to return—and as then, so now, I linger to bid them a fond good-bye.

In the autumn my father returned. He remained but a few days, and when the hour of parting came I dreaded, as never before, to say good-bye.

I recommenced my roving in the woods. Months passed away, and yet my father did not return. Winter came, with its bleak winds and heavy snows, but I went to school in spite of them. Sometimes the snow would drift, and I have waded through it when it was nearly as high as myself; I enjoyed it hugely, and when the snow would freeze and bear me, I would slide down the hills until I reached the valley. I was just as happy playing on the ice and in the snow as I had been in the summer rambling in the woods.

CHAPTER VI

DEATH OF MY FATHER—I WORK FOR "GOOD MARKS" IN THE BOOK OF LIFE.

My Childhood's Religion.

SPRING came; and one beautiful April morning I went to the post-office. My happiness was too great when the clerk handed me a letter to my address. I did nothing but kiss it, and read my name on it. It was my *first* letter. I did not open it, nor feel any need to do so. I was sure that it must be from my father. I ran with it as fast as I could towards the school-house, near which I saw Aunt Huldah standing at her barnyard gate. I rushed over to her, crying out as loud as I could: "Look, look, Aunt Huldah, my father is coming; here is the letter." She took the letter, and I went into the school-house; but in a few moments she came after me exclaiming, "Your father is dead! your father is dead!" She took me by the hand, led me to her house, and read me the letter. I threw myself on the floor, and wept as though my heart would break. My anguish was increased by the fear that my mother might come after me. My relations believed that she was dead, and I had never breathed her name.

Ever since I had come to my uncle's house I had always said my prayers before going to sleep. The night of the day on which I had heard of my father's death, I began to weep at the thought that I should never see him again on earth; but I trusted that, if I were good, I should meet him in Heaven. Then I began to repent of all the wicked lies I had told before I came to Amenia; and feeling that he knew all now, it made me wretched to think that he should know how bad I had been. I said the Lord's Prayer, and then burst into tears, saying: "O Lord, I ask you, as many times as there are grains of sand on the sea-shore, to forgive me for being so bad;" and that prayer I continued to say for years afterwards. Sometimes I would change it by saying: "A million times as many as there are grains of sand on the sea-shore, and drops of water in the ocean, or stars in the sky."

The next day after I had heard of my father's death, I answered my sister's letter. Part of my letter I composed myself, and a part of it was dictated. I recollect that whenever I wrote my father's name, I would begin it with a capital letter, and would commence all other names with small letters. That was one way of showing to my father more honour and affection than to any one else.

For a long while I could not play, but would go out into the woods and weep, without speaking to any one, except my father, whom I imagined to be near me.

One day Uncle Horace told me that every good action was recorded in the book of life, and so was every bad one; and that, after death, we were all to be judged from the record of that book. I said to myself that I would go to work and try to have more good marks than bad ones. So I took up the New Testament and began to read. After I had read a chapter, I ran to ask my aunt if she believed that God would give me a good mark for every *chapter* I read in the Bible. She said: "Certainly." I went back and began to read again; and, as I read, I felt a glow around my heart; it was a feeling I had never experienced before, and in spite of the thought of my father's death, I was consoled. I no longer wished him back; and I was impressed with the assurance that I should meet him in Heaven. I did not finish the chapter, before I went to my aunt again, and asked her if God would give me a good mark for every *verse* I might read. Again she said: "Yes." I went back, feeling happier than ever, took up the Bible, and felt such joy that I skipped about a few moments before I commenced to read. I then hardly read three verses before I ran to my aunt again, and asked if He would give a good mark for every *word* I might read. She said, "Yes, yes." "Why," said I, "how good He is!" and the warmth around my heart began to increase. I was so happy that I could not sit still and read. So I read and walked the floor until I was tired. I then went to a room where my aunt was busily engaged. She said impatiently: "If you bother me so, God will give you a black mark." I instantly felt a sharp pain around my heart. For I would have denied myself anything at that moment, sooner than offend God. I told her that I came only to look on, and not to talk. Then I said to myself: "You will not give me a black mark now, will you, God?" I continued reading the Bible with this same intention for several weeks; and every time I felt the same glow around my heart.

When my uncle and aunt spoke to me of God, they always

taught me to fear Him, and never talked to me of loving Him ; yet they would often refer to the love of God for us.

In speaking of our Saviour they would always refer to His divinity, and but little to His sacred humanity. They dwelt upon the truth that Christ is God ; but this they seemed to understand as if the human nature had been changed into the divine. They did not seem to appreciate that if Christ is God, it is only because God *became* man, and *is* man. And least of all did they seem to realise that the Divine Person, in uniting a human nature to the divine in unity of person, made *His own* the actions and sufferings of that human nature, the thoughts of that human mind, and the affections of that human heart.

Under their teaching I learned the truth that Christ is the Creator, most powerful, omniscient, and Lord ; but I did not understand that in Christ the eternal wisdom and love of His divine nature were *translated* by the divinity itself into the thoughts of a human mind and the affections of a human heart, so that on account of the unity of *person* these thoughts and affections were the thoughts and affections of a God ; and while the divine nature in itself could not suffer nor labour, yet in His human nature God was truly sad and weary, and laboured and suffered, and grieved and wept, and died. I feared Christ as my judge rather than loved Him as my Saviour. I felt that it would be presumption in me to pity One so great and mighty ; that I had great need of His mercy, but that He could not need, and could hardly desire my compassion.

Such were the ideas of God which gave shape to the religion of my childhood. I do not mean to imply that my teachers entirely ignored, much less that they denied, the humanity of Christ and all its logical consequences ; but in the Sunday-school, and in my uncle's house, such as I have described was the tendency of the teaching, or, at least, this was the way in which my infant mind seized the instruction.

In their efforts to enlighten me in regard to the truths of the gospel, they awakened no emotion of love in my breast for God. So long as I could keep His threats in my mind, I tried to obey Him ; but in this I was actuated by self-love, for I feared hell only for its torments, and I longed for heaven only to join my father.

I soon began to call on God for everything. When I went out to gather berries I would call on Him to lead me where I would find the most fruit. Sometimes I would thank the Lord for every berry I gathered ; and it is a well-known fact that I used to gather more fruit than any other child in the country.

I was renowned for it; but I was selfish, for I never told my
secret lest the other children should ask Him, and He would
help them too.

CHAPTER VII.

THE ILLEGITIMATE CHILD.
"The Sins of the Parents."

WE had been for months expecting a letter from my father's
brothers.

It came at last. It was from my uncle Milton, who said that
my father had died penniless; that all his children were illegitimate, and that they had no claims on the St. John family, who
refused to either recognise or assist them.

A few weeks after my uncle Milton had written, my uncle
Chauncey St. John and his wife made their country cousins a
visit, and told them how my father had forsworn himself to pass
off Maria Monk's child as his own, and that she was the mother
of his two children. Although it was only months afterwards
that I learned all this, yet I began immediately to feel the evil
effects of this visit on myself, for the family did not attempt to
conceal their indignation against my father. But what mystified
them was that I should not have remembered my mother, and,
for a long while, they thought that I must be some other woman's
child.

One day my aunt began to question me, and asked if I remembered my mother. I denied at first all remembrance of her.
She then told me what my uncle Chauncey had said. When I
saw that she knew so much, I told her all about my mother.

"What!" she exclaimed, "you, but a child, could be so deep,
as to deceive us all in this way so long? Why did you just
now deny that you knew anything about your mother?" I
was on the point of telling her that I had done so in obedience
to my father, when she commenced to talk of the dreadful
punishment which awaits all liars, and said that if my father
had not sworn to a lie, we might have been *respectable* children;
for my uncle Chauncey had said that it might be true that he
was married; but, as he had forsworn himself, the executors had
refused to recognise his children as heirs, unless he should prove
his marriage, which my father would not do. She told me that
my uncle Chauncey had repeatedly spoken of the strong resemblance which I bore to the St. Johns; but, as my aunt had

assured him, that I had forgotten my mother, and that she had
died when I was very young, they had felt sure that I was not
one of the children whose names had been registered and then
crossed off.

I wept bitterly at my aunt's taunts, and begged her to forgive
me. I promised that I would never deceive her again. I threw
my arms around her and tried to kiss her, but she pushed me
away, declaring that she would never believe another word I
said, I had to bear it all, and I *never* told her that my father
had strictly forbidden both Georgina and myself ever to mention our mother's name. My brother could not remember her.

Aunt Mercy tried hard to make me understand what an
illegitimate child was, but she could only explain the word as
a dictionary would have done. She knew only the name; but
the venom had never reached her—she had never felt the sting.
She told me, it is true, how the world turns its back on those
whom Providence places under the ban by this name ; but she
did not tell me the heart-rending sufferings to which the
illegitimate child is heir. It is only those who have lain
beneath its pall that can ever know the extent and constancy
of the tortures covered by this ignominious title. Not only
does the world shun them, but the very blood of their kindred
curdles against them, as a living reproach to their own unsullied
name. Nor is the measure of their miseries full in being bereft
of fortune, honour, and affection. The interests of society require that they shall not share that which in one or two syllables
conveys to the legitimate child so much of the history of its
blood ; that which contains so much of warning or incitement;
that which strikes so many tender chords of the sweetest ties of
kindred and affection—a name. The illegitimate child must
have no name or only one that either tells a lie or says nothing.
For it is a sort of theft practised on their kindred if these
children dare to take the name of their own father.

There is seldom any hand, however feeble, raised in defence of
the illegitimate child.

It certainly is but proper that the secret sin of the parent
should be concealed, as far as is consistent with justice and
kindness to the innocent. But is it not characteristic of the
pride and selfishness of the world that, while it is so ready to
condone the sin, it can be so hard and cruel to the child, who,
by its mere existence, may be the unwilling, even unconscious,
means of revealing it ? But why dwell on the hardness of
remoter kindred, when this same pride and selfishness so turn
awry the current of natural affection in the parents themselves,

who are often the first to abandon it? The smiles and caresses of such a child become to them reproaches; and, to drown remorse in forgetfulness, they will abandon their offspring to the hands of strangers, and oftener to the still colder hands of public charity.

Should such a child inherit only low and grovelling instincts from parents who abandon it, and kindred who oppress it, its lot, in the worldly view, were even then hardly so pitiful, as when nature enkindles in its breast a spark of her sacred flame, to make it aspire to something higher and nobler. The world, or, rather, society, too indifferent to give its hate, will give but grudgingly that fame which is its highest incentive and reward, and that credit which is due to moral energy and real worth.

Even now I can hear the world's familiar words—they have often grated on my heart—" It is always so with illegitimate children; they are always more clever than others. Pity that it should be so; but so it is." "Of course, *you* couldn't be other than intelligent, *my dear*." Thus will society encourage the efforts of the illegitimate child, too often paralysing its energies and stifling in their conception its generous resolves to persevere and overcome misfortune. If it does persevere, it will find society but too ready, at the very hour of triumph, to force upon its brow an ignominious crown, putting the sin and shame in which it was conceived, above the honour of a life of toil and sacrifice.

In vain does the world attempt to exonerate itself by scriptural phrases, which, it pretends, authorise its cruelty towards the illegitimate child. In vain it will tell you, with the Bible in its hand, that they are the children of sin, and that it is the law of God's providence that they should suffer for the sins of their parents. Too well do we know that God's providence permits all this, and reverently do we bow to His dispensations. But from that very legacy of hereditary woe itself, have they not all the greater claim upon Christian charity? Do the holy Scriptures tell *us* to judge one another? Do they tell *us* to mete out to these children the punishment due to the sins of their parents ? Do they not strictly forbid us to judge one another, and command us to leave that to God ?

It is willing instruments of His mercy, and not of His justice, that God seeks among men. Let these would-be followers of God humbly acknowledge their own unworthiness and offer Him their grateful thanks that, in His mercy, He has spared them a similar misfortune. By their charity to the less fortunate let them try to win for themselves His love and

His protection against the hour of temptation, when, if not assisted by His grace, they, too, might entail upon the innocent that inheritance of suffering which is inseparable from the lot of an illegitimate child.

CHAPTER VIII.

NOBODY'S CHILD.

The Plaint of Nobody's Child.

FROM that, for me fatal day, my aunt conceived a dislike for me which she never tried to conceal. She attempted to treat me with justice, but she never offered me one word of sympathy or affection. She felt that I was bad, and that I deserved to suffer.

But my worst enemy, that was lodged in my own breast, was aroused by such treatment. My wounded pride made me reckless and obstinate, and its exhibitions were sure ever to bring down upon me new humiliations and trials, as galling to my pride as they were repulsive to my will. I would go into the woods where I had passed so many happy hours in sportive dalliance with nature; but, instead of songs and laughter and the merry words of childhood, those rocks and hillsides would echo back my wails of impotent rage, and my imprecations against God and those whom I had learned to fear.

I began to hate God, and would often reproach Him for permitting me to be an orphan, and poor, and the daughter of Maria Monk.

I dreaded the very sight, too, of that home, where, but a few months before I had been so happy, but within whose walls now I found nothing but suffering.

My aunt was sorely vexed to see me so dejected. She thought that I assumed this air to annoy her, and by injurious words she would try to force me to be natural. But my answers would so exasperate her, that sometimes she would strike me and nearly stun me with one blow. To punish my pride she would force me to work and do the most menial services about the house; but she little understood all that I was writhing under, and how I was goaded by the sense of *shame*. Even the school-children knew that my mother was Maria Monk: they used to throw it in my face and call me a bastard; and as I therefore became just as bad at school as I was at home, my conduct there made me generally disliked.

As soon as I had become misfortune's mark all my ways were scrutinised, and faults which would have been easily overlooked when my father lived were exaggerated into crimes the moment I became an object of charity.

The children would keep away from me and tell me that their parents had forbidden them to associate with me. They would taunt me and ask me what was my name, and would tell me that they knew it was not St. John; that I was a girl without a name. Sometimes the school-children would whisper among themselves, and I would overhear my mother's name; she would then appear before me in one of her most hideous forms, and I could see her again, as I had seen her in her drunkenness, when she would seize me, beat me, and curse me at every blow.

When I would hear that name on the children's lips it would humiliate me so, that I would have gladly gone back to her, and have borne all of Maria Monk's cruelty rather than be known to anyone else as *Maria Monk's daughter*.

One day I begged my aunt to let me leave the place. She asked me where I would go, and said that no one who had ever heard of me before would take me, and that strangers would want to know all about me. As for herself, she could not say anything in my favour; so that she did not see any other place for me but the poor-house. If I chose to go there I might. I answered by saying that I would run away at the first chance. "Yes," she replied, "do it if you dare, and the State will seize you as a vagrant, and bind you out to some family until you are eighteen." This frightened me, for I knew several orphan girls who had been bound out by the State until they were eighteen; and they were treated like slaves. "So," said I, "I cannot do as I please until I am eighteen: I have five years more, therefore, and then I shall be free." I went away by myself, and, after shedding a flood of tears, I became somewhat resigned to my lot, and began to think how I could pass the time until the five years had rolled round. Five years at that age seemed like an eternity. But hope filled my heart and began to infuse into me an indomitable energy, which enabled me to resist and to fight against my destiny. I made a resolution not to be sad, nor to care for anything or anybody, since I saw that there was not one on earth who cared for me.

CHAPTER IX.

THE TRIBULATIONS OF BETSY DOT.

Sweet Revenge—Woof and Warp—An Alibi.

FROM that hour there was nothing bad which it was in my power to do, and which could give me a moment's gratification, that I did not do; and the more mischief there was in the thing the more I enjoyed it. I did not care for the consequences. To experience a moment's pleasure I would risk any punishment. I became as adroit as a Spartan thief; and the only sense of shame I ever felt for all my evil deeds, was when I did them so bunglingly that I could be found out. Then I blushed at my want of caution, and would be more angry with myself than those who reproved me.

My aunt soon noticed a marked change in me, and was not long in discerning that it was boldly for the worse. But this, instead of increasing her bad opinion of me, only gave her encouragement; for she thought that I was becoming less deceitful and less hypocritical. From that time I was more to be feared than despised, and I soon became the terror of the neighbours by reason of the mischievous tricks I would play upon them to avenge the slightest offence.

Mrs. Dot, our neighbour, one day made two charges against me, of both of which I was innocent. One was that, instead of going into the woods to gather berries, I had gathered them in her garden, for she had seen little tracks in the ploughed ground. The other charge was that I had stolen a piece of rag-carpet for my play-house, for she had found it among the rocks.

In return for the first injury, I never let an opportunity slip of gathering her fruit; and, to disguise my tracks, I would put on an old pair of men's boots.

As to the other charge, it seemed to me that no ordinary revenge was sufficient to repair my wounded honour. The idea of my stealing a piece of old rag-carpet was too much for my pride, and I could hardly rest in my perplexity to devise a punishment equal to the offence.

One morning I saw all the people go to a funeral, leaving nobody in the neighbourhood but aunt Lavinia and myself. I felt that my hour had come. The "Dot" family had a favourite cat—a tremendous animal—which they had educated, petted, and doted upon for years. My first exploit was to catch this cat, tie it up together with a big stone in a bag, and throw it into the pond. Then I determined to get into the house, and made a thorough survey of the premises. The weaving-room was on the first floor in the rear. In one of the side windows, close to the door, a pane of glass had been broken, and its place supplied by an old straw hat. As I found the window fastened, I pushed in the hat, thrust my arm through the place of the broken pane, pulled out a corn-cob, that was placed in the staple to fasten the door, and then went in.

Betsy Dot's room contained a piece of white flannel, which she was weaving for the Ketchums, the aristocrats of Dutchess ; and Mrs. Dot was taking all pains to make a beautiful piece of cloth, to secure their patronage.

She had left everything in the room in perfect order. I spooled some yarn for the shuttle, and snarled all the other skeins I could find. I then began to weave, but with great difficulty, for, on account of the shortness of my arms, I had to push the shuttle from one side and pull it from the other.

In pulling it through I drew the thread tight, so as to make the edge of the piece as uneven as possible.

I wove about the eighth of a yard, and I could put my fingers into the holes, which I left by not fastening the thread, when it broke. Getting tired of weaving, I threw the shuttle across the room, where it fell behind a box ; and I turned everything in the room topsy-turvy. I then threaded a darning-needle with a long piece of yarn, attached the thread to the crown of the hat, stuck the needle into the sash by the broken pane, went out, and from the window fastened the door with the corn-cob, with the thread pulled up the hat, and placed it just as I found it, broke off the yarn and threw the needle into the pig-pen, and then went home and remained with my Aunt Lavinia the rest of the day.

She begged me to go away and not worry her ; but I kept near by, and she could not get rid of me.

The next morning as I saw Betsy Dot coming, with head erect and quickened step, towards our house, I felt a weakness coming over my limbs, and sat down, trying to look unconcerned.

The woman entered, and looking unutterable things, commenced : "Well, you have done it this time ! This beats all the capers *I* ever heard of in *my* born days."

She went on in this strain until my Aunt Mercy interrupted her, bidding her to tell what the child had done.

They must see for themselves, she said, for no one could believe it on her word alone. And forthwith she told her story.

In answer to my aunt's interrogations, I said : " Mrs. Dot is bound to get me into trouble. She accuses me of stealing first

her berries and then her carpet, and now she says I have been
helping her to weave."

At my mention of the word *carpet*, " Ah !" exclaimed Dame
Dot, " you vixen ! I know now what you did it for ;" and she
began another volley of objurgation far more forcible than
elegant.

Aunt Lavinia, who was very much given to scolding me herself, would take my part against anyone else. She protested
that I had not left the house. " I told her several times to go
out," said she ; " but it is well that she stayed with me, since
people are so ready to invent charges against her."

My Aunt Mercy remarked, that to leave the house open was
to invite strangers in, and it was just as likely that somebody
else should be the culprit. " That is the strangest thing of all,"
screamed Betsy, stamping her foot indignantly, " that I found
every door and window fastened just as I had left them, so that
she must have come down the chimney or have false keys." My
aunt then doubted the whole stroy, and, as Aunt Lavinia had
proved an *alibi* for me, I was honourably acquitted.

CHAPTER X.

MY MOTHER'S TRAGIC END.

My Sister again—" The Way of the Transgressor "—A Maniac's Cell—
Forgiveness.

MY sister and I had corresponded regularly, but I had never
led her to suspect how miserable I was. She used to send me
newspapers ; sometimes the *Home Journal*, but constantly the
Flag of our Union, a journal entirely devoted to romances and
trash. I had found a large number of books stored in a closet ;
they had been left by my cousin Lorin, a Methodist minister.
I would take some of the papers and books into the woods, and,
instead of gathering fruit, for which I was sent, I would read
most of the time. Although in my fourteenth year I would play
school with the trees and the bushes, and, while reading to them,
I always took a note of the words I did not understand, and
would look up their meaning in the dictionary when I got home,
and would explain them to the trees when I returned to the
woods.

The novels had filled my head with romantic ideas, and I used
to imagine myself some meek Cinderella, and a gallant knight
falling in love with me and carrying me off.

I was constantly copying much of what I had read, so as to learn how to spell. When my aunt would scold me for *wasting* so much paper, and would refuse to give me more, I would tear the blank leaves from all the books I could find; and after they were consumed, I would still continue to copy off whole pages on the margin of newspapers.

One day my aunt caught me with a book on mythology, which I had found in the closet. She asked me what I was reading, and snatched it out of my hand. I told her that it was a very pious book, which spoke of nothing but gods. She took it from me, saying that I was heathen enough without learning their religion, and I had better stick to my sewing instead of filling my head with such trash. She condemned the book: that was a sufficient reason to make me like it, and I studied it until I knew it by heart.

One day I found my sister at the house. We had not seen each other since my father died. After my father's death she had passed through many vicissitudes.

I was delighted to see her, and we embraced as affectionately as though we had always been the best of friends. She never would have known me she said. My nose had become less of a 'pug, and the whole outlines of my face had altered. Yet I was still very slight, short, and thin.

I did not see her alone till we went to bed. I then asked her about our mother, and where she was living. She answered angrily: " I don't believe that you even take the trouble to read my letters, for I wrote to you over two years ago that she was dead." I told her that I had received a letter in which she had merely said: " Your parents are both dead now," and that I thought she had written thus to blind the country people who might want to find my mother, in order to send me to her. I then made haste to soothe my sister by saying that I was very glad that our mother was dead. But, as I said the words, she pushed her hand towards me as though she would strike me. " Yes," said she, " you are like everybody else, you blame her for everything. She was not half as bad as she is represented." " She was bad enough, anyhow," said I, " and if she had beaten you as she has beat me you would not love her much." " She hated you," she answered, " because you were St. John's child. She knew that it would be found out that I was not his child. She was afraid that you might rise above me some day, and, to avert that danger, she exposed your father's perjury. But," she continued, " if you knew how our mother repented before she died of all that she had done, you would not feel as you do towards her.

"It grieved her to death to be separated from her children, and the one thing that prevented her from killing herself was the hope of seeing them again. Remorse and grief drove her to distraction, and she died insane. After her death, your letter, in answer to mine informing you of your father's death, was found in her bosom, and it was buried with her."

I wept bitterly at the dreadful recital of my mother's last days; yet I could not but feel that there was a retributive justice in her tragic end. I understood not then the nature of her chief offence, and I thought that she must have been punished for her cruel treatment of my father and myself.

A remark to this effect, which escaped me, enraged my sister, and she began to heap blame upon my father. Besides my mother's own mother had always been cruel to her, and had turned her into the street when a mere child.

"What!" I exclaimed, "had she *a bad mother, too?* Then I pity her." I wanted to say, but I dared not: "Why did she not treat her own child better, having suffered so herself?" I tried to quiet my sister, for she had become very excited, and said that she wished she had never come near me; that she thought by my letters I must have changed, but she found me the same torment I had ever been since I was born.

Thus the conversation ended. It was not renewed until sixteen years later, when my sister disclosed to me other facts in regard to my mother, which I will reserve for their proper place.

Maria Monk is now long dead. Her spirit passed away in a maniac's cell. She was my mother, and I hated her. But another mother has since taught me that I must love my erring parents. She has taught me not to judge my mother's soul, but leave her to her God. His creatures know not that soul's temptations, nor the graces He may have bestowed on it at the last hour. We know that she had a cruel mother, and had been misfortune's prey from her childhood. We know how she lived, and erred, and suffered, and died. But we do *not* know whether suffering did not wring from her wretched heart the tear of true repentance, which can cleanse and soften the hardest heart. We know that God is ever good and merciful, and we do *not* know that Christ may not have taken pity on her tears, and descended in mercy to breathe upon that dying maniac's brow peace and pardon for her sinful soul.

CHAPTER XI.

EVERYBODY'S HAND AGAINST ME, AND MINE AGAINST EVERYBODY.

Vanity *versus* Nature—The Pursuit of Knowledge.

My aunt soon discovered how much my sister disliked me, and there sprang up a strong intimacy between them. My sister exchanged stories with her, and gave her a long account of my early delinquencies. I had nearly driven my mother wild; and there never had been any peace in the house while I was in it. My mother had always predicted that I would come to some bad end.

I began to wish that my sister had not come, and I longed for her departure.

After she left my lot became harder than before. My aunt was determined to conquer me, and showed me no mercy. She often repeated to me that my sister had told her that she must not pay any attention to my tears, which I had always at command. She now made me go barefooted; and when there was company I was not permitted to sit at the table; and when her nieces would come, who were about my age and had always been my playmates, she would not permit me to play with them or sleep with them. She kept me continually in the kitchen.

In spite of my earnest determination to be happy, all this would gall me; and I would weep at night, long after the rest were asleep.

My aunt Lavinia died, and I was left a great deal alone. My aunt and uncle visited a great deal, and I would be left whole days by myself. I would pass a part of my time studying, and the other part looking in the glass. I had heard a great many say that I was growing handsome. This turned my head, for I had always been taunted with my ugly looks. I no sooner discovered that I was admired, than I commenced building castles in the air, and imagining myself the wife of a prince. I no longer thought of Nature, and would pass a greater part of my spare time trying to arrange my hair becomingly, making muslin mittens to protect my hands and arms from the sun, and arranging ruffles and trinkets of all sorts with which to adorn myself. One of the first things my sister had said on seeing me was: " But where is your pug-nose?" " It is gone," I replied; but I did not tell her how it had gone. I will here make the confession to the reader.

The school-children used to tease me on account of my ill-shaped nose, and would make horrid profiles on their slates, and write my name under them ; so I determined to bring my nose down into proper proportions. At night I would take a long garter and fasten it around my face, drawing it so tightly over the tip of my nose that I could hardly breathe through my nostrils. During the day I used to pull on the nose. In two years I succeeded, and the pug had disappeared. How much did I not suffer for this vanity ! It would often bleed copiously. But it never hurt me half so much to bring my nose into shape as it did to look into the glass and see that the school-children had been drawing correct likenesses of me.

I always carried a little comb, with a looking-glass attached, in my pocket ; and even in the woods I passed a great part of the time looking at myself.

The more perverted I became the more I became puffed up with self-esteem, and the greater became my contempt for my persecutors ; and the more they shunned me the more I esteemed myself above them.

I was determined to gather all the knowledge I could, and to do my own will, no matter how many stripes it might cost me ; for I knew that I never could be a lady unless I was educated, and I could not educate myself and perform faithfully the duties my aunt set before me. I felt that my whole future was at stake, and I set myself earnestly to work at my task. I would take a book with me wherever I went. After passing the whole day and returning with little fruit, a sharp reprimand was sure to await me ; but, by the force of my will, I rendered myself deaf to my aunt's vehement threats and just reproaches. She supposed my silence was actuated by a fear to provoke her more and a desire to calm her anger, which it often had the effect of doing. But the good woman little knew that while I stood before her my mind was far away, imagining myself courted and beloved by some noble heart that would lead me to the altar, where would be blotted out the name they so much grudged me, and I should be raised above my misery and shame. Sometimes my very listlessness would provoke my aunt the more, and she would give vent to her indignation by giving me a push that would send me reeling across the floor.

CHAPTER XII.

MY UNCLE IS OF OPINION THAT THE DEVIL MUST HAVE BEEN BORN
IN ME.

I make a Vow—Voltaire.

ONE day I was rambling in the forest. It was early spring, and the trees were just putting forth their leaves and blossoms. Yielding to the influences of the time and the place, I fell to building castles in the air, in the building of which the new self-consciousness produced by my vanity had no small part. I alternated my reveries with the admiring of myself in the little glass. But my dreams were suddenly interrupted and my castles destroyed by the dread of my aunt's displeasure, when I remembered that, meanwhile, I had neglected an errand upon which she had sent me. I looked round for sympathy to the trees, and talked to them as of old. But a change seemed to have come over them. For though all was beautiful as ever, yet nature did not breathe happiness and joy to me as she had done before, and I wondered that my spirit could be darkened in the midst of all that I loved.

I childishly wondered, could the winter just passed have chilled Nature's love for me? I knew not then that it was my own heart that was chilled by the breath of pride, which, drawing me to self, must needs draw me from the heart of nature; of which can be said what was said of the Wisdom that created it, that its conversation is with the simple. I suddenly exclaimed: "I know what it is, old friends! you despise my cowardly fear of that woman. But now I swear to you that I will never show my face among you if I permit her to strike me without returning the blow." I raised my hand as I swore, and sealed the vow by kissing myself in the glass. Then I threw a kiss towards the mountains, and ran home with the courage of a lion. But, strange to say, my aunt received me with more than wonted kindness.

Three days before I had met my Aunt Huldah, when my improved appearance attracted her attention. "Ah!" she exclaimed, "You were the lucky child, after your faither died, to have such a good home, where they clothe you so nicely, and send you to school!"

"Hang the clothes and the school!" I replied; "What do I learn there, where they strive to insult me? I learn more by myself, roaming over the hills. You call that a good home, do you, where I am beaten like a dog for just nothing at all?"

Saying which I pulled up my sleeve, and showed her the marks Aunt Mercy's lashes had recently left on my arm.

"Who did that?" she exclaimed. "Did Mercy dare to strike one of *his* children like that?"

"Oh!" I cried, "she dare do more; you should look at my shoulders!"

Aunt Huldah was much moved at the sight.

"Well," said she, "if anyone strikes you again come to me, and I will protect you."

I gave her a kiss, and started for home.

Days, weeks, and months, passed without blows, and I feared that I should never have an excuse to flee to Aunt Huldah's protection.

When summer came I was no longer sent to school, and would spend most of my time in the woods, where from May till October I went to gather berries in their season. I drove the cows to and from pasture, and would have to sit for hours on the lawn, watching for the swarming of the bees. But amid these occupations I was ever eager to learn, and found constant companionship in my books.

One Sunday I heard a Methodist minister denounce Voltaire from the pulpit. It was the first time I had ever heard the name. He commenced by saying: "Voltaire was a philosopher!" and he repeated the sentence. "What a beautiful name!" I exclaimed to myself. He spoke of Voltaire's learning, his genius, and the wonderful versatility of his gifts. Then he denounced him as the worst of men for having abused these gifts for the destruction of the Christian religion; and concluded by describing his death-bed as most wretched and harrowing. The sound of Voltaire's name had charmed me; in spite of all the minister said against him, I was irresistibly drawn towards the man, whose name was Voltaire. I kept thinking of the name, and of what the preacher had said. Weeks afterwards I asked my uncle what Voltaire had done that the minister should abuse him so. My uncle answered that he was a bad man. But I insisted upon knowing what he had done. My uncle lost patience, and said, that he did not know anything about him, nor did he wish to know: it was enough for him to hear what Brother King (the preacher) had said; that was proof enough for him that Voltaire was a scoundrel. "Yes," said I; "but perhaps the preacher did not speak the truth." My aunt, who had been listening to the conversation, flew into a passion, and said: "What! do you even dare to doubt the preacher?" "I don't know," said I, "anything about it; but I felt as though he was

lying about the man. What a pretty name he has—Voltaire !—
Voltaire !" At these words my uncle joined in with my aunt,
and said, that it was plain that it did me no good to go to
meeting ; that the devil must have been born in me. "Yes !"
exclaimed my aunt, with a sigh, "it was sufficient that Brother
King should say that Voltaire was a sinner, to make her like
him ; and she wants to know all about him, in order to imitate
him, I suppose."

* * *

CHAPTER XIII.

I KEEP MY VOW, BUT LOSE MY FRIENDS.

Aunt Huldah and I—Pluck—Homeless.

I was now in my fifteenth year. One morning, as I was
starting for school, my aunt Mercy asked peremptorily for an
article I had been using the day before, and said that I should
not go to school till I found it.

I instantly thought and said that she but sought an excuse to
keep me home to work.

She was incensed, and seizing me by the arm, she struck me
two severe blows over the shoulders with a little stick. In an
instant I caught her by the hair, and as she raised her arm to
strike another blow, I snatched the stick from her and broke it
over her head. I then fled to the woods, where I lurked for
several hours, and in the afternoon I started for Aunt Huldah's.
When I told her that I had come to live with her, she indignantly
commanded me to go home. I reminded her of her promise to
take me if anyone should dare to strike me again. She would
not admit that she had made such a promise. . "And besides,"
she added, "do you think that Horace would carry my butter
and eggs to the station if I should step in between you and
them ?"

"Now be a good girl," she said soothingly, "and run home."
She went on to say that her health was so poor that she could
not get along without "help," and the father of the "help"
would never let her remain in the same house with me. "And I
don't blame him for that," she added.

I offered to take the place of the "help." "What !" she exclaimed, "you be my help ! I wouldn't give a good broom for
a dozen like you. Oh, I know all about the hard times Mercy
has to bring you up. All you care for is to gad the lots.
Nobody could ever make anything decent out of you. One
thing is certain, I am not going to be bothered with you."

"But," said I, "I thought you would be good to me on my father's account." She hesitated a moment, shook her head, and said very gravely: "I am *not so sure* that you are *his* child." I still entreated, and said that I should never go. At last she said: " You will sleep on the door-step, then, for I cannot permit you to stay in the house," and with that she gave a push toward the door.

I had learned from Aunt Huldah, that my brother, the "help," and another girl had gone to the river to fish, and, when repulsed from her house, I hastened to join them. As I went, the country appeared more beautiful than ever. I felt free once more, for I was determined to live in the woods sooner than return to my uncle's house. My bosom began to glow as it did in former days, when I used to loiter for hours and converse with Nature. The sky was a deep blue, filled with massive snow-white clouds, and the whole landscape was draped in the varied and beauteous colours peculiar to our American autumn. I paused at every step to look upon the scene, every now and then exclaiming: " Beautiful country ! Why are not the people like you ?" and I would stoop and kiss the ground. I wished that I, too, were one with irrational, or even inanimate, Nature; and then my position thrust itself upon me, and I wept.

When I reached the river my brother handed me his fishing-rod, that I might fish awhile. Presently he annoyed the two girls by some trifle, and both attacked him.

When I saw this, I dropped pole and line into the river, and sprang upon them. I took my brother away and sent him home ; and then began a furious fight between me and the two girls, which ended in their running away. When at a safe distance they loaded me with opprobrious names.

On my return Aunt Huldah received me with open arms, for my brother had told her how I had fought for him.

" Well, you have good blood in you anyhow," said she, " no matter where you come from. I will be your friend. I like people that can fight ; but," she added, " I am afraid that that is all that you are good for," and she laughed.

My pugnacity purchased me a bed for the night, at least.

The next morning Aunt Huldah had come once more to a lively sense of the great inconvenience of protecting me. She offered to accompany me home, but I protested that I would never go into the house unless they would promise never to strike me.

When we arrived at the house, my aunt Mercy angrily forbade me to enter, till I should consent to take the whipping and beg pardon on my knees. I defiantly refused to submit, and said, that if they would give me my clothes, I would never trouble them again. My aunt Huldah tried to extenuate her own fault in harbouring me by telling how she had at first repulsed me, and to say something in my favour by telling how well I had fought for my brother. Her tactics did not succeed, for her praises of my pluck but added fuel to their indignation, and they answered her very sharply. She in return taunted Aunt Mercy for her cruelty to the orphan child of Mr. St. John, and ended by promising to pay my board to anyone who would take me.

As my aunt Huldah descended the hill I took the road towards the mountain, little caring where I went or what became of me.

My heaviness of heart grew less at every step as I hastened from the house. I walked about a quarter of a mile, and then threw myself down by the side of the road under a large chestnut tree near to a neat little cottage surrounded by fruit trees. My heart went out towards that little cottage, and I wished it were mine. I could be perfectly happy, I fancied, if I owned such a home, and could live by myself, and do as I pleased. It was situated in an isolated and picturesque spot. Nature never displays her charms more peacefully and lovingly than she does at every season of the year in the country which surrounds this little cottage. I would doubt the morality of anyone who could stand on that spot and remain unmoved at Nature's aspect—whose heart would not instinctively raise itself to God with thankfulness for the gift of life, and sense to enjoy His wondrous works. As I gazed on that lovely landscape, I forgot my wretched existence—I forgot that I was an orphan, without a home, and hardly a friend in the world.

When, after a little, I saw that I had attracted the attention of the inmates of the cottage, I walked on until I was out of sight, at a spot where the road was bordered on one side by a ledge of rocks, and on the other by a beautiful pond. I sat on the ledge of rocks and looked intently at the reflection of the sky in the water of the pond, when suddenly a gust of wind arose, and the placid surface was covered with numberless waves. A tremor came over me: I rushed down from the rocks, knelt in the road by the edge of the pond, and burst into a flood of tears. For a moment I was bewildered ; I knew not what had brought me down so suddenly, nor why I wept. I rose to my feet, impatiently dashed the tears from my eyes, and was about to climb the rocks again, when I cast another glance at the water, and again saw the waves. I dropped on my knees, buried my face in my hands, and wept long and bitterly. Ah, those waves !

I understood at last. They spoke to me of my father; of the
days when we would cross the river together, and when, as the
boat touched the wharf, he would have to drag me along by the
hand, as I would linger to catch a last look at the waves.

I remained on my knees looking at the waves for a long time:
every ripple would bring a fresh outburst of tears, and I could
once more hear my father's voice, as he used to say: "Come
along, Tick; I shall have to carry you if you don't." I looked
up to heaven, and cried imploringly: "Father, father!" At
last the breeze ceased, the water became tranquil, and so did my
breast. As I turned to climb the rocks I looked over at the
mountain, and saw that the sun had just set. I ran a few steps
towards my uncle's cottage, before I remembered what had
happened: then I turned and ran the other way.

CHAPTER XIV.

I BECOME READER TO A SHOEMAKER.—HIS OPINION OF ME.
Taming a Lion—Exit from the Den.

AT a short distance from the pond lived a shoemaker, who was
cross-grained, conceited, and miserly, and had never been known
to speak a good word of anyone. The last time I saw him he
drove me out of his house with a strap for having taken from his
bench a piece of black wax, with which I fastened back his cat's
ears tight to its head. He disliked everybody, and particularly
myself, but as he was fond of money, I was sure he would take
me, when I would tell him that Aunt Huldah would pay him.

When I entered his cottage he received me with a sort of
growl; but I ran up to him as though he were my best friend,
and told him what Aunt Huldah had said, and that I had chosen
his house because it was near the woods. He then told me to
sit down, and that Polly (his wife) would get me something to
eat. I went to bed, however, without my supper, for they had
nothing in the house that I could eat. The next morning it
was the same thing. But I went into the garden, gathered some
green apples, which I roasted, and then took some bread and
browned it, and this, with a glass of water, made my breakfast.

In the house of this shoemaker there were a bureau and table
loaded with novels. He handed me one, and begged me to read
aloud to him while he worked. I did so. After reading to him
for several days, he began to speak kindly to me, which really
touched me. His wife kept constantly repeating that she hoped

I would always stay with them, because Eleazar had never been so good-natured before.

Two children came to the door one day to jeer at me. The shoemaker defended me so warmly that I felt happy that I had a friend; and I tried in every way to please him.

Days passed on. My only diet was cold water, burnt bread, and green apples or peaches roasted or stewed. I grew very weak. I exerted myself to the utmost to read, but I could hardly speak aloud. Then the shoemaker became cross, and began to ill-treat me. He would tell me that. the neighbours had said that he would soon find me out. He would repeat to me how he had defended me, and how he had succeeded in enlisting the sympathies of others for me; and how a great many, from what he had said, blamed my aunt for her cruel treatment. I was so pleased to hear this, that it gave me strength to read a little farther;—but, if he happened to be interested, at the moment I paused he would hold up a long strap, and make a motion towards me, as if he would strike me; and he would say that he had always thought that I was an imp of the old boy, but now he was sure of it.

One day, when I had fainted from want of food, instead of sympathy, I only excited the shoemakers's wrath, and provoked his abuse. I awoke the next morning with the feeling that he had become as intolerable as my aunt. I left his house without saying a word, and ran across the lots to my uncle's, so as not to pass the neighbours' houses. My aunt met me, saying: " You look half-starved." The truth flashed upon me that the cause of my weakness was want of food. I told her that I had come for my clothes, and that I was sure Aunt Huldah would as soon pay my fare to New York, as pay my board. She urged me to wait, at least until spring, and told me that I might come back to her house; but that I should never expect to be treated again *like one of the family*, for they could never forgive what I had done. The whole country, she said, was abusing Uncle Horace and herself on account of the reports which the shoemaker had been spreading. I told her she might scold as much as she chose, but that she should never strike me. This she promised; and I remained with her, and never went back to inform the shoemaker, who abused me everywhere for my ingratitude.

CHAPTER XV.

MY ENTRANCE INTO THE WIDE, WIDE WORLD.

The Mercy of Strangers.

ON the 17th of March, 1853, I was fifteen years old. It was arranged that one of my father's brothers and his family should come to spend the summer at Uncle Horace's. I protested indignantly that I should leave before they came; that I would never be a servant to one of my father's brothers, who had refused to receive him, and who persisted in regarding my brother and myself as illegitimate children. My protests were answered sometimes by argument, to prove to me my folly, and sometimes by derision and angry outbursts on the part of my uncle and aunt. I never yielded to either; and my persistence finally induced my uncle Horace to seek a situation for me, which he found in a family in the village of Kent, Connecticut, about five miles from his house. This family kept a little "variety" shop, and made calico shirts for the trade. I was to assist in the housework, and might sew the rest of the time; and I was to be paid for the shirts I might make at the rate of *ten cents* apiece. I gladly accepted the place, as the alternative of the dreaded humiliation of acting the menial to the family of my father's brother.

My aunt and I quarrelled, because of my demand for the elegant garments which my father had given me. She wished to give them to her niece, and I, although I had outgrown them, desired to have them as mementoes of my father. She yielded most reluctantly; but, to punish me, deprived me of some of the clothes which I needed for actual use.

My uncle came and placed my trunk on the waggon. I got half-way down the stairs, when I went back and kissed the sill of my little bedroom, saying: "Little room, I bid you a long, a fond farewell." The little dog came running up to me. I kissed him on the forehead, and bade him, too, good-bye; and I then rushed out of the house, for my heart softened at the thought that I might never see it again. My aunt bade me a formal good-bye, without a kiss or a kind word. I sprang into the waggon, and my uncle drove off. I glanced over at the west mountains, and, with a wave of my hand, bade them adieu.

As we drove along my uncle spoke very kindly to me, and said that he was very sorry to have me go away; that he had always liked me, and that he would have done more for me. "But," said he, "you know how I am situated. A man has to please his wife ; and your aunt Mercy is one of the best women in the world, but you must always let her have her own way."

When we arrived at my new home, and my uncle bade me good-bye, he begged me to be a good girl and write to him. " I will never write to you," said I, " nor will you ever see me again until I am a lady."

I remained at my new home just two weeks. I arose at four in the morning, and I worked so steadily that I fell ill. I had made the acquaintance of the family that resided next door. It consisted of a lawyer and his wife. They took a fancy to me, and invited me to stay at their house a few weeks. There I made the acquaintance of some of the best people in the town, and was treated by everybody like a lady. The lawyer's wife lent me her clothing, and tried to dress me well when I went out to drive or to church ; and for that too brief period I found it better to be at the *mercy* of strangers than to live with my relations, and " *be treated like one of the family.*"

CHAPTER XVI.

A Nun's Charity—An Artist's Stratagem—Frequent Change of Base.

THE moment my sister knew that I had left my uncle's house she came to see me, and took me back with her to New York.

I tried for some time in vain to get a situation. My applications were often met with the answer that I was too small and too delicate to work.

One morning I commenced in Broadway, at Fourteenth Street, and stopped at every " fancy " shop asking for employment. My appearance was so much against me that, after a hurried glance, the answer was invariably one of those " no's " from which there is no appeal. My heart kept growing sadder and sadder, until I passed Bleecker Street, when I saw in a window a card stating that three hundred sewing-girls were wanted. The forewoman of that establishment engaged me at three dollars and a half a week, and I went to board with the family of one of the sewing-girls.

It was a very poor Irish family, whose humble home was often but scantily provided with fuel and food, but ever lighted up with cheerfulness.

I told my story to the forewoman of the establishment ; an

intimacy soon sprang up between us, and she got me a situation
as forewoman in a children's clothing establishment in Broadway,
owned by Mrs. Dwinelle.

In my new situation I had higher wages and much less to do.
I resided with the family, and was treated like a member of it.
Mrs. Dwinelle and her husband would often remark that they
would like to see me accomplished; and regretted that they
were not able to send me to school.

One day, as several of Mrs. Dwinelle's friends were speaking
of my going to school, one of them said that the Catholics would
be most likely to take a scholar gratis. I decided at once on
the first step I would take.

I had often passed through Houston Street, and used always
to linger, as I passed St. Catharine's Convent, with an almost
irresistible desire to go in. So the next day I went, and was
kindly received and encouraged by the Superior. She told me
that their institution was not for education, but simply for
charity, and advised me to go to Madam Hardey, Superior of
the Academy of the Sacred Heart, at Manhattanville.

Shortly afterwards I went to Manhattanville, accompanied by
Mrs. Dwinelle's sister, and asked for Madame Hardey, who in a
few moments made her appearance. She invited me to be
seated beside her, and questioned me about myself.

I merely told her that I was a Miss St. John; that I was
poor and an orphan; that I wanted to educate myself, and, if
she would take me, I would be for ever grateful.

While I was speaking, Madame Hardey looked me full in the
face—she did not appear to notice my companion. Her attention was drawn from me, for a moment, by a religious coming
in and asking " if the dog should go with them too." " Certainly," replied Madame Hardey; " they expect to see the dog
as much as they do you." As she spoke those words, she smiled
so sweetly and her face lighted up so beautifully, that I felt I
could be happy near her, and I waited with breathless impatience for her reply. She paused, as though waiting to hear
if I had anything more to say; and, as I looked up into her
eyes to catch her words, she spoke—and her words thrilled my
very soul. She said, in a kind, decided tone: " I will take
you; you may come as soon you choose." I sprang to my feet,
and thanked her with all my heart. I had never met a stranger
who received me so kindly. My friend was as much moved by
Madame Hardey's generous manner as I had been, and she
dwelt on the fact that Madame Hardey never asked for a reference, but took my word.

It appeared as though happiness had once more dawned upon me.

On the morning of the day appointed for my departure, a young girl accompanied me to a daguerreotypist's. We childishly told the man my reason for having my portrait taken on that day, and he soon had the whole of the story. He several times inquired about my family. I told him of my sister, who lived very near (and I gave her name and address), a cross, cruel beauty, who cared but little for me; and I rattled on about the *convent*, the good Superior, and the beautiful convent grounds. But at the word *convent* he would knit his brows, shake his head, and abuse the Catholics. He tried to prevail on me not to go; but I told him that nothing in the world could prevent me. Suddenly he arose and begged us to excuse him, as he had an engagement down the street, which might detain him ten minutes, not longer. He came back appearing very much excited.

I little suspected the trick he had played us. The daguerreotypes were soon despatched; and, as I came out, I saw my sister on the other side of the street. I tried to get away from her; but she soon tapped me on the shoulder, and insisted on accompanying me home.

After an introduction to the Dwinelles, my sister, in their presence, asked me to accompany her to her home. I tried to excuse myself; but she would not be satisfied, till at last I lost patience and told her all. She calmly replied that she was well aware of it. (The daguerreotypist had told her.) I defied her. She leaned over and whispered in my ear my mother's name. She then asked, in a triumphant manner: "Now will you go home with me?" I durst not refuse; and I went with her. She upbraided me at every step for giving her so much trouble.

When I reached her home, the lady, her employer, talked to me as if I had committed an act disgraceful to my sister as well as to myself. I pleaded, in extenuation of my fault, that I wanted to be educated, and no other opportunity had offered.

They sneered at my eagerness for improvement; and, when I spoke of the good superior, they sneered again.

"After all your mother did to injure the Catholics, how dared you go among them?" asked the lady.

I replied that they did not know who I was.

"If you go into that convent," she threatened, "I will go myself and tell them who you are, and that *good* superior will tear you limb from limb."

Her threat so frightened me that I nearly fell from my seat. All that I had suffered for being Maria Monk's daughter flashed through my brain. She had conquered. I rose and told her that I would not go.

When I reached Mrs. Dwinelle's they were indignant when I told them I would not go. They were curious to know what my sister had whispered to me that had made me change so suddenly. I refused to give them any explanation. Mrs. Dwinelle plainly showed her displeasure, and remarked that she felt that she had been rash in introducing me to her friends without knowing anything of my antecedents. She begged me to be frank with her, and promised to forgive me, no matter what I might have done. But my lips were sealed. She reproached me for my want of confidence, and accused me of ingratitude.

The next day she got me a situation in a shop in the Bowery.

From that moment I began to sink. My spirit was crushed. I had no heart to look forward and hope for a better lot. In one day all my bright visions for the future had vanished, and all my friends, too, had vanished with them.

At the end of two weeks I was discharged. I then engaged at a ribbon shop. I had not been there long when two of Mrs. Dwinelle's gentlemen acquaintances called on me there. One was a handsome young man, who excited for me the envy and jealousy of all the girls in the shop. From that day I was watched with an evil eye, and they were not long in entrapping me. One day I wrote a note to the young gentleman, to say that I should be pleased to have him call to see me again. But, in the flowery manner, which I thought becoming to the epistolary style, I told him of the "pleasure which his presence afforded me." I misspelt *presence*, and wrote it *presents*.

As I finished writing the proprietor sent me, on some pretext, out of the shop in great haste.

When I returned I could not find my letter, and all in the shop declared that they had not seen it.

Early the next morning I was sent for, and, in the presence of several of the elder girls, my letter was read aloud to me, torn in two, and thrown at me, with the remark, that no respectable girl would accept *presents* from men. I denied having ever received any, at which all turned on me like furies, and asked me how I dared to deny it, after having written it with my own hand. I was dismissed immediately.

I had none but the bitter alternatives: to go to my sister for shelter, or to sleep in the street.

When I called on my sister I had to confess the truth, as she knew some of the employees in the ribbon-shop. When she had heard what I had to say, she broke out upon me in an avalanche of abuse. She then left me, and, after nearly an hour, returned to tell me that her employer had given me permission to remain *for the night.*

I was then ushered into the parlour, where the lady was seated, and she and my sister took turns in lecturing me. They both concluded that I would be far better off in the country.

The next morning I left the house with a fixed determination never to put my foot into it again. The word *country* had frightened me thoroughly. Towards evening I succeeded in engaging myself as an apprentice to a basket-maker. At the end of a month the establishment was bankrupt, and I was once more alone and without a home. Every piece of furniture had been taken out of the house: I and my trunk alone remained. I sat on the trunk and fell to thinking. I passed my whole life in review, and comparing each unhappy or painful scene with the present, I asked myself where I preferred to be: where I was then, or where I had been.

CHAPTER XVII.

A NEW TURN OF THE WHEEL OF FORTUNE—MY MARRIAGE.

A Sunbeam—A Prayer for a Husband—The Prayer answered.

I REMEMBERED an old woman who had once been good to me. I went to her, and she received me kindly into her humble home. Being able to write an eligible hand, I sought for weeks, but in vain, a situation as copyist. One afternoon, disheartened and discouraged, for I had called at least at twenty different places, I met a gentleman leaving his office. I approached him, and begged him to give me employment. It was Judge ——. He asked me for a reference, and my name and address. I referred him to the old woman with whom I was staying, but I had no sooner pronounced my name than he began to question me about my family. I commenced to tell him my story, beginning with my father's death, when he interrupted me, saying: "Your father and I were old friends. I got him out of that scrape with his brothers that your mother got him into." The judge was from Dutchess Co., and was acquainted with my relations there. He had as strong an aversion towards the Methodists as my uncle Horace had towards the Catholics, and he believed every word I told him against my cruel old aunt. He took me to his home, and as good as adopted me; his wife became a mother to me, and he was generally recognised as my guardian.

I was then eighteen. The troubled life which I had led since my father died began to tell on my constitution, and I fell ill.

The physician proposed that my guardian should send me away to a boarding school in the country. The judge agreed to the proposal, and on the first of April, 1856, I was enrolled a scholar at Monson Academy. Monson is a small village in Hampden county, Mass. I was received most cordially by Professor Tuffs, the principal, and his wife. They introduced me to the leading people of the place, and I was frequently invited to their entertainments and receptions.

The moment I arrived at Monson I tried to become oblivious of the past.

I studied assiduously, and conformed to all the rules. Everybody showed me confidence and esteem; yet my soul was sick; I was not happy. The climate, by an alternation of rain and fogs, seemed to be in sympathy with the condition of my spirit.

One afternoon we had holiday. Having studied hard all the morning, I began to think what I should do to improve it. Suddenly a bright, unwonted sunbeam shed its rays through the room.

My heart lighted up as it did in childhood; and I sprang towards the beam to embrace it, as I used to do in the woods. I burst out into a hearty laugh at the silliness of my action; but, in an instant I was on my knees, kissing the rays as they fell upon the floor, I got up and drew back the curtain as far as I could; then threw myself upon the floor with my head lying in the sun; and as its rays played upon my cheek my eyes filled with tears; it was the innocent kiss of other days. When it disappeared I waited for its return, and each time it seemed to bring greater peace to my heart. As the sunbeam slowly crept away, I gave it a parting kiss on the window-pane—and then I raised my eyes to heaven, and said: "At last I have had *one* happy day."

From that hour I began to be more like myself. I became cheerful and light-hearted, and looked forward as hopefully towards a happy future as any of my companions.

At the close of the term I returned to New York; and, as I was still anxious to pursue my studies, the judge's wife proposed that I should go to the select academy of Madame Martinet, in West Twenty-first Street.

Miss Julia Martinet, from the moment that I entered the school, took more pains with me than with the other scholars. She was just to all, but she was more than just to me. She used to take me alone to the parlour and teach me the proper pronunciation of historical and mythological names; for I pronounced them as I had taught myself when I first undertook to educate myself in the wild woods.

In the latter part of January, 1857, Madame Martinet gave an evening party to her scholars, to which some of the best people of New York were invited. The judge's wife took upon herself the arrangement of my toilet. She dressed me most becomingly, and on my head I wore a wreath of exquisite natural flowers. As I merrily tripped down the stairs I said half aloud: " Now, Lord, you must get me a husband to night ; *be sure* that you do."

When I entered Madame Martinet's drawing-room I noticed a tall, handsome, gentleman, about thirty, who made way for me to pass.

My friend and teacher exclaimed: " How beautiful you are to-night, Lizzie ! You look as lovely as the flowers you wear." Then, turning to this gentleman, she presented me to him, saying: " This is my daughter; I am very fond of her, and you will soon acknowledge that I have done you a favour by introducing you." She then addressed me, and said : " This is Mr. Eckel of Tennessee ; he has just returned from Chili ; you will find him very interesting."

Mr. Eckel, by his suavity of manner and the sprightliness of his conversation, was a good type of the cultivated southern gentleman.

I was at once dazzled by him. He had a vivid imagination ; and his poetic fancies, as he uttered them, so bewildered me, that once when he paused for my reply, and looked full into my face, instead of answering him, I returned his earnest gaze. But our glances had different meanings. He was thinking of me, and was trying to read into the depths of my soul ; while I was thinking of myself, and was sadly pondering in my mind whether I would ever become an accomplished lady, that I might dazzle others, as he did me.

We were standing by a vase of flowers. While admiring them, he said something of their different *genera* and *species;* and said that he had learned to know and love flowers and birds in South America. He pointed to a flower and asked me the name of it, which he had quite forgotten, as this flower was peculiar to the North. Said I: " I am very ignorant; I know nothing about flowers or anything else." He laughed and said, rather timidly: " Would you like to be taught ?" " I long for nothing else," I replied ; " I think of nothing else. But Nature herself is against me ; for whenever I study steadily I fall ill,

and have to lay aside my books; then I become discouraged."
He told me afterwards that it was while I was making him this
reply, that the thought flashed into his mind that he would
marry me and become my teacher.

A few days afterwards, as I was returning from school, I met
Mr. Eckel. We walked until dusk. We repeated the same
thing for several days, when one afternoon he called on me, and
asked me to be his wife.

I told him that I was poor, and that my guardian supported
me. "I don't care," he replied, "if you do not own the hat on
your head." I could not believe that he was serious, and I told
him so, and asked how was it possible that he should offer himself to a lady that he knew nothing about? He said it was
sufficient that Miss Martinet had introduced me to him; and
he repeated her words.

He said that he had the greatest confidence in Miss Martinet's
judgment, and that he saw that she loved me. Then I began
to speak in the most disparaging terms of myself. But he soon
grew impatient, and his hand trembled as he took mine, and
said to me: "I fear that I am mistaken in you, and that you
are a confirmed coquette, instead of an innocent, artless child."

The next day I placed my hand in his and promised to be his
wife. We appointed the 20th of August for our wedding day;
and Mr. Eckel left for Washington.

I kept my engagement, for a long time, a secret. I first told
the judge's wife, who arranged me a most beautiful trousseau.
A few weeks before my marriage I disclosed it to Miss Martinet.
She tried to persuade me not to marry him, as she was sure Mr.
Eckel would make me miserable.

On the appointed day I repaired with Mr. Eckel to a Methodist parsonage, and was married by the Rev. Dr. Crawford, in
the presence of the judge's family, my sister, my brother-in-law,
and two lady friends.

CHAPTER XVIII.

MY FIRST LESSONS IN INFIDELITY.

Misanthropy—An Infidel—Immortality—A Light goes Out.

MONTHS had passed since our marriage, and my husband
continued to shower upon me those delicate attentions which a
devoted heart alone knows how to bestow. He never wearied of
telling me how fondly he loved me, and how his happiness

depended on me alone. He would press my head to his bosom, and search in my eyes for a reply, and his loving heart imagined that mine responded to his own. But an early life of misery and misfortune had left its traces in my heart; except when sickened at the sight of penury and want, it seemed to be dead and to remain icy cold to everything, save ambition. I had only one thought—one desire: to improve my mind, to educate myself. Not that I prized knowledge for itself. I loved it, as a vehicle to success—nothing more; for anything else would have answered me just as well that would have gratified my ambition.

One afternoon my husband was giving me a Spanish lesson, when suddenly he closed the book, and said: "What happiness it is to call you my own dear wife! that is all there is in life worth living for; to love and be loved; to be united till death." "And after death?" said I. He paused, commenced to speak, but hesitated, as though he wished me to urge him to say what was already upon his lips. But I wanted him to go on with the Spanish lesson, and tried to take the book from him; but he held it clinched, as he looked me steadily in the eyes, and said: "Do you believe in Jesus Christ?"

I startled at the way in which he pronounced that name, for I had always heard it spoken with reverence. It was a name I had ever feared and had never loved; but a chill passed through me at the cold and mocking tone in which he pronounced it. I answered him earnestly: "Of course I believe in Him." He shook his head, and slowly, and in a low tone of voice, as though afraid of wounding me, he gently said: "*But I do not.*"

"But," said I, "I have read the Bible; and it says that only those who believe in the name of the Lord Jesus Christ, can be saved." "But, my dearest wife," he replied, "the Bible is a lie from beginning to end. Read Genesis, and any geologist will tell you, that the world was created thousands and thousands of years before the epoch given there. Just look at the first chapter, and you will read as pretty a fable as was ever invented; how God first created a man and a most silly woman, who was deceived by a lying serpent." "But," said I, "King David, who wrote such beautiful psalms, must have been inspired; when, for instance, he said: 'The Lord is my shepherd!'" "Beautiful poetry," said he, impatiently interrupting me; "but the truth is that when David was young, he was a sort of roving troubadour, but afterwards he became nothing more nor less than an old filibuster."

"What *do* you believe?" I asked. He replied that he did not

LIBRARY
UNIVERSITY OF ILL

believe in the divinity of Christ, in the individuality of a devil,
or the locality of a hell. "You only tell me," said I, "what you
don't believe; but tell me what you *do believe.*" The question
seemed to puzzle him for a moment, but he soon recovered himself, and answered that he believed in an Intelligence,—a God,
if I preferred the word,—which pervades all space, all matter ;
and the spark of intelligence which he himself possessed, proceeded, he believed, from God, and would return to Him again,
as the dew-drop on the mountain returns to the ocean.

I asked him what he called his sect. "We are infidels," he
said, "but the fashionable term is Unitarian Universalists. I
am an infidel." I shuddered ; for I had read a story called "*The
Infidel's Bride,*" which had left a painful impression on my
mind. It depicted the wife as supremely wretched, just because
her husband was an infidel. At that moment Miss Martinet's
words flashed on my mind: "He will make you miserable."
Miss Martinet was a Catholic. She probably knew that Mr.
Eckel was an infidel, and the thought came to me that this
might have been her reason for opposing our marriage. I withdrew a few steps from him and sat down upon the floor, and
leaned my head against the bed.

I felt sad. There was something in the word *infidel* that I
did not like; it made the same impression on me as did my
mother's name the first time I heard it. I wished my husband
were not an infidel, without fully comprehending what an infidel
was ; but the word seemed to forbode me evil.

We remained for a few moments without speaking. I broke
the silence by asking him if he believed that all man's person-
ality, and all his hopes of eternal bliss and glorious immortality,
that I had so often heard the Methodists speak of, were to be
swallowed up in the grave.

"Nonsense," said he ; "if I had my choice I should choose
oblivion. The sleep of a thousand years is no longer than that
of an hour. Why should we make such an ado about nothing?"
With an anxious tone I asked him did he not believe in a future
punishment. A contemptuous smile passed over his face as he
replied : "A bugbear, that mankind has been obliged to trump
up from the beginning in order to keep thieves and liars in subjection. But, beloved, how frightened you look!" At those
words he knelt down near me, and said that *my* future punishment should be, throughout eternity, to be adored by my most
devoted husband. "Then," said I, "you *do* believe in the individuality and immortality of the soul?" A nervous spasm
passed over his face, which he tried to conceal. But I quickly

said to him: "It is now your turn to be frightened. Why do you turn so pale and look so sad?" "Because," said he, "my whole conviction of the immortality of the soul is merely based on a simple fact, which actually occurred to me in Chili; and I am as sure of its reality as I am of my own existence. But it recalls one of the saddest hours of my life, which I have been trying to forget."

He opened his trunk, and from a small portfolio took out a piece of paper, and continued: "When I was in Chili, a few months after my wife died, I took my child to Valparaiso, and left her with Mr. Albert Campbell's family, who were devoted to me and also to the memory of my wife. I then returned to my post.

"One morning my wife appeared to me. I cannot tell if I was asleep or awake; but I saw her distinctly, holding the child in her arms. The clock struck four. I arose and rushed towards the spot where she appeared, but the vision had fled, and I burst into tears and nearly fainted, for I was sure that my child was dead. I was as heart-stricken as though I had just received the news. I dressed myself and walked up and down the beach. I cannot tell how long I had been there, when my secretary came and handed me a despatch. It was from Mrs. Campbell. Here it is," and he handed it to me to read. It read thus: "Mr. Eckel, your child died this morning at four o'clock." I asked him if that was the only reason that he had for believing that the soul is immortal. "I am sure," I added, "that the Bible will give stronger assurances than that. But why have you not told me all this before? I have ever been living more in the dread of hell than in hope of heaven; for I have always heard more about hell than heaven. But I am not sure that you are right yet." "Read Gibbon and Hume," he replied, "and you will soon be convinced that the Christian religion is a gigantic humbug." Said I: "*I wish it were so.*"

I had always feared the name of our Lord Jesus Christ, through dread of the punishment due to my sins; and when I said that I wished to disbelieve in His name, I spoke it from my heart, and longed to be convinced that there was no punishment for sins.

In an instant I felt a light go out of me. I cannot describe it: it was one of those supernatural impressions, impossible for anyone to understand who has not felt them. I had often violated the *laws* of God; but the moment I dared to go so far as to wish to disbelieve in the sacred name of Jesus, my whole being became enshrouded in a moral darkness, which was never dispelled until the light of Faith once more gleamed upon my soul.

"Yes," said I, "I wish I could know that you are right : I should be so happy." "Be happy, then," said he, "for I will soon convince you. If I have never told you these truths before, it is because I did not know how much your mind might have been prejudiced. There are minds which have an insane reverence for the name of Jesus; but I am glad to see that you are more reasonable, and are willing to be instructed."

From that day my husband took every pains to make me what he was himself, an infidel. He procured me Gibbon, Shelley, Hume, and other writers, whom I devoured with eager attention.

These impious authors soon became my passion and my delight; yet, in spite of all their subtle reasoning, a feeble ray of doubt still lingered in my mind; for, amidst such moral darkness even doubt itself becomes a ray of light.

CHAPTER XIX.

AN INFIDEL'S INTERPRETATION OF SCRIPTURE.

The Religion of the Bible—A Wondrous Mechanism—Piety and Cock-fighting—Miseries of Unbelief—Venus *versus* Minerva.

WHEN alone I passed the time learning foreign languages; but when we were together we would read and converse on those infidel writers. Once my husband said to me that the ignorance of the Christians themselves in regard to their doctrine was most astonishing; that a Protestant to him was the most unreasonable of beings; that any man of sense, who had a knowledge of sacred or profane history, must either be a Roman Catholic or an infidel—that there was no compromise between the two. "But," said I, "I could never be a Roman Catholic!" All that I knew about them was what I had read and heard in Amenia. "I suppose," said he, "you judge of their doctrine from what you see of the Catholics themselves. If I only knew their religion from what I have seen of the majority of professed Catholics, I would pronounce the greater part of them idiots, and the lesser part knaves.

"If I believed the Bible," he continued, "I would become a Roman Catholic at once; for were the Bible true, their doctrine would be unanswerable. I have studied the question long and thoroughly, and have made the machinations of the Roman Church itself an object of special research. It is one of the

most magnificent structures of human policy ever conceived
by the mind of man. It is after you have examined it
long and analysed it well in all its sinews, its fibres, and its
breathings, that you become amazed at the harmony of its
movements; and you feel as though you stood before some
monstrous body possessed of human reason and supernatural
sense, and whose magnitude fills the globe on which it stands.
Always moving, always conquering, even when it appears to halt,
and its adversaries pronounce it crushed or receding, its strength
never wanes; for, in proportion as they have weakened it in one
part, they have strengthened it in another. It has, ever since
its existence, retained its equilibrium like the universe itself.
It is the masterpiece of human wisdom, and the Pope is the
pivot on which the whole of this sublime machinery turns.

"A Roman Catholic has to believe," he continued, "that the
Pope is infallible, or he might as well throw up the whole game;
for the Church of Rome finds just as much reason to believe in
that, founded as it is on the words of Christ Himself, as it does
for believing in the rest of the juggleries of Christianity; and
they cannot be called anything else; for to cheat a man out of
the pleasures of this life by a mere *promise* of eternal happiness
is the greatest fraud ever invented by human skill!" "Where,"
said I, "do the Catholics find in the New Testament that Christ
said that the Pope is infallible?" "You will find it," said he,
"somewhere in Matthew, where Jesus one day was questioning
Peter, and the old fisherman paid him a compliment which
pleased Him so much that He promised him that He would
never abandon him or his church, and that hell itself should
never prevail against either of them."

"Then," said I, "you believe the Pope, cardinals, bishops,
and priests, to be knaves, and their adherents so many dupes?"
"By no means," he answered; "I am convinced that they are
sincere, and that is the most marvellous part of the whole
business: that they actually do believe themselves in the
divinity of the whole edifice. Therein lies the enigma which
eighteen centuries have not yet been able to solve, and which
alone is sufficient to excite one's admiration for this great con-
trivance, whose workings and whose results soar above reason
itself. In the face of the Church of Rome Reason itself lies
dethroned."

I could not see, I said, how he could say that this great piece
of machinery had always held together, for it seemed to me that
Luther and Henry the Eighth had carried off two of its big
wheels.

" Nonsense !" said he, " they were only the offal which the wheels threw off; but they were not a part of the machinery itself; for it became much cleaner and brighter, and ran on much smoother without them. It was such Catholics as Luther and Henry the Eighth that impeded rather than impelled the course of this mighty work ; for the Church has always tried to grind down pride and licentiousness, and your Luther and your Henry the Eighth were a fair mixture of both."

I then recollected how my uncle Horace used to abuse the Blessed Virgin, and I asked my husband how he could be in earnest in his admiration of a church which worshipped the Virgin Mary as equal to God. " That is a lie," said he, " for they do no such thing. I know the Catholic catechism by heart, and it only teaches to honour the Virgin as being the mother of the Messiah ; and why should it not ? How can a man worship Jesus Christ as a God, and then *repudiate his whole family?* It is simply ridiculous !"

Said I, " I have lived among the Methodists, and I know they are good people." " Good !" repeated he, " but what do they amount to ? I never bother my head about these different sects. You never know where they begin, or where they are going to end; but the Catholics have something tangible. I have often attended the Catholic service in South America, and I have seen more real devotion in one Catholic church than I have in all the Protestant churches I have ever entered. Your Protestant women have not serious religious convictions. They go to church when they are young to catch beaux ; and, after they are married, they go to show off their fine clothes, and to make the other women jealous ; and when they get old they go to set a good example for their children. There is less dissimulation among the Catholics. In Catholic countries they attend to their sacred duties in the morning, and divert themselves the rest of the day. I was intimate with a priest there whom I know to be an honest man, and what Christians would call a pious man : I loved him for his uprightness and integrity ; yet I have heard him celebrate mass on Sunday morning, and have met him going to the cock-fights in the afternoon, with two big feathered fighters, one under each arm ; and I would trust that man farther than any man I ever knew." " What !" I exclaimed, " break the Sabbath in that way !" " It is easy enough," said he, " to see that you have been bred among a set of Puritans."

" Well," said I, " I never edified them with my piety. But I never met so big a sinner yet as would not have said that a

priest who went to a cock-fight on Sunday did wrong." "Well,"
said he, " I don't mean to say it was the best thing he ever did
in his life, but I do not see where the harm lies. They say that
if a man labours the whole week, they do not believe that the
Lord will grudge him a little innocent diversion on Sunday.

" It is by drawing the reins too tightly on us poor mortals,"
he continued, " that we are set a-thinking. If we have time to
examine the matter, we protest; and as we become enlightened,
we keep on protesting, until we protest against Protestantism
itself, and then we become Infidels, Freethinkers, such as I am.
But we have to go through a galling process before we reach the
pinnacle on which we stand, and whence finally we can take a
good survey of all that lies beneath us. We have to traverse
Protestantism, because Protestantism is the first step towards
Infidelity.

" You never hear of Catholics falling suddenly into Infidelity,
and you never heard of a sincere, enlightened Catholic turning at
all. There is no need for them to change, as the Church admirably adapts itself to all natures and all climates, without changing an iota of its fundamental principles, which they believe
have been handed down to them directly from Christ Himself.
After they have inculcated and tried to make practical the three
great theological virtues—Faith, Hope, and Charity—they let a
man alone to exercise his own free will, and save himself, by the
help of God ; but they don't take upon themselves the care of
their neighbour's salvation by meddling with his affairs and
neglecting their own souls, as the Protestants do. These will
put a strait-jacket on you that will chafe a man so that, unless
he is a lunatic, he will not stand it long. So we throw off the
whole yoke and become freemen." "And then," said I, " you
are happy." He replied : " I do not mean to say that, for I
believe, and my experience has proved it to me, that the happiest
men here below are those who have lived and died in the illusion
of Christianity, when they have had the courage to live up
to it."

He became thoughtful, and after having paced the room
several moments in a hurried, anxious way, he continued :
" There have been moments in my life when misfortunes have
borne heavily upon me, in which I have tried to drown despair
in pleasure ; but pleasure itself, the gay deceiver, like the apples
of Sodom, would turn to ashes in my mouth. In such moments,
dearest one, I have wished that I had never doubted."

He paused for a few moments, and then commenced to speak
jocosely, as though he would drive away all serious thought. " I

do wish," said he, "that those Puritan Yankees, while they were teaching you their catechism, had taught you a little order, for it would have been of more use to you." "Let us be just," said I, "and not reproach them for that. It was the least of their faults. Aunt Mercy" . . . "Aunt who?" said he, interrupting me. I repeated the name. "*Caramba!*" he exclaimed; "what a name for a woman!" "Ah!" said I, "you should have lived with her once, and have been treated by her *like one of the family*, and then you would have agreed that her name was *most* appropriate. Well, this old lady was nearly six years trying to teach me to hang up my sun-bonnet, and to put things back where I found them. The truth is, I heard such a noise about *order* in those days that I took a dislike to it, and we have been bitter enemies ever since."

"It is of no use," said he, "to try to pass over so serious a defect in that way; for if you have fallen out it is time you were reconciled." "It is enough," I replied, "for me to find my things; I never think about the rest. But I know people who devote more time to putting their things straight, folding them, and arranging them, than it would take me to learn all the natural sciences." "And they would be far better employed," he remarked, "doing those very things you so much despise. I find only one defect in you, dearest, and that is, you are too ambitious. I wish you would take life more calmly: you are too restless, too eager to learn; you place too high a value on mental acquirements. I love you as you are; and where is the man who does not prefer Venus to Minerva? Give me a woman that can neither read nor write, and I would prefer her infinitely to a blue-stocking. Let us enjoy life while we may —'*dum vivimus vivamus*,'—and say with Horace, 'Let kingdoms and empires pass away, but give me the moment as it passes by.' You told me the other day that you were seeking for happiness. You don't know how you wounded me; for where can happiness be found but in our mutual devotion? Happiness consists in small things; in the picking up of a pin, or the turning over of a leaf. *Carpe diem;* Let us seize the present, and not sacrifice to the future, who is an ungrateful dame and would be sure to cheat us."

CHAPTER XX.

WASHINGTON.—MY HUSBAND AND I CHANGE PLACES.

The Study of Men—The Blackguard Vote.

IN January, 1858, I accompanied my husband to Washington, and entered into its intrigues and frivolities with a zest and earnestness, of which only a giddy mind, filled with vanity and self-love, is capable. To be thrown among prominent men and to receive their adulation, was what my heart had craved; and now it had obtained its desire, and for the first time in my life, my ambition was gratified. It was in Washington society that I first learned the magical power of woman over man, and even over the destinies of a state.

For awhile I threw aside my books to study men. Our apartments soon became a resort for many of the distinguished men of the capital. They would pass the evenings discussing politics, playing cards, or trying to form new political combinations.

We remained in Washington about eight months. When we returned to New York we stayed at the St. Dennis Hotel, where I resumed my studies.

A few weeks after our return my husband was ill, and I was seated at his bedside. He then gave me for the first time some account of the state of his affairs, from which I found that he had been living since our marriage on the generosity of his family, who now refused to give him further assistance; and that just before our marriage he had lost all he was worth by the total loss of the ship *Obed Mitchell.*

"There is nothing," said I, " I so much dread as poverty !" " The grim spectre," he replied, " has been chasing me for a long while; and the thought that you would sooner or later discover it has tortured me to distraction."

" Misfortune, dearest," said I, " shall never separate us; it will only draw me to you. I have suffered, and I know how to pity you."

It surprised him to hear me speak so, for I had never revealed to him my past history. " I have often pondered," he said, " as to what would become of you if you had no one to take care of you;" and he dwelt on my peculiar child-like helplessness. I reminded him that in acting hitherto such a part I had been but fulfilling a promise which he had exacted of me on our wedding-tour. I reminded him how he had said that it is the duty of a husband to take care of his wife, and of a wife to lean upon and cling to her husband, as the ivy does to the oak, and that he had made me solemnly promise that thenceforth I would let my husband stand between the world and me. "But now," I said, "I am tired of being a puppet. I believe that it is as much the duty of a woman to assist her husband as it is the duty of the husband to take care of his wife. It is now your turn," I continued, "to promise that you will henceforth let *me* stand between *you* and the world."

He clasped me to his bosom and said: "You are so good! I only wish you were as affectionate as you are noble and generous. Do anything, anything you choose; I can see no hope; I am so discouraged that, were it not for you, I would light a handful of charcoal, and all would soon be over."

The next morning I went to the St. Nicholas Hotel, to see Col. Bilbo of Tennessee, one of my husband's most devoted friends. I told him how we were situated, and succeeded in enlisting his sympathy.

He named over several things, but quickly decided that it would be of no use to offer any of them to my husband, as he was too indolent for one, too proud for another, or not qualified for a third. He continued: "It is the most difficult thing in the world to set men up who have dabbled in politics. They become like gamblers who refuse to work, and spend the rest of their lives taking their chances." Finally he said: "I will take you to Hon. Fernando Wood's office, and introduce you to him. He is the only man that can do anything for your husband, for he must have a situation under the Government, where there is a good salary and nothing to do."

After receiving his friend in the most cordial manner, Mr. Wood turned to me and asked the Colonel if I was his daughter. "Yes," said the Colonel, "for I have just adopted her. She is the wife of a Tennesseean; and you know that we are still one family in the dear old State. Promise me," continued he, "that you will be a friend and a father to this lady." Mr. Wood gave me his hand, and told me that I had only to make my demands.

When he learned that my husband had been consul: "Please give me his name," he said, "and I will get him a situation in the Custom House."

"Are you in earnest?" I asked wonderingly. "Certainly, madam," he replied. "Did you not hear me promise the Colonel?" "Why then," said I, "you are a good man! I thought you were the worst man that ever lived." "I suppose you read the newspapers," said he. "Yes," I replied; "and if you are innocent, why do you not contradict what they say?"

" Why," said he, laughing, " the best service they can render a man in this city is to abuse him: it will secure me the whole blackguard vote in the next election without costing me a cent. They have said so much against me that I am now sure to win." I left, assuring Mr. Wood that I would try to induce every man I knew to vote for him.

In less than a week my husband received an appointment in the Custom House. It was at one of the *abstract* desks, and just such a place as the Colonel had proposed, where there was a salary and but little work. From that moment my husband began to look up to me as a marvel and a· genius, and would depend upon me for everything. We took more spacious rooms in the hotel, and our evening receptions became almost a repetition of what they had been in Washington, with the exception that I now took every advantage of using those who visited me for my own profit. I was always trying to obtain an appointment for someone, whom I would make remit me a quarter of his salary if I succeeded. Not content with that, I would use my influence in obtaining contracts for my friends, upon which I received a percentage. In a short time my income far exceeded my husband's salary.

CHAPTER XXI.

I REVISIT MY AUNT—SHE DOES " HER CHRISTIAN DUTY" BY MAKING MY HUSBAND JEALOUS.

The Temple of Nature—A Husband's Honour—Virtuous Assassins—A Review and a Moral.

THE unusual tension of nerves required for my new part of intriguer and lobbyist, soon caused a reaction which made me wish myself again in the woodlands of Dutchess. My health began to fail, and with the consent of my husband I revisited the scenes of my childhood's joys and miseries in the summer of 1859. My uncle and aunt received me as if I was their long-lost child.

I passed several days rambling alone in the woods, and sought out the spots which were dear to me when a child. All things were unchanged in their exterior aspect; but they spoke to me a new language which my conscience could not but understand. I found remorse wherever I turned my eye. The woods seemed to frown upon me, and to whisper to me to begone; and one evening, beneath a glowing sunset, I gave them a long, parting look, and sadly went away. I have never since returned.

From that time I was constantly drawn to the pond, whose
waves had once made me weep. One day I sat near by upon a
little mound, which gave a fine view of the surrounding scene.
The sun was setting, hidden by a cloud. I had not been there
long before I felt the peace of other days come back again, which
I had vainly sought amidst my old favourite haunts. Almost
unconscious of what I did, I raised my eyes to heaven and repeated a little prayer that I had composed when a child. I had
hardly finished it when the sun escaped from behind the cloud,
and shone forth with dazzling splendour, and its peerless
brightness illumined the whole landscape. In the same instant
I heard the mellow tones of an organ, which proceeded from the
neighbouring cottage. It was soon accompanied by a child's
voice warbling a little hymn. The whole scene seemed to
vibrate upon my soul, and filled it with an unknown and
ineffable sweetness. There was a pause in the music; but it
recommenced, and repeated the same melody. After the hymn
was ended I longed for the spell to last, and the hymn was
commenced again. I listened, like one entranced; and when
the music had entirely ceased, I thought, and exclaimed aloud :
" Oh, that I could build here a church, that these hills might
ever resound with sacred music! It is just the spot in which
to worship God !"

I arose to go, and, as I turned, the sun sank behind the
mountain. And I, too, sank again into the foul depths of
infidelity, and peace left my heart.

One day the little girl, who filled my former position in Aunt
Mercy's house, expressed to me a desire to go to New York,
and return a lady, as I had done. I was stung with remorse,
and felt my apparent success a shame—a decoy to invite others
to ruin.

I had the appearance of having all that I could desire ; yet
He who reads hearts knew that I was wretched, and rarely saw
a happy hour. I had formerly studied, believing that knowledge would bring happiness ; but now study became a resource
to enable me to forget. Still I clung to the pleasing delusion
that *more* knowledge might bring happiness, and I resisted the
arguments of my husband to induce me to give up the pursuit.
I would not permit him to point out to me the road to happiness, as he had not found it himself.

My aunt was annoyed that my husband should be so blindly
attached to me as not to see my faults, and she sought to open
his eyes to my defects of character. I rather encouraged her in
this, believing her to be a woman of sense, who would do me no

real harm. Besides, I had so great reliance upon my husband's sense of honour (to which he seemed to cling more than to life) that I was confident that her attempts would redound to her humiliation. Alas! for me—fatal mistake!

Just before setting out for Amenia, I had almost decided not to go. A dread foreboding had taken possession of me that some evil would befall me there. I could not shake it off, till one day, amidst an outburst of tenderness on my husband's part, I had said to him: "Is your love so strong that you are incapable of believing evil of me? I have enemies in the country—would you believe their slanderous tongues? I admit," I added, laughingly, "that I have ever done but little to conciliate their goodwill or their good opinion."

He had taken it very seriously, and had said: "I am a man of honour and self-respect. Do you think me capable of permitting anyone to speak disparagingly to me of my wife? Has a man anything more sacred? I would consider that he offered me a personal insult who would even refer to my wife's faults in my presence; and so would any gentleman." I was delighted with his reply, and had decided to go, sure, that I had nothing to fear.

But the breath of slander is so insidious that it steals upon us unawares, and never is this poison infused into our minds more subtley than when we receive it from the lips of those whom we believe to be our friends, and the friends of those whom we hold most dear. And even while they are undermining them in our affection, the worst of all is that we cannot hold these murderers of our peace guilty of an *intent* to kill our happiness; for these virtuous assassins are often so deluded in regard to their own sanctity, that they *really imagine* that their advice is prompted by a sentiment of charity, when it is nothing but jealousy and hate.

I had been in Amenia but a few weeks, when several of my cousins came on a visit. One of them was a gentleman from the South. He was about my own age, tall, handsome, and accomplished. Among these cousins were also two young ladies. The gentleman showed me a marked preference by inviting me to drive, to ride, to shoot, and to fish. He liked me better than the others because I had seen more of the world. I preferred him—not only because of his excellent qualities, but also because it provoked the envy of the rest.

My husband came frequently, and my aunt took it upon herself to render him an accurate account how I passed the time in his absence. I had told him all myself; but hers was, of course, a different version. He became furiously jealous, and requested my immediate return to New York.

I was quietly packing up, but in no humour to hear a sermon, when my aunt came and told me how much she regretted to see me so indifferent to so devoted a husband, and that she hoped I would reform. I knew that she was the cause of my being obliged to leave, and she had hardly pronounced the word *reform*, when I retorted upon her with a volley of words such as only an enraged woman can command.

She flew to my husband, and they remained together for an hour. When he spoke to me again he was a changed man. I knew that it was useless to question him, for his pride would never permit him to acknowledge that he had allowed anyone to speak to him against me. He spoke to me in a tone, and with a manner and a look, such as he had never used before, and sullenly resisted all my efforts to soothe him. I soon lost all control over myself, and ran to my aunt, who was looking perfectly composed and happy. I reproached her sharply with having tried to influence my husband against me, remarking that she had succeeded but too well in her efforts. She admitted that she had done what she considered to be her *Christian duty*, by letting him know my true character.

"Yes," I retorted, "and it is out of *love for me*, that you have done it." And I prayed, with unutterable bitterness of heart, that such love should have its fitting reward.

As we drove to the station, my aunt, in blandest tones, said to me: "I suppose you will come to see me again next summer?" "You will not see me again for ten years," I pettishly replied. She laughed and said that I could not keep away from the woods so long. I replied that the woods were like herself: they did not treat me well; and I never cared to see either her or them again.

As the train bore us away I took a rapid review of what I had seen and heard during my stay in the old place: and as I recalled, one by one, the different expressions of envy and disdain that I had seen on the faces of my old school companions, and remembered the sly hints that some worthy dames had frequently given me, both by look and words, to show that they felt themselves above me, I wound up my reflections by a meditation founded on the following moral of Gil Blas: that if a person had risen from poverty to wealth and could roll around in his carriage, it would be idle for him to imagine that he could go back and live in *peace* in the place from which he went away barefooted, *for the country people would not stand it.*

CHAPTER XXII.

WHAT JEALOUSY LED TO—AN ANGEL'S VISIT, AND ITS DEPARTURE—
THE WORD OF GOD.

THE poison of jealousy administered by my aunt Mercy seemed to have killed the affection of which my husband had previously been so lavish. From the day we left Amenia he treated me with respectful but distant formality. He uttered no word of complaint, but the ceremonious attentions which he paid me were more galling to my pride and self-respect than the most outspoken upbraiding could have been. My nature was hungering for the affection which my pride would not permit me to beg. The demon of drink seized hold of the discontented husband, and I, the wretched wife of a drunkard, was left to the insulting pity of enemies and would-be friends.

I expostulated, but to no avail: the spell was broken; my influence had gone. He no longer invited his friends to call on us; I passed the greater part of the time alone, and I became low-spirited, and was wasting away for want of excitement.

I sought for consolation in those authors whose style fascinated me most, and whose ideas were in harmony with my new convictions. Voltaire, Rousseau, and Gibbon were my constant companions. These three authors so absorbed and delighted me that I at last became indifferent to my husband's coldness and dissipated life.

At the moment when I found myself most contented, and perfectly resigned to be left to myself, an event happened which brought back to me his estranged affection. I was to become a mother. He was so overjoyed when I announced it to him that he fell at my feet and asked me to forgive him his past neglect, and immediately recommenced his former devotedness.

He again invited his friends to visit us. They were curious to know the cause of my husband's jealousy; for to that they all attributed my late seclusion. I threw all the blame of our quarrel on my pious old aunt.

It was in the latter part of May, 1861, that I gave birth to a daughter. My husband's cup of happiness seemed to be brimming over. He ceased to attend to his official duties and remained constantly by my side.

Months passed, and our home was truly happy. But a cloud soon overshadowed it again. Our little one died, and with her expired all our domestic happiness.

My husband covered the little bier with flowers, and remained by it all the while, weeping, and pressing the marble forehead with his lips.

Many thought me cold and unfeeling in that I did not show sorrow as my husband did. At the grave I could not weep. But at midnight, when the rest had ceased to mourn, I would stretch out my hand to find my infant's head, and my hand would fall heavily on the spot where that little head had lain. Then it was *my* turn to weep. A mortal sickness would come over my heart, and I would sob for hours. For months I would weep at that same hour, until at last my hand forgot to seek its treasure, and then I wept no more.

Months afterwards my maid told me that my French teacher had baptised my child shortly before she did.

From the day that our child expired it seemed as if my husband had determined to do himself to death by drink.

We were staying again at the St. Denis Hotel. One morning a happy ray of sunshine flitted over my heart when · I discovered that I was once more to be a mother. At the announcement my husband, to my surprise and sorrow, burst into tears. " I can never love another child," he said : " I have never looked at one since ours died, and even the perfume of flowers falls like a pall on my heart, for it ever recalls the night we first met and our beloved one's bier. I never want to see another child." He tried to persuade me that it could not live, because of the fatality that was hanging over him. He wore me out with his entreaties, and when he saw that I would not yield he treated me unkindly.

One day he dealt me, as if by accident, a terrible blow. Instantly the thought flashed upon me that it was done for a purpose.

Still writhing with pain, I placed my hand on my heart and made a vow, as if speaking to the little unborn : " I will protect you," I· said, " while I have breath."

I could then realise how intemperance can harden the kindest heart and benumb the affections of the most unselfish.

The next morning, when I resolutely refused to do his will in regard to my unborn babe, he ill-treated me as he had never done before.

That day I left him and went to my old friends, the family of the judge. Shortly after I went to live in Brooklyn, so that I might be near my sister during my illness. Soon after I left my husband he lost his position iu the Custom House. I tried to have him reinstated, but without success. Afterwards I would occasionally send him money, for I knew that he must be utterly destitute.

One day I received a package containing a little Bible neatly bound. No name, no message came with it; and to this day I do not know who sent it.

I was displeased that anyone should send me such a token, for I felt that it was intended as a silent reproach.

I was about to put it away among other books, when the thought struck me that I should open it, and would apply the first verse I laid my eyes upon to myself. I knelt down and prayed that God would say something to me that would console me. I then opened the Bible, and my eyes fell at once on a verse which spoke threateningly to me, and called me by a name which made me shudder. I closed the book with a slam and threw it on a shelf, saying, "Stay there, I will never open you again." What I had just read depressed me so that I began to weep. *I felt that God Himself had spoken to me.* I tried to shake off this impression, but I would shudder every time I saw the book which had so wounded me. My eyes fell on my own old neglected Bible. I exclaimed: "I will consult you, and see if you will treat me better." I knelt down and opened it, and behold, my eyes fell on a verse in another place which spoke as threateningly to me, and called me by the same vile name.

I closed the book, and placed it beside the other one with a clash, saying: "I have done with you too." I wished I had not consulted the Bibles, for they troubled me night and day. The very sight of them lying together on the shelf importuned me so that I hid them out of sight amidst the other books. But I could always feel their presence, and even in my sleep the menacing words which I had read would loom up before me in letters of fire.

CHAPTER XXIII.

ADRIFT.

A Mother's Vow—Intrigues—Bound Fast.

ON the 5th of October, 1862, I gave birth to a little girl. When the child was placed in my arms I laid it on my breast, and prayed God that her life might not be as sad as mine had been; and placing my hands over her, I made a vow that I would be a good mother. I thought of my own mother, and I pressed my child closer to my bosom, as I said: " Lord, I know

that You will forgive me all my sins if I become a good mother."
It was in trying to be faithful to that vow that I finally found
peace.

Our civil war had then been raging for nearly two years, and
from the extensive acquaintance that I had made in Washington of men who had since risen to high positions in the Federal
service, I became very useful to several prominent men in New
York and Brooklyn, who were then holding high and lucrative
offices under the Federal government. Several of these gentlemen were closely allied by blood to men who were in open
rebellion against the government. Some of these persons, having
large families, had been cast into prison, and they appealed to
their Northern relatives for assistance. But the latter did not
always dare to do what they would have wished in favour of their
Southern kindred. The government had hosts of spies, even in
the post-offices, who were ever on the alert, and too willing to
report against those who appeared to be disloyal. I went
earnestly to work to secure the liberation of some of these men,
without compromising their friends whom I was serving. In several
cases I was able, by merely writing energetic letters to persons
in power, to release them, or at least to alleviate their condition.
Their Northern friends were very grateful to me, and wished to
remunerate me by large sums of money, which I refused to
accept.

I wanted their *influence*. I knew that they had become
gratefully attached to me on account of the discretion which I
had used in serving them, and I knew that I could rely upon their
serving me whenever I needed them. I refused their money that
they might not feel that their indebtedness to me had been
acquitted. I had another class of acquaintances, some holding
lucrative positions under the government, and others not so
fortunate, but both united in their endeavours to ship contra-
band goods to the South. So I made use of the former, whom I
had served to assist the latter, who paid me liberally for it.

I had no sooner left my husband than all his affection for me
returned. It was in the midst of these exciting intrigues that
his entreaties for forgiveness would reach me, which, together
with the menacing words I had opened at in the Bible, made
me carry a heavy and dejected heart. I was like one who had
sold herself to so many friends, and they held me as their
slave. They gave me to understand that I was no longer
free; that it was my duty to protect them : and with anxious
looks they would tell me all the danger to which I would expose
them by renewing my relations with my husband. Then they

would dwell on the risk which I would run myself; for, when the first ebullition of happiness had passed, he would surely demand explanation. They pictured to me his revenge. And, lastly, they insisted on the wretched condition to which he was reduced.

I longed to return to him, but I yielded to the persuasions of those who held me bound, as in a coil; and I never permitted him to see his child, or even to know where I was.

I left Brooklyn in the latter part of November 1862, and came to reside in New York.

CHAPTER XXIV.

A POET'S DEATH-BED.

Somebody's Daughter—The two Coffins—Grave Flowers.

IT was a bitter cold evening in January, 1863, when one of my husband's acquaintances called to ask me for money to aid my husband, who was ill. He showed me a letter, which he had just received in regard to him. The letter was written in an elegant feminine hand, and evidently by a lady of culture and refinement. I handed the man some money, and begged him to let me accompany him; but he firmly refused, alleging as an excuse the lateness of the hour and the severity of the weather. He even refused to give me the address, lest, as he said, I might persist in braving the cold to go to my husband.

I passed a feverish night, and awoke from a disturbed slumber just as the clock struck five. I anxiously awaited the dawn, fully determined to go at once and urge this gentleman to give me my husband's address.

As I was about to go out the judge's wife and one of my husband's friends came to tell me that my husband was dead.

His friend said that he could not tell me where his body was, for my husband had made his friends promise that they would never let me know. But the judge's wife gave me the address, and I immediately drove to the place.

The carriage stopped before a row of newly built tenement-houses in the upper part of the city. We ascended a dark staircase, which brought us to the entrance of the rear apartment on the second floor. The door was slightly ajar, and I pushed it partly open. The first thing I saw was a woman of about thirty, with bloated face and bewildered looks, standing in the middle

of the room, with her face towards us. She started when she
saw me, and springing forward, placed her hand on the door, and
asked what I wanted. When I told her that I had come to see
my dead husband she withdrew a few steps in apparent confusion.
As she recovered from her emotion she looked steadily at me and
said : " I know you now ; I have seen your portrait. You are the
cold, ambitious one ; you will find him in there ;" and she pointed
to the bedroom.

Just as I was about to enter she seized me by the arm, and
drew me with a frantic gesture to the middle of the room, and
began to weep.

For a moment I wondered if we had not made a mistake,
feeling that such a debauched-looking woman could hardly have
been the writer of that note, when I saw my husband's portfolio
on the table. I pushed the woman from me, and went alone
into the bedroom. There, upon an old straw mattress, without
sheets or any covering save an old worn blanket, and no pillow
but his folded coat, lay the lifeless form of my husband. He
was beautiful in death. His face had the genial expression
which it wore in happier days. My grief was so poignant that
the blood seemed to congeal in my veins. I rested on the side
of the bed for support, and having looked steadfastly at him for
a few seconds I leaned over his dead body, and, with bowed head,
I humbly asked God and his departed soul to forgive me, for I
felt that had I been a devoted wife this might not have been.

The woman came and stood beside me sobbing and weeping.
She looked at me, then at my husband. At last she sobbed out :
" This is what he dreaded most, and what tortured his last
moments. He feared that *you* would come and find him here,
and he begged rather to be dragged to die in the street. Ah !"
said she—and she pushed me towards the corpse—" *you* broke
his heart, for you would not let him see his child. He waited
three months, daily and hourly hoping to get a message from you
to come ; but it never came, and he said he could not live, and
so he died by drink. I wanted to die with him. I knew him
long before he knew you. I loved *him ;* but *he* loved *you*. You
abandoned him, but I closed his eyes in death. I knew he was
dying ; the physician told me that he could not live till morning.
I feared that the candle would go out and leave us in the dark,
and that he might die when I could not see to close his eyes.
But it lasted just long enough, and you see I did it well."

She gently passed her hand over his eyes, and then leaned over
and picked up from the floor, at the head of the bed, a tin
candlestick, on whose top clung a small black wick burnt to a

crisp. She showed it to me, then gave it a tender, grateful look, and replaced it carefully on the floor. "But," said I, "did not Mr. —— come last night and give you some money?" "No," she replied; "he came this morning, and when he found that Mr. Eckel was dead he left me without saying a word."

I handed some money to the woman, and told her to buy fuel, for the room was so cold, that although wrapt in furs, I was shivering. I left the bedroom and came into the room I had first entered. This room had two narrow windows, which gave but a cheerless light, on account of the projection of another building. It seemed that no ray of sunshine could have ever penetrated there. The furniture consisted of two wooden chairs, a table, and an old cooking-stove. I asked the woman how they had managed to live. She told me that they had sold or pawned nearly every article of clothing and furniture to provide bread, until all was disposed of but the few pieces I saw in this room. She added, that my husband from time to time wrote poetry for the *Sunday Atlas* and the *Evening Post*, and these journals paid him well.

The following was written in lead-pencil, and lay carelessly on the table :—

> Say who be this so strangely fair,
>   That meets me on life's fitful river?
> Deep shadows loop her raven hair,
>   And stars upon her forehead quiver.
> O who be this so strangely fair,
>   With step so light, yet cold her breath?
> O she will take my vacant chair,—
>   I know and love thee now, *sweet Death!*

A few days before he died, he had risen at midnight and written some verses. He told her the next day that if he should die she should take them to the *Atlas* office, and she could bury him with the proceeds. Saying this, she took up the portfolio, which lay upon the table, and held it closely to her, as though she were afraid that I might claim it and its contents.

I inquired how my husband had spoken of me, and I dreaded to hear her answer. She replied that his mind was ever running on me, and that he would often say: "How could she treat me so? not to let me see my child! It kills me, it breaks my heart." "I have heard enough," I exclaimed; and I rushed out of the room. I was descending the stairs, when the woman came after me, and seizing me with both hands drew me back into the room. She begged me not to leave her. She had no money to bury him, she said, and no clothes even, nor a bonnet,

with which to go out. I told her that it was my intention to do
everything that was needed. At this she threw her arms around
me and kissed me.

"But," said she, "let me tell you all." "Ah, no!" I cried,
"for he must have cursed me." "No, no!" she said, "he
always loved you. The one thing he said was, that you were
too ambitious, ever sacrificing the present for the future. But
let me tell you how, just before he died, his countenance lit up,
and that sweet expression came over his face which it still
retains, and, stretching forth his arms, he pointed upward, and
exclaimed: 'The portals of Heaven are opening;' and he
nearly screamed out: 'There, there are my wife and child,—
the same as in Chili. Oh, see! she beckons me to come to her
now. Oh, welcome Death! how glad I am to leave this world.
Come, sweet Death! and take me quickly. I long to go.'
Those were his last words. After he had said this he made
but a few respirations at long intervals, and then all was still.
He was dead! I closed his eyes, and crossed his arms upon his
breast, as you see them now. I had hardly done so when I
heard a neighbouring clock strike five, and then the candle
went out, and I was left in the dark. I took the blanket off his
corpse, wrapt it around me, and walked the room till morning.
Then I wrote two letters, and a neighbour took them to his
friends."

When the woman had ended her story I begged her to tell
me who she was. She told me. Her father lived in Syracuse,
and her husband, who had abandoned her, was a captain in the
Federal army. "I will give you some money," I said, "and
you must go back to your father." "Ah, never, never!" she
replied; but she begged me to give her money that she might
get the clothing which she had pawned.

This strange being was highly educated, and her manners
were those of a refined lady, yet she was one of the most debauched-looking creatures I have ever beheld. Her face was
something revolting to look upon, and the contrast between her
speech and her looks was such, and her intonations were so softly
refined, that if you looked upon her face while she spoke her
words would appear like so many sparkling dewdrops oozing out
of some stagnant pool. She implored me not to leave her, for
she dreaded to be alone, and it was only through the assistance
of my friend that I could disengage myself from her. She
followed us down stairs to the sidewalk. My friend got into
the carriage. Before I did so I turned to bid this woman good-
bye, but she had gone. We had hardly driven twenty paces

before I caught sight of the woman, standing before the counter in a rum-shop, in the act of handing to the man behind the counter a bank-note—the one I had just given her.

How events repeat themselves! Why should that woman have stood there, just at that time, to recall to me the last time that I saw my mother? It was only years after that I found the answer to this question—when the devil, taking advantage of my dejection, sought to enlist me in the ranks of the unfortunate women who vainly attempt to drown sorrow in the cup. The remembrance of the circumstances under which I last saw my mother, and of that wretched woman who had closed my husband's eyes—as I saw her in the bar-room—saved me from the abyss. Those sad scenes were, as I have since learned, among the greatest graces that I had received from God.

After making all other arrangements for the interment, I returned home with a heart bowed down with grief. I clasped my child to my bosom, and renewed the vow that I would be a good mother. I tried to nourish her; but my emotions had been too much for me, and from that day my breasts refused all nutriment.

The 11th of January, 1863, was a bleak, wintry day. I was in Greenwood, standing by the side of an open grave, waiting while some men disinterred my babe; for I had insisted that her remains should be placed upon my husband's breast. His coffin had been lowered into the earth; but not a clod had yet been thrown upon it. The wind blew mournfully around me, and kept up a doleful melody, as though nature were moaning a dirge for the departed. I was standing all alone: for the friends who had accompanied me had withdrawn, and were walking up and down among the graves. They had tried to persuade me to leave, assuring me that my wishes would be obeyed. But I must see for myself so sacred a trust fulfilled, and I persisted in remaining.

At last I saw two men coming, bearing a little coffin. My heart melted: for the first thought that came to me was, that in contained that precious little head whose touch used to thrill my heart with so much joy. I bade the men place the little burden on his breast, and when I heard the two coffins touch I felt relieved. I leaned over and gave them both a long, parting look; but, as I saw my tears drop into the grave, I felt how different all would be could I place my hand upon my breast and say that I had always done my duty as a wife.

The following Sunday a friend brought me the *Atlas*. It contained the poem which my husband had written a few nights before he died. It always makes me sad to read it, and often have I moistened it with my tears. For I cannot read it without seeing his sickly form sitting by that table, during a cold winter's night, in that cheerless room, with his debauched companion. There he sits, regretting sunnier days; and, by the feeble glimmer of a candle-light, he writes this poem, believing it may pay the expenses of his burial.

[*Written for the New York Atlas.*]

EVENING MUSINGS.

BY THE LATE SAMUEL ECKEL.

(HIS LAST POEM.)

The evening star is in the sky,
   The balmy wind is whist; but, oh !
My soul is very sad, and why ?
   I'm thinking of the long ago.

The maple-leaves have gone to sleep;
   The lonely moon is still awake,
And by her gentle light I weep:
   My heart can bleed, but cannot break.

The days of childhood, sweet as morn,
   My playmates, too, each with a toy—
That blest the home where I was born,
   And made me happy when a boy,

Have vanished like an April gift
   Of crocus-blooms when fields were green—
When singing-birds on pinions swift
   Gave life and beauty to the scene.

The hours of youth, with dreams of bliss,
   All filled with starry hopes for me,
Have faded, too, and left but this—
   A dark and gloomy YET TO BE.

January 5th, 1803.

One summer's day, when the sun shone brightly, I went to Greenwood, and by his grave I passed the day. On his bosom I planted the rose, the heliotrope, and the violet—his favourite flowers; and at his. head I placed an ivy, which I entwined around a little marble slab, whereon is simply inscribed :—

TO

MY HUSBAND

AND

MY DARLING BABE.

CHAPTER XXV.

PARIS—THE AMERICAN COLONY—I AM PRESENTED AT COURT.

Peering into Futurity—Paris and the Pantheon—Saint Geneviève—Literature, Languor, and Learning—I am introduced—I utilise " Les Inutiles "—Feminine Diplomacy—Capture of a Diplomat—Ancestry —An English Heart.

I RECEIVED more congratulations on account of my husband's death than were offered me at the time of our marriage. But they would send through me a bitter pang, for I sincerely mourned him. Yet I tried to conceal my grief, lest others should suspect me of affectation. My sorrow would betray itself, however, in spite of all my efforts to conceal it : for I soon lost my ambition and energy, and became despondent and discouraged.

I then began to seek encouragement and hope by consulting fortune-tellers, spiritualists, and clairvoyants—a habit I had indulged in during my married life, but which, after my husband's death, I carried to great excess. I had faith in whatever these persons told me. For a while, indeed, my faith in the spiritualists was somewhat shaken, as they had all predicted that my child would be a boy. I called them to account for having deceived me, as I had already selected a boy's name, and had marked some of the baby-clothes with the initial. All the satisfaction I got from them was, that they appeared as much surprised as myself.

As soon as my husband died I went to a strange medium, whom I happened to see advertised. I had hardly sat down at the table before this woman wrote out my husband's name. This restored my confidence, and I would go regularly to consult the spirits whenever I became doubtful and sad in regard to the future. But spiritualists and soothsayers would occasionally contradict each other. Notwithstanding their disagreement in minor things (and I consulted everyone I saw advertised), they were all of an accord in the one all-important matter, that I would marry a tall, wealthy distinguished blonde ; that he would die very suddenly and of an accident, about five or six years after marriage ; that I would inherit his estates and would marry again for love ; that I would outlive number three, and live to a good old age.

My maid was a young German woman, whose husband had abandoned her, and had left her heart-stricken and wretched.

She would lull my babe to sleep, singing to it the most melancholy German airs. She had a sweet, sympathetic voice, and those plaintive melodies were the only sounds that accorded with my saddened heart. I sought to be alone with her and my child. My old exciting mode of life had become distasteful to me ; and, one by one, my friends abandoned me. I had lost all my gaiety and energy, and was consequently incapable of serving or diverting them.

In a few months my parlour was deserted by all, with the exception of two or three faithful friends, and they happened to be the few whom it had never been in my power to serve. I was speaking with them one day about the future. I proposed to study two years more, and then go to Europe. But they all advised me to go at once.

These gentlemen gave me letters of introduction to their acquaintances abroad, and I left with my maid and child in July, 1863.

Our steamer glided over the Atlantic as smoothly as if we were sailing on some silvery lake. Not a gale arose, hardly a cloud appeared in the horizon, from our departure, till we came within sight of port.

Never shall I forget my feelings when I first laid eyes on the shores of France. The very air infused into me a new life. In an instant every trace of sorrow disappeared from my heart, as though it had been touched by some magic wand. I felt like a happy child. As we passed through the streets of Havre, I kept looking up at the sky and constantly exclaiming : "What a beautiful blue !"

My maid, too, for the first time threw off her grief and began to smile ; and my babe clapped her little hands and gladdened us both with her infantine laughter.

We went along like a group of merry birds that had just discovered a genial clime. I kept continually stopping to embrace my child. My heart was so flooded with delight that I could have kissed the very pebbles over which we walked. I did not feel like a stranger who had just arrived in a foreign land, but more like an exile who had just come home. The genial expression of the passers-by—everything, in a word, gave joy. Even the signs which hung over the shops seemed to welcome us with a bewitching grace ; and I remember distinctly the first sign which attracted my gaze. It was an immense picture of our Lord carrying a lamb, and the shop was named " *Au Bon Pasteur—Of the Good Shepherd.*" We looked into the shop to see what it meant, and we began to laugh when we saw it filled with children's clothes, and a lot of little children there trying them on.

We got into the train, and it seemed as though we were passing through one continual garden, from the time we left Havre till we reached Paris.

I kept humming to myself, all the way, the first verse of an old French song, called "*Ma Normandie.*"

> "Quand tout renait à l'espérance,
>   Et que l'hiver fuit loin de nous;
> Sous le beau ciel de notre France,
>   Quand le soliel revient plus doux;
> Quand la Nature est reverdie;
>   Quand l'hirondelle est de retour;
> J'aime a revoir ma Normandie—
>   C'est le pays qui m'a donné le jour."

Of which I would submit the following, as an attempt at a translation :—

> When to new hope from their long trance
>   All things revive, and winter flees;
> 'Neath the sweet sky of our loved France,
>   As milder suns embalm each breeze:
> When earth dons her green livery,
>   And swallows homeward wing their flight;
> Fain would I see my Normandy
>   Once more, where first I saw the light.

Just before we reached Paris we heard a voice from an adjoining coach exclaim: "*Voilà Paris!*" I looked, and the first things I saw were the Arch of Triumph and the dome of the Pantheon. I see them still as I saw them then, and even now they send through my heart a pleasing thrill. In that instant the earth, the sky, the air, the Arch of Triumph, and the dome of the Pantheon, all seemed to bid me a joyful welcome, and to foretell a happy future. They have kept their promise; but the Pantheon was the last to put the seal of fulfilment on that which then spoke so vividly to my soul, and said: "Thou shalt be happy yet!"

We put up at the Hôtel du Louvre. On the steamer I had made the acquaintance of a lady and gentleman who were on their wedding tour. They were Cubans, and as I spoke Spanish we soon became friends, and they proposed that we should visit the monuments and churches in Paris together. "Yes," said I; "but we will visit first the tombs of Voltaire and Rousseau." I felt as if it were a homage that I owed to the memory of those two philosophers, who had contributed so much to enliven my solitude when neglected by my husband.

We went to the Pantheon, and at once descended into its
vaults, and walked through their serpentine passages until we
reached the tomb of Voltaire.   I became mournfully sad during
the few moments that I stood by this tomb.

As I reflectingly gazed on his statue, I regretted not having
brought a garland to hang on the lyre, which his statue represents him holding in his hand.   After remaining there a few
moments we passed on to Rousseau's tomb.   No marble statue
was there to honour his memory.   A small monument, on
the side of which was sculptured a sinewy arm and a hand
bearing a lighted torch, did honour to the dead philosopher.
Some one remarked that the device meant that Rousseau
came into the world to bring Discord.   I turned to the speaker
and replied that that was a misinterpretation, for the torch
meant that he came to enlighten the world.   " Then," answered
the speaker, " if such is the *light*, I prefer the obscurity which
preceded."

As we ascended the steps leading from the vaults I thought
what a pity it was that two such men could not have been
immortal.   All at once I discovered that I was separated from
my companions, who were placing themselves in positions to
get a good view of the frescoes on the concave ceiling of the
rotunda.

I merely threw them a fugitive glance, and then continued
to walk along, without caring which way I went, or even
remarking what was before me, until suddenly I found myself
before a railing which barred my progress.   I looked up, and
to my surprise I was standing before a beautiful altar erected
to Saint Geneviève, patron saint of Paris.   Directly over the
tabernacle was placed an antique statue, which represented the
saint in the garb of a shepherdess.   I first looked steadily at
the statue, then at the altar, and then at an elderly priest who was
sitting to the right in the sanctuary saying his beads.   By his
side were many lighted candles, which the faithful had placed
there in honour of Saint Geneviève, whose intercession they
implored.

I was deeply impressed by the devotion which was paid to
this saint.   Crutches and other memorials of gratitude were
hung about the sanctuary.   Old men, women, and children were
kneeling around the altar, and with upturned faces and clasped
hands were earnestly invoking Saint Geneviève's protection.
After making a slight reflection, on a sight that was to me so
strange and yet so interesting, I looked up again at the statue,
and this time I mentally exclaimed :

" I wonder if there is anything in it?"

" I will try you, good saint," said I, " and if you answer my prayer I will offer you a memorial which will far exceed anything that I see offered to you here."   I knelt down by the railing and implored Saint Geneviève to intercede for me, that I might be presented at court, that I might have plenty of money, and that the first men of the empire might be at my feet.

I then arose and went and knelt down by the priest, and asked him to give me his blessing.   He arose and blessed me.   I then asked him why those candles were burning there.   He told me their meaning, and expressed his surprise that I was not a Catholic.   Said he : " Did I not see you this moment invoking Saint Geneviève ?"

"Yes," I replied : "I asked her for three things ; I just want to see if there is anything *in it.*"   " But, my child," he continued, " why did you ask my blessing ?"   Said I : " I hardly know myself ; but I felt that it would bring me good luck."   He continued : " You are a Protestant ?"   " Yes," said I, " inasmuch as I protest against all religions ; but I am what you would call an infidel ; for I belong to the school of Voltaire, and it was to visit his tomb that I came here to-day."   He sadly and faintly smiled after I had finished speaking, and was going to resume his seat.   But, as I lingered near the altar—for I was strangely drawn to it—he came to me again and said to me : " You have a Spanish accent, my child ; but I never knew that Spain ever educated one of her daughters to be an infidel."   " I am an American," I answered.   He smiled, nodded his head, and making a Frenchman's movement with his hands, uttered; " *Eh bien,*" which meant that it was all clear to him then.

I took apartments in the Champs Elysées, where I settled at once, as though I were to make Paris my home for the rest of my life.   I had not been there a week before I engaged two experienced teachers, and began a thorough course of Italian and French literature.

My Italian teacher taught me how to paint my eyes, so as to give them that dreamy languor so much admired in the ladies of the East.   She was an adept in the art, and she pronounced me an apt scholar ; for, in two short lessons, I profited so well that she declared the colouring was so well blended with my complexion that no one could suspect that it was not natural.

After four months' study I delivered my letters of introduction. I was received most cordially, and was invited to receptions and entertainments.   As I had never dissipated, I appeared much younger than most ladies of my age, and I pretended to be still younger.

I had always been fond of studying encyclopædias, and I had acquired a large amount of superficial knowledge, which I had tact enough to display to the best advantage. I soon acquired a reputation for learning. I had a smattering of many things, but the knowledge of nothing; and my tact consisted in never going so far as to let others discover how little I knew. I have often conversed with persons on subjects I knew nothing about, and on which they instructed me at every word; yet I am sure that I have left them under the impression that I knew more about the subject than they did themselves. In fine, I soon acquired the enviable reputation of trying to conceal my knowledge, whereas the truth was I only succeeded in disguising my ignorance.

It is needless to say that I was at once detested by the women, and adored by the men. The ladies when conversing with me would invariably turn the conversation on myself. They would ask me who were my relations, and whom I knew in America. As for my relations, I knocked them all at once on the head by declaring that they were all dead, and I gave them a list of the acquaintances I had made in Washington, who were among the best families at home. The only account I would give of myself was that I descended from the family of Lord Bolingbroke; that my husband had been United States consul; that I had always had, *even as a child*, a morbid distaste for society;—which I could say truly when I thought of my life in the Highlands of Dutchess;—that I had always preferred solitude and study; and that even now I only went into society at the earnest solicitations of my friends, and not that it gave me the· slightest gratification.

I chanced to meet several gentlemen who had known my husband on the Chilian coast, and who had been particularly fond of him for his melancholy and laconic humour, which made him one of the most pleasant *convives* in the world. These gentlemen introduced me to their acquaintances as the wife of their bosom friend. My four months' solitude and my demeanour verified my words in regard to my indifference to the attention of others. I never sought anyone's acquaintance; I made no advances, and made everybody come to me first.

In a few weeks I was obliged to have a reception-day, as I found that I was constantly interrupted by callers. But there were some few of my newly-made friends whom I would permit to call on me at appointed hours during the day, which gave me an opportunity of conversing with them. These were chiefly idlers, or, as the French call them, "*Les Inutiles*," who sought

me at that time only because my apartment faced on the Champs
Elysées, and it gave them a chance to kill time by looking at
the horses and equipages as they passed to and from the Bois de
Boulogne.

Les Inutiles Americains in Paris are not usually men of
sentiment, but are men of leisure, whose principal occupation
during the day consists in making calls and in lounging about the
reading-rooms of the American banking-houses.   Their evenings
are usually passed in gambling in their bedrooms, or promenading
in the disreputable gardens of the metropolis.   They are the
repositories of all the gossip that floats among the American
colony in Paris.   I cultivated a few of the species, and reversed
their calling by making them extremely *useful;* for they
brought me a daily bulletin of all they heard, either good or
bad, in regard to myself, and all that their information cost me
was a few French biscuits and a bottle of wine.

By what I learned from “ *Les Inutiles,*” I saw that my position
could only be maintained by a continual struggle.   I heard with
regret that the envious had succeeded in prejudicing our American minister, Mr. Dayton, against me ; and that he had said
that he should not present me at Court.   I heard also that the
ladies who frequented my receptions were my bitterest enemies,
and their caustic remarks and broad insinuations would be repeated to me just as they had fallen from their lips.   I was a
mystery they thought, and there *must be something wrong* that
so young a lady should be travelling alone without any protection.
Even such accomplishments as I had they turned against me by
saying that it was evident that I had only been educated in order
to attract and inveigle the opposite sex, with *no good* design, as
was *clear* to every woman who had laid eyes on me.

I was kept so well informed of everybody's sentiments towards
me, that I was always prepared to manage my adversaries whenever I came in contact with them.   But instead of using their
own weapons, which my position then was too weak to justify, I
tried to conquer them by treating those with the most civility
whom I had the most reason to hate.   I avoided giving them a
chance to suspect that I knew what their sentiments were in
regard to me ; and those whom I had the most reason to distrust
I would treat apparently with the greatest confidence, and every
one of my words would be repeated to me, with additional
remarks, by *Les Inutiles.*

But I soon got tired of the strife, for it gave me little or no
satisfaction, even after I had succeeded in weakening my
enemies.   I saw, in spite of all I could do, that I was losing

ground ; and I began to lose courage, and was ready to give up
the contest and leave Paris. I could go to Florence, where I
had excellent letters to old residents, and there begin anew. I
fell into my old habit and went to consulting the fortune-tellers,
who all predicted for me a bright future, a splendid marriage,
and great worldly success.

One day I found Mr. Pennington, Secretary of the American
Legation, waiting for me. He had come to tell me that the
first ball at the Tuileries would take place on the 6th of January,
and that, if I wanted to be presented to their Majesties, I must
make my application at once. "I know too much," I said, "to
make an application when I am sure to be refused." Then I
told Mr. Pennington that I had learned from Mrs. ———, that
Mr. Dayton had said that he would not present me at Court.
" The old vixen !" exclaimed Pennington, " she is the very woman
who came to the Legation and prejudiced Mr. Dayton against
you." I was surprised to hear this, for I thought her the only
true lady friend I had in Paris. She had feigned to be exceedingly sorry when she came to tell me what Mr. Dayton had said ;
and she was always inviting me to her house to dine, and always
coming to my receptions. " Well," said I, " if such is the case
I am disgusted with Paris, and I shall leave at once for Florence."
Pennington broke out into an ironical laugh. " Florence," said
he, " is, of all places on the face of the earth, the ——— ;" and
he used, in the superlative degree, a participial adjective de-
cidedly and dedecorously more forcible than polite, to express his
utter condemnation. " Why, Paris is a heaven to it ;" he continued ; " here people only know how much money a man has in
the bank, but in Florence they will tell you how much you have
in your pocket. All that people do there is to mind one another's
business. It would ruin anyone who has a good name to live
there ; and I wonder what chance you would stand. Why,"
said he, " there would not be a hair left on the top of your head
at the end of the first week." " But," said I, " my head feels
pretty sore now, and I have got enough of it ; I give it up."
" If you cannot get along in Paris," said Pennington, " you can
never succeed anywhere. At any rate, Mrs. Dayton is your
friend, for I have often heard her speak sympathizingly of you.
She knows that it is nothing but envy that has turned the
women against you. Write her a note ; make your application
to her. I will choose a good time to give it to her. If *she* asks
her husband to present you he will do it." " But," said I, "why
do you not ask it for me ? You ought to have a good deal of
influence, being Secretary of Legation, and being with them

most of the time." "How foolishly you talk !" said he, " they all know just what kind of a man I am. I will run you down when I present the note, then Mrs. Dayton will be sure to stand up for you. You ought to know that people of sense are suspicious of a woman whom all the men are praising and all the women abusing ! "

I wrote the note, and the next day I received a letter from the Legation, asking would I like to be presented at Court on the occasion of the first ball, which would take place on the 6th. I replied in the affirmative, and a few days later I received a letter, saying that my application had been granted.

I made a most extravagant outlay on my toilet. I wore a pearl necklace, a set of diamonds, and a white silk dress puffed with tulle. Pennington introduced me to a courtier, who escorted me into the supper-room, where I supped at the first table, near to their Majesties, and with the Diplomatic Corps. Mr. Dayton saw me. He came up and spoke to me, and complimented me for being so handsomely dressed, saying that he was glad to see America so well represented. He took his place beside me, and remained by me during the time we were in the supper-room, which must have been three-quarters of an hour. I felt that my opportunity had come to undo the mischief that my rivals had done me, and I was determined to profit by it.

It was easy to read Mr. Dayton's character, and it would have been difficult to mistake it, for his frank, high-toned, generous nature was stamped on all his features.

For a moment I was perplexed, I did not know what art to use in order to win him and make him my friend. I knew that my future in France depended on being sustained and protected by the Daytons. I finally came to the conclusion that the best art to use with such a man was to use no art at all. So I threw off those allurements and that air of languid indifference which had never failed to captivate those who were as deeply steeped in dissimulation as myself, and I behaved towards him like a plain, honest, frank, outspoken woman. This was a hard part for me to play, for the contrary long habit had almost become to me a second nature. I commenced by attacking his gallantry, and gave him to understand that I knew that I was not indebted to him for the pleasure of supping that evening at their Majesties' table. I then tried to enlist his sympathies by exposing to him my real position, and telling how grateful I felt towards Mrs. Dayton ; and I appealed to his generosity by begging him not to let the envious so poison him against me that he himself should seek to break that slender support which I had in the protection of his wife.   In an instant I saw that I had conquered, for he reproached himself at once for his prejudices, which he acknowledged to me.   "I give them all up," he made haste to say, "for I never was so mistaken in anyone in my life. Why you are nothing but a child!   I have often watched you, and have tried to study you, and I came to the conclusion that you were a confirmed diplomat."   "And so I am," I replied, "and I have just given you a good proof of it by throwing all diplomacy aside the moment I came into the presence of my master."   He smiled and slightly inclined his head in acknowledgment, and he assured me when we parted that evening that I could count on his protection whenever it would be in his power to serve me.

The Americans received me better after my presentation at Court, for there was still a doubt whether I might not rise after all.

Among my American acquaintances was a family whose son had married the daughter of the Count of ——, who was brother of the Duchess of ——.   I was introduced to this family, and, for a short time, was a general favourite.   They invited me to their dinners and parties, and introduced me to their friends.   But in a short while it was only a repetition of what had occurred among the Americans.   I gave umbrage to the women.   They felt that I took a position that no lady had a right to aspire to, unless she could trace her genealogy back to Charlemagne, or one of his paladins ; and they tried to disembarrass themselves of me, by not inviting me to their houses, nor coming to my receptions.   But, to their great chagrin, we were constantly meeting in the drawing-rooms of those to whom they had introduced me.   One was that of Madame O'Gorman, and another that of an English lady, Mrs. Admiral Ross.

I was passing one evening alone with Mrs. Ross, at her house, when, in a most adroit and lady-like way, she very delicately remarked, that the great affection she had for me gave her a strong desire to know all about me, as, from my manners and education, it was evident to all that I had not descended from anything vulgar.   I felt that she had put the question very sweetly, yet I had become chafed by the treatment I had received from her noble French friends, with the ducal connection ; and I got tired of hearing ancestry discussed from morning till night, especially for the reason that I did not care to resuscitate my own.

I answered her laughingly, " I see that it is all over with me here, and that you are going to court-martial me, so as to go over to the enemy." She was unprepared for any such outburst on my part. She had supposed that I would not be quick enough to detect her object. She was so embarrassed that she could not reply, but blushed crimson. I took pity on her, and continued: "My relatives are all dead, at least they are all dead *to me. Requiescant in pace;* and if their resurrection depended on me, I am afraid that they would be permitted to continue for many a year to enjoy their present *shady* condition. I was fondled by them one day as a pet, and the next day was thrust into their kitchen like a Cinderella. But it was not in their kitchen that the gallant knight Eckel fell in love with me, for I had already wandered from it! Now, madam, be satisfied, for I shall tell your no more. But if I should judge of myself by what I know of my kin I could swear to you, madam, that the *worst* blood in America flows through my veins. So now give me my hat, and let me go." At that I advanced towards the door of the antechamber.

My friend burst out into a hearty laugh, sprang after me, and caught me, before I reached the door. She kissed me on both cheeks, took my hand, and led me back to the sofa, saying, " I want to be your friend. Sit down, and I will open my heart to you." She told me the efforts that others, even the Americans, had made to prevent her visiting me. But henceforth, she said, nothing should separate us. " I give you my heart," she said ; " and in fact you have had my sympathies from the first moment that I saw you." And in the enjoyment of her friendship I soon learned to know the priceless value of a true English heart.

CHAPTER XXVI.

MY OCTOGENARIAN BEAU—A NOBLE IRISH FAMILY AND AN IRISH M.P.

Marrying a Title—The Duke de Morny—I prove that I was Born—The Life of Jesus—Systematic Theology—My Friends.

ABOUT this time I was engaged to be married to a Mr. S——, from Boston. One night, as I was going to bed, I implored God to send me a true dream, and to let me know if I was ever to marry Mr. S——. I dreamed that I was standing in a garden, and that I saw a gipsy coming towards me. I went up to her and asked her to tell my fortune. She instantly unrolled a scroll which she held in her hand, and on it was written, in letters of gold, " *You will never marry S——.*" I saw it plainly, but beneath the scroll was a word that could not be seen so distinctly, for it seemed to float in a mist; but it was plain enough for me to read. The word was " Laferrière." The gipsy then disappeared, and I instantly awoke. The dream was just as vivid before me as anything I had ever seen, yet I did not believe it, and said to myself, " Dreams always go by contraries." But in a few weeks Mr. S—— and I had a quarrel, when we both confessed that we would sooner be shot than marry each other, after which we parted the best of friends.

My next suitor was the Count de V——, an octogenarian, who pretended to be much younger. I made his acquaintance at an evening party given by the Countess de Loyauté. Everybody knew that I wanted to marry a title, and he offered me his in exchange for my fortune, which he proposed to divide with his daughter the Countess de F——. I then cast a look over my money affairs, and I saw that I must either retrench my expenses or give up the idea of marrying a count. My friends in America were still faithful to me, and I was constantly drawing interests on contracts, wherein it was understood that so long as certain men should give me a per-centage, they would have the preference—justly or not.

One evening Dr. Johnson called on me and asked me why I did not try to marry a title. I told him that for the present the only man of title who presented himself was an octogenarian, and that to take him would seem like being led to the altar by Satan himself. " So much the better," said the doctor, " the older he is the sooner he will die, and then you will be Madame la Comtesse, without any encumbrances." He talked to me in this way for about an hour, until he actually persuaded me that I ought to jump at the chance.

I at once conferred with Mr. Dayton, who said all he could to reason me out of it. But I became inexorable, for my head was full of all the advantages that Dr. Johnson had persuaded me would accrue to me the moment I would be ushered into the drawing-room as Madame la Comtesse. Mr. Dayton then told me of the danger of marrying a Frenchman, on account of the civil law in regard to marriage; that it was a difficult thing for an American to be legally married in France, as the most necessary article was a certificate of birth, which not one American out of a hundred could produce, as required by French law. He might marry me to a Frenchman at the French Legation, and I might be married again at the church; yet in France my marriage would not be considered legal, and my right to the title of Countess could be disputed after my husband's death by anyone whose interest it might be to lay claim to it. As I had suffered all my life from the fact that it had not been proved that my parents were legally married, notwithstanding their allegations that they were married—and it is my firm belief that they were—I was determined not to run any risk, but to be perfectly sure of my success before advancing any farther. So I bade society a short farewell, and went to studying *le Code Napoleon*—the civil law of France. I made the Count bring · me all his papers so as to satisfy myself of the genuineness of his title.

In the midst of this laborious occupation, Mr. Dayton introduced to me the Duke de Morny. The Duke called on me one day, and was exceedingly amused to see a lady's boudoir turned into a law-office. He proposed to relieve me of a task which my instinct of self-preservation against French chicanery had imposed upon me, and took home with him the two or three hundred papers of the Count, which must have proved his ancestry as far back as King Pepin.

In a few days the Duke brought me an answer that my certificate of birth was the most important paper, and that I must have also papers to prove the death of my parents, besides my marriage certificate and the certificate of my husband's death, signed by the French consul in New York. I sent at once to America and procured the two last. But to produce my certificate of birth would be impossible. To obtain a certificate of the death of my father would be possible, but I would certainly never apply to the insane asylum for the certificate of death of my mother.

The Duke de Morny confided to me his own history which had been full of vicissitudes. As he was the illegitimate son of Queen Hortense and half-brother to the Emperor, he had passed a part of his life in a palace and another part in misery. I saw that illegitimacy in his eyes was no disgrace, so I told him how I had been done out of my birthright—justly or not there would ever be a doubt—but that I had smarted from it just as much as though I were really an illegitimate child. My story interested the Duke, and he promised to do all in his power to aid me, and he was sure of success. As soon as he became thoroughly informed he called on me again, and told me that there was a law in France which made provision for cases where foreigners could not procure their certificate of birth. I would have to go before a magistrate and make a declaration that I was the daughter of such and such persons; I must give my mother's maiden name. " Which," said I, " I will never do! " (I had not confided

it even to him.) My declaration must be signed by seven
witnesses, and this paper would answer the purpose of a certificate of birth.

I secured the seven witnesses, and we all met at the court-
room of a justice of the peace. The witnesses should have
declared their own knowledge of the alleged facts, but on account of the powerful influence that was aiding me they were
permitted to confine themselves to declaring their belief in the
truth of my statement, as this was all that they could do con-
scientiously.   So the whole burden was thrown on my conscience.
I quieted my scruples in this way : I gave the name of my father,
and as my mother had come from Montreal, which is a city, and
ville is the French for city, I gave my mother's first name and
her second name as *de Ville*, which, in English, would be Maria
of the City.

When I explained to the Duke how I had gotten out of the
difficulty he laughed heartily, and said : "What is your religion,
that you can arrange your conscience to suit such an emergency?"
I was surprised that he should even suspect me of having
any religion at all, and I did not reply. "Do," said he
seriously, "tell me what is your belief."   Said I : "I believe
in Venus and Mars—love and fight." "I am a convert too,"
said he.

The next day he brought me Renan's "Life of Jesus." We
read most of it together. I will never forget how I was affected
by reading the last chapter. I was alone, and had passed the
whole afternoon perusing the book. I had been reading that
part where it speaks of the Saviour's perfections as man, and of
His divine generosity in being willing to die for His doctrine,
which He believed would secure the happiness of mankind.
Renan speaks admiringly of so much magnanimity. Then he
spoke of His delicate organisation, and of His crucifixion. I
closed the book, burst into tears, and exclaimed : " What a
pity that He is not God ! for I feel like falling down and
worshipping Him." It was the first time that I had ever shed
a tear over our Lord's sufferings. I felt that He *must* be God ;
but I did not *want* to believe it, and I at once set diligently
to work to re-read those passages in Jean Jacques which had so
thoroughly convinced me of the contrary years before. But I
had to fight against the grace that was given me at the moment
that I had finished Renan's work.

There was something so beautiful in the description of the
Man-God, even as pourtrayed by the pen of an unbeliever,
that I could not divest myself of the feeling that He *must have*

been Divine, as no mere *man* could ever have been like that man.

Mr. Dayton regretted having introduced me to De Morny, and was always warning me to beware of him. The Duke knew it. Mr. Dayton once said to him that he was afraid he had thrown the lamb into the lion's arms. The Duke answered: " Which of us is the lamb ?" The moment I made the Duke's acquaintance I scarcely needed any longer the influence even of the American Minister; for through the Duke I could get invitations everywhere, even to " *les petits bals*," of the Empress ; a favour which Mr. Dayton could not have obtained for his most intimate friends.

The Duke also sent me boxes for the opera and theatres. In fact I had everything my own way, and was enjoying life to my heart's content.

The Count de V—— had introduced me to all his friends, but the moment I became intimate with them they advised me not to marry him, for it was evident that I would be most miserable if I did. He was already so jealous of me that he endeavoured to control my relations with others. This I would not allow ; but he threatened to enforce his will in the matter the moment I should be his wife. All this did not decide me to give up the idea of marrying him. It was only when the Duke, on bringing me a report of the genuineness of the title, told me that his secretary had discovered, in looking over the genealogy of the family, that for the five last generations all the male ancestors had lived nearly a century, and when he remarked that there was a prospect of the present Count outrivalling them all in age, from his present hale and hearty appearance, that I became frightened and dared not run the risk, for I had only counted on one or two years at most. I had done everything to attach him to me. Being fond of literature, as he was gifted and talented, we used to pass whole days together while he instructed me. It is one of the sinful acts of my life, which I now regret the most, that I embittered the last days of the Count de V——. He died two years afterwards ; but he was wretched until the day of his death, on account of the manner in which I had treated him, for it humbled him in the eyes of all his friends, to whom he had boasted of his future happiness.

But I forgot him the moment he was out of my sight. Yet, with a "systematic theology" of my own, I looked upon our acquaintance as providential, for it had incited me to obtain a certificate of birth, which might be of great service to me in the future.

I felt that I owed all my success to God, and I used to thank Him for everything I received. I believed that He showered favours upon me to remunerate me for the injustice He had done me in my youth. I did not believe that He would hold me responsible for my sins, as I was sure that if I ceased for one day to be a rogue, that day I would be lost.

As soon as I had secured friends among the best families in Paris, I at once ·swept my rooms of "*Les Inutiles.*" This created for me a new host of enemies, for they wished to make use of me to extend the list of their acquaintances, and they revenged themselves upon me by injuring me as much as they could. I had weighed all that before I waged war with them, and it was only when I had secured a position too strong for *them* to pull me down that I ventured on such a battle.

I left the Champs Elysées and took a spacious apartment at the Hôtel du Louvre.

About this time the O'Gorman returned from Berlin, where he used to spend the greater part of his time. His return was hailed with great joy by his friends in Paris. I was invited frequently to their house, and the happiest hours I ever passed in society were spent under their roof.

They were of a noble Irish family, highly cultivated, witty and refined, generous and charitable to the last degree, never doing another a wrong, nor suspecting it in others. *They knew who they were themselves*, and therefore did as they pleased and judged for themselves whom they should like, and whom they should not. They were not always thrusting their nobility in your face, yet you could see it in all their ways. I always left them with one regret, and that was that there were not more like them in the world. Whenever I went to the O'Gormans I was obliged to throw off the mask I wore in the world, and tried to behave like a woman of sense; for in a house where so much candour and honesty reigned, deception and craft were ill at their ease. I would cast them off at the sill of their door, where I would resume them again to make a fool of the beau who escorted me home.

It was at Mme. O'Gorman's that I made the acquaintance of Pope Hennessy and Edmond de Lesseps. Hennessy was then an Irish member of the British Parliament, and Lesseps had just returned from Lima, where he was the French consul-general. Hennessy was full of intelligence and wit. It was impossible to dine where he was, for he would keep us constantly laughing at his sallies and repartee. One evening, as we had just left the table, I asked him if that *was* the truth he had been telling, for he had nearly affirmed with an oath all that he had said. "The truth!" he exclaimed, with astonishment; "who ever heard of such a thing as telling the truth at a dinner-table? Why, you would not have me put all the people to sleep, would you?" "But," said I, "the O'Gorman has just told me that you are a good Roman Catholic, and I cannot believe that you are sincere." Hennessy became serious, and assured me that there was not a better believing or a worse practising Catholic in all Ireland than himself. "Then," said I, "how dare you tell such lies, if you believe you are going to be punished for them?" "Ah," said Hennessy, "that is all right; for I have two sisters at home who are constantly praying for me—they will keep me out of hell." "But," said I, "why don't you pray for yourself?" He replied: "So I do; for I pray that God may listen to them." I did not, and could not, believe him confessing against himself. As I pen these lines the thought occurs to me that the day may come when I shall take Hennessy's place, and he mine; when it will be much easier for me to convince him and the world that all the lies I ever told were truths, than to make them believe me now when I speak the truth.

CHAPTER XXVII.

MACHIAVELIAN SUCCESS—A NIGHT OF HORRORS—ALONE WITH A CORPSE—MR. DAYTON.

The American Minister—A Judge of Horseflesh—The Prospects of Rat-scratch—Death—The Hand of God—Despair—The Son—The Wife and Daughter—Where Death had been—Retrospect of a Night.

On the last evening in November, 1864, I was standing in my bedroom before a wardrobe mirror, admiring myself, and contrasting the past with the present. I felt happy and contented. It seemed as if I then realised all that I had ever hoped for or dreamed of in life. I was courted and flattered by the fashionable world of Paris, and my life was but one continual round of gaiety and pleasure, which never gave me a moment's time for sadness or reflection. In the midst of it all I had kept my heart perfectly free. I enjoyed everything, yet loved nothing but what I called success.

I had made the "Prince" of Machiavel my breviary, and I

never doubted that its maxims pointed the way to happiness; for had not the following of them paved my way to success?

I was contented with the present, and felt that the future was secure; for I believed that all lay in my own hands—that I had only to continue in my Machiavelian course, and that pleasure and enjoyment would always be mine.

I had just finished my evening toilet. I had on a dress which was fitted to my form with artistic simplicity, and my hair-dresser had becomingly arranged my hair with bands of ribbon in the Grecian style. My maid had gone to her room, and I was alone. I was waiting for Mr. Dayton, whom I expected to come and pass the evening with me; for I had written him the week before that I wished to see him on a matter of importance. It was in regard to an American, whom I will designate as Mr. Ratscratch, who wanted to be Chevalier of the Legion of Honour. He had promised me five thousand dollars if I would get the ribbon for him, and I wished to get Mr. Dayton's influence in the matter.

Mr. Dayton had called the previous evening in my absence, and had left his card, with word that he would come again the next evening. As I felt chilly I threw an opera-cloak over my shoulders, and took another admiring glance at myself in the glass; and this time I exclaimed, half aloud: "Who would have believed it ten years ago?" I burst out laughing at the thought of what kind of faces my old acquaintances would make if they could see me just as I stood there then, and I promenaded before the glass, talking to myself as merrily as could be, until I heard a rap. I flew to the door, and the Hon. William L. Dayton stood before me. He was surprised at my toilet, and withdrew a step, saying: "You are going out?" "No," said I, "not at all; I have been waiting for you." "But," he continued, "you are dressed to go out." "No," said I, "I am dressed to receive you." He smiled and came in, and, as we passed through the antechamber into the parlour, he said that he had just got away from Willie, who had gone to the theatre Palais Royal.

"Now," said he, "tell me what the important matter is that you intimated to me in your note." I went and got a paper. It was Mr. Ratscratch's application to the Minister of Foreign Affairs. "Nonsense," exclaimed Mr. Dayton, as soon as I told him that Mr. Ratscratch desired to be decorated; "what fools Americans do make of themselves the moment they cross the Atlantic. I always feel ashamed of myself whenever I put on my uniform, for I feel as though all that tinsel were beneath an American citizen."

I then read him the application. Mr. Ratscratch had founded a new branch of industry in France, which had greatly enriched the department in which it was established ; and it was for that reason that he laid claim to be decorated as Chevalier of the Legion of Honour.

Mr. Dayton promised me that he would have the application drawn up at his office in proper form, and that he would present it at once to the Minister of Foreign Affairs, with whom he was on excellent terms, and that he would press it so as to get it through before he left. "What !" said I, "are you going to leave France ?" "Yes," he replied, "I am going to send Mr. Seward my resignation very soon, for I am tired of this position, where I spend about six thousand dollars above my salary; and I want to go home on Willie's account." Said I : "How sorry I am that you are going away, for you alone can protect me against the envy and jealousy of the Americans."

He told me that he would recommend me strongly to his successor, and would do all he could for me. I then asked him to introduce me, before he left, to two French noblemen, who held good positions at Court. "Why do you want to know them ?" he asked. Said I : "I want their protection." "Yes," rejoined Mr. Dayton, "that is all very well *for you*, but who is going to *protect them ?*" and we both began to laugh. He continued : "You know too many people now, and you have all the young men abusing you." "Yes," I replied, "all the *petits crevés* whom I turned out of doors." "No, no," said Mr. Dayton, "something better than they. It was the Marquis de T——, who told me a few days ago that he found you on your reception-day surrounded by a pretty fast set; and I was very sorry to hear it too." "What," said I, "did that little English Marquis dare to speak so to you of me ? He was piqued that I did not take a fancy to him. You know yourself that he has a face of the colour and shape of a lobster, and that he walks like one too. He met none but his superiors here, the envious little fellow !" "Tut, tut," replied Mr. Dayton, interrupting me, and taking the Marquis's part, "I know better, for he is considered the best judge of horseflesh in Paris." Said I : "I would not trust him to buy me a jackass." Mr. Dayton could no longer restrain his laughter. But I continued : "And to prove to you that he has even less sense than a well-bred donkey, I will tell you what happened a few days ago at a dinner-party, where the Marquis was invited.

"All the guests were assembled excepting the Marquis, and it was already twenty minutes past the dinner-hour. Finally the

host gave him up, and we all sat down to the table. The first
course was served, when the waiter handed the host a piece of
folded paper, which was so soiled and misshapen, that anyone
could have guessed it had been written in a stable. Our host
took the note, but could only make out the meaning of one
word, and that was the signature, which he believed to be that
of the Marquis. 'Ah,' said he, 'this must be the Marquis's
excuse;' and we all remained silent, expecting to know why we
had been deprived of his company. But it was too much for the
host, so he handed the note to a lady who sat next to him, but
she could not make out a word of it either, and passed it to the
next, until it went round the table. Each one had his remark
to make, which would set the table in a roar. The ludicrously-
shaped note coming from an English nobleman, and the witty
remarks of the *convives*, afforded such merriment that the
dining-room was deafened with laughter. It had just reached
its full height when who was ushered into the dining-room but
the Marquis himself!

"His presence fell upon us like a bomb, and in a second our
peals of laughter were changed into a death-like silence, and
each one looked down straight into his plate, as though he were
making his examination of conscience, for the thought came
simultaneously to us all that he might have heard what we had
said. There was not a smile on the face of one of us during the
rest of the evening, and we all waited patiently for him to leave
that we might have our fun, but he outstayed the whole of us !
Now what do you think of that ?—to write a note of excuse,
which it would puzzle a magician to read, and which, to this
day, no one has ever been able to make out, and, after frighten-
ing us, to bore us to death ! I have not recovered from it yet."

Mr. Dayton laughed all the while that I was relating this silly
story, which I finished by asking him if he would let such an
ignorant jockey pass judgment on me. "No," said Mr. Dayton,
" I retract, and pronounce judgment in your favour." "And
well you may," said I, "for he only met the most charming
gentlemen in Paris here; but who keep their horses in their
stables without eating and sleeping with them, as the Marquis
does."

In this frivolous strain we kept our conversation for about
twenty minutes. I appeared reckless and overjoyed, but I was,
in reality, serious and anxious, for I was thinking all the while
about the five thousand dollars, and what he had said to me
about his leaving Paris.

Mr. Dayton had always been a good friend to me. I liked

him and esteemed him more than any gentleman who had taken
an interest in me. But I very seldom saw him, as I rarely
passed an evening at home. So I now felt that the time was
precious, and that I must do all I could to enlist his sympathies,
so that he would go to work at once and press my application
through the different departments, for, after being approved by
the Minister of Foreign Affairs, it had to pass through the hands
of the Minister of Agriculture and Commerce. Mr. Dayton told
me that his relations were good with both these gentlemen, and
he felt confident that he would succeed with them, for he considered that Mr. Ratscratch had a good claim to set forth. I
was so overjoyed when he gave me so much hope that I was
profuse in the expression of my gratitude.

Mr. Dayton was an open-hearted, candid, pure-minded man,
and one who was totally off his guard against the seductions of
any woman like myself. I began to assume a dreamy sadness,
as if at the thought of his departure. I was partly in earnest,
for he was my sincere friend, and had been of great service to
me, and he was a friend that could be relied upon. He was all
that I needed to protect me against the malice of the Americans,
who by this time had become exceedingly bitter against me, on
account of my pretensions, my indiscretions, and my success.

He was touched and moved at my expressions of tender regret,
and even surprised ; and he candidly admitted that it was only
the persecutions of others that had drawn him to me.

"I have often thought," said he, "what a pity it is that you
have not your family here to protect you." "Ah," I replied,
"then it is to my misfortunes alone that I am indebted for so
much sympathy ? If such is the truth I shall hereafter call them
by some other name." And thus we continued to converse,
until he at last arose and began to walk the room like a man
struggling to master an inward strife. But he soon resumed
his seat, and in a few minutes pressed his hand to his forehead
and exclaimed : "Oh, my head ! I feel sick ! get something that
will relieve me." I rushed into the bedroom and got some bay-
rum.

When I returned he was seated in the middle of the sofa with
his head bowed down upon his breast. I raised his head and
began to bathe it. "Do not leave me alone again," he said.
"Oh, I am so sorry I came ! I am so sorry I came !" and he made
an effort to disgorge. I sent the maid at once for a physician
When I returned I found him sitting as I had left him, but his
eyes were closed. Said he: "Do not leave me alone again, I
cannot see; you must not leave me alone." I moistened a

handkerchief with bay-rum, and supporting his head with my
arm, I placed the handkerchief on his left temple. That seemed
to relieve him, for he thanked me and said: " You are a good
child, but do not leave me alone again."

For a while neither of us spoke. At last I broke the silence,
and asked him if he would not like to lie down. He answered
by a slight motion of the head. I ran into the bedroom,
snatched up a pillow, and returned as quickly as possible. I
found him as I re-entered the room with his head down on the
sofa—he had fallen on his right side. I supposed that he had
tried to lie down. I placed the pillow on the arm of the sofa,
and told him to lay his head on the pillow; but he did not
move nor answer me. I finally succeeded in placing the pillow
under his head, and stretching his form upon the sofa, but I
nearly fainted with exhaustion in the effort. He began to
breathe loudly and harshly. I thought he had fallen asleep.
He continued to breathe thus for several minutes. Then there
was a pause—a deep silence. He drew one long last breath—
and was dead.

I thought that he slept soundly. The fire had gone down in
the fireplace, so I took off my opera cloak and threw it over him,
and wrapt up his right hand in the ermine hood. I took the
candle and placed it on the floor on the other side of the chimney
that the light might not shine on his eyelids. I looked at the
clock, it was twenty minutes past nine. I thought that I should
let him sleep until ten, and that it would then be time for him
to go home. I moved softly about the room that I might not
wake him.

The maid returned and told me that the doctor who resided
in the hotel was absent. " It is all over now," said I; " he is
asleep, and he will probably have recovered from his headache
when he awakes."

I then returned to the drawing-room and sat down by the side
of the *sleeping* man. I remained by his side for more than half-
an-hour, thinking, meditating, and building castles in the air,
as unconcernedly as though that evening was to end for me as
brightly as it had begun.

The clock struck ten. I uncovered his hand, which I had
wrapt up in the hood of the cloak. I took hold of it, expecting
to find it warm, but to my surprise it was cold, and without
suspecting why, I shrank instinctively from its touch and dropped
it instantly.

I tried gently to rouse him, and spoke to him. I called him
again, and then again, each time raising my voice. I thought

he had fainted, and I at once began to apply the few remedies I
had at hand to revive him. I felt for his pulse, and I imagined
that it feebly beat. I then thrust my hand into his bosom, and
placed it over his heart on his breast; it was bathed in a warm
perspiration, and from this I took hope, and still believed that
he had only swooned away.

I now called the maid to help me to revive him. I shook him
and called him as loud as I could. Again I took his hand, but
this time I was so excited that I was insensible to its death-like
touch. But the maid and I perceived at the same instant its
deathly palor, and the dark circle which had settled around the
nails, and we simultaneously uttered a shriek. The maid became
livid with fright, and fled from the room. I rushed after her,
caught her, and threw my arms around her neck, and implored
her not to say one word to anyone in the house, but to go for
Dr. Baillard, Mr. Dayton's physician. " Anything you ask me,"
she said, " but to go into that room again, for I am afraid of
the dead." " Dead !" I exclaimed; " he is not dead; I am sure
of it, for his breast is moist and warm. He has only fainted."
" But, madam," replied my maid, " the white hand !" " That
is nothing," I replied; for in spite of all I had seen I could not
believe that he was dead.

The maid went for the doctor. I fastened all the doors of my
apartment, and then returned to the drawing-room. I raised the
body up, and placed my mouth near his ear, and implored him
to wake. His face was flushed, and looked as natural as in life;
and there still lingered on it that kind and genial expression,
which it always wore. I laid the head again upon the pillow,
and placed my hand again upon his breast; it was still warm.
I got my hand-glass, and, kneeling beside him, held it over his
mouth ; and, while I held it there, I prayed. I held it several
minutes, fearing to look at its surface, for on it hung my last
hope. " O God !" I cried, " have mercy on me !" At last I
ventured to turn the glass. Ah, never shall I forget that look !
What did I see ? Instead of moisture nothing but my own
affrighted face. I shrieked : " It cannot be ; he is not dead !
I did not hold it long enough !"

I tried again, and pressed the glass more closely to his lips,
and held it longer than before, all the while imploring God to
have mercy on me. Then with trembling hand I turned the
glass and looked again, and saw my face as clearly as before.

I rose and staggered to the table, and my first thought was—
" This is the *hand of God !*" I felt that God was there, and I
knelt down and implored Him to forgive me ; to have mercy on

H

me ; to take pity on me, and to give him back his breath, just long enough for me to get him to his home. I prayed, and prayed with faith, believing that God was all-powerful, that as He had taken away his breath, He could give it back to him again.

I then arose and turned towards the dead man, expecting to find him alive. I could not be resigned. I raised him up again, and implored God more fervently than before, to give him back life, only for an hour, just long enough for him to reach his home, so that his family might never find him there. I held him up, and prayed until I lost all hope, then instantly my strength failed me, and the corpse fell from my grasp with a heavy bound back upon the pillow.

Trembling with fear I left his side and knelt in a corner of the room, the farthest from where he lay, and there I prayed once more.

But this time I invoked the sacred name of Jesus. Years and years had passed since I had called upon that holy name, and as my lips pronounced it the hills of Amenia came up before me as in a vision, and I remembered the days of innocent childhood, and the delight that my soul then found in the Word of God. For an instant a ray of comfort lighted up my desolate soul, but it as quickly passed away. For my doubts at once thrust themselves upon me and quenched that light, and I was left alone once more in darkness.

In that instant a feeling of unutterable despair came over me, and, like my husband, I too wished that I had never doubted.

I remained in the corner of the room, almost afraid to stir, until I heard a knocking at the door. I was afraid to open till I heard my name feebly pronounced, and recognised the voice of my maid. I learned from her that the doctor had retired, and refused to come before morning. "Did you tell him," I enquired, "that it was for Mr. Dayton ?" "No," said she, "I was afraid to speak his name. Ah, madam, how can you stay in that room ? The doctor asked me if you were ill. I told him no, but that you wanted to see him." "Oh, horror !" I moaned, "and must I wait here alone *another hour* while you get the doctor ?" I sent her again to say that Mr. Dayton had been taken very ill in my parlour. I sent a servant for the bookkeeper, whom I told that the American minister was taken very ill in my rooms, and I requested him to send word to his family to come in their carriage for him.

Alone once more with the dead body.

I soon became calm, and I made up my mind as to what I

should do. I was the only one who knew that he was dead, and I determined to get him home before the police should know anything of it.

It was nearly midnight when Dr. Baillard arrived. He and Mr. Dayton were bosom friends, and the doctor loved Mr. Dayton as a brother. He leaned over him, placed his fingers on his pulse, and instantly I saw his hand tremble and his face turn pale. He placed his hand on the dead man's heart, heaved a sigh, and then opened one of his eyes, which was fixed and stared glaringly at him. He quickly closed it, staggered back a few steps, then came up to me and stood in an attitude as though he were going to strike me. I looked at him as calmly as though I had not the slightest suspicion of what was passing through his mind. Said he: "Do you know that *he is dead?*" "Certainly," I replied, "he must have died a few moments after nine, but I knew it not until after ten, for I thought he was asleep. I did all I could for him, and have been sending for doctors in vain till now." The doctor began to question me, and was eyeing me closely meanwhile; but I answered his questions indifferently, and began to lament over myself for all that I had suffered. "But," said he, "how am I to break this news to his wife?"

It was as much as I could do to appear calm. But I rallied, as I knew that everything depended on my self-possession. At that instant Willie Dayton came in, and rushed up to me, shook hands, and began to apologise for coming so late. Then he asked what was the matter that I had sent for them so urgently. But before I had time to reply he saw his father lying on the sofa; he rushed over to him and said: "What is the matter, father? are you ill?" Said I: "Willie, he is dead." The son uttered a shriek, and threw himself on the dead body of his father, and began to kiss him, and screamed out: "Oh, father, speak to me, speak to me!" The doctor came and took him off the sofa and supported him, or he would have sunk on the floor. Then Willie said to the doctor: "I am so glad you were with him." Then, as though recollecting himself, he turned to me and said: "But how came he here?" Said I: "He came to call on Mr. Vanderpoel (who was then residing at the Hôtel du Louvre), but it appears he was out, and so he came up to see me. He came in very ill. I sent out for a doctor at once, but he had gone to the theatre. I did all I could for him." Then the doctor said to me, surprised: "Did he come in ill?" Willie answered: "Certainly, for he must have left me a few moments before, and he complained of having a headache."

The doctor's manner then became more gentle towards me.
Mr. Dayton's youngest son also arrived, and I drove home with
him and Willie to break the news to Mrs. Dayton. As soon as
we left, the doctor called two of the porters, and told them that
Mr. Dayton had fainted, and would have to be carried down to
his carriage. The porters seated the dead man in a chair. The
doctor assisted them to put him in his carriage, and they drove
off as quickly as possible. All was done so promptly, and with
so much discretion, that the police did not get the slightest clue
to what had happened until the following morning.

When I arrived at the house, Mrs. Dayton was standing in
the corridor, looking over the balustrade, and the moment she
heard the door close, she called out: "Willie, is that you? I
wonder where father is, he has not got home yet." I began to
tremble, and shrank back; but Willie pushed me forward and
told me to go upstairs first. Mrs. Dayton was greatly surprised
to see me. I was wrapped up in my opera-cloak, and the first
thing she said to me after shaking hands was: "Are you going
to a ball, or have you just returned from one? What is the
matter?" I could not answer her. By this time Willie was in
the room. He threw his arms around his mother's neck and
burst into tears.

Miss Dayton took me into her bedroom and begged me to tell
her what was the matter. But I could not utter a word. Said
she: "How very pale you are!" She then arranged her bed
and helped me to lie down, and begged me to speak, asking if
anything had happened to my child. The very thought that all
was well with her gave me breath, and I replied: "It will kill
you to know." She became deathly pale, and assured me that
she was prepared for anything. I then repeated to her what I
had told the rest. She did not weep, but the mental agony
which depicted itself on her face expressed more than tears could
have done. She walked the room with her hands tightly
clenched, and would now and then exclaim: "Poor ma!" At
last the body was brought in. I heard the valet give orders,
that it should be laid in the grand saloon. It was there that we
used to dance. I heard a shriek and a moan—it was Mrs. Dayton's voice, and it pierced me through and through. Miss
Dayton continued to pace the room, and every time her mother's
voice would reach us, a new pang seemed to wrench her heart.

I could stand no more. I sprang to my feet and said: "I
must go." "No, no," said Miss Dayton tenderly, "you must
not think of going home to-night. Try to sleep. You look so
pale, and your hands are cold." She went into her mother's
room and brought in a warming-pan, which she said her mother

had placed in her father's bed to take the chill off. She put it at my feet and told me that I must try to sleep. "Sleep!" thought I; "would that I could sleep and thus forget!" Miss Dayton recommenced to pace the room. I closed my eyes and feigned to be at rest. But I lay there as though I were stretched on a bed of flaming fire—I did not dare to move or shed one tear.

How long I lay there agonising I cannot tell, for it seems to me even to-day like a century, so poignant were my sufferings. Finally they overpowered me so that I could lie still no longer: I rose and declared that I must go home. Miss Dayton did all she could to prevail upon me to stay, and it was only after I pleaded that I could not remain away from my child that she yielded, and called the valet to accompany me home. But the doctor had need of his assistance and he could not go. "Never mind," said I, "I will go alone." It was past two o'clock; but nothing could have induced me to remain till morning. The carriage was still at the door waiting to take home the doctor; they told me to take it, and let it return for him.

Paris was enveloped in a dense fog, and, as we drove through the Champ Elysées, the lamps shed through the mist a weird light, which, added to the gloom and loneliness of the hour, seemed to increase the terrors of my soul.

When I got to my rooms I found my maid weeping. "What are *you* crying for?" I exclaimed; for I felt at the moment as if no one could be wretched but myself. "Who could help crying," she answered, "to see that good man carried out dead? The doctor told me that he was dead, and that you, madam, were the most heartless woman that he had ever met. But I never thought so until to night; and you did not shed a tear!"

Before I reflected where I was going I found myself in the drawing-room. Everything was strewn about the room in great disorder, except the pillow that lay on the arm of the sofa and showed the print of his head. It was like going into a banquet hall where Death had come to make it suddenly desolate and deserted, and as if he had but just taken his departure.

I quickly left the room, and when I reached my bedroom I said: "Now it is my turn;" and I threw myself on the floor and gave vent to the torrent of grief that was raging within me.

The sight of my distress made the girl weep for me. She raised me from the floor and placed me in an arm chair, and began to undo my hair. She raised it off my temples to loosen the ribbon. She started back, and then brought me the very hand-glass that I had held over Mr. Dayton's mouth. "Go!" I

exclaimed, " I can never look into that again." " But," said she,
" do madam, look and see ; look at your hair." I did as she
told me ; many of my hairs had turned grey. Then she began
to weep and pity me for all that I must have suffered.

I too wept until I was bathed in tears. I chanced to look up
and saw that I was sitting in front of the wardrobe mirror, just
where I had stood admiring myself with so much satisfaction,
when Mr. Dayton rapped. But I had to recollect myself, for it
seemed as if a year had passed over my head since then. What
a change ! and I began to contrast the beginning with the ending
of the night. I remembered my reflections just before Mr. Dayton
came, and I thought that if my old acquaintances could see me
then, as I sat there, they would see very little to envy me for ;
and thinking of them brought back to my mind the hills of
Amenia, its free forests and happy plains, and for the first time
since I had left them I wished that I had never seen beyond
their horizon.

CHAPTER XXVIII.

THE RECOLLECTION OF THE PAST SAVES ME FROM A DRUNKARD'S
GRAVE—THE " SISTERS OF HOPE."

Medicine for Melancholy—The Nun and the Child—It is the Lord's
Prayer.

THE sudden death of the American minister in my apartments
soon became the talk of Paris. The American colony was very
much excited, and in a few days an American official solicited
an interview, and requested me to state to him the circumstances of Mr. Dayton's death, in order that he might inform
Mr. Seward.

Just before I saw him Mr. Ratscratch told me that he was the
worst' enemy I had in Paris, and repeated to me some of his
remarks. To be revenged, yet to satisfy him, I gave him a long
account, drawing minute and pathetic circumstances merely from
my imagination, while to protect myself I carefully concealed as
much as I thought desirable of the Ratscratch business, which
had led to Mr. Dayton's visit.

One evening I was accompanied home from an evening party
by Edmond de Lesseps and a young Irishman. I felt myself
plunged in profoundest melancholy and grief. My conscience
seemed to reproach me with every sin that I had ever committed.
My young Irish friend undertook to prescribe a remedy that would
certainly cheer me, and ordered for me a hot " sling ;" and I

suppose to encourage me to take the medicine, he ordered one for himself. I drank it nearly at one draught. Hardly had I taken it when all my sadness disappeared, and I felt as gay and merry as ever in my life. In a few moments he ordered another, and I drank that too as quickly as the first. As soon as I felt the effects of the draught I exclaimed : " Whenever I am sad I shall know what to do to chase grief away ! thank heaven I have found an antidote to sorrow ! I will never suffer again so long as this medicine is within reach." " It is a wonder," said my young friend, " that you never thought of it before. It is the only thing that will drive away care. Look at yourself in the glass ; you look as animated and fresh as an Hebe ;" and he ordered a third.

Lesseps looked sad and would not drink. He seemed to be displeased at the scene, and to look reproachfully at me when I turned to him. I began to wonder why it was that I had never resorted to this means of excitement before, when all at once I was startled by a recollection of the past. In an instant all my strength left me, and I sank in my chair as though I had been pushed back by a blow. All my sadness and depression returned, for I remembered two women, whom I had seen standing in two different grog-shops ; and the thought passed through my mind that there would soon be a third, and that would be myself.

I now refused the proffered glass, and in a determined tone said : " Never." Lesseps seized my hand and kissed it ; and, as my young friend still urged me to take the glass, I took it and threw it into the fireplace. The thought flashed upon my mind that the past would save me, and I raised my heart to God with a feeling that He had always been good to me after all. I had often reproached Him for having haunted my life with such horrible recollections. But in that moment I thanked Him for them. It was the first time that I had ever raised my heart in loving gratitude to God for having bred me upon sufferings.

When my friends took their departure I had hardly strength to stand. I grew weaker and weaker, until all at once that same sad feeling took possession of me again, and I fell senseless upon the floor.

I awoke early the next morning, and found the housekeeper of the hotel watching by my bedside, my maid, she informed me, being too ill to attend me. She also handed me the card of Mr. de Lesseps. I attempted to rise, but was seized with convulsive pains, and was not able to move. I was in a burning fever.

She brought Lesseps to my bedside.

He said that he was not surprised to find me ill, and that he had noticed how greedily I had seized on every kind of excitement to keep up my spirits since Mr. Dayton's death; and that I must have wonderful vitality, to have resisted so long. He begged me not to be sad, but to keep up my spirits; and promised that he would see that I had every attention. My hair was dishevelled, and the housekeeper in arranging it off my forehead, showed Mr. de Lesseps where it had turned grey on that fatal night. Mr. de Lesseps was moved to tears, and said to the housekeeper: "How the world misjudges us when it judges from appearances! But," said he, "I knew this lady was suffering, in spite of that mask of reckless indifference which she always wears. Yet it is for that that the world applauds and admires her; because it believes her to be as heartless as itself!"

The housekeeper's duties obliged her to leave me: and the question arose: who should attend me? My maid was nearly as ill as myself; and there was my child too. Mr. de Lesseps at once decided what should be done. "I have a cousin" said he, "who is superior of a convent in Spain; and they have a branch of their institute here, about ten minutes' walk from the hotel. Their vocation is to attend the sick, and they receive five francs a day for their services. The institution is called *Les Sœurs d'Espérance* (The Sisters of Hope)."

He proposed to go immediately and get one of the Sisters of Hope to take care of me.

The Lessepses were related to the Empress Eugenie, and were, at the time I write of, one of the most favoured and popular families in France, not alone on account of their relationship to the Empress, but for their own intrinsic merit and worth.

Lesseps soon returned, accompanied by a boy with a large bundle of toys that he had purchased for my child. When the Sister came, my child at once left her playthings, and took hold of the crucifix, which was suspended from the beads, that hung by the Sister's side. The Sister said to her: "Kiss it, dear child;" and, at once, the child placed it to her lips, and covered it with kisses. The Sister was so pleased, that she caught the child up in her arms and kissed her on her forehead. After pressing her to her bosom, she placed her on the floor, in the midst of her toys; but the child left them again, and took hold of the crucifix, and began kissing it. The Sister then said to her: "What a good little child you are to love Jesus so!" My child was then over two years old: it was the first crucifix

she had ever seen ; nor had she ever heard the name of Jesus.
I saw the expression of the Sister's face change when Mr. de
Lesseps told her that we were not Catholics, and that the child
had never been baptised.

Sir Joseph Olliffe was the physician who attended me. He
came towards dusk and began his treatment, but the next morning I was worse. The following evening he became alarmed,
and the next day he brought the celebrated Trousseau to hold a
consultation. They found my condition most precarious. While
there was no disease, yet there was a total prostration such as
they had never witnessed, unless caused by long physical suffering, and usually just before death. They spoke to me plainly
because, as they said, my life depended on my own will. If I
would only keep up courage and drive from my mind everything
that troubled me I would soon get well. At the very mention
of the word *trouble* I burst into tears.

Sir Joseph, without my knowledge, drove directly to see Mrs.
Dayton, and told her that I was dangerously ill from excessive
mental excitement. Miss Dayton and Willie came at once to
see me. In the afternoon Mrs. Dayton sent me a beautiful box,
with following note :

" MY DEAR MRS. ECKEL,

"I regret exceedingly to hear that you are still suffering so
much from the excitement through which you have passed.

"I send you by the bearer some very fine tea, presented to me
by Mr. Burlingame, our minister in China. Please accept also
the box in which it is contained.

" Ever gratefully yours,

" M. E. DAYTON.

" PARIS, *Dec.* 21st, 6, RUE DE PRESBOURG."

On the fifth day I was able to move a little. The physician
then prescribed strengthening tonics, but so soon as I had tasted
and found them disagreeable, I would send them up to my maid.
I did so in fact with nearly every prescription that the doctor
left me ; and I would amuse myself during the day laughing at
the success of this little strategem. As Sir Joseph Olliffe always
spoke to me in English, which the nuns could not understand,
they thought that it was all right. The result was that I recovered long before my maid.

During my illness much of my time was passed with the
Sisters and my child. My child became fondly attached to the
nuns, and would not leave them to play with her toys. No

matter how often she would awake in the night, she would call
out at once; "*Ma Sœur, ma Sœur.*" As soon as the nun
would reach her, the child would say to her: "*Je veux embrasser
le petit Jesus.*" (I wish to kiss the little Jesus.) The nun
would hardly know whether to scold her or not, for the child
would frequently awaken her out of a sound sleep, after she had
passed a fatiguing day by my bedside. I told the Sister that
she must not permit the child to call her up in the night for
such a purpose. The nun would tell *me* to scold her for it. I
told her that I had not the heart to do it, for I loved to hear
her. "And so do I," replied the nun; "it is a sacrifice to get
up, but I offer it up to God each time." This was a new
language to me, which I did not understand.

One evening the Sister retired later, and more weary than
usual. She had hardly got to sleep before the child called her.
"This time," thought I to myself, "you will lose your patience."
The nun quickly lighted the candle and flew to the child's side,
believing something ailed her; for she called her as though she
were in distress. But the moment she reached the bedside the
child said to her in one of her sweetest baby-tones: "*Ma Sœur,
je veux embrasser le petit Jesus.*" When the nun returned she
lay down again on the sofa without saying a word. I remarked
that it was too bad that she should be so disturbed; but she
instantly replied: "Oh, madam, if you could only have seen her!
for the dear child was hardly awake when she asked me to let
her kiss the crucifix, and she dropped to sleep while she held it
to her lips. I can never forbid her to call me, if I should never
get another hour's rest."

I could not understand why she should feel so, for the love of
Jesus Christ was to me then a deep mystery, which my obdurate
heart could not comprehend.

One evening the child was asleep. I felt much better and
stronger. It was about nine o'clock when the nun crept softly
to my bedside, and asked me if I would not repeat a little prayer
after her before I went asleep. She knelt down by my pillow,
and in one of the gentlest and sweetest accents she began to
say the Lord's Prayer. I repeated her words every time she
paused. When we had finished I told her that I had learned
that prayer at school when I was a little girl, and that it was a
Protestant prayer. "Oh, no," she replied; "it is the Lord's
Prayer." "How sweet it is in French," said I; " let us say it
again." She answered: "It must be sweet in all tongues;" and
she knelt and we said it again. Just as we had finished I
stretched out my hand and placed it on her head, to prevent her

from rising, and I said to her: “Sister, *once more ;*” and we repeated it again. Then she rose and kissed me, took my hand and pressed it, and said to me, with a feeling that I know must have gushed from her heart: “ Oh, madam, how I wish that you and your lovely child were Catholics! I pray for it constantly.” Said I: “ Don't pray for that, Sister, for that *can never be.* But pray that I may get well, and that I may yet be happy, and that my heart may be at rest, for I am troubled and long for rest.” “ I do pray for that,” said the Sister, “ and only. for that ; for you can never know rest until you love our Lord.” “ Sister,” said I, “ don't speak to me in that way.” “ I am telling you the truth,” said she. “ But,” I replied, “ I do not believe in it ; you can never change me from what I am.” “ That is very true,” she answered ; “ I can do nothing, but our Lord can change you, and I pray earnestly that He will.” “ How good you are!” said I ; “ but you little know the woman that lies here before you ; if you did, I am sure you would never have kissed me.” At those words she covered my cheeks with kisses, which so affected me that I began to weep. I told her that had it not been for my child, whom I saw playing before me all day, I would hardly have had the courage to breathe. She told me how great had been my danger. “ Why,” said I, “ I would have loved to die could I have taken my child with me.” “ But,” I added musingly, “ she is so delicate, I am sure she cannot live long.” “ Do let her be baptised,” exclaimed the Sister to me imploringly. “ That would do no good,” said I ; “ she never did wrong. She would go straight to heaven now.” “ Well,” said the Sister, “ you believe in sin. You tell me you have sinned, and perhaps your parents, too, have sinned before you.” These words pierced me, for the Sister had nursed me most tenderly, and I thought if she only knew who my parents were, and what an enemy one of them had been to her religion, how different might be her feelings towards me.

CHAPTER XXIX.

LAFERRIÈRE.

The Spectre of the Feast—In High Life—The Viscount—Tête-à-tête.

IN January, 1865, I received an invitation to the first ball at the Tuileries. Edmond de Lesseps escorted me there, and took me into the *Hall of the Marshals,* and gave me a seat with his family, who had their places in the seats reserved for the family

of the Empress, which was on the left of the throne. I wore a
magnificent toilet of white tulle, and a wreath of ivy interspersed with diamonds.

That evening I made the acquaintance of the best people of
the Court. The Empress, of whom Edmond de Lesseps was a
favourite, came up and spoke to us, and of course everybody
else followed her example. I was elated with my success, until
Mr. de Lesseps led me into the supper-room. He happened to
conduct me to the very spot where I had conversed with Mr.
Dayton a year before. Here I found the skeleton of the feast,
and what a moment before I had enjoyed like a triumph, seemed
suddenly changed to a hideous "dance of death." I tried to
disguise my feelings, and to appear gay and indifferent, but,
after a little, I could stand it no longer, and I said to Lesseps,
"Enough, let us go." "What!" said he, "I did not expect
that you would leave before morning." Descending the stairs,
he said to me, "I hope you were satisfied with your evening,—
in fact these were the only happy hours I have ever passed
under the roof of this palace, for I have never been here before
to a festivity that I did not come away mournfully sad. But
to-night I was happy to see you so happy;" and he continued
to express himself in this way until our carriage came. He
handed me in. I threw myself back in the seat ard burst into
tears.

I preferred Mr. de Lesseps to any of my friends, yet I did not
love him. But he loved me. He was the youngest son, and
had no title; but he had a heart. I was ambitious to marry a
title: I felt that only a title would make me happy. He knew
me thoroughly, and deplored that I should be the slave to such
an illusion; but he was charitable, and attributed all my faults
and follies to a bad education.

On the last Sunday in January, 1865, I was invited to an
evening party at the Princess Sulkowska's. Lesseps called on me
early in the evening. I was low-spirited, and he had been trying to cheer me up. The Prince de Monléard had promised to
call for me to take me to the party. It was nearly nine o'clock,
and Lesseps proposed to leave me that I might make my toilet.
I told him that I had not the heart to change my dress, and that
I was going as I was. Said he: "You are dressed very becomingly, but not at all suitably for an evening party." I had on a
black velvet dress with train, fitted to my figure in the Gabrielle
fashion. My hair was thrown off my face, and looped up at the
back with a diamond comb. Lesseps tried to prevail upon me
to change my dress, as others might say that I had only chosen

that costume in order to be singular. I begged him to leave me to my caprice, and said that others might think what they pleased, but change it I would not. "But," said he, "the Prince will not accompany you." At that moment I heard a rap, and said to Lesseps, before I opened the door: "Hand me my scarf and cloak, and he will not know how I am dressed."

When we arrived, and I was ushered into the saloon, I was confused, for there were a few ladies assembled, and they were all dressed in the most elaborate style. I excused myself at once to the Princess, and told her that I had misunderstood her invitation, and supposed it to be a mere informal reception. The Princess, to make me feel at ease, redoubled her attention to me, and excused me to her friends by accusing herself of not having made her invitation sufficiently clear. She conducted me to a sofa, and introduced me to the Countess de ——-, one of the largest and homeliest women in France, but a lady of rank, which lessened in some degree in the eyes of many her excessive plumpness. I sat on the sofa beside this lady, and was at once reconciled to my toilet; for I could easily believe that the contrast between us as we sat there together was not disadvantageous to me. I tried to arrange myself on the sofa, so as to bring myself out in high relief, and to make the enormous form of the Countess serve as a background to the figure. The door opened, and the valet announced the Viscount de Laferrière.

As the Viscount entered the room our eyes met. In an instant the Princess was at his side, and when she spoke to him he appeared like a man who had forgotten himself for a moment. After exchanging a few words with her he retired into an isolated corner of the saloon directly opposite to where I sat. My eyes followed him, and when he saw that I was still looking at him a slight flush passed over his face, which he instantly controlled, and his whole countenance assumed an expression of haughty indifference.

I recommenced my conversation with the Countess; but, in a moment of absent-mindedness, my eyes reverted once more towards the Viscount. He was not prepared for my glance, for I caught him this time looking attentively at me; and, with a desire to revenge myself for the expression of indifference which he had assumed, I instantly turned my eyes from him with an air and a look in which I tried to express a feeling of disdain. I then looked triumphantly at him to see the effect. But this time his face was calm, and on it was seated a deep shade of melancholy, to which my heart at once responded; and his own must have instantly divined what was passing in mine, for his

face brightened up for an instant, and then he turned and left
the spot where he was standing, with the air of a man who was
displeased that another should have been able to divine his
thoughts.

The Viscount de Laferrière was tall in stature, and had
passed the middle age : his hair was *blonde* and slightly tinged
with grey. On his left breast sparkled the insignia of the
different orders that sovereigns had bestowed upon him. His
bearing and manners were courtly, but extremely reserved.
The outlines of his features were noble and beautiful ; they bore
the impress of deep thought, shaded by a tinge of melancholy.
This he tried to conceal by affecting an expression which it is
impossible to describe, but which is more or less assumed by
men who can read at a glance the thoughts of others, but who
are not willing to be read themselves. I chanced to see him
several times again during the evening. He was always looking at me ; but these times he did not try to avert his gaze,
but remained like a man who was looking at one object while
his thoughts were on another. I felt nettled that he should not
have asked the Princess to introduce him to me. It was only a
small gathering of between thirty and forty guests, and all those
whom I did not know were presented to me—he was the only
exception.

The same week I was at another ball at the Tuileries. I had
just entered the *Hall of the Marshals*, and had left my escort
in the adjoining room. I was conversing with the Countess de
Lesseps, when a lady asked me if I would not permit her to present to me the Viscount de Laferrière, who would escort me to
the other side of the room where there were two vacant seats.
I paid no attention to the name, and before I had time to
reply the introduction was made, and he offered me his arm. I
told him that I did not come to be seated, but to dance.
"Then come with me," he replied, "and I will get you a
partner."

I took his arm, hardly looking at him or he at me until we
had crossed the room, and I turned to thank him, when we
looked each other full in the face, and both started with surprise. The Viscount exclaimed : "Did I not have the pleasure
of seeing you last Sunday evening at the Princess Sulkowska's ?
But how come it that a royal Polishwoman like you can stoop
beneath the Prussian flag ?" (He thought I must have been
presented by the Prussian minister.) Said I : "I am not from
Poland. I came from a land that is free." "Ah," he replied,
"that must be a happy land." "Yes," said I, "happy for

others, but never for me." "I thought," he said, "seeing you at such a brilliant party dressed in black that you must belong to one of Poland's royal families, and were so wedded to the thought of your country's wrongs that you would not cast off your mourning even for a night. But tell me who you are?" Said I: "I am an American and a princess, for in my country every man is a sovereign."

My answer displeased him, for he did not know whether to understand it as a sentiment of patriotism or as a thrust at his own government. He continued: "I refused to let the Princess introduce me to you the other evening, because I thought that you were one of her compatriots who wanted to be a martyr— your black dress deceived me so." "How extraordinary," I replied, "that the order of things should be reversed in me, for it is usually the woman herself who deceives, and not her dress." Said he: "I hope you have learned that from books, and not from experience. At all events I was entirely deceived in you, for I was sure that you were a Polish lady who had no heart for anything but her country." Said I: "They tell me that I have no heart at all. I sometimes believe it; but I am sure of one thing, and that is that I have a conscience." (I did not tell him that I knew this chiefly by its *sting*.) "Ah," he replied, " you are very lucky, for that is a very rare thing in this country." As we promenaded the different rooms he was surprised to see so many of his friends salute me, as he thought I was a stranger, and he wondered that I should be so well known, and that he should never have met me before.

He lead me to a secluded part of the palace, into a room which belonged to the private *suite* of the Empress. We sat in an alcove and talked a great part of the evening. He told me that it was the first time he had abandoned his post, for it was his duty, as one of the Imperial chamberlains, to remain in the *Hall of the Marshals* until their Majesties retired. "But," said he, " I could not resist the temptation of having a long chat with you."

I was frank with him, and open-hearted. Sometimes I would make him laugh, and then again it seemed, as if he had to suppress his tears. I wondered would I ever see him again. I gave him my address, but I did not dare to ask him to call on me. He conducted me to my carriage, and bade me a formal goodbye, without even touching my hand; which disappointed me, for I expected he would kiss it, as he assisted me into the carriage.

When I got home, I embraced my child with rapture, for I felt really happy. It was one of the happiest evenings I had ever known. Never had I met a gentleman before, whom I had so much admired, so much respected, so much loved at first sight.

The next day M. de Laferrière left his card ; and the day after, he sent me a note, asking me, if I had received an invitation to Prince Bonaparte's ball. The day following he called, and from that moment he was my constant visitor. He treated me as he would a child, and always addressed me, as " his dear child : " " *ma chère enfant.*" All my gentlemen acquaintances quarrelled with me, on his account, and ceased to visit me ; because Laferrière, no matter how long they stayed, would always outstay them, and made himself, during their visit, as disagreeable as he could. He treated them, even his intimate friends, when he met them in my rooms, with a cold and studied reserve, which they well understood ; for it plainly showed them, that every one of them was one too many. I was willing to sacrifice them all for him ; for I found no pleasure nor happiness, unless he was near, or my thoughts were upon him.

***

CHAPTER XXX.

IN LOVE.

The de Montalemberts—I visit the Viscount—Master and Servant—
The Viscount's History—I tell my Story.

ONE morning Laferrière brought me the news of the Duke de Morny's death. In three months I had lost three of my most valuable friends ;—Mr. Dayton, Mrs. Ross, and the Duke de Morny. But I became insensible to misfortune from the day I met Laferrière ; for he seemed to replace everything I lost. For the moment, his friendship seemed sufficient to wipe out the bitter remembrances of the past, to fill up the present, and to give me bright hopes for the future.

It was about this time that the Princess Sulkowska introduced me to the family of the Count de Montalembert. The Princess chaperoned me several times to their evening receptions. There I met a society that I was totally unfitted for, and in order to conceal my unfitness there was required on my part a double amount of dissimulation and tact, for I was constantly put to the test. A part of the time I felt as though I were on the wheel, for the Count and Countess would address to me questions concerning the political constitution of my country, which I knew nothing about, but, being too proud to acknowledge my ignorance, I was in constant dread of having it exposed. So

that I never descended their stairs without saying to myself
that certainly I was never made for that.

With the O'Gormans I was perfectly natural, and did not try to
conceal how little I knew, therefore they never tried to enlighten
themselves by talking with me, but would always treat me as
though I were their child. With them I felt perfectly at home.
I soon found that I might have spared myself much annoyance
if I had been equally frank from the beginning with the De
Montalemberts, for I soon learned that where true nobility
reigns honesty, candour, and simplicity are always at their ease.

The Count de Montalembert called upon me several times,
but it happened whenever he came that I was surrounded by
some of the Emperor's *suite*. I met him one evening at a party,
and he told me that I received a class of people who did me very
little honour, and that, for himself, he would not associate with
them. I was too much dazzled by the flash of the Court to be
capable of appreciating such a man as the Count de Montalembert, and I frankly told him that I believed that he was
jealous because the Emperor had not given him an appointment,
and therefore he opposed him ; but that if he chose to snub the
Emperor's adherents on that account, it was no reason why I
should. The answer amused him, and he laughed heartily
over it.

One morning Laferrière did not call at the usual hour, and
his valet came with a note, which told me that he was ill, and
could not leave his room. Without thinking of the impropriety
of such an act, *I drove off at once to see him.* When the servant
answered my ring, and I asked her if the Viscount was at home,
she gave me a reproachful look, which said as plainly as words :
" How dare you come here and ask for him ?" and then she told
me that Monsieur the Viscount was out. " I know that he is at
home," said I, " and he would do well to teach you to speak the
truth !" and without further ceremony I opened one of the doors
which led from the antechamber. It happened to be the door
of the parlour. In defiance of the remonstrances of the servant
I went in, took a seat, and handed her my card. But she still
insisted that Monsieur was out.

The servant took my card and returned in a few seconds ; but
this time, in a most subdued voice. She said to me that Monsieur would be in in a moment : and she disappeared as quickly
as possible. I did not have to wait long before the Viscount
entered, with a nervous step and troubled look. Without even
saying " Good-day " he came quickly towards me, and, raising
both arms, exclaimed : " You imprudent child ! Why did you

I

come here ? Who saw you come in? Who knows it? Whom have you in your carriage ?" Said I, "I came all alone. But what is the matter ?" "Oh, my dear child ! if anyone knew that you called on me your reputation would be lost." I burst out laughing, and said : "I should *like* to lose it, for it is a very bad one. But what a strange way you have of receiving your friends !"

The Viscount became impatient and vexed that I would not acknowledge at once my fault, and he took hold of my arm as though he would like to give me a good shaking. "What !" said he, "have you not been in France long enough to have learned *something* about the conventionalities of society ? If it were known that you called on me alone every door in Paris would be closed in your face. How am I to get you out ? Suppose someone should meet you on the stairs ;—and what does my servant think?" And the poor Viscount acted as though he were frightened out of his wits. "What do I care what your servant thinks of me ! My opinion of her is that she is a shrew." "That servant," said he, "has been in my family twenty years, and when servants remain so long we are but nominally their masters : they rule us to a certain degree." "Yes," said I; "and I would prefer changing mine every week to being reduced to such servitude." "Ah, but a trusty servant," replied the Viscount, "is a precious thing, and we ought to have consideration for them; their virtues entitle them to it. Besides it is for our interest, for what should I do if I did not have trusty persons to guard my things ?" and he threw a glance around the room, which, for the first time, I discovered was filled with antique ornaments and souvenirs.

"I am thankful," said I, "that I never had any ancestry, and therefore have no heirlooms to guard. But I would rather have servants who would carry off half my things than become the slave of one of these *trusty* dames whose very look will make you quake, if you happen to jar in the slightest degree their ideas of propriety." He began to laugh in spite of his vexation. "But," said he, "this servant is none of that kind, but a most worthy-person, whom I greatly esteem, and I do not wish her to have less regard for me than I have for her. I am sure that she must have taken you to be one of the *demi-monde;* for what other lady would ever call on a gentleman alone in this way? How imprudent ! how imprudent ! You might have met some of my family here. And the woman too read your name on the card. How can I account for this?" His hand was placed all the while on the knob of the door, just ready to open it for me to leave.

He bade me good-bye, and told me I must go, for he did not know what the servant would think. Said I : " I am ready to go, and I am not at all sorry I came, for it has relieved my mind. I feared you might be seriously ill. I am satisfied with my visit, although it was like forcing my way through the ranks to get to you. But I have seen you : I am happy now and am ready to go." Said he, " I will go and tell the servant that you are an American lady, and that it is not against propriety in America for a lady to visit a gentleman." " That would be defaming the American ladies a little," said I ; " but I owe them a grudge, so let us hit them all a rap with one sling. Go and tell that prude in the kitchen that all well-bred American ladies visit their gentlemen friends at their residences when they are ill.

He left the room, and when he returned his face was radiant with smiles. " It is all right now," said he, " and I am delighted you came, for I was thinking of you and wanted to see you." He begged me to forgive him for having scolded me ; he would sacrifice anything sooner than be the cause of diminishing in the least the esteem others had for me.. " But," said I " you know that everybody abuses me." " No, no," he replied, " it is only the envious who abuse you ; for I know some estimable people who are very fond of you. But I can well understand now how it comes that you are traduced if you are capable of such reck- lessness as this." " Nonsense," said I : " this is one of the smallest things I ever did to get a bad name." Said he : " You are one of those who are always calumniating themselves. But I never pay compliments, so do not resort to that means if your motive is to receive a compliment from me." " I am telling you the truth," I said ; " and as for your compliments, the greatest one you can pay me is to abandon society and pass all your time with me, as you do. I do not desire any greater com- pliment from you.

He invited me into his library. Most of the pictures that were hanging on the wall were family portraits. I threw them all a fugitive glance until I came face to face with the portrait of a lad of about fourteen summers. One would have at once taken it for the portrait of Laferrière himself when he was a child. I asked him who it was. A sad smile passed over his countenance as he said to me : " How much I love you for having noticed the only portrait in the room which is dear to me !" He was about to continue, but the tears choked his words. It was several moments before he could master himself sufficiently to continue, when he told me that it was his grand- child, who had died a few years before. The Viscount had never

spoken to me about himself, and I had never had an opportunity
of asking others about him, for from the moment he first called
on me, nearly all our time had been passed together. Nor did
he know the first outlines of my history. All that we knew of
each other was that we were perfectly happy in each other's
society. We did not care to know more. A strange, mysterious
sympathy existed between us, which neither of us could account
for. After passing the livelong day together we always complained of the hours passing too quickly; and when we bade
each other adieu, we already longed for the morning to come,
that we might see each other again.

From the day I first met Laferrière, I became more thoughtfully serious, and less selfish and ambitious. I could enjoy
nothing unless he was by my side; and we mutually agreed to
refuse all invitations where we were not both invited; for it was
too great a sacrifice to make for society to be separated from
each other, even for a few hours.

The Viscount's family, with the exception of his father, had
always adhered to the old order of things. But his father, in
his youth, had joined the ranks of the followers of the first
Napoleon, and became his Chamberlain. The Emperor conferred
upon him the title of Count. He was a Marquis under the
Bourbons, and could have resumed that title after the Restoration,
but he always preferred the title given him by the Emperor.
From the moment that Laferrière's father espoused the cause of
the Bonapartes, all intercourse between him and the other
members of his family was broken off. The Viscount himself
had never had any communication with his father's family, as he
had inherited the sentiments of his father, and had always been
a strong supporter of the Bonapartes.

The Viscount had graduated at the Polytechnic School ;—had
entered the army, and served on the general staff in Greece.
He became enamoured of the only daughter of the Marquis of
Saron, whom he married, and by whom he had one daughter,
who was now living, and was the wife of General the Count de
Bernis. The young lad, whose portrait had affected Laferrière
to tears, was the only son of the Countess de Bernis. The Viscount told me that during his short military career, he had seen
enough of the world to make him thoroughly convinced, before
he was twenty-three years old, of the futility of seeking happiness in sensual gratification. He loved his wife devotedly, and
his married life had been a most happy one, the whole of which
he had passed in the château, which he had inherited from his
ancestors. He was then member of the Council General of his

department, and had been elected, for the past twelve years, chief magistrate of his own township.

The Emperor Napoleon III. had written to him during his married life, inviting him to come and accept a position at Court; but he had strenuously refused, as he had no illusions in regard to Court life. His wife died. The Emperor wrote him a letter of condolence and renewed his offer, which the Viscount again refused, for he had filled the void that his wife's death had made in his heart by his affection for his little grandson, Raymond de Bernis. But the premature death of this promising youth again cast him into the slough of despair.

"As soon as the Emperor heard of the death of my child," said the Viscount, "he wrote me again, and iterated his offer, which this time I accepted, hoping that the distractions of a Court life would make me forget my sorrows. But they have only aggravated them. Still I cannot resign myself to go back to the château to live: for when I see the trees which we planted together, growing up, each one of them tells me a tale of the past, and speaks to me continually of my buried hopes. I remained here in Paris and mingled in its frivolities; but my heart was dead to everything around me until the moment we met, and that was the first time I have ever been consoled since Raymond died. There is something about you that reminds me of my boy, and yet you are totally unlike in appearance. But you have filled up, in a measure, the void that that dear child's death made in my heart; and it is only now, my child, that you can understand how much I love you."

I wept while the Viscount related his heart's sorrow to me; but when I told him that I could understand how deeply he suffered, he replied: "Ah, no, my child, you can never know nor understand all that I have suffered, for you have never lost a beloved child."

"Yes," said I, weeping as though my heart would break, "I lost an infant, and I have but *one recollection* connected with her, which, whenever I recall it, tears my heart open anew. I can well imagine what your grief must be, when you have your heart full of many remembrances,"

He took my hand and, for the first time, he pressed it to his lips, and then placed it on his cheeks until it was bathed in his tears. "Yes," said he, "I feel that our hearts sympathise. It was thus that Raymond and I used to sit and converse for hours. When my wife died he consoled me. But when he died I was left entirely alone, and it used to make me mourn to see how soon the others forgot him." Then he continued to tell me all about his darling's little ways, which wound him so around his heart. I then told him how I used to sleep with my babe, and of the feeling of loneliness that would come over me after her death whenever I awoke, and, before I thought, would reach out my hand to feel that little head. "Ah," said he, "I understand it well, for I have had that feeling come over me at every step I took about the château."

He then tried to console me by saying that I had reason to be happy, since God had given me back my child. "Ah, no," I replied; "a thousand other children can never replace the child that dies." "But," said he, "I love you as I loved my Raymond, and that is saying much, for never did I love a being on earth as I loved that boy."

A few evenings after this visit I opened my heart to Laferrière, and told him my history, naturally disguising my own defects, and making out my relations to be so many hyenas. The old aunt would hardly have recognised herself, if she could have seen how I painted her to Monsieur de Laferrière. He then understood better my position in Paris among the Americans, and told me that henceforth I should look upon him as a father.

The Viscount was blind to my defects, and had unbounded confidence in me. He believed me to be just what I represented myself to be, and I tried to become worthy of his esteem. He was always reserved with me, although his manners were tender and his words were always full of fond devotion. I was timid with him. I ceased from that moment to play the coquette, for I had become indifferent to the praise and admiration of anyone but himself.

CHAPTER XXXI.

A GENUINE REPUBLICAN IN SEARCH OF A TITLE.

I Interpret for Ratscratch—The Ribbon is earned.

ONE day the Viscount proposed that I should dine with him, and desired that I should invite some lady or gentleman to join us. I proposed that Mr. Ratscratch should be the "one too many." The Viscount exclaimed: "Oh, no, he would be a terrible bore, since he can't speak French." Said I: "That is just the reason to invite him." I then told the Viscount how desirous this gentleman was of obtaining the ribbon, and that as the gentleman had promised me a large sum if I would get it for him, I wished that the Viscount would aid me, which he promised to do.

One evening found Mr. Ratscratch and myself seated at the Viscount's table. The Viscount and I were so full of talk that we nearly became oblivious of the presence of Mr. Ratscratch. At length the latter ventured to ask me what we were talking about that seemed so very interesting. I knew Mr. Ratscratch's hobby, so to put him in good humour I told him that the Viscount and myself were discussing the American war.

This immediately loosened Mr. Ratscratch's tongue. He talked volubly, and begged me to interpret his sentiments to the Viscount. I continued the former conversation with the Viscount for a few moments, and then turning to Mr. Ratscratch I rattled off some remarks on the war, which I had heard the Duke de Morny make, and which delighted Mr. Ratscratch so much that he wished me to express to the Viscount his high appreciation of him for taking so clear and just views of the subject.

I continued as before my conversation with the Viscount, when I saw Mr. Ratscratch looking straight into the Viscount's face, evidently expecting him to make some sign of acknowledgment for the compliment he had desired me to pay him. I told the Viscount to look at Mr. Ratscratch, take his glass, bow and smile, and then drink Mr. Ratscratch's health. As he did so the Viscount discovered, by Mr. Ratscratch's gesture and brightened countenance, that I must be making game of him, and was seized with an impulse to laugh, but I checked him just in time, telling him that he would ruin me if he laughed then, as it would be in the wrong place.

In the meanwhile Mr. Ratscratch had said something else, which I had not heard, and as the Viscount at that moment put on a serious look, the better to control his laughter, Mr. Ratscratch, misinterpreting it, anxiously asked of me if the Viscount disapproved of his last remark. I then told the Viscount to smile and say "*Oui*," which was about all the French that Mr. Ratscratch understood. Finally Mr. Ratscratch was satisfied, and he began another long sentence for me to interpret. We kept it up for some time, until I happened to have a moment's distraction.

I then got things so mixed that I no longer knew where I was, either with the Viscount or with Mr. Ratscratch. I asked the Viscount to pardon me, and told Mr. Ratscratch that I was tired talking politics. The Viscount saw that I had gotten into as bad a predicament with Mr. Ratscratch as I had with himself, and he lost all control, and laughed till the tears started from his eyes.

Mr. Ratscratch could not understand this, and he turned to

me again for an explanation. I did not have ready a satisfactory answer, so I pretended to get provoked with him for giving me so much trouble; I protested that I wanted to eat my dinner, and not act as interpreter all the evening, and I proposed to him to defer the war question till the Viscount should have learned English, or he should know a little French. So the question was adjourned that night, but it was renewed every time we three chanced to come together.

After Mr. Ratscratch had dined with us several times in this way, the Viscount declared that he had richly earned the ribbon, and that he would do his endeavour to have the name of Ratscratch enrolled on the list of the Chevaliers of the Legion of Honour.

CHAPTER XXXII.

I GO TO CHURCH—A PREACHER DRAWS MY PORTRAIT.

Giving for God's sake—Compelled to Surrender.

THE Princess Sulkowska was the most devoted friend I had. She was really attached to me, and I, too, was attached to her. But there was one thing which I could not endure with patience —she was ever seeking to make me a convert to the Roman Catholic faith. No matter where we were—at the opera, at a ball, or out for a drive—she would always find an opportunity to say something to me about my soul; and her request in varied keys and tones was ever the same, that I would let my child be baptised, and become a Catholic myself.

I would beg her to let me alone, and would quote Rousseau and Voltaire, when she would stop her ears with her hands in horror. She was ever begging me to go with her to Mass. One day she insisted, and called in the Viscount to aid her to prevail on me. One look from him was worth a volume of her entreaties. I saw that he wished me to go, and I yielded. She took me to a little chapel erected on the Street of St. Philip *du Roule*. It was dedicated to St. Joseph.

A small, insignificant-looking *abbé* preached, and the first thing he did was to attack Voltaire. I was sure that the Princess had put him up to it, and from that moment I was satisfied that the sermon was prepared for me. I listened attentively, but only with the intention of contradicting whatever he might say; for I sneered at the thought that that little *abbé* could convert me to his views or teach me anything.

He began to expose the reasons which prevented sinners from believing. It was, he said, because they were afraid that religion would restrain them in their course of wickedness. It would be easy enough to make intelligent and candid minds believe, if that belief did not enforce self-denial. Sometimes divine truth would flash upon unbelievers, in spite of their opposition to grace ; and, for an instant, they would feel that it *must be so*—that Jesus Christ is the Son of God. Then they would begin to reason, and would throw into the balance of their fallacious reasonings their worldly interests and their sensual gratifications, and, just because it flattered their self-love not to have it so, they were determined that it should not be so—that Christ was not God ; and they would return to their infidel writers, as the dog returns to his vomit ; and they would do so, in order to bring back their incredulity which had been swept away by one breath of the Holy Ghost.

They would consult these works to quiet their consciences, he continued ; for, when grace infuses its light into a soul, conscience awakens, and it requires just such poisons as the mind distills from authors like Voltaire and Rousseau to put it to sleep again.

Thought I to myself: That little *abbé* is drawing my portrait ; for what he had said was exactly what had happened to me. The Princess watched to see the effect of his words, particularly when he attacked my favourite philosophers. But I would look away from the speaker when his words moved me most, and would affect the greatest indifference and even weariness, which was most disheartening to my zealous friend.

After the preacher had finished, the Princess said to me : " I am sorry that you did not pay attention, for that priest's words would have converted a heart of stone." " Yes," said I, " he must have been an infidel himself to know so much about them. Tell me, Princess, how often does that little *abbé* come to see you ?" She assured me that she did not know him, and had never spoken a word to him in her life ; " and," she continued, with a smile, " it must have hit you pretty hard, or you would not have suspected such a thing." For a moment I was struck, as the thought flashed through my mind that the God who reads all hearts might have inspired this man what to say. But in another moment I doubted the Princess's word, and felt sure that she *must* have advised him.

When we reached the church door, a poor woman with an infant in her arms stretched out her hand and asked me to help her for the love of God. I handed her a piece of money, and, turning to the Princess, I said : "Dear Princess, this is my religion, you will never convert me to any other." She instantly replied : "That is Charity, which is one of the corner-stones on which our religion rests ; but there are two others necessary to poise the edifice, which are Faith and Hope, and those you have not. You do right to relieve the poor, but at the same time you do wrong to neglect yourself. If in giving your money— had it been but a farthing—you had been actuated by a spirit of Faith and Hope, then you would have done it for God, and it would have benefited yourself more than the poor creature you have relieved." "But," said I, "it gave me pleasure." "Yes," she replied, "it gratified your generous nature, therefore you have already received your reward. But if you had offered it to God to please Him, and you had not thought of yourself, you would have performed an act of Faith, Hope, and Charity, and you would have given like a Christian, and would receive a Christian's reward."

"Don't be afraid, Princess," said I ; "speak it out, and say that I gave just like a Pagan." "Yes," she replied, laughing ; "and that is just what you are, a charming little American Pagan."

While we were waiting for the carriage a lady came out of the church elegantly dressed. Turning to the beggar she said : "My good woman, I have no money with me ;" and as she pronounced those words she kissed the child that the woman held in her arms. The poor face lighted up and her eyes filled with tears as she exclaimed : "Oh, may God bless you, madam." The Princess remarked that that lady, in kissing the beggar's child, had given her more than I ; she had done the woman's soul an everlasting good ; she had helped her to love mankind. For the charity of the poor is to love the rich.

"You must not," she continued, "confound liberality with Christian charity. The one helps us to obtain the other, it is true. A glass of water is a very small thing ; but given with charity, in the name of Jesus, it is the price of eternal life."

Our conversation ended with the usual entreaties on her part, that I should have my child baptised, and with sharp remonstrances upon my neglect of so important a matter.

When I reached home, the Viscount was waiting for me ; and his first question was, If the Princess had made me set a day for the baptism. "No ;" I replied, "but it was hard to get away from her." Then the Viscount informed me, that she had made him promise that he would try to influence me. "What!" said I, "will you too join the attack ?" and I tried to laugh it off ;

but to my surprise, I found him as importunate as his friend, save only that he went more adroitly to work. He took the child on his knee and began to caress her, and asked her would she like to have him for a godfather.

The Viscount was a fervent believer. He had endowed monasteries, had erected two hospitals, and had given a large tract of land to the Trappists.

He told me how deeply he was interested in the child's future, and begged me to yield. I had no more power of resistance when I saw that the Viscount earnestly desired it. I was hemmed in at home as well as abroad, and I had to surrender at discretion.

CHAPTER XXXIII.

A LITTLE CONVERT—THE LITTLE OLD SHOE.

A list of Names—I part with my Child—A Dream comes back—
Homeward bound.

IN the beginning of April, 1865, I received a letter from New York, which decided me to return to America. The letter was from one of my friends, informing me that an affair in which I had used influence before my departure, had been decided favourably; and begging me to return at once, as he feared the other parties interested might cheat me. I made immediate preparations to leave, expecting to be absent about two or three months.

As soon as I announced my intended departure, the Princess and Viscount gave me no peace, until I named a day for the baptism of my child. The Princess was godmother, the Viscount godfather. The ceremony was performed in the church of St. Germain l'Auxerrois. When the ceremony was over, the Princess took from a casket a beautiful child's necklace of torquoise and gold, whose pendants were a cross in the centre, and on each side a finely-wrought medal bearing the image of the Virgin Mother. She made the child put to her innocent lips the two medals, which bore the likeness of that mother, under whose protection she then placed her. She clasped the necklace around her neck, covered her face with kisses, and pressed her to her bosom, saying: "God bless you, sweet child; may the Blessed Virgin always protect you, and we will all pray that your mother may soon learn to love Jesus."

The child was baptised by the names of Marie Geneviève Dominique Ferdinande Lenore. The Princess's first name was Marie; Laferrière's name was Dominique; Mr. de Lesseps wished the child to be named after his cousin Ferdinand, then at Suez. The Princess said that she ought to be called Geneviève, after the patron saint of the city, where God had led her to be baptised; and I wished her to be called Lenore. To satisfy all parties, the priest gave her the whole list of names.

About one week before I left Paris, my maid informed me that she feared the sea, and would not accompany me. My child was delicate; I had no experience in taking care of her, having always abandoned the entire charge of her to a maid; and I dreaded crossing the Atlantic with a strange one.

I took my child in my lap, and asked her what I should do with baby, if Fanny the maid should leave us. "Do you like Fanny?" I asked. "No," she answered in her baby-French; "no, mamma, I don't like Fanny; I like the Sisters."

The thought struck me instantly, that I should ask the Sisters to take care of her in my absence.

In less than half an hour I was at the convent door. The Superior told me that their institution could not receive children; but that another branch of it was for education; the nearest house of which was at St. Mandé, a suburb of Paris. She advised me to go there, and I drove there immediately.

At St. Mandé the Superior received me kindly and agreed to take the child at once. But she had not seen the child, and supposed her to be much older than she was. As soon as she saw her she was taken aback and exclaimed: "Why, that is a baby; we don't take babies here." "But," said I, "she is two years and a half old." "We have never taken a child under five," she answered, "and," she continued, taking another look at the child, "this one does not look much over a year." I blamed the maid for having put on the child a dress which she had outgrown; and I insisted that it was this that made her look so small. The Superior laughed, and said that I might put any dress on her that I chose; I could not make anything but a baby out of her.

The Superior called the child to her and seated her on her knee; but the child soon got up and stood on the nun's knee, and began playfully to hide her face in the frill of the Superior's cap, and to kiss her as she did so. All of a sudden, as though an idea had just struck her, she got down saying: "*Je vais embrasser le petit Jésus;*" and she began to fumble in the skirt of the Superior's dress searching for her beads. The Superior wondered what she could be doing. But the moment the child found the crucifix she caught it in both hands and covered it with kisses. She then looked up into the Superior's face and laughed, and then kissed the crucifix again and again.

The Viscount could hardly refrain from weeping; while the Superior actually wept, and catching the child in her arms, kissed her most tenderly, and pressed her to her heart, saying: " I will take this child. I will run the risk." " It will only be for a couple of months," I remarked. " Never mind," replied the Superior, " I will keep her, and take as good care of her as I can till you return."

I felt worse on separating from my child than if I had always been a devoted mother, as I felt a keen self-reproach for having neglected her.

When I entered my bedroom the saddest feeling imaginable came over me. The room was in perfect order—no playthings strewn about, and no child's voice. I felt so desolate that I sat down in the middle of the floor and began to weep. I was all alone, and I wept and sobbed until I could weep no more. As I arose I chanced to see something peeping out from under the bureau. I made a spring for it as though the child herself had come back to greet and cheer me. It was one of her little old worn-out shoes of which the child had made a plaything.

I took it up and kissed it as tenderly as though it were the little foot which had worn it. I then put it into my jewellery-box, and completely covered it with my diamonds and pearls, and I said to it: " You dear little shoe, how happy you have made me!" I uncovered it again and began to talk to it as before. But this time the sight of it made me sad and I recommenced weeping, for the little shoe seemed to reproach me for having been faithless to the vow that I had made to God on the morning of my child's birth, when I pressed the first kiss on her baby brow. I had promised that I would be a good mother, and I felt that I had kept the promise but indifferently.

I covered the little shoe with kisses and wet it with my tears, and then put it back among my jewels and said: " Stay there, little shoe, and whenever I look upon you, you shall remind me of my vow, and I will yet become a good mother." I renewed my vow to God, and I felt better, stronger, happier, and more resigned. I must crave pardon from some of my readers for my childishness; but if it is a mother that peruses these pages I need ask no pardon, for mother's know how to love little feet, and know that few things have the power to speak so tenderly to a mother's stricken heart as a little old shoe.

I wept long after I lay down to sleep that night. Separation made me feel with exaggerated keenness my former want of devotion to my child. I asked God to forgive me, and I thanked Him for His goodness and mercy, especially for having given me such a friend as Laferrière. I repeated his name over several times—for to me it was the sweetest name on earth—when, for the first time, I recalled the dream that I had had when living in the Champs Elysées. I instantly sprang out of bed and began to pace the room, wild with delight, for I remembered that I had seen the name of Laferrière written in a sort of haze that floated under the scroll whereon was written: "You will never marry S——." I was now sure that I should marry Laferrière, for a part of that dream had come true, and I was astonished that I had not recollected it before.

To marry Laferrière was all that my heart or my ambition craved. He had titles, wealth, and position, and even without those advantages my heart would have taken him for himself alone. He was the embodiment of principle and honour; I always felt the ascendency of his superior worth, and I tried to resemble him. He had given me a better opinion of the whole human race; and I began to believe in honesty, friendship, and truth, and to love virtue in proportion as my love increased for him.

CHAPTER XXXIV.

"LES MISERABLES."

My Monitors.

ON a bright morning in April I embarked at Liverpool and sailed for my native city. After a pleasant voyage, as we anchored in New York harbour, the passengers were all on deck admiring the beautiful scene. Every face was beaming with gladness; but I felt lonely, and my heart remained unmoved amidst one of Nature's most beauteous prospects. I preferred the Arch of Triumph to the whole of it; and while each passenger was pointing out the view that pleased his fancy most, I almost wondered how anyone could admire with so much enthusiasm a scene that lay so far from the Seine.

After parting with my friends on board the steamer I experienced a feeling of isolation, which none but those whose kindred have disowned them can ever know.

I remained at the Fifth Avenue Hotel a short time. As I was alone I found it exceedingly unpleasant, for a young lady alone at a hotel, no matter how retiring and modest her demeanour may be, becomes at once the object of special remark, and often of suspicion. At every boarding-house at which I applied there was objection to taking a single lady alone.

It was then I began to consider and to pity the condition of young women alone and without protection. If I had not had plenty of money I know not what would have become of me. I sincerely pitied other women with a scanty allowance, for I could well understand how much they must suffer, particularly if young, since their youth, which should call forth the sympathies of their own sex, seems only to inspire envy or distrust.

I have often forgotten my own troubles reflecting on the suffering, that such a state of things must entail on thousands of women situated in the world like myself, and far more deserving, while far less capable of battling with such injustice. I began to conceive a great dislike for a country where, it seemed to me, there was so much narrow-mindedness, so little real charity and true sympathy among women for each other. I longed to leave it, and thought only of getting away as soon as I could, with the determination of never putting my foot on its shores again.

I longed to leave a country where so many of the women seemed to be pushing one into the streets, and so many of the men enticing one to ruin, and where so many of the latter seem to look upon a young woman without protection as their legitimate prey. These men will apparently smpathise with us, and then play upon our better nature to drag us to the abyss. Our happiness depends so much on the sympathies of others that when we see ourselves unjustly trodden upon, if we find not in religion that strong arm of Faith, which alone can sustain us, it is difficult for woman's heart not to receive with gratitude the hand that offers sympathy, and equally hard for her trusting nature to suspect at first the devilishness that prompts it.

And what was it then that saved me? It was my child and Laferrière, for Laferrière was constantly writing to me. His letters were full of sympathy and encouragement. He had an exalted opinion of me, and I strove to become worthy of it. And my child would ever come up before me whenever I saw that little old shoe, in the same way as a Christian is reminded of his Lord by the sight of a crucifix. That little shoe had become the monitor of my conscience. And when, to give the last touches to my toilet, I would open the jewellery-box, I was sure to see it, and to go out into the world fortified by my recollections.

I set diligently to work to arrange my affairs, so as to return to France as quickly as possible. My illusions, as to the sincerity of others in having my interest at heart, were soon dispelled. I found everyone disposed to swindle me, and to take advantage of my evident impatience to return to France, by delaying payments due to me, in the hope that I would leave without waiting for them. In order to turn my vexatious delays to some advantage, I began to study again ;—I engaged teachers and laboured assiduously.

Through the ingratitude of those whom I had befriended, and the malignity of others who hated to see me on the road to worldly success, it took me eighteen months to arrange my affairs. As soon as I had concluded my business in New York, I hastened, with 'all the yearnings of a mother's and a lover's heart to return to France.

Shortly after I left France Laferrière received an unexpected promotion. The Count de Bacciochi, the First Chamberlain, died, and the Emperor appointed Laferrière to replace him. He left his apartments and resided at the Tuileries.

When I had fixed upon the day of my departure, I wrote to Laferrière, requesting him to secure for me the apartments I formerly occupied at the Hôtel du Louvre.

He replied that his own apartments were vacant, and begged of me to occupy them ; that I would be well and conveniently lodged, and that my establishment would cost me one-third less than what I would have to spend at the Hôtel du Louvre. He added, that he had several excellent servants to place at my disposal, who had been in his family for many years. He had no need of these servants, but retained them through gratitude, because they had taken such excellent care of his wife.

I took passage on board the *Pereire,* which sailed Nov. 17th, 1866, from New York for Havre. When the ship moved from the dock I hoped that I was bidding my country an eternal farewell. Nothing could have given me more pain at that moment than to imagine that I should ever see its shores again.

CHAPTER XXXV.

AWAKING FROM A DELUSIVE DREAM—SACRIFICED ON A FAMILY ALTAR.
Jealousy—A Dream of ill Omen.

THE Viscount was at the station when I arrived in Paris. He caught me in his arms as I alighted from the train, drove me to my new home, and introduced me to my servants.

He came early the next morning, and offered me his carriage to drive to the convent, where I found my child alone in the Superior's parlour, playing with a doll. I caught hold of her; she cried out, "Who is it, who is it?" I told her, "Mamma," then she jumped up on my lap and covered my face with kisses.

I wanted to take her home with me; but she said she would not leave the good mother.

To avoid a scene, the Superior said she would bring her to me the next day. She brought her, but the child had not been with me an hour, before she began to ask me to take her back to St. Mandé. Laferrière persuaded me to let her go, as she would be much better taken care of there, than she would be with me.

So the next day I took her back to the convent. The arrangement did not suit me, but I yielded to the entreaties of the child and the advice of the Viscount.

Laferrière had the distribution of the Imperial boxes in all the theatres and opera-houses of Paris. These were usually proscenium boxes, with drawing-rooms attached. We passed most of our evenings at the theatre; but if the play did not amuse us, we would retire and converse in the drawing-room. In that way we passed the first few weeks after my arrival, and those days passed away without a cloud.

The Viscount introduced me to his family, and his daughter treated me like a sister. Everyone knew of Laferrière's devotion to me; for he never sought to conceal it, not even from his family; and I was constantly receiving congratulations upon my triumphal return.

Madame O'Gorman was among the few who were displeased, and who did not congratulate me on my apparent prosperity. It grieved her to see me sought after only by those who were seeking favours at court; and she was sorry, too, that I should have accepted the apartments formerly occupied by Laferrière. She said that it had given the Americans a chance to attack me, and they were doing all they could to prejudice the new American Minister, General Dix, against me; which was the worst turn they could do me, as it would injure me much if I were not received at the American Legation. But as soon as she heard how well I was received by the Viscount's daughter, she became less anxious, and hoped that I would soon become the Vicountess de Laferrière.

Laferrière and myself had never spoken definitely in regard to our marriage, although he knew, since my return, that I expected to be his wife; and he never discouraged me from thinking so, but rather encouraged it, by apparently concurring in all my projects and schemes for the future.

One evening he called on me later than usual, and for the first time since my return, he appeared downcast and sad. He told me that he had just had a scene with his daughter; that the rumour had reached her that he intended to make me his wife, and that some Americans had embittered her against me. He told me that if we were married it would separate him from his family; that he would be willing to sacrifice for me all of them, except his daughter; and it was only on her account that he hesitated; and he asked me if I wished him to make such a sacrifice. His words and looks pierced my heart. I loved him most devotedly, and would have sacrificed all things for him, save his love for me.

He had supposed that his age would have prevented me from ever becoming more attached to him than as to a fond parent or to a devoted friend, on whom I solely relied for sympathy and protection.

My misfortunes had endeared me to him. He looked upon me as some lone child whom sorrow had driven away and estranged from its native land, but over whom God had ever kept a watchful eye; whose Providence had taken compassion on it, and had brought it to him, in order that he might solace and protect it.

It was that very isolation, for which the world reproached me, that bound me to him; and his desire to marry me was chiefly in order to give me perfect protection. He felt grateful too to Providence for having sent me to him, because I had filled the void in his heart, that the death of his beloved child had made. My disposition always diverted and amused him, while my misfortunes called forth his most heartfelt sympathies. Yet our dispositions were totally unlike. The perversities of human nature, of which he had only been an observer, would inspire him with misanthropy and hate; whereas I, who had ever been their victim, was ever ready to forgive, excuse, and pity. He loved this in me; for he attributed it to the noble impulses of a generous heart, whereas it might only have sprung from a morbid insensibility, and from that exaggerated self-love which so absorbed my reason and my senses, that it rendered me incapable of peering as deeply as he did into the depths of malice. I could oftentimes only laugh at and ridicule that which would inspire in him hatred and disgust.

His daughter, who was his only child, had been an invalid from her earliest years. The Viscount could hardly recollect of ever having opposed his daughter's wishes. Her physicians had lately pronounced, that one of her lungs was entirely gone; although she had all the appearance of health.   Her physicians had recommended diversion and excitement to recreate her mind.   I, who had been her companion of pleasure, and who did not see with the eyes of the physician, could not discern anything in her condition to excite my compassion or sympathy.

I assured Laferrière, that he had killed all my desire to marry him, since I saw that he did not love me well enough to sacrifice everything for me; and that if he loved me, as I loved him, he would never hesitate a moment on account of his daughter.   He admitted that what I said was true; but he implored me to consider his years, and then ask myself if it were possible for him to love with the ardour of youth.   He said to me that, if I could take twenty-five years off his head, nothing on earth would prevent him making me at once his wife; but that he had reared and buried nearly all his family, one child alone remained, and she too had but a short while to live; and he felt it a sacred duty to sacrifice his own inclinations and mine to his daughter's happiness.   In my bitterness of soul I said : " You are sacrificing our happiness to your daughter's selfishness and pride."

I fancied that I knew the chief objection that the Countess de Bernis had to her father marrying again ; namely, that while she filled the place at Court that his wife would hold, she was exceedingly unwilling to cede it to anyone.

He said all he could to restore my confidence in his affection, and repeatedly called me his own dear child.   For the first time, this appellation of *child* chilled me, and I begged him never to call me his child again; for it was *too much ;*—and yet it *was not enough !*   But he answered me, that I should ever be his child, and that he would ever be a father to me.   He offered to do anything that I asked, provided that it did not interfere with his daughter's happiness.   But what could he give me, to replace the illusions which he had just taken from me?   From the moment I loved him I had lost my ambition, and all I had asked was his love in return ; and I foolishly had thought that he loved me with the same ardour with which I loved him.

For two whole years I had been living on that illusion.   It had completely changed me.   I was no longer the ambitious, unscrupulous woman, that I was before we met.   I began to love virtue, to loathe vice, and to hate deception.   My love for him had become a purifying flame that had cleansed my heart ; and I loved him, too, for having raised me to a higher and a purer life.

He told me that he believed that, on account of the difference of our ages we would be happier to remain as we were, and it was only on account of the world and my isolation that he ever wished to marry me; that he loved me, as he would some fond child, whom Providence had sent to him, to bring back to his seared heart the freshness of happier years.

When he uttered these words it seemed as though my heart's most cherished idol had changed suddenly before my eyes into a heartless, icy skeleton. I hated him in that moment, and would not have married him for worlds. And yet, a moment after, I would have crawled at his feet, and have become his slave, his household drudge, if he could have only given me back my illusions; and I would have felt happier to be with him, in such a state, believing that he loved me, than I would to have become his bride, when I knew that he only loved me as his child.

It is only sensitive and impassioned hearts that have loved that can understand my feelings, for they know that love can only be satisfied with love. Offer it the whole world in exchange for the heart, which it believes to be united and blended with its own, and the whole universe will appear worthless, compared to the priceless value it sets upon that heart. There is nothing holier in nature than a parent's love. But the parent robs nothing from his child when he loves another. For the first time in my life the demon jealousy entered my heart, and I feared that if he only loved me as his child his heart was still free, and he could love another. I thought that perhaps he did not love me because of his love for his wife, who was in the grave. For an instant a sort of frenzy took possession of me, and I imagined that he loved everything else but me, and only loved me because I consoled him for the absence of those whom he loved. I became jealous of the memory of his child, of his departed wife, and even of my own misfortunes, for I looked upon them all as so many rivals whom he preferred to me. My heart was so rent with agony that it distorted my whole body, and I writhed in excruciating pain.

He was the first and only being that I had ever really loved. In my childhood I had fallen in love with nature while rambling alone over the hills of Amenia. But my guilty conscience soon divorced us, and since that time until I met Laferrière it seemed as though my heart had fed on what was most uncongenial to it.

Others had thought that they had won my heart; but when I really loved I could not find courage to express my love. It was that want of courage which had deceived Laferrière as to the ardour and depth of my attachment. It was ever my great defect to be too frank and too confiding; and this was the last passion in my heart that Laferrière thought I would have been able to conceal.

When he left me that night, and I was once more alone, I felt like one who was for ever wedded to sorrow : for it appeared to me that I could never recover from this last blow, which seemed the most cruel that God ever dealt me.

That night I could not sleep. I wept and sobbed for hours; but, in one of the darkest moments of despair that I had ever known, I remembered the dream I had had in the Champs Elysées, on which I had so strongly built my hopes that I would be his wife. It came back to me like a ray of hope. I began to be consoled, and to believe that he really loved me. I reproached myself for having doubted him and for having been so violent, and I longed to see him that I might ask his forgiveness. I recalled with delight the happy moments we had passed together, and the many times he had told me that he loved me. I thought of his letters, too, and then I was sure that all would yet be well—that I would one day be his wife. For had I not seen his name in my dream long before we ever met?

I prayed God to give me another true dream that night, and begged Him to let me know in it if I was really destined to marry Laferrière. It was nearly morning before I closed my eyes, and, when I did sleep, it was not with the sleep of peace which refreshes. My rest was broken by a dream of ill omen. I dreamt that the very same gipsy who had told me that I would never marry S——, appeared, bearing in her hand a placard, on which was written distinctly : *You will never marry Laferrière.*

As I saw these words I awoke, and became very sad. I tried to console myself by remembering the old adage, and taking hope that it was a true one : That dreams always go by contraries, just as I had done before in the Champs Élysées.

CHAPTER XXXVI.

VANITY OF VANITIES, AND VEXATION OF SPIRIT.

I dispense Favours—Enemies and Beggars—An unwelcome Visit—The Ways of the World.

THE following day, when Laferrière called on me, I could see, from the painful expression of his countenance, that he was suffering mentally as much as I. When I told him again how unhappy I was that he did not love me as much as I did him, he earnestly assured me that he considered his love for me far more lasting and less liable to change than mine. He mentioned the qualities of my heart, on which his love and attachment were founded, remarking that there was too much passion and imagination mixed up in my affection for him.

I asked him how I should hold up my head when the world would congratulate me upon my future nuptials, as it had often done.

He replied: "So long as I live you need not fear the world, for I will bring it to your feet; and when it is there you will see how hollow and worthless it is, and I am sure you will toss it from you as you would an old programme of a play."

From that hour it seemed to be Leferrière's constant study to make me happy. He showered everything upon me that it was in his power to bestow. He never refused any favour that I asked him to confer on my friends or acquaintances, that was consistent with his duty. And whenever a poor wretch appealed to me for assistance, I had only to recommend him to the Viscount, and he was sure to obtain relief.

As soon as it was known that I had so many privileges, those who had sought by every means to pull me down were among the first to throw down their scalping-knives, and to pay court to me and besiege me for favours. I tried to oblige everybody, but with those who I knew hated me, and were obsequious only to use me, I would never associate; and while giving them whatever they asked, I would never permit them to express their thanks in person if I could avoid them. I would at times have contentions with Laferrière for giving the preference to the poor over the rich.

Sometimes I obtained invitations to a court ball for educated and refined ladies who were too poor to buy a decent court dress, and I would have to dress them up in my own clothes, so that they could appear. These things would irritate Laferrière, for he never knew, he said, how far I might go. He once said that he feared that I would have people received at the Tuileries in the evening whom the Empress would find the next morning domiciled in the Charity Hospital.

At last he despaired of making me reform in this respect; and once he asked my forgiveness after having given me a reproof, and acknowledged that he was blaming me for the very faults that endeared me to him. He knew me so well that, if I recommended one person more urgently than another, and appeared particularly anxious, he would remark: "I am sure it is an enemy or a beggar."

I knew some correspondents of journals, among whom were some ladies, who had families to support. Most of them had been slandering me both with tongue and pen. Laferrière had conceived an intense dislike for them, and implored me to have nothing to do with them. But their malice did not lessen my compassion. I once made Laferrière laugh by saying, when he was pressing me hard, that I pitied their poverty so much that I was delighted that they could make a little money by abusing me, even though it were in order to gratify the malice of those whose favours they sought.

In less than three months I became so cloyed with pleasure and amusements that I could no longer enjoy anything. I tried to conceal my weariness and to appear perfectly contented and happy; but Laferrière would sometimes unexpectedly join me at the theatre, and find me sitting in the back of the box weeping, while those who accompanied me were merrily enjoying the play.

Sometimes at a ball, while surfeited with the insipid compliments and obsequious attentions of those who had formerly never noticed me, and now only sought me for my influence, I would be wounded to the quick to see my old and true friends stand off and avoid me; and, on returning home, I would be seized with such a moral nausea that the moment I entered my room I would throw myself on the bed in all my finery, and would tear the jewels from off my neck and arms and throw them across the room. My maid would sometimes remain beside me until the day dawned, trying to console me, and I have felt her tears fall on my neck and arms as she would lean over to unlace my dress.

In such moments, when I became sufficiently calm to reflect, I looked back with regret to the days when I used to be called "Tick," and used to pass long hours on the curbstones, swimming my shoes in the gutter, or roaming bareheaded through the alleys, building castles in the air. I found that I was happier building them than I was living in them.

My weariness grew to such a pitch that my health began once more to give way. It required a stronger constitution than mine to resist such a constant strain of nervous excitement, and I began to loathe and hate that flash of worldly pomp and show which formerly I had so much coveted; for I found it to be but gilded misery.

One evening, as I was trying to persuade Laferrière to consent to let me leave Paris for a short while, my valet brought me a letter from my brother-in-law. He wrote that my sister was about to make a visit to the Holy Land, and would like to remain a few weeks in Paris, and he asked me whether she could remain with me. My mind was thoroughly made up to leave Paris, and it went hard with me to remain just to oblige a sister who had, I thought, but slender claims upon my gratitude. I consulted the Viscount, who said, "If she has not behaved like a sister to you your duty is to set her an example, to show her how one sister should behave towards another." I remarked that my sister was rich, and that I could not see that she needed me sufficiently to require me to make such a sacrifice.

Said the Viscount, "Her money cannot buy for her the advantages that your position can give her? She abandoned you in adversity? Well, she is only like the rest of the world, as she will not refuse to live with you in prosperity."

I soon repented of having spoken so severely of my sister. My conscience reproached me, and to quiet it I said that if she had treated me harshly, it was because she believed that my life was not as blameless as it should be ; that I never gave her my confidence, and we had seen each other but very little since we were children; that, in fact, I was quite like a stranger to her.

"Well," replied the Viscount, "if she knows none of the particulars of your miraculous escape from poverty, I do not see why she should have a better opinion of you now than she had then. My dear child," he added, "you will find out that the world will be indulgent to our faults the moment it finds it to its interest to be so. Your experience this winter ought to convince you of the truth of my words. Mankind does not honour us for our virtues ; it is only God who loves us and rewards us for these. Men prefer our vices, when they prove successful, to our virtues when they entail upon us obscurity and want. I will give you another winter in Paris, to become as great a misanthrope as myself. I try to live up to the precepts of the Gospel; but don't suspect for an instant that I seek to benefit others from any other motive, for I have a horror of the human race. There are not half a dozen people among all your acquaintances who seek you for yourself, and esteem you for your virtues, or who believe that you have any."

I laughed as I said : "You say all this for fear that I may fall in love with somebody else."

"But it is true," he replied seriously. "I think you have too much human respect, and fret too much lest the world should misjudge you; and I want you to feel more independent of the world and its judgments. Do what is right, and look up to God for the rest; but do not expect any reward or satisfaction from the world, for it will surely cheat you."

"But," said I, " Mme. de Staël says that a man should brave public opinion, but a woman should bow to it." "My child," answered the Viscount, " you will always misunderstand me as you do half of the maxims of our French writers. Your heart is all right, but your head is all wrong—*Votre cœur est bon, mais votre esprit est à travers.*

"Of course it is a man's duty to fight for his principles in the public arena, even to the death; while woman's is an obscure, but not less important mission. But when she has conformed to established rules and customs, and has a clear conscience, why should she not be happy? and why allow those to make her miserable who choose to find pastime in attacking her conscience?"

I replied that all this was the least cause of my unhappiness. A far greater was that our hearts never beat in unison; that I was miserable and alone even when near him because condemned to feel that our hearts could never be united. And it were less pain, I added, to be separated from him altogether.

"Does it make you any more miserable than it does me," he asked, " that I am unable to forget or to make you remember the difference of our years? Your love for me is the greatest solace of life; and the day may come,—but God knows I am not anxious for it, for I would willingly lay down my life if it would ensure a few happy years to my daughter,—but the day may come when I will ask you to make the sacrifice to become my wife. A sacrifice indeed it would be, although you at the time might not deem it such. I fear you will discover when too late that Autumn and Spring consort better as father and child than as husband and wife. Marriage is a great disenchanter. When two beings are united by an indissoluble bond, it requires great virtue and much mutual sacrifice of taste and inclination to preserve through life those sentiments, and to keep alive that warmth of feeling which first animated them."

CHAPTER XXXVII.

MARIA MONK'S CONFESSION.

A plea of Guilty—Recommendation to Mercy.

MY sister arrived in June with her eldest daughter. I brought my child home, thinking that the companionship of my niece would reconcile her to absence from the convent. I did my best to amuse her and wean her affections from the Sisters. I would take her to the Champs Elysées to see *Guignol* (the French Punch and Judy), but the moment the excitement was over she would importune me to take her back to the good mother.

One morning as soon as she awoke she recommenced her usual petition. I said: "Not to-day, but to-morrow." She put on a sad countenance, and that morning she fainted at the breakfast-table. As she slowly opened her eyes she looked piteously and beseechingly in my face and said: "Mamma, won't you take me back to the good mother?" I regretted that I had ever left her at the convent, and I began to hate the Catholics for having robbed me, as I thought, of my child's affection. I took the child back that same afternoon.

The next day I was abusing the Catholics in conversation with my sister, when, to my surprise, she seemed inclined to defend them. I asked her how it was possible for her to think well of them after all our mother had said against them.

She replied: "But do you not know that that book of our mother was all a lie?"

Said I: "I believe every word in Maria Monk's 'Awful Disclosures.'"

My sister was quite irritated and said emphatically: "I know, that the '*Awful Disclosures*' of Maria Monk are all lies! SHE HERSELF TOLD ME SO." Said I: "Why did she write it then?" "In order to make money," my sister replied: "some men put her up to it; but she never received one cent of the proceeds of the book; for these men kept all for themselves."

When my sister told me that my mother's book was a lie, a tremor passed over me at the thought that such a woman should be my mother; and I felt humbled to the earth. I had not the charity in my heart for her then that I have now. I now feel that my mother was not so much worse a woman than anyone else who lives in sin.

I have been told that my mother at eighteen was handsome and quite prepossessing. She did not write her book; in fact the book itself admits that she did not. She only gave certain facts which were dressed up by the men who afterwards helped to cheat her out of the proceeds of her crime.

A young girl of eighteen, with her disposition, unrestrained either by education or religion,—thrown penniless on the world, the victim of a licentious man, and driven to seek refuge in a hospital—would naturally try to make friends among the visitors and attendants, by representing herself as the helpless victim of circumstances. And in order the better to enlist their sympathies, she would take care to shape her story so as to suit the prejudices and partialities of those whose protection she sought.

The visitors and officers of Bellevue Hospital, at the time Maria Monk was a patient there, were notoriously anti-Catholic. These men gloated over the horrid fictions of her diseased imagination, and published them to gratify their prejudice, and with the less sentimental object of swelling their own profits.

My mother may have known a few of the external observances of the Catholic religion, but she knew nothing of its spirit,—and she could not have been conscious of the full extent of the enormity of her crime, when she made herself an accomplice of the work which bears her name.

We should not forget to take into consideration her youth and her misery at the time that these men gave her the hope of rising above poverty, if she would allow them to publish in her name such calumnies against the inmates of the Hôtel Dieu.

Most Catholics shrink with horror at the very mention of the name of Maria Monk; but God is more merciful than His children;—He judges the intent and not the act.

I seek not to exonerate my mother. It was indeed a cruel and nefarious thing on her part, to try to blacken the characters of unoffending and holy women, entirely dedicated to the service of religion and humanity. But bad as she was, she did not destroy her offspring; and let every woman who has sinned, and to hide her shame has committed a still greater sin, examine her own conscience before daring to pass judgment on Maria Monk (*See* Appendix.)

CHAPTER XXXVIII.

LAFERRIÈRE AND GIBBON—THE LADIES OF THE HOLY FAMILY—
THEIR HOME AT ST. MANDÉ.

A new-fashioned Postulant—My unexpected Paradise.   A historical Mirror.

MY sister stayed with me a few weeks, and then left France. I was heartily tired of the life I was leading, and determined to leave Paris.   I consulted Laferrière, and told him how I was grieved to have lost my child's affection.   He sympathised with me in my regrets concerning my child, but he could not see why I should not be content in other respects, as I had everything else my heart could wish for.

He too readily forgot that I had everything except just that which was the one desire of my heart.

The thought came to me that I should go and stay with my child, as she would not stay with me.   Laferrière was much pleased with the proposal, and suggested that I should stay in the convent for a month while he went down to his château, as he disliked to have me go to a watering-place without him, and his accompanying me might give scandal ; while I would not go to his château, as I had never spoken to his daughter since I knew that she was the only obstacle to our marriage.

My chief objection to go and live in the convent was that I was full of prejudices against the Catholics, notwithstanding all that my sister had said to me in regard to the great wrong my mother had done them.   I had no faith in them, and looked upon them as partly dupes, partly rogues, and partly hypocrites.

It pained Laferrière to hear me speak of Catholics as I did, and he tried quietly to convince me of my error, and that it was only my total ignorance which made me so prejudiced.   I tried hard to make him acknowledge that he himself had little or no faith, and that he was only a Catholic because his mother had him baptised one.

I thought that I would have but little trouble in making him a proselyte to infidelity, and I began to give him my Voltarian theories, and I accused the Catholics of being narrow-minded and of stifling the efforts of the intellect.   I told him that if he would read Gibbon I was sure that writer would convince him that the first Christians were the greatest of imbeciles.

At the mention of Gibbon's name his face assumed the air of one trying to master his temper.   He answered me, with great earnestness and decision, that he was more familiar with Gib-

bon than with Bossuet, and that Gibbon was the least adapted
to convince him of anything.

Villemain's Criticism on the writers of the eighteenth century lay on the table. He took up the second volume, and
began to read where he describes some of the early events of
the sceptic Gibbon's life; how he became a Catholic—not by
chance, by poverty, or caprice, as Rousseau did, but after having
read the eloquent work of Bossuet on the Variations of the
Protestant Churches—and how his father, who belonged to the
Established Church, was so displeased with the conversion of
his son that he sent him to Lausanne. In the words of Villemain : " Gibbon was here subjected to a pretty rough course of
treatment, which brought him back, in reality or in appearance,
to his old religion. His soul does not seem to have been
exactly made for the practice of resignation to sacrifice, and
resistance to undue pressure from authority."

Gibbon himself says that the life there was too sad, and that
they set too bad a table —both of which things hastened his re-
conversion. Upon which Villemain remarks, that a man who
makes such a start in life and in the theological career does not
seem to him well-fitted to conceive a very disinterested enthusiasm for the martyrs.

Laferrière continued to denounce my favourite historian,
occasionally referring to the book which he held in his hand.
He was not willing that I should even tolerate the principles of
such an author, much less be prejudiced by them. He did not
withhold his admiration for the intelligence and rare talents
displayed in Gibbon's works, which, as Villemain had said, it
was far easier to censure than to equal; but he wondered how
a person like myself could be influenced by a writer who was
ever siding with the executioner against the victim, and who
kept all his enthusiasm for material greatness, while his heart
remained cold and his genius mute before the sufferings, the
combats, and the triumphs of the moral order.

He could not, he said, conceive how an American could
admire a historian who looked upon the military despotism of
the Roman empire as the masterpiece of civilisation, and whose
great spite against Christianity arose from the fact that it had
succeeded in overthrowing the empire of the Cæsars.

There never was a historian, he said, so thoroughly destitute
of sensibility as Gibbon; and he had often wondered how a
being possessing human instincts could have so cruelly and
heartlessly mocked and derided men whose only crime was to
die for their fidelity to conscience.

"For my part," he continued, "Gibbon inspires me with more horror for his cold insensibility than he does with admiration for his genius and learning. I for one cannot find it in my heart to weep over the monuments of tyranny and despotism, which have crumbled into dust at the feet of moral worth and religious truth."

He continued to talk in this strain, until I put a stop to it by bringing in Voltaire and Rousseau. "Rousseau," said he—and he caught up the book and threw it contemptuously on the table—"Rousseau always used to put me to sleep, and, as I don't feel like dozing in your charming society, we will throw him aside; but Voltaire, who is the king of geniuses and the prince of mockers, I always read in the same way as I go to the theatre—to be delighted, amused, and interested. But if I wanted to strengthen my mind, and to give it a force that would enable it to withstand alike good and adverse fortune, I would not go to Voltaire—I would do better; I would read the lives of the saints and martyrs, which, my child, I would much prefer having you study, as stupid as you might find them, to seeing you infect and enervate your mind with the anti-Christian theories of the philosophers of the eighteenth century.

The next morning I called to see the Princess Sulkowska, who had become my bosom friend since my return to Paris. The moment I told her that I thought of going to the convent to remain a few weeks with my child, she ordered the carriage, and we drove at once to St. Mandé.

When I mentioned to the Superior my desire to board at the convent, she was startled at the thought of taking so worldly-minded a woman, and made every possible objection to my coming. The Princess overruled all her objections. The Superior changed her tactics, and tried to frighten me out of my design by enumerating the stringent rules which I would necessarily be subjected to, from which she could not exempt anyone within the walls of the convent, as she herself had to be as observant of the rules as the humblest Sister. She told me that I could not receive any gentlemen, except in the common parlour, and then only from two until five; that I must be inside the convent by nine, and could not go out alone, and could not look out of any of the front windows.

Said I: "I subscribe to all that." "Oh! no," she said, "my dear child, you would not be contented to remain here twenty-four hours." "My good mother," I replied, "I am thoroughly sick of the world and long to get out of that constant whirl of excitement; it is killing me."

I spoke with an earnestness that quite amused the mother, for she thought that I was incapable of having one serious thought. The Princess said that she was willing to go bail that I would be contented. It but made the mother laugh the more to see how I had succeeded in persuading the Princess of my seriousness. She said that it would be a moral impossibility for one like myself, who had never been subjected to any restraint, to be contented there, where no one, not even herself, could ever do her own will; and she assured me that it was on my own account that she wished me not to come, as she knew that I would suffer, and she too would be unhappy that she could not grant me any more liberty than the rules allowed.

I finally said that if she would not let me come I must take away the child, which frightened the child so that she climbed into the mother's lap and wept, as if she were to be the chief sufferer by the mother's refusal. The Superior made the child take my hand and walk with me in the garden, while she stayed with the Princess.

After some time they joined me, and by the joyous expression of the Princess's face, I could see that the conference had ended in my favour. The Superior had agreed that I might stay there during the summer vacation, which would begin in a few days and would last eight weeks.

I could readily understand that the Princess had brought the mother over with the idea that there was a chance of converting me, which the Princess had never despaired of since the day she first made my acquaintance. She had always been praying for it, had even made novenas, or nine days' prayers, for it, and was constantly telling her friends that if I could only be converted, she believed I would do a great deal of good.

The mother was not so sanguine in this respect, in fact she looked upon my conversion as almost hopeless, for she was well acquainted with my aversion for the Catholic religion, as I had never attempted to conceal it from her. I had been equally frank with the Princess, but she would never pay any attention to my railleries.

The Superior conducted the Princess and myself across the street, to show us the apartments which would be assigned to me during my stay, and, as we waited for the portress to unfasten the door, the lugubrious aspect of the street, with its high sepulchral walls on each side, made a chill pass over me. But the moment the massive door was opened a magnificent garden spread itself before us. It was an enclosure of about twelve acres, surrounded by a high wall, the top of which was thickly garnished with broken glass. To the right, as we entered the garden, was an old château, which had formerly been a country-seat of Foquet, the Minister of Finance under Louis XIV. The grounds which surrounded it were artistically laid out in beautiful lawns and serpentine alleys, shaded on each side by lilac bushes, which had grown very tall, and were so thickly interlaced, that they formed almost as impenetrable a barrier as the wall which surrounded the whole enclosure. In the centre of a wide lawn, which lay in front of the château, stood a large tree, a cedar of Lebanon, of more than two centuries' growth. The wide-spreading branches of this beautiful tree, and its lofty head, which towered majestically above the château and the surrounding trees, amply justified the name which the nuns had given it of " The Monarch of the Garden."

At the farthest end of this lawn was a walk shaded by sycamore trees, which led to a high mound covered with shrubbery, through which had been cut a winding path, by which we ascended to the summit, where we found a dilapidated kiosk, which had been entirely hidden from our view by clusters of rose-bushes and grape-vines. On reaching the top of the mound we had a most commanding view of Paris.

These spacious gardens contained every variety of fruit, and plant, and vegetable. The grassy lawn and the borders of the walks were thickly strewn with violets of every hue, and the gentlest breeze would impregnate the whole garden with their odour. The Princess and myself were equally taken by surprise to find there so enchanting a spot, and we were enraptured with the beautiful prospect.

The château, which was to be my home till the end of vacation, was unoccupied. I was to have a suite of rooms facing on the garden, consisting of a spacious parlour and bedroom, a dining-room, a room for the maid, a room for my toilet, and a bath-room. The saloon presented the sombre appearance of a past age. There were the antique mouldings and furniture, the high chimney-piece, and large fireplace, and immense mirrors.

The mirror directly opposite the chimney-piece filled the space between the large windows. It was broken at the top. It was behind this mirror that the papers were found which convicted Fouquet. It is said that when Louis XIV. used to go hunting in the Park of Vincennes he would stop and refresh himself at the château, and that he had often paced this very saloon.

The convent ground, which lay on the other side of the street, extended to the Park of Vincennes, and one of the entrances into the convent grounds was by a gateway through the park-railing on the west side.

The Superior inquired how I would pass my time. The Princess told her of my fondness for study, and the Superior offered to let me have during the vacation as many of the ladies to instruct me as I wished.

Laferrière was delighted that I had determined to stay at St. Mandé during the summer. When I had described to him the furniture of the château, and told of my intended studies, he proposed to complete the latter by sending me a harp teacher from the Conservatory, and to send me a part of the furniture in his apartments, so that I might be as comfortable at the convent as I was in Paris.

It was the first week of August, 1867, that I went to reside in this convent château. The community was called: *The Ladies of the Holy Family; Les Dames de la Sainte Famille.* It is the educational branch of the convent of the Sisters of Hope.

CHAPTER XXXIX.

LIFE AMONG THE NUNS.

Books for Use and for Show—An Encyclopædic Nun—Crumbs of Comfort—Cloistered Happiness—"The Bread of Life"—Wrestling in Prayer for Me.

As the day appointed for my admission as a boarder into the convent drew near, I began to realize the fact that I could not be happy without Laferrière. On the day of our separation, when my heart was weighed down under a sense of my lonely position and dependence on another, for all that makes life endurable, Laferrière proved himself the true friend. He encouraged me in my good resolution and helped me to keep up my courage, by reminding me that it would be only for a short time—three or four weeks at most.

His tears fell on my hands as he kissed them, when he helped me into the carriage. Said he, "My child, you are doing what is right. God will reward you for it, and I will never cease to love you."

When I arrived at the convent, my child, who had been watching for me the whole day, ran towards me, holding in her hand a nosegay of violets, which, she said, she had gathered for her little mamma. She called the Mother Superior *the good mother,* but me she always called *the little mamma.*

L

The Superior was in the château, waiting to receive me. By her side stood a young Spanish nun, to whom she introduced me. It was Madame St. Xavier. After conversing for a few moments in her native tongue we embraced; and then, turning to the Superior, she thanked her for having chosen her to be one of my teachers.

Madame Xavier might have been in her twenty-seventh year. She was about the medium height, of slender and delicate mould, with a face that expressed all the sweetness and innocence of an angel, while it bespoke a firmness and a courage, which would have graced the brow of a hero.

The convent bell rang and the nuns left me. The garden appeared to me more lovely than ever, lighted up as it was by an August sunset. I began to run through it like a wild fawn, over the lawns and through the alleys, imagining all the while that I was talking to Laferrière. After rambling for an hour, I found myself once more near the garden gate. By this time I was tired, and I took it into my head to cross the street and talk with the Mother Superior. But I found the massive door locked. I called in vain for some one to come and open it.

As I had never yet known locks or bolts to prevent my doing anything I wanted to do, my first impulse was to try to climb over the wall. I stepped back a few paces to see what my chances were; but the wall appeared twice as high to me then as before, and the sight of its coping of broken glass made me recoil still more. I ran into the château. The thought struck me that I should go into the basement and get out through a window. I found them all protected by a strong iron grating that would hardly permit a cat to pass. I then went upstairs to the first floor, but found all the rooms that faced on the street locked. Then I remembered that it was one of the rules of the convent never to look out of a front window, and I congratulated myself upon having escaped a violation of rules into which I would have thoughtlessly rushed. I hastened to my rooms feeling thoroughly checkmated, and I began to realise that I was in a convent.

In packing up my books to come to the convent I had put all the infidel writers into a little trunk by themselves. This trunk I hid in a closet. But Fénélon's works and other, as I supposed, approved writers, I put out on the table. Among them were two little books which I had never read. One was called " The Words of Jesus." It was given to me before I was married by a lady friend. The other was called " Evidences of Christianity." It was given to me by Mr. Elise Charlier, after the death of my husband. I had always intended to read "Evidences of Christianity," because Mr. Charlier, when he put it into my hands had made me promise that I would read it. "I am sure," said he, "that you cannot read that book without becoming a Christian." I laughed and told him that I would read the book to please him, but I was sure no book would ever convert *me*. Nearly five years had passed and I had never had the courage to open it. The very title set me against it. I put these two books on the table on account of their respectable titles, and to make thus a good impression on the nuns.

Ever since I had placed my child in a convent, and had determined to educate her in one, I had marked certain passages in Voltaire and Rousseau which I intended to read to her when she would be older, believing that the reading of those passages would undo in one day all that the nuns would have effected in years. I had brought these books with me as weapons of defence in case the nuns should attack me. I felt that it was my duty not to bring confusion into their midst unless they should choose to bring it down upon themselves, and that was my reason for keeping these books so well guarded.

To my surprise, no one ever said a word to me about religion, unless I introduced the subject myself, and even then they appeared rather disinclined to converse with me upon it. I saw that they were all happy and contented, and I soon became more curious to know their views than they seemed willing to tell me.

The day after my arrival in the convent, the Mother Superior introduced me to a religious whose name was Madame Marie de St. Paul. She was a fine scholar, well versed in history and general literature. She seemed to me like a living encyclopædia. She was always ready to answer any question or give any date, no matter how remote or obscure the fact inquired about might be. Sometimes she would sit down and instruct me in history, much in the same way as one would relate a story to a child, to impress the events more vividly on my mind. At the same time she would delineate the striking traits of character of the personages in the events of which she spoke, and she would do it more graphically than any biographer I had ever read.

My friends thronged to see me in my convent home. Laferrière, before he left for his château, drove out nearly every afternoon.

I had more peace of mind than I had had since the night Laferrière told me that our marriage must be deferred until after his daughter's death. Yet I was not happy, and at times I was miserable. In spite of all I could do I found it impossible to forget my cruel disappointment, and every time that the thought of it came to me, it would send an acute pain through my heart.

I tried every means to attach my child to me, but, in spite of all my endeavours, she always preferred the Mother Superior to me. She would sit on the mother's lap and fall asleep with her head reclining on her bosom, while with me she never seemed to feel at ease.

Sometimes, while sitting on my knee, she would put her hand on my heart, and say: " Mamma, I wish you had Jesus there, then I would love to lie there." She had repeated the same thing to me so often that I one day asked Madame Xavier what she meant.

Madame Xavier then explained to me the real presence of our Lord in the Eucharist; and she told me that it was that bread of life which they received at the altar, that gave them strength to remain true to their vocation.

" It is simply your faith," said I, " that makes the bread and wine become for you the body and blood of Christ." "Ah, no," she replied, "for our Lord said : ' *This is* my body,' and ' *This is* my blood.' It is not a receiving of mere symbols of our Lord, but this most intimate personal union with Him that gives us strength to overcome our natural inclinations, to leave all and follow Him, and to be ready to die for Him, as the martyrs have done. No, it is our Lord, whether I choose to believe it or not."

Said I : " If I should receive it, would it be just as much the Lord to me as if I were a Christian ? "

" It would be the body and blood of our Lord to you," she answered ; " but you would not receive the spiritual benefit unless you were rendered worthy to receive Him by the virtues of Faith and Charity. The possession of the latter virtue necessarily implies the cleansing of the heart from sin. And if we receive our Lord unworthily, we receive Him, as the Apostles tell us, to our own damnation."

" What is sin ?" I asked. She replied : " Sin comprehends an infinity of evils, which I could never enumerate ; yet it may be summed up in the statement that it is a violation of that law which requires that we should believe God and love Him for His own sake, and love our neighbour for God's sake. And therefore when we injure our neighbour, when we nourish hatred in our hearts against him, when we refuse to forgive those who injure us, and when we feel envious of those whom it has pleased God to favour more than ourselves, whether temporally or spiritually, then do we sin also against God."

"Well," I insisted, "I love my neighbour; I hate no one, I forgive everybody; I am not envious. Why should I not eat of this bread?"

"I would that you could," she said, "for I can never be happy until you do. But you must love your neighbour for God's sake, and must first believe and love our Lord before you can receive Him worthily."

"But," said I, "I *cannot* believe." She firmly replied: "*You will believe;*" and then, as if recollecting herself, she started to leave me. I tried to detain her, and begged her to continue to talk with me. "No," she replied, "I must go to the chapel and pray." I implored her to remain with me a little longer, and reproached her for not loving me enough to make such a trifling sacrifice. "You force me to betray to you my secret," she replied: "I love you more than you can ever know, and I promised our Lord that I would make the Way of the Cross every day for your conversion until you are converted, for I must have your soul;—I want it to offer to our Lord."

I accompanied her to the chapel, and sat down in a corner to wait for her, expecting that she would hurry knowing my impatience.

"I had not the slightest idea of what Madame Xavier meant by "making the Way of the Cross;" and when I saw her go and kneel before a picture, and remain there for a few minutes with her body almost prostrate on the floor, and then repeat the same thing before each one of thirteen similar pictures distributed around the walls of the chapel, I took such compassion on her that I began to pray for her; but when the thought struck me that she was doing all this for me I was in agony.

When she had finished, she came to me, her face radiant with smiles, although I could see that she had been weeping. This was too much for me, and as soon as we left chapel I said to her: "I will never forgive you if you repeat this thing. For what effect can it have upon me, that you should go every day and remain with your body bent to the ground for an hour before those paintings; no matter what they represent? I pitied you so, that it was as much as I could do to keep from snatching you off the floor." My ignorance of the Catholic forms of worship amused her so much, that she sat down on the grass, and began to laugh like a child.

"Well, what must you think of us all here?" she exclaimed. Said I: "I am sure that you are all good; but I am not so sure that you are all in your right minds." She told me that she had performed the same devotion every day since I had been among

them, and she would continue it until I was converted. Said I:
"It is impossible to make me believe; and you are afflicting
both of us for nothing." She replied: "I do not blame you for
not believing; for how can you believe in what you know nothing
about? I know you cannot help your unbelief; therefore I
am imploring our Lord to do for you what you cannot do for
yourself."

She then explained to me that when she made the Way of the
Cross, she did so to unite herself with the sufferings of our Lord
on His way to Calvary; and gave me to understand that this
pious practice had its birth in the very cradle of Christianity.
She related how, after the ascension of our Lord, it was the
practice of the early Christians who resided at Jerusalem, to
visit the consecrated spots which had witnessed the sufferings
of our Saviour, and which had been sprinkled with His blood.
"These visits soon became pilgrimages," she said; "and for
centuries it was the constant practice of the faithful to visit the
scenes of Christ's mission and passion. But when the Holy
Land fell into the hands of the infidels and became difficult of
access, images were made emblematical of these holy places, so
that the faithful, by kneeling before them, could make this journey to Jerusalem in spirit, and thus be able to meditate on the
agonies that our Lord suffered for our salvation in the last hours
of His life.

"This devotion is known as the Way of the Cross, and will
be found in all our chapels and churches. We only make use
of these pictures and images to remind us of our Lord's sufferings."

CHAPTER XL.

GENERAL ROLLIN'S "AUNTS."
The General's Love.

WHEN we left the chapel and had returned to the garden, I
said to Madame Xavier: "Some people call you idolaters for
kneeling before these pictures." "Yes," she replied, "because
they do not know our interior life; they only judge us from the
exterior, as you did a little while ago. With us everything is
interior, and therefore only interior minds can understand us."

That afternoon General Rollin drove out to see me. The
general was a man over seventy years of age; he was adjutant-
general of the palace, and occupied the first floor in the east

wing of the Tuileries. He had always been a man of the world, and knew as little about his religion as many Catholics do. We were walking in the garden when the thought struck me that I would ask him how it was possible for him to believe in a religion so contrary to reason. "General," I asked, "are you a Roman Catholic?" He looked at me with astonishment, as if to see if I intended to insult him, then, knitting his eyebrows, he asked me: "What do you take me to be? Do you think I am a Huguenot?" Said I: "General, I don't wish to offend you, but when you see the priest raise the Host, do you really believe that Host to be the real body of Christ?"

He withdrew his arm from mine, struck his cane firmly to the earth, frowned more deeply, 'and then, in a most indignant tone, asked me: "*Did these women teach you that?*" "Yes, they did; but of course I could not believe it." "Well," said he, "you did well; but you ought to leave this place or they will make a fool of you. I never wanted you to put your foot here, and I told Laferrière to prevent it if he could, for I know the nuns. Why, do you know that I was actually bred among them? I had three aunts, all professed nuns. Two of them were abbesses, and the other was procuratress. I tell you that I got enough of them in my youth to last me the rest of my days. They are crazy themselves, and they bewitch everybody who comes within shooting distance of them.

"I once fell in love with a beautiful girl, she was as sweet as a flower, and she took it into her head to go into one of these places for a week before she would decide to have me. I was fool enough to consent to it, and *mon Dieu!* that was the last I ever saw of her. It has given me an anti-cloister fever that I shall never get rid of. Besides, my mother used to make me go to one or the other of these old aunts to be taught the catechism, and it was the ugliest of the three that prepared me for my first communion. I have been through many a hard-fought battle, and would willingly go through them all over again sooner than be obliged to submit to the drillings that she used to put me through."

Said I: "General, speaking of your aunt, reminds me of the old woman who brought me up." "Why," said the general, "did she teach you the catechism?" "She tried to," said I; "and she succeeded about as well with me as your old aunt the abbess seems to have done with you. But I think that you and I resemble each other in this respect, that neither of us is piously inclined."

"Oh, my dear madam!" he replied, "don't trust to that disposition for protection. If you wish to escape the influence of these women, you must clear right out, otherwise they will have you; and, if they once get you, that is the last of you." "They have actually set me thinking," I rejoined; "and I ask myself: are they crazy or am I?"

"Oh," said he, "I see they are getting the best of you, and I tell you to beware of that Spanish nun. She is one of the worst kind. I can see in her eye that she is bound to have you: she will stick to you night and day until she gets you. And you ought to know that she is personally interested, for it would be considered a great triumph here if she could wrest a lady like yourself from the claws of the devil. That is just the view these women take of it. To hear my old aunts go on you would think that a man was only born to die." "Well," said I, "by the rate at which our friends are dying off it looks very much like it." "Ah!" said he, "is it not dreadful? There is my daughter, my son-in-law, poor Bassano's daughter; and then Tascher's daughter, too; and now the duke's wife,—all gone! I tell you there is a fatality that seems to hang over the east wing of that palace."

The old general wiped away his tears, and then continued: "It is the least that a man can do to try to console himself by making use of the good things in this life without becoming a voluntary martyr." "But," said I, "you are surfeited with the good things of this life, and yet they do not seem to console you." "I would like to know," he replied, "what there is on earth that can replace or console us for the loss of those that we love?"

"The nuns say," I answered, "that they replace them with the hope that they will soon meet again, and they console themselves by still rendering them services by their prayers and their good works." The old general wiped his eyes, heaved a deep sigh, and said to me, in most despairing tone, "My dear lady, *they have got you;* for, when you said that, it sounded just like one of them!"

CHAPTER XLI.

A SPLENETIC SPINSTER.

A perverse Nature—A Nun's Revenge—Rare Christian Charity.

NIGHT after night I was thrown entirely upon myself during those hours which, for years, I had devoted to dissipation and pleasure. The religious would leave me about half-past eight, and I had never been accustomed to retire before midnight. The moment I was alone I would begin to think of Laferrière, and wonder what he was about. I imagined that he could not always be alone in his palatial apartment, and then I would be seized with a fit of jealousy, which would render the loneliness of my position harrowing.

There, too, was my maid Josephine, who would have driven me frantic had I not been firmly resolved to resist her influence. She was a nominal Catholic, but one who had a hatred towards nuns. She was one of those Catholics, and the Church is full of them, who pride themselves in the title of Catholic, but who disgrace the name of Christian. Hers was an odd and strangely perverse nature, for nothing escaped her *but the good.* The good she could never see, for she belonged to that class of evil-minded people who ever remain blind to the good, the true, and the beautiful, but will find evil everywhere and in everything. They are ever searching for it, and they cannot fail to find it, for they have the faculty of perverting everything that is good and beautiful into what is bad and hideous.

Josephine was always prying to find something to tell me against the nuns. Her object was to make me dislike them, and to make my stay among them so disagreeable that I should have to leave; for Josephine's horror was the restraint, monotony, and loneliness of a cloistered life. She had already been counting the days that still remained before the vacation would end; but when the Mother Superior informed me that the Superior General had given permission that I might remain with them as long as I chose, and I had decided to make the convent my future home, her impatience turned into despair, and she raved like a mad-woman. There were two reasons for not discharging her: one was that it was extremely difficult to get a maid who would reside in a convent, as one of the rules that applied to her was that she should not receive male acquaintances. Josephine said that she had none, and nobody doubted it; but it would have been difficult to find another girl in France who could say as much. Another motive for keeping her was one of compassion, for it would have been difficult for her to get another situation.

To give an accurate description of this lonely and disconsolate maid, who so much more preferred the din and bustle of Paris to a life of quiet and calm in a cloister, would be impossible. She never appeared twice alike, but I have a vague recollection of her being tall, lank, and sallow, with protruding eyes. She always reminded me of someone who had just escaped from the flames, for she always looked frightened to death. And I have a distinct recollection of her waterfall which seemed to justify my fancy, for it resembled nothing on the earth, or in its supernal or infernal surroundings, as far as they are known to us, so much as a parcel of scorched rags twisted together, covered with a net, and nailed to the back of her head. She looked about forty, but she gave herself twenty-five.

It was not, however, her awkward address and homely face that prejudiced me against her; for I was always too much of a woman to be displeased with another woman on account of her being homelier than myself. Josephine was always finding fault, or was angry with someone. She disliked everybody in the convent except a Switzer, the gardener, who was the only man on the premises. She was the personification of curiosity and inquisitiveness. What she could not otherwise find out she was sure to learn from the gardener, who knew everything that was going on; and she was thus able to retail to me all the doings of the Sisters, laying always particular stress on the evil intentions which she imputed to them.

One day I was cognizant of a vile trick that Josephine had been playing on a little old Sister, who was known as Sister Madeleine, whom she accused of being a hypocrite because she refused to resent it. In strolling through the garden I happened to surprise Sister Madeleine praying before a statue of the Blessed Virgin. She started, and appeared as confused as though she were committing an offence. But the moment she saw that it was I, she told me how I had frightened her; for she feared it might be Josephine for whom she was just praying.

"What," said I, "were you praying for that rogue, who is the plague of the convent?" "I don't know of anyone who needs it more," answered the Sister.

I began to sympathize with her, and told her that I was sorry for her. But she was not pleased with my remark: for, in a determined tone she said to me, "Don't pity me, but pity Josephine; for, no matter what tricks she may have played off on me, I have always got the best of her." I was astonished to hear her speak in this way. She noticed that I did not comprehend her meaning and continued: "No matter what she has done to me, God has given me the grace to forgive her; and there I get the best of her. But, madam, she will not *forgive me for forgiving her*, and that is what makes me so wretched. I feel a little down-hearted to-day; I don't know what more I can do in order to make her do better; and I was just asking our Lord to inspire me when you caught me." At these words Sister Madeleine burst into tears.

There was a lesson for me in Christian charity, which far exceeded anything I had ever imagined. As I turned away from the Sister and saw her humbly kneeling on the ground to continue her prayer, I asked myself, "What is there in this religion that can bring souls up to such perfection ?" for I knew that Sister Madeleine was thoroughly insensible to all the wrongs that this perverse creature could do her, and that she only grieved because the girl offended her Lord.

CHAPTER XLII.

POWER OF A CHILD'S REPROACHFUL LOOK.

Perversity itself—A Moral.

ONE day I asked the Mother Superior to permit my child to dine with me that afternoon. She at first hesitated because a late dinner disagreed with the child.

She took the child by the hand, and said to her : "My little dear, you may dine with your mamma this afternoon ; but you must not eat any dessert." The child threw her arms around her neck, and kissed her as she replied : " No, good mother, I will not eat any." The Superior then turned to me, and requested me not to offer the child any, and I promised I would not.

When the dessert came on the table the child's eyes sparkled, for it was her favourite kind ; but in an instant her eyelids drooped, and she looked sad, for she remembered the prohibition of the good mother. I said to her : " I will give you some." The child shook her head and said : " No, mamma, good mother does not wish it." Said I : " Never mind the good mother ; she will never know anything about it ;" and so saying, I was about to put some on her plate when she prevented me by raising her hand and pushing the spoon away, saying as she did so : " Oh, mamma, I would not disobey the good mother."

I dropped the spoon and reddened with shame that I should have given my child so bad an example ; but thinking I could make it all right I began to praise her obedience. While I was speaking the child looked thoughtfully with her eyes fixed on the table ; and when I had finished she looked up into my face, with an inquiring glance, and said : " If I am such a good girl for obeying good mother, why do you disobey her ?"

This time it was my turn to look down at the table. I was so humiliated that I could have burst into tears, for what reason could I give the child, if I spoke the whole truth, but to tell her that I was perversity itself, and that was the reason why I disobeyed the Superior, and thus set her such an example. The child waited an instant for me to reply, and I was going to speak, when she continued : " If it displeases God for us to tell lies, mamma, why do you tell them ? for you told good mother that you would not offer me any dessert." This last question was too much. I was completely crushed.

The moment the Sister returned to clear off the table I made her open the gate, and taking the child by the hand I rushed over to the good mother, to whom I confessed the whole thing, telling her that my confusion and shame was only equalled by my gratitude to her for having brought up my child so well. The good mother embraced me. This seemed to delight the heart of the child, for she had expected that I would be put in penance for my disobedience, and for having told a falsehood. I told the mother that I never could have believed that a child of that age could resist such a temptation. But the mother was not at all surprised at the child's conduct, and she said that all the little girls in the school were brought up in the same way, and that the first thing that a true Christian mother teaches her child when it leaves the cradle is to love and fear God, and to keep His commandments.

She then took the child on her knee and excused me to her, telling her that as I was not a nun it was no sin for me to disobey her. But the child spoke up and answered her : " But then she should obey God like the rest of us, and He forbids us to tell a lie ; and you know, good mother, she promised she would not offer me any dessert." The mother found it harder to get out of that. But she still excused me as well as she could. The child listened attentively, and at last appeared impatient at the mother's ineffectual efforts to defend me. Then she sprang off her knee, looked up seriously into her face, and said : " I know, good mother, that mamma cannot understand these things, for she has never been baptised." " That is it," replied the mother. " Now go and kiss your mamma good-night ;" and the Superior accompanied me back to the château, laughing all the way at my child's ingenious way of settling the affair.

From that day my child kept away from me more than ever, and I noticed that she even sought to avoid me. It was the severest punishment I had ever yet had inflicted upon me for disobedience and falsehood; for my child's reproachful look would cut me to the quick. I had read somewhere that the best lessons on morality that parents can give their children are nothing compared to their good example.

But the case with me was now so strangely reversed that, as far as my reading went, it seemed to have escaped the moralists. So I sat down and wrote out a moral for myself—

Put together all the beatings and scoldings, the sermons and lessons, that a perverse woman may have received during her whole life to induce her to speak the truth, and they will not have as much power to reclaim her as one reproachful look from her little child.

CHAPTER XLIII.

THE PANTHEON.—"SERMONS IN STONES."

Petitions granted—More Petitions—The Column Vendôme—A Patriotic Nun—A Parallel.

MADAME XAVIER was with me a great deal. I loved to hear her talk of her native Spain, and explain the beauties of Catholic faith and practice. We had been passing one afternoon in the kiosk in the garden. She had been explaining to me the honour that the Church teaches should be paid to the saints.

"We beg of the saints," said she, "to plead in our behalf. Hence it is that we make use of two forms of prayer; but they differ widely from each other; for in speaking to God we say: 'Have mercy on us,' 'Hear us;' whereas in addressing ourselves to a saint we say no more than: 'Pray for us.'" I objected that I could not believe that the saints could hear us. She then quoted the passage in Scripture, which declares that the repentance of a sinner on earth causes joy among the angels in heaven. "St. Peter," said she, "knew the criminal deception perpetrated privately by Ananias and Sapphira (Acts v.);—and when feeble mortals can know so much by the mere light of grace, what is there not possible for them to know, when their spirits are freed from this dungeon of the body, and have the light both of grace and of glory?"

As we rose to leave the kiosk, we threw a glance over on Paris, which was resplendent in the fiery light of the setting sun. For a moment Madame Xavier remained silent, and appeared lost in thought before the brilliancy of the scene. At last she said to me: "This reminds me of Spain. It is like a Spanish sunshine." Said 'I: "I should think you would long to return to Spain; for a Spaniard is seldom weaned from his native skies." "Ah," she replied, with a joyous smile, "all lands are alike to me, since I have given myself to God. The land that pleases me best is the land where I can serve Him most." Pointing to the sky, she exclaimed: "There is my country; for it is there that He dwells whom I love."

Said I: "I have always loved the sun, and I think that I would have made a devout Parsee." And I told her how, when a child, I used to roam over the hills, through a wild woodland, and my signal to return home was the sun's touching the mountain top; and as I went along leaping over the rocks and through the bushes, while the sky was all on fire and the hills were lighted up by the sun's departing rays, it filled my bosom with such warmth and rapture, that I felt that I could kneel and worship it.

"Your bosom would be filled with a far greater rapture," she replied, "if you would but kneel and worship Him that enlighteneth every man that cometh into this world, and is the Son of God. The solar light is but a faint reflection of the glory which surrounds His head. But the light which He has shed over the world we must not merely admire but follow."

She pointed out to me the different churches in the distance, whose spires and domes, as the sun illumined them, seemed encompassed by a halo.

At last I fixed my eyes on the dome of the Pantheon, which reared its head aloft above the rest, and sat like a crown on the brow of the great city; and I fell to musing on the past; for the Pantheon was associated with my first recollections of Paris. Was it not its dome that had put its seal on the vision of bright hopes that filled my bosom at the first glance I caught of the gay capital? And had not its augury proved true? I felt that that happy vision had been fulfilled, and would never come again. Yet, while gazing steadily on the Pantheon, my hopes seemed to revive. I loved that beautiful dome, I could not tell why: there seemed to exist between it and me some hallowed mysterious bond; and I inwardly exclaimed: "Oh give me peace! give me hope! Oh give me back again my joyful heart!"

I had hardly offered up this mental prayer when I instantly recollected having once prayed beneath that dome; and, all at once, the beautiful altar, St. Geneviève's statue, the priest, the lighted candles, all came back to me; and I remembered the petition that I had offered to God through the intercession of this saint. I remembered well that I had asked without faith, and only to test if there were anything in Christian piety.

A crowd of events which had happened since rushed through my mind, and, throwing my arms around Madame Xavier, I was so overcome that I could scarcely speak. It seemed as if my tongue cleaved to the roof of my mouth, I was so anxious to tell her all in a word. Pointing to the Pantheon I exclaimed: "*I do believe in one of your saints—I believe in St. Geneviève; for she has given me everything I asked for.*"

I was so excited, and spoke in a tone so loud and so discordant with our former quiet musings, that Madame Xavier had not time to recover from her astonishment and ask me what I meant, before I told her how, nearly four years ago, when I first arrived in France, I had gone to the Pantheon to visit the tombs of Voltaire and Rousseau; how I had suddenly found myself in front of St. Geneviève's altar, and had asked her for something just to see what a saint could do, and that I had promised her a beautiful present if she granted my request. Said I : " She is a powerful saint ; for she has obtained for me all that I asked. I prayed her that I might have plenty of money, that I might be presented at Court, and that the first men of the empire might be at my feet;" and I began to count, by running over my fingers, the names of my different conquests.

I have heard it said that nuns never laugh. I wish those who think so could have seen Madame Xavier after I had told her of my faith in St. Geneviève, and my connection with this saint. She laughed until the tears ran down her cheeks. Said she : " We must go and tell this to the Mother Superior." She made me tell the whole story over again ; and when the mother could recover from her laughter, she said to me that it was evident that St. Geneviève had taken me under her protection ; and she gave us permission to go the next day to the Pantheon, and offer our thanks, telling me at the same time that I could put in the poor-box whatever I chose ; but she was sure that the saint would be more pleased with my faith and my gratitude than with any other present I could offer her. " Yes," thought I, "probably more so than the *curé* of the Pantheon."

The next day Madame Xavier and myself started for the Pantheon As she had a great devotion to our Lady of Victories we drove there first. The walls were covered with marble slabs, on which were inscribed the pious ejaculations of praise and thanks, which faithful souls had placed there in testimony of the favours they had obtained through the intercession of the Blessed Virgin.

When we reached the Pantheon we went straight to St. Geneviève's altar. Madame Xavier knelt in prayer. I stood leaning against one of the massive columns, and thanked the saint for her kindness to me. I then put a small sum of money in the poor-box. I felt that it was almost a fraud to requite the saint so poorly, for I was sure that she had assisted me. But I quieted my conscience by thinking over what the mother had said to me, that the saint preferred my faith and gratitude to any other gift. "But," said I, "one of these days, good saint, I will do all I promised."

I was then ready to leave, and was impatiently waiting for Madame Xavier to rise, when the thought struck me that I would ask the saint for something else, hoping she would intercede for me again.

I knelt and said: "Good saint, I believe you to be all-powerful with God. I am sure that you can obtain for me whatever you like. Now do not refuse to offer up my petition; and, if you obtain it, I will be good to the poor for the rest of my life, and that shall be my offering of gratitude to you. I want to marry well, and I want you to take away this pain from my heart." Then I hesitated a moment to think what else I should ask for, when I happened to glance at Madame Xavier, who was kneeling with her body nearly prostrate to the floor.

I knew she was praying for me. My heart went out in pity towards her in that moment. I shuddered at the sacrifices she was making to a mere delusion; for Madame Xavier was beautiful, refined, and accomplished.

It seemed to me that she possessed every charm and grace that was lovely in woman. I threw a glance up at the statue of the saint, and, pointing to Madame Xavier, I said: "Good saint, *if there is anything in this I want to know it.*" I wished the saint to tell me if the Catholic religion was all true, and if the soul was eternally benefited by so many sacrifices made on earth for God's sake.

Returning home we passed along the quay that borders the left bank of the Seine. Madame Xavier called my attention to the statues of Voltaire and Henry the Fourth, and said: "I am sure you would not have thought of these men at this moment had you not seen their statues."

When we reached the end of the Rue Castiglione, and approached the Column Vendôme, we saw that its base was freshly covered with immortelles, and the railing decorated with wreaths and other tokens of affection. They had been placed there by the adherents of the Bonapartes on the day of the Assumption which is also the feast of the Napoleons.

I felt moved at the sight of the generous tokens which lay there in honour of the illustrious dead, and I exclaimed: "How beautifully touching are those wreaths of immortelles!" "Yes," she replied, "it is very beautiful; but it does not move me in the least, although I know that the whole column is moulded of cannon captured in battle by the French armies, and it is embossed with scenes which represent the victories of the conqueror. I admire the enthusiasm which placed it there, but I would that that enthusiasm and gratitude were expended on a more worthy object than a tyrant."

I reproached Madame Xavier for her severity, and intimated that her being a Christian ought not to make her insensible to talent and genius. But she interrupted me, and tightly clinched my hand as she spoke: "Remember that I am a Spaniard, and a religious. I admire that column as a work of art, and admire the generous enthusiasm which prompted it, but I, a spouse of Christ, to be true and faithful to Him, must ever espouse His cause and cling to its standard, which is the cross. And how can I venerate the memory of a man who would seize that standard to make of it a mere ladder for his ambition, or would trample it under foot when raised to check his perfidious course?"

After a pause she continued: "As those statues but a few moments ago served to remind you of the illustrious dead, so do the images and pictures which represent our Lord and His Blessed Mother serve to remind us of them. The promptings that impel the world to raise monuments to its great ones spring from the same source as those which animate us when we raise a statue to represent Him who redeemed the world. If a stone or a canvas bearing His sacred image recalls Him to our minds we should cherish it most dearly; and nothing is unworthy of our affection if it has the power to help us to give one thought to God. There are our altars, which represent the tomb of our Lord. You were not shocked a moment ago at the wreaths of immortelles that were strewed at the foot of a monument in honour of the memory of a man, but you are at the flowers you see me place on our altars, which are placed there as an act of honour and adoration to our Creator and our God."

When we reached the convent the Superior insisted upon my telling her what I had asked for this time. But I refused to do so, and all she could get out of me was that my prayer this time was a slight improvement on the first.

M

CHAPTER XLIV.

AN OLD SOLDIER'S VIEWS.—SOCIETY IS EDIFIED.

The Pope and the Emperor—General Rollin on Nuns—Feminine Philosophy
—Job's friends condole.

GENERAL ROLLIN became my most constant visitor and confidential adviser. My aged and honoured friend thought it his solemn duty to protect me against the machinations of the nuns, especially Madame Xavier, "that Spanish one," in whose eyes the valiant old soldier thought he saw a fixed determination to rescue me from "the claws of the devil," and shelter me within the walls of a cloister. He would pass the whole time he was with me trying to persuade me to leave them.

I said to him one day: "General, I wish you would explain the Mass to me. The truth is that it always looks to me like a comedy." "Hush," replied the general, "I don't like to hear you speak so disrespectfully of the Mass." "Oh!" said I, "I only do so to you; I would not dare to say so much to any one of these ladies. But it is the truth, and I cannot help feeling so. But do tell me about it." "Tell you?" he replied. "What is there that you don't understand? Why, it is simple enough; the Mass is—is —the Mass! I have always attended Mass." "Yes; but explain it to me." "Why," said he, "there is nothing to explain. You can see it and understand it better than I can explain it to you; that is all there is about it."

I felt that he knew as little about it as I did. He begged me not to let my mind run too much on those things for they would never do me any good; he had heard them talked over so much when he was a boy, that he had got enough of them then to last him the rest of his life. He then recommenced his persuasions, and tried to make me promise that I would return to Paris at once. But failing to obtain from me a decided answer, he grew impatient, and told me that I was as headstrong as the worst of them.

"Yes," I replied, trying to find a change from his entreaties, "what powerful wills these ladies have!" "Well!" he exclaimed: "you might as well try to reason with the thunder, or with the roar of the cannon, for all the effect it would have on one of them when they once get 'convent' into their heads. It is a mania they never get over. They carry it with them to the grave." "After all," said I, "it is a most fascinating kind of insanity." "Well," he sorrowfully replied, "if you think so I pity you, for it shows that they are getting you.   But just wait until Lent comes, and you will see that they will starve you to death. Don't I know them ? and have I not listened to them.   Just as though a man had nothing to do or to think about but to save his soul.   They are moral maniacs ; that is the only name for them."

"General," said I, "where were you on the 15th of August ?" "Why, you know I was with the Emperor.   We headed the cavalry that marched from the Champs de Mars to Place Vendôme, where we hung fresh wreaths around the column.   Why do you want to know ?"   Said I : "The thought just struck me that you preferred the monument to a crucifix ;" and then I related to him how beautifully Madame Xavier had explained away my prejudices against religious images.   The general frowned ; he would have preferred that she had chosen some other monument to draw her comparison from to teach me Catholic doctrine.

Said he : "All these communities are opposed to anything that has the scent of Bonapartism.   They never forgave the first Emperor for having arrested their Pope."   "*Their* Pope !" said I ; "is he not just as much your Pope as theirs ?"   "When he behaves himself," said the general, "then I acknowledge him ; but when he refuses obedience and submission to the civil authorities, then I denounce him.   Napoleon did right to arrest him ; for what right had he to interfere with the Emperor ?" "It appears to me," I replied, "that the Emperor interfered with the Pope."   "Interfered with him ?   Of course when he found him unmanageable, and when the Pope refused to render to the Emperor lawful allegiance."   "Yes," said I, "the Pope refused to obey Bonaparte when he ordered him to publish an embargo against the English allies ; he also refused to annul the legitimate marriage of Jerome Bonaparte.   He further declined to hold the same position to the Emperor as the Archbishop of Canterbury holds to the Queen of England.   Those were a few of the grievances that the first Emperor had to complain of, were they not ?"

The general threw me an indignant glance, and replied : "*Is that the way these women teach you history ?*"   "Oh, no," said I, "I learned that before I came here" (which was not true). "Well," said he, "that has a mighty strong odour of the convent, and I am surprised that you should have ever heard so much outside of one, for I never did.   I tell you these women falsify everything, and whatever facts, theories, or principles they lay down you must believe just the contrary, and then you are sure to be right.   When these women tell you that the Emperor was wrong, you may depend upon it he was right; and when they tell you that man was born to suffer I will swear that he was born to enjoy himself.   I have even had them tell *me* that a man's happiness depends on the mortification of his passions, when *I know* that he is only happy when he indulges them.   I have always lived up to that principle, and I have always found it a true one."

"So have I lived too, General," said I, "but I don't think I am any the happier for it."   "You think so now," said he, "because they are getting around you.   I am tired of telling you to look out for them.   I beg of you to be particularly on your guard against that Spanish woman, for she is the most determined of them all.   But they are all determined to have you, and there is no power on earth that can resist them.   The only safety is to flee from them."

"But," said I, "you seem to have resisted them pretty well."

"Oh," he replied, "because I am a man, and it seems to be a part of their vocation to repel the men and to draw the women. If I did not know them so well I would not be half so anxious about you."

We had just reached the garden gate and the general was taking leave, when he started back as though he had seen an apparition.   "Where," said he, "did that woman come from ?" "That is my maid," said I.   "Well, she looks like a very hard case (*mauvais sujet*). Who made you that present ?"   "She is not a gift," said I, "she is a loan."   "Well," said he, "if I were the lender I don't think I should ever call for her.   To whom does she belong ?"   "The Princess Sulkowska," I replied, "but she will hardly ask for her again."   "I might have expected as much," said he, "for it is only our best friends that will palm off their broken crockery on us."   "Why, General," said I, "her bad looks are the only thing I can find to recommend her."   "Oh, *mon Dieu*," exclaimed the general, "deliver me from a homely woman."   "Deliver *you* of course, because you are a man.   But you know the old French proverb : *Du temps immémorial femme prudente choisit singe coiffée pour con- fidente et pour l'ombre au tableau.*"   (From time immemorial, a prudent woman chooses for her confidant a dressed-up monkey to serve as a background to the picture.)

The general's face lighted up; he retreated a few steps, took off his hat and made a profound bow.   "Madam," said he, "I congratulate you on your powers of resistance, *these women haven't caught you yet.*"

The autumn had come, and Laferrière had returned from his château. His surprise was indescribable when I assured him that I would make the convent my home. He was not willing to let me make such a sacrifice; but the more he opposed it the more determined I was to remain. Such is the perversity of the human heart when untutored by faith, that when we have suffered we take pleasure in afflicting those who have caused our sorrows, even though they be our hearts' idols. Laferrière became miserable on my account, for he felt that I must be wretched there, as he could not conceive of anything more incompatible with my nature than a cloister. Yet I was much happier there than I had ever been since the night he sacrificed me to his daughter. He became more devoted to me than ever, which devotion daily increased the number of sycophants who sought my influence.

When it was known that I was to pass the winter in the convent it created a great deal of sympathy in my favour, and many began to feel that they had treated me unjustly. I deserved no credit, however, for the sacrifice I was making. It was a mere stroke of policy on my part: "*C'était retirer pour mieux sauter.*" (It was only drawing back in order to jump the farther.)

But I soon found that it was not so easy to keep my resolution as it was to make it, for the gay season had begun, and everybody was enjoying himself. As the season advanced I became more and more miserable.

Towards the middle of October the evenings began to be intolerably long. Every afternoon would bring me some votary of the *beau monde*, who, after relating to me her triumphs of the preceding night, would then condole with me for not being there to witness them, and would wonder how it was possible to remain locked up in such a place.

CHAPTER XLV.

THE ANGELUS BELL:—ITS CHIMES TOUCH THE DEADENED CHORD OF FILIAL AFFECTION.

All Souls' Day—"The Quality of Mercy."

IN the midst of the varied emotions of jealousy, weariness, and disappointed ambition; while my heart raged with the most turbulent passions, and the devil not unfrequently whispered in my ear *self-murder* as the panacea for all my ills, there was one gentle soul whose sympathy and consolation reconciled me to life, and snatched me from the power of the tempter. Madame Xavier was, I firmly believe, sent in my way to rescue me from the depths of despair, and remove the clouds of prejudice and passion which hid from my view the sublime truths of revealed religion.

She took occasion from the approach of the day of "All Souls" to explain to me the doctrine of praying for the repose of the souls of the dead. She pointed out to me the passage in 2 Machabees, ch xii. v. 46, which says: "It is therefore a holy and a wholesome thought to pray for the dead that they may be loosed from sins." She then referred to our Lord's words, where He said that sins against the Holy Ghost would not be forgiven in this world or the next, which shows that some sins are remitted in the next world. She added:—

"It would be one of the saddest thoughts to me in this life if I believed that I could no longer be of service to my departed parents and friends. It is one of the sweetest consolations that I have it in my power to help the loved ones who have gone before me."

The first of November being All Saints' Day, and a holiday of obligation, Madame Xavier was free from the duties of the school-room. She passed the greater part of the day with me. Her explanations made me see the Catholic doctrine of praying for the dead in a pleasing and, to me, poetical light.

At midday she left me to my own reflections, and returned about 2 o'clock with a joyful smile, as she announced to me a message from the bell-ringer of the parish church. St. Mandé's parish church adjoined the convent outside its walls, but was separate from the convent, and entirely independent of it.

For several weeks back I had been bribing the bell-ringer to ring the "*Angelus*" in the morning so softly that it would not disturb me in my sleep. The religious were in the secret, and remonstrated with him, but to no avail, as my money would always stifle any remorse that their words might have raised in his conscience. They became at last resigned, and would frequently laugh at a corruption which they had not the power to prevent.

Whenever I gave the bell-ringer money the following morning it was barely possible to hear the bell at all, but every succeeding morning it would ring a little louder, gradually increasing until it would get to a pitch that made me uncomfortable. Then I would send him more money.

Now I had sent the bell-ringer some money the previous day, and had gone to bed flattering myself, that I should not be disturbed, when, to my horror, the bell this morning had pealed louder and shriller than ever. I at once suspected that Josephine, who was my agent in this negotiation, had kept the bribe; but during the interval of the strokes I heard an angry murmur proceed from her room, which I regarded as a solemn protest of her innocence. I felt perplexed the whole morning and angry, not knowing what more to do to abate the din of that bell.

At last I resolved that I would double the fee, when Madame Xavier came in, with her smiling face, to offer me the bell-ringer's excuses. It was All Saints' Day, and he had always had a great devotion to the saints; and he feared, if he had not rung loud enough that he might incur, not only their displeasure, but that of the *curé* himself, who would certainly have called him to account, as it was customary on feast days and other memorable occasions, to ring the morning *Angelus* longer than on ordinary days: and to-morrow morning, which would be All Souls' Day, he would be obliged to ring it louder and longer than ever. But he promised to compensate by ringing gently the rest of the month.

Madame Xavier then explained to me the signification of the *Angelus* bell, which in all Catholic countries, and in all religious communities, is rung three times a day in honour of the mystery of the Incarnation. That evening, when she bade me good-night, Madame Xavier begged me to have faith in prayer, and not to forget to pray for my deceased friends in the morning when I heard the *Angelus* ring. It was near midnight before I closed my eyes, and I awoke towards early morn. I had scarcely awoke when the church clock struck four.

I had been dreaming of my mother. I do not remember ever having dreamed of her before; and it was such a vivid dream, I saw her so distinctly, that the same feeling came over me which I had often felt in her presence when a child. It was a sensation of fear and shame; for, when the children in the street, or in the alleys, would point her out and say to me, "There is your mother," I used to shrink at the very name of mother; but if I saw that she was not looking for me, shame would take the place of fear, and I would turn away, so as not to see her.

As I awoke, the thought of my mother revived most bitter feelings, for my dislike for her had increased with years. I seldom thought of her; but there were times when her memory would thrust itself upon me like some weird phantom, and I could hardly realise that the past had been a stern reality. I then fell to thinking over my troubled life, and I accused my mother of being the cause of it all. I even hated her, because I could not wrest my heart from Laferrière. I felt that if I had known a mother's, a father's, a sister's or a brother's love and care, my heart never would have knitted itself to his as it had done.

That night too, the recollection of my mother humbled me, and when that sense of fear and shame passed over me, I felt beneath Laferrière, and I wondered how I had ever dared to aspire to be his wife, when I was the child of such a woman? Then one by one those scenes which I had witnessed in my childhood came up before me, but the sense of shame soon turned into rage and anger, and I burst out into imprecations on my mother. Those scenes of drunkenness and wanton cruelty appeared to me still more hideous, when I contrasted them with the daily examples of those who surrounded me.

The recollection too, that she had not only brought disgrace and misfortune upon her children, but had defamed, by wilful falsehoods, those holy beings who were so many living monuments of self-sacrifice and untiring devotion,—whose every thought and aspiration was for the eternal good of souls,—nearly drove me mad. I was furious at the thought that she had poisoned so many souls against them, who would never know the truth. To know that this woman, this woman-monster, was my mother! And I stretched out my hand, as though I would have strangled her.

I next turned to God, and began to upbraid Him for having given me such a mother. I asked Him, how He thought I could be good, with so much to struggle against; and I kept on reproaching Him, until at last I burst into tears and cursed the day that I was born. But my tears did not relieve my anguish; —they only aggravated it. They seemed to bring back other recollections of the past, which began to grow thicker and thicker upon me, and were coupled with the smitings of my guilty conscience; until, maddened with remorse and despair, I sat up in the bed and spoke to my mother as though she were standing before me, and I said to her: "If *you* had not been my mother, all this would not have been!"

In the midst of my angry ravings the *Angelus* began to ring. I threw myself back upon my pillow, but I was so excited that its vibrations did not disturb me, they rather soothed me as I lay there quietly listening to its chime. I thought at once of Madame Xavier. I knew that she was in the chapel praying for her departed friends. The thought of her brought me comfort, and all at once I recollected her parting words : " Have faith in prayer, and do not forget to pray for your deceased friends in the morning when the *Angelus* rings." An instant afterwards found me kneeling beside my bed praying for my mother ; and my prayer kept cadence with the tolling of the bell, as I three times exclaimed : "God forgive her ! God forgive her ! God forgive her !" I then lay down again, and listened in breathless silence to the ringing of the bell.

What a change had come over me ! All my anger, and that hatred which I had nourished for years, had gone. My bosom was peaceful and at rest : *I had forgiven my mother.* It was a great grace that God bestowed upon me, and it was as effectual as it was lasting. Years have passed away since that merciful hour, and since that time I have never cherished but kindest sentiments of sympathy and regret for my unfortunate and erring mother.

Infidel as I was, I was not unconscious of the effect of my prayers. I attributed it to my nature, and not to grace ; but I was so overjoyed, that I resolved that henceforth I would pray for my mother whenever I heard the *Angelus* ring.

From that morning the ringing of the Angelus never disturbed me ; for I hailed it as a chime that summoned me to a pleasing duty. If all those who nourish hatred in their breast against departed souls, will but raise their hearts to God and pray Him to forgive those souls, they too will feel what I felt on that All Souls' Day, the first time I prayed for my mother, as the *Angelus* rung.

———

CHAPTER XLVI.

A FEMALE "INQUISITOR."

An intimate Enemy—A Visit and a Comedy—Music and a Tableau—The Object of the Visit—The After-piece—Flying in the Face of God.

THE world of fashion had just returned from the summer resorts, and nearly every afternoon some one of its votaries would call on me. These visits had anything but a salutary effect. The moment I was left alone I would brood over my solitary life, contrasting it with the gay and exciting scenes of which they told me.

These visitors would occasionally drop some word that would excite my envy and jealousy to such a pitch that I felt like rushing out at once into the whirlpool of fashion and pleasure.

Among this class of "intimate enemies," as the French call

them, was a Mrs. Sham, a recently married lady. She had formerly been a " belle " in America. When I met her in Paris she was a widow of thirty-five, who loved show, and had only a moderate income to support it.

I knew that she was dying to get married, and I was always giving her all the opportunities I could by having her invited to the Tuileries and the ministerial balls, and sending her boxes for the theatre and opera. I looked upon her and treated her like what she really was, a dashing object of charity; for she was fine-looking, clever, graceful, and refined, and I felt it a pity that so many natural gifts should not have a chance of success, since it was on them alone that she relied for securing a husband. On account of her age, besides, I felt that no time was to be lost; so I did as much for her as if she were the most serviceable friend I had.

One day she came to me and confided to me that she was engaged to a wealthy American, and shortly afterwards she was married. At the wedding my friends gathered round me, and told me that they expected that it would be my turn next, and wanted an explanation why I deferred my marriage so long. Their inquiries brought back vividly to me my disappointment, and I almost wished I had not come to the wedding, for I trembled lest someone should see my emotion. I concealed it as best I could by railing at the marriage state and vaunting my own position, declaring that there was no condition in life so enviable as to be young, wealthy, and a widow.

I was glad that my friend had succeeded so well, for her husband was immensely rich, and belonged to a good old family.

Laferrière escorted me home from the wedding, and remarked that he was glad that she was married and out of the way, for she was the most selfish intriguer he had ever met. He told me that several old ladies had come up to him and warmly thanked him for all the favours he had showered upon Mrs. Sham that winter, and had talked to him condolingly. He divined at once what it all meant, that Mrs. Sham, my charming *protégée*, had made them believe that he was in love with her, and wanted to marry her; and he could see by the expression of her husband's face and his manner towards him, that he was most deluded of all.

The Viscount had always tried to make me drop this lady; but I would not listen to him, and frequently I would favour her without his knowledge, asking him for tickets in some other name. But this time he touched a sensitive chord, when he intimated that she had made others believe that he was in love with her; for I was extremely jealous that everybody should think that I was the only woman in Paris whom he cared for, and that the delay in our marriage should be attributed more to me than to him. I was too proud to let any one suspect that he would not marry me in spite of his daughter.

About the time I came to the convent, this lady and her husband went to Baden Baden, and other fashionable resorts.

She returned to Paris elated with her success. She had captivated numberless crowned heads, princes, dukes, and so on, down to cavaliers.

She was constantly calling on me and telling me how happy she was, and how her husband let her have her own way; that she was as free as a widow, and she wondered why I did not get married myself. She was always sure to mention Laferrière's name, and her conversation would so upset me that the moment I was left alone I found the convent as gloomy as a prison cell.

Laferrière would beg of me not to listen to this lady, who was telling me these things simply to make me unhappy. "Why," I asked, "should she wish to make me miserable, when I was the best friend that she ever had?"

"For that very reason," he replied. "Do you suppose the woman will ever forgive you for patronising her? Never in this world; and she only comes here now to take her revenge by tormenting you. I have noticed all my life," said he, "that you have to be extremely cautious about assisting some people, unless you are willing to create for yourself implacable enemies. Take a cold-hearted, proud, ambitious woman, and, if you could read her heart, you would see that the depth of her enmity towards you, is in proportion to the amount of benefits she has received from you."

One Sunday, in the middle of November, the rain was falling in torrents. There was a bright fire blazing on the hearth. I was standing by the window, amusing myself by turning now and then from gazing at the dismal autumnal scene without, towards the fire, which threw such a cheery and pleasant light on everything within.

A Sister came and announced that Mrs. Sham and her husband had arrived in an open barouche, and wanted to know if I could receive them. The thought struck me that they must have started for the races, but the storm having overtaken them had driven them to the convent for shelter. Besides, I was sure that she had come to ask some favour of me.

"*Ma chère belle!*" she exclaimed, as she entered the room, "I don't think you have another friend in the wide world that loves you as I do.   Only think, to drive out six miles in this awful storm, just for the pleasure of embracing you!"

Said I: "How sweet of you, dearest! But you know that you have but one rival, and that is this solitude, of which I am enamoured.   But the moment I see you I become faithless to it, and feel that I still prefer solitude for two."   "Tell me, dear one," she continued, "are you as happy and as contented as ever?"   "Oh, yes, this claustral life is what my soul has ever yearned for, and it is only after drinking long and deeply of its peaceful joys that one can truly appreciate the boon of being immured with angels."   (At that moment I would have preferred being in Paris among the demons.)

"I saw the Viscount last week," said she, "at the opera, and he was looking so well! I tried to catch his eye, but he had his lorgnette fixed the whole evening on a beautiful blonde who sat in the proscenium opposite.   He seemed thoroughly oblivious to everything else."

This time she wrenched my heart; but I burst out laughing as I exclaimed: "The poor old Viscount! how glad I am to hear that he was looking well, and that he was trying to amuse himself! it completes my happiness to know that he is happy too."

"You call him old.   Why, he is the handsomest man I know; he doesn't look over forty."   "Well," said I, "he always seems to me like an old papa.   You know how it is; after a man has been devoted to you so long as the Viscount has been to me, we would get tired of him if he were Apollo himself."

The husband did not relish this remark, for they both exchanged glances and appeared confused.   "On no," she replied, blushing up to the eyes: "that has never been my experience, and God forbid that it ever should be; for with me it is just the contrary; each hour increases my affection!" and she gave her husband her hand, and he pressed it to his lips.   "Oh," said I, "I can understand that, when we have once consented to wed a man.   But I mean these *cavalieri serventi*, these men who become our willing slaves, men whom we never intend to wed; I believe that as their love increases for us we become tired of them."

The husband remarked that that was too hard on the men. "Oh," said I, "they deserve it all, and even worse than they get, for their inconstancy."   "But," said he, "it appears that you think woman to be the inconstant one."   "Only such women as your wife and myself," said I; "who have lived and learned;

but she has had better luck than I had to have found one on whom she is willing to risk all.

"Your wife, however, has a far more confiding nature than I have. The truth is that I have been perverted by Italian literature. An Italian author says: 'Men are inconstant; inconstant in love, inconstant in hate, constant only in their inconstancy.' My own experience made me an easy convert to this belief, which is the principal doctrine taught in my Catechism; and I have found in it an excellent spiritual exercise; for, by making it my daily meditation, I have succeeded in subduing my ingenuous confidence in the other sex, which formerly led me into so many errors."

She appeared scandalised, and exclaimed: "How can you use the phraseology of a divine to make such a confession?" Said I, "If it displeases you I will come down to the common vulgar style, and tell you that the only way to get even with the men is to know them as they are, and not as they appear to be, and to deal with them accordingly." "What would the world come to," asked the husband, "if it were made up of such women?" "What is it coming to," returned I, "filled with such men?" "Well, well," exclaimed his wife, "what an enigma you are! I always imagined you were dead in love with the Viscount."

"How could you think such a thing when you see me seclude myself from him and persist in deferring our marriage indefinitely?"

"Your coming here," she replied, "was a stronger proof than ever that you were beside yourself in love, for I always look upon this seclusion as the master stroke of an arch coquette."

The harp was uncovered. "Do play me an air," said she; "you have so much time to practise, I am sure, that you play beautifully. My engagements, I am sorry to say, have condemned me to abandon my harp altogether. Play me Laferrière's favourite." "Ah," said I, "he loves them all, it would be hard for me to choose. I will play you my favourite air by Gounod. It is taken from the parting scene in the opera of Romeo and Juliet, where the love-sick swain says:

> "'It is the dawn, it is the lark,'

and Juliet replies:

> "'Oh non, ce n'est pas le jour, ce n'est pas le jour;
> C'est le doux rossignol, qui chante ses amours.'"

While I was playing my friend threw herself listlessly on the rug before the fire, with her face turned towards me, and, in a half-reclining posture, she assumed a careless artistic pose, as though

she were listening enraptured to the music. The whole formed a
pretty picture. The outlines of her graceful figure were delineated
by the blazing fire, which made a most bewitching background. Her
husband soon approached her. She reposed her head against
him, then slowly and languidly she raised her hand towards him,
which he clasped in his; then curving her head gently back-
ward until their eyes met, they both remained motionless, as
though spellbound by each other's glances, and lost to all the
world beside.

The picture now displeased me, for I found the tableau too
living. I nervously seized the strings, and by a spasmodic
movement of my hands, two of them snapped in twain, which
instantly startled them from their reverie. I sprang towards
them as though I coul d have killed them both for having excited
emotions in my breast which made the convent seem to me a
hell.

In an instant she was on her feet, and looking intently at me,
she exclaimed: "Why, how you tremble! the strings snapping
frightened you as much as they did me."

"I am superstitious," said I, "and whenever a string snaps
amidst a train of thought I look upon it as an omen that my
hopes are mere illusions." "But," said the husband, "how can
you have illusions when you have lost all faith in men?"
"Oh," said I, "I build them on everything else." "But," rejoined his wife, "what else is there worth building them on?"

I pretended not to hear the question, for I did not know how
to answer it, and we continued to converse until the husband
remarked that it was getting late and was time to leave.

I accompanied her to the door. She placed her arm around
my waist and drew me near to her heart, and then repeated:
"*Au revoir, ma belle;* how I wish you were as happy as I am,
and how sad it makes me to leave you in this dreary place."
She had already descended three of the stone steps, when she
turned around, as though an idea had just struck her, and asked
me when the Corps Legislatif would meet. "On Wednesday,"
said I. "What!" she exclaimed, "so soon?" By this time
she was back into the corridor. "How sorry I am," she continued, "that I did not know it before, for then I could have
secured my tickets. But now it is too late, for every ticket
must be disposed of. But how glad I am that I happened to
think of it, for you, dearest, can always do impossibilities. I
would not miss going for anything, for I want to hear the
Emperor read his speech.

"I think it is one of the most beautiful sights in the world to see that hall filled with the deputies, senators, and the diplomatic corps, all dressed in their uniforms. Besides, how queenly the Empress looks as she passes among them wearing her long train ! and how gracefully she ascends the throne and bows ! She must have practised several days in advance, for it is impossible to manage such a tremendously long train, make such a short curve, and do it so gracefully and faultlessly as she does unless she has had some pretty sharp practice. Why, she does it so admirably that one would think that the train itself was a part of her body ; and she smiles so sweetly when she bows amidst the uproar of voices ! I don't know anything more exciting than to have your ears deafened by the cries of *Vive l'Empereur ! Vive l'Impératrice ! Vive le petit Prince !* And her figure comes out in such charming relief as she stands in front of the *Cent Gardes*, who, with their steel trappings, look so ferociously beautiful. Besides, their brilliant armour shows off the Empress's costume to such advantage.

"Do, dearest ! see that I am not disappointed. See that I have a ticket for my husband and myself, and, if it is possible, another for a friend. I know you will not disappoint me." "But," said I, "you know that Laferrière adores you ; you have only to drop him a line, he will send them instantly to you if he has any left." That remark pleased her so much that it would almost have compensated for a disappointment. She looked at her husband to see if he had taken it, but instantly continued in a tone that meant to convey to him that it would almost be encouraging Laferrière too much if she made such an advance. "No," said she, "after all his kindness I feel that it would be indelicate for me to write to him. No, I prefer to depend entirely upon you, *chère belle*. Don't fail me this time, for it would break my heart."

Said I : "I will write to Laferrière as soon as you leave, and the strongest argument I can use in your favour is to tell him the claim you have on my gratitude ; for, really, to come out so far to see me in such a storm !—"

"Yes," she replied, interrupting me, "the moment I saw the heavens cloud over I ordered the carriage, for I feared you might be lonely, and our stupid coachman took the barouche, thinking we were going to the races."

"Why," said I, "your beautiful costume made me suspect the same thing." "Oh, my darling," was the answer, "don't you believe that I would make as much display to call on you as I would to be seen by thousands ? Your eyes are worth more to me than all of them, for I know you love the beautiful ;

and what is there that I would not do to gratify your taste for
it ?   But I don't know how you can stand it here, for it would
kill me."   And, after making me reiterate my promise, that I
would not fail to procure her three tickets for the opening of the
chambers, she embraced me tenderly, and we parted.

As I turned to go into my room I could hear the rain patter-
ing without, and the wind moaning through the stone corridors
of the château.   My retreat never appeared to me so lugu-
briously sad.   The blazing fire recalled the tableau I had witnessed but a few moments before, when I had seen *my friend*
and her husband drinking happiness in each other's eyes.

Envy, jealousy, anger, hate, and sorrow raged in my heart.
The storm without but too faithfully reflected the troubled
state of my mind ; and, as I looked and listened, the same sad
feeling as before came over me again.   I uttered a shriek to
relieve my heart, and the shriek resounded through the whole
château.   My maid had gone to pass the day in Paris—no one
was near to hear my wail, which made the loneliness seem more
ghastly.

I flew to my writing-desk and began to write ; but my fingers
pained me, and it was an effort for me to hold the pen.   I
looked at my fingers and saw that they were swollen—the
result of having pulled with such force on the strings of the
harp, when they snapped—a thing that I heeded not at the
time.

But I soon became so furious that I did not mind the pain,
but kept on writing at a rate which tried to keep pace with my
thoughts.   Every other sentence was something to this effect:
"How I *hate* that woman !   Not because she is selfish, not
because she is ungrateful, not because she delights to torment
me—I forgive her all that—*but she has actually married the
man she loves !*   She loves her husband !   Forgive her for
that ?   Never !"   It was the only bliss on earth that I coveted,
and to think that that woman should possess such an advantage
over me !   "Talk about God being just !" I said ; "there is a
specimen of His justice in that miserably selfish, cold-hearted,
ambitious, ungrateful, intriguing, envious woman being able to
marry the very man she happened to fall in love with !"

And I had the effrontery to declare that I was her opposite,
and that God had refused to a deserving child what He readily
granted to one of the most odious women that ever were born.
I had supposed that she married so as to have someone to pay
her debts.   I never suspected for a moment that she was in love
with the man.

I had never envied her ; but now I envied and hated her, and I took my revenge by writing to Laferrière to erase her name from the list, and to see that her form never darkened that palace again.

I related to him all that had passed : how she had torn my heart by pretending that she had seen him pass a whole evening admiring a blonde; but what I dwelt upon most was the scene before the fire, which so exasperated me that I had nearly dislocated my finger-joints by wrenching the strings of the harp. Altogether, I was the most miserable being on the face of the earth.

I then wrote to Mrs. Sham that I had just penned a letter to Laferrière expressing her wishes; but it was useless for me to press him to oblige her, for the moment he knew her desires he would consider them as sacred as his sovereign's commands. Hoping that she would enjoy herself, and that she would not fail to command me whenever she thought it was in my power to serve her, I remained, as ever, her most truly devoted, etc.

I knew that it would make her furiously angry if I threw all the blame on Laferrière.

The Viscount answered that, if Mrs. Sham was happily married, I ought to rejoice, instead of letting another person's health be the sickness of my soul.

CHAPTER XLVII.

A PEAL OF LAUGHTER SOUNDS THE RESURRECTION NOTE OF A SOUL LONG DEAD IN SIN.

The Power of Pride—A Prayer repeated—The Prayer granted.

THE peace and solitude of the convent ill-assorted with the turbulent passions which raged in my breast. I felt as though I were in a prison, and every time I would go by myself to the top of the mound it required the strongest effort of my will to resist leaping over the wall and running back to Paris. It was my pride alone that prevented me; for I had told everybody that I would remain, and I had already received the congratulations of my true friends, and the condolence of those who cared nothing for me. If I returned I was afraid that everyone would suspect that my weakness for Laferrière was the real cause of my giving up the world, and I was afraid of being laughed at. I knew that my reign was for ever over if I once fell under the ban of ridicule.

I saw no alternative but to remain.

I then learned how envy, jealousy, and hate can goad a mind on to commit the foulest crimes. At night, when all around me was as breathless as the tomb, the solitude and stillness would seem appalling, and the conjurings of my brain would make me desperate. I would imagine that, while I lay counting the long weary hours, Laferrière was chasing away the *ennui* which my absence caused him by the side of some coquettish *débutante*, and in such moments I felt as though I could have killed them both. My heart would beat so wildly that I would almost tear the flesh from my side trying to seize it in order to quiet its throbbing. It was so full of pain and anguish that it sometimes seemed to me that it would break.

Sunday came. It was a bright, genial, autumn day. I was surprised that I had not heard from my friend, Mrs. Sham, and I was expecting her every moment. I passed the morning trying to devise some plan to crush her by a single word, and I was longing for her to come to give me the chance to do it ; for I was fully determined that she should go away as wretched as she had left me the Sunday before. Twelve o'clock came, and yet she had not arrived. As I impatiently awaited her I tried to kill time by thinking over the past. But this day I was incapable of reflection. My bosom was so filled with fiery passions that they silenced reason, and I was ready to commit any deed just to gratify them. My heart pained me incessantly. I could not drive the disappointment of my marriage from my mind, and I seemed to feel it that day keener than ever.

The convent clock struck one.

A few moments afterwards, I heard the garden door slam heavily to. I was sure that my friends had arrived, and I rushed to the window. But it was not they. It was some religious who had just entered the garden, and had come to pass their recreation there.

I left the window disappointed and went into my bedroom, where the sun shone brightly on the walls and floor. I looked for a second at the effects of the sun's rays as they streamed through the cedar of Lebanon, and for a moment I forgot all ; but my frenzy soon returned, and I sank back into a chair, almost powerless under the weight of so much mental agony. I remained there suffering as I had never suffered before, until a peal of laughter from the garden awoke me from my reverie of hate, and touched a chord in my heart which had never before vibrated. I sprang instantly to my feet, looked out the window, as another peal of laughter still merrier than the first greeted me, and saw the nuns, who had just entered the garden, and who were standing warming themselves in the sun directly under my window.

There could be no deception in such laughter. I felt that it rang from their hearts, and I knew that they must be happy. I was just as much convinced that they were happy as I was certain that I was miserable, and I cried out: "O God! what is there in the love of Jesus Christ, that it alone can give such joy and happiness, and can replace all things?"

I threw a glance over my beautiful chamber, and compared it with the gloomy cells of the religious. Surrounded as I was by every luxury, I was wretched: they were happy. There was no denying it; that peal of laughter alone spoke volumes to me of the true bliss that is hidden in the love of Jesus Christ. As I stood there watching them, their cheerful voices, their happy smiles, and the bright sunshine seemed to shed a halo around them.

I looked up to the heavens and asked God what it meant, that I alone should suffer while every creature that surrounded me, and even Nature herself seemed, to rejoice?

I left the window and began pacing the room, and my eyes fell on the little book entitled "Evidences of Christianity," that Mr. Charlier had given me years before. I took it up, thinking I might learn from it the source from which the nuns drew their happiness. I opened the book at random, and read an account of the conversion of St. Paul. This miraculous conversion, the writer maintained, was a sufficient evidence of the truth of Christianity. I was unable to refute him and thought to myself: "How well the fellow defends his case!" I tried to defend my own convictions against his assertions, but, being unable to do so, I grew impatient, threw the book on the table saying: "I know it is a lie."

The argument was a forcible one. It had seized hold of my mind, and I could not drive it away. Again I took up the book, and again I opened it where it spoke of the conversion of St. Paul; and I read how, from a persecutor, he became an apostle. That pleased me, and I knelt down and began to pray. Said I: "Lord, relieve my heart of this pain: if Thou wilt take it from my heart, I will believe that Jesus is Thy Son." I prayed fervently and hopefully; but I did not obtain relief. I recommenced reading the same chapter. In a few minutes I knelt down again, and prayed more earnestly than I did before, making the same request; but the pain did not cease. Up to this time, my thoughts were divided between the book and my friend, Mrs. Sham, whom I expected every moment. After I had prayed the second time, without obtaining relief, I took up the book and recommenced what I had already read. At last I threw the book across the floor. My thought was, when I made that impetuous movement, that God must answer my prayer this time, or the whole thing was a lie, and I would never look into the book again.

I knelt down the third time and implored God to take away the pain from my heart, and as soon as I had made this time the request, I promised Him that if He would relieve my heart I would be good.

I wrestled for several moments with all the powers of my soul, and after firmly resolving if God would only answer my prayer, to lead henceforth an irreproachable life, I uttered a shriek, which seemed to rend me through and through, as I cried out: "If Jesus of Nazareth is the Son of God, and is as powerful as God, let Him remove this pain from my heart: then I will believe in Him, and will ever adore Him."

As I pronounced those words, a moral light seemed to illumine my soul; and it brought to me a conviction that Jesus Christ was God,—just the same as that peal of laughter, which had thrilled me but an hour before, told me that the nuns were happy. But this answer to my prayer was still more vivid and impressive, so much so that, for a moment, I was bewildered. As soon as I recollected myself, and remembered what I had just been praying for, I rose to my feet, but instantly sank down again on my knees, and kissed the floor; *for my heart was relieved*, and my bosom was filled with peace.

My first reflection was that, ever since my husband had made me an infidel, I had been deluded by a lie. I compared at once my present buoyant feelings with that light which I had distinctly felt go out of me the instant I *consented* to disbelieve, and I felt that it had just come back again. And as I stood there, trying to recall the past, and how dark everything had seemed to me since that time when I ceased to ask forgiveness in the name of Jesus, I began to feel the same glow around my heart as I had felt in my uncle's cottage when as a child I used to read the Bible; and which I had also felt for an instant, while I was praying, the night that Mr. Dayton died.

All these thoughts and recollections crowded upon me quicker than I have been able to relate them.

I ran out of the château and met the Rev. Mother. I threw my arms around her and was so overcome that I could hardly speak. At last I said, "Oh, good mother, you don't know what has happened to me." "Speak, my child," said she: "I feel that you are no longer happy here, and that you are going to leave us."

"Never, good mother," I replied; and I related to her all that I had suffered, and what had just happened to me in answer to my prayer. The Rev. Mother observed: "All this, my child, is the grace of God." "What!" I exclaimed, "is this the grace of God?" If this is the grace of God I want more of it. Tell me, good mother, how I shall get it?"

"Pray, my child, always pray as earnestly as you did then, and God will not fail to grant you all the grace you need." "Oh! if it only requires prayer, good mother, I am willing to pray all the time."

I was so afraid that the pain around my heart would come back again, that I instantly left the Rev. Mother, and entered the château and recommenced praying. But my heart and mind remained as calm and as peaceful as though the storms of passion had never swept over them.

In the evening I wrote to Laferrière. I did not explain to him the great change which had taken place in me: I merely told him that I had forgiven Mrs. *Sham*, and that he would please me by doing anything he could to oblige her.

CHAPTER XLVIII.

"DIAMOND CUT DIAMOND."

Prayer, with a " Distraction"—A Wife's Philosophy—Married Bliss.

I FOLLOWED the Rev. Mother's advice, and prayed continually. Whenever I felt a sentiment of envy, jealousy, or hate, I would instantly resort to prayer, and continue to pray until I felt that love and charity had taken their place. Prayer became to me like an invincible instrument of defence against any evil passion that rose in my breast. I would resort to it just as a man seizes hold of a weapon to defend himself from a blow.

The aching pain around my heart returned; but, by prayer, I could assuage it. Whenever I thought of Laferrière, I felt it acutely. I was always trying to drive him from my mind; but his image constantly intruded itself upon me. Even in my prayers, he would come up before me like a bygone sorrow, or a future hope.

My first appeal to God usually was, "Lord, take the memory of him from my heart."

I soon discovered that my success did not depend on the length of my prayer, nor on my words, or my cry—it depended more on a secret movement in the interior of my heart, which was produced from my faith in God and by an act of my own will: and I have sometimes felt that my prayer was answered before I knelt down—but this was rare; for the effort it requires on the part of the will to produce this effect in the interior portion of the heart is almost a superhuman one, and it requires the strongest opposition to our own natural inclination; and even then we can do nothing unless assisted by divine grace, which I was not aware of then; for I supposed I did it all myself by the force of my own will.

From the day I had experienced my change of heart, I had been hourly expecting a call from Mrs. *Sham*, but she never came. I feared she was angry with me: so I decided to call on her.

I found her by herself, and low-spirited, and my presence alone seemed to put her in a worse humour. I remarked at once her dejected mien, and told her that I was not prepared to be met with a frown, for I expected to find her happy.

"Happy" she exclaimed, "*quand je m'ennuie? Ah! que je m'ennuie!* Happy! when I am wearied to death!" "What!" said I. "It is hardly fair that you should suffer with *ennui* during the honeymoon. There will be time enough for that during the other moons,—what is the name the French have for them?—*les lunes d'absinthe* (the wormwood moons). I suppose *you* do not believe in them, as they have not risen for you yet."

"Hush," she replied, "this nonsense. Why have you prevented Laferrière sending me boxes? *Ah que je m'ennuie!*" "Upon my honour," said I, "I even implored Laferrière to do so; but he will not. *You* talk about having *ennui!* Why, I actually thought that you were in love with your husband!"

. "In love with him!" she exclaimed; "do you take me for a bigger fool than yourself, to fall in love with any man? I would like to know how you would expect me to manage him if I did." "Well," said I, "I was sure you were in love with him; how you looked at each other, and how you dallied with him when you were on the rug before the fire in my room." "*O mon Dieu!*" said she, "that was all *put on.*" "What!" I exclaimed, "do you mean to say that that was all a farce?"

She burst out laughing, and I laughed too, as I thought to

myself, "The rogue, the rogue! how she fooled me! and how I hurt my hand for nothing."

"Why," she asked, "did you suppose that I could ever fall in love with such an old man? Now you know how it is yourself: these old fellows are *sensitivissimi*. If you don't happen to respond to all their tenderness, they imagine at once that you are tired of them, and then you'll have a pretty time if they once get that into their heads: for they are sure to cage you up like a bird."

"Why," said I, "I did not suppose that your husband was much older than yourself: he doesn't look so."

"Well," she replied, "without wishing to tell you my age (yet I don't care what age you take me for), I will tell you in confidence: he is more than twenty years older than I am." Said I: "The old deceiver! Does he dye?" "Ah," said she, with a sigh, "he will never die! but you hold your tongue, and don't ask me any questions. I manage him just as you do Laferrière. But how you fooled me! I used to think you were dead in love with him. I can now understand how you can immure yourself, for I feel sometimes like doing it myself. I get so tired of hearing his insipid endearments; and I am weary to death of his attentions and caresses: *Ah, que je m'ennuie!*"

"I should think so," said I, "if that is the way you pass your time; for *toujours du plaisir n'est point du plaisir* (pleasure all the time is no pleasure). But when are you coming up to see me?" She did not reply, and I repeated my question, and as she hesitated, I said to her:

"I don't suppose I shall see you any more, now that I cannot prevail on Laferrière to patronise you." "Ah!" she quickly replied, "*that* is not it." "So" said I, "then there is a reason?"

She did not deny it, and I urged her until she intimated that her husband was displeased with me, and had refused to drive her out to see me.

She then began to scold me. Said she: "Why did you go on that way before him, and show out just what you are? You might have known the effect it would have upon him. That is the way you create so much opposition; you are always throwing yourself open to criticism. You cannot imagine the bad impression you made on him."

"Then," said I, "I suppose he is afraid to have you associate with me, for fear I might corrupt your morals?" She seriously assented by a nod of the head. This provoked me to a fit of laughter, which made her look into my face inquiringly, to know what I could find to laugh at.

Her husband made his appearance, and she instantly resumed her mask—by showering upon him epithets of endearment, and treating me with a cold, haughty reserve. I thought that the comedy had now reached a pitch where my part was the most disagreeable one to play: so I took leave, without either of them inviting me to call again. Since that day I have been slower in envying other people's happiness.

CHAPTER XLIX.

A MAN OF GOD.

My Idols upset—A Short Biography of Satan—The Bishop on Spiritualism —Spiritism and the Church.

DURING my residence at St. Mandé I was accustomed to attend Mass regularly every Sunday. Although I had no faith in the doctrine of the Real Presence, yet the solemn grandeur of the ceremonial and the happiness and peace of mind plainly visible on the countenances of the nuns, produced an impression on my mind, and begot in it feelings of reverence and hope and a hitherto unknown confidence in the goodness of God. One Sunday, Mass was celebrated by a strange priest.

He was a tall old man, who looked worn out with age and hard labour. The expression of his face inspired veneration, while his whole attitude bespoke the most perfect humility.

After Mass, Madame Xavier and I took a stroll in the park of Vincennes. On entering the convent garden, which joined on the park, we met the Lady Superior, who introduced me to Bishop Semeria, the venerable celebrant of the morning Mass. He was an Italian who had resided for many years in the Indies as a missionary. He was the Bishop of Olympia, Vicar Apostolic of Jaffna in Ceylon, and was a member of the Society of Oblate Fathers.

After the Rev. Superior introduced us we exchanged a few words and then parted, never expecting to see each other again.

The next morning I told the Rev. Mother that I would like to talk on religion with Monseigneur. She consented reluctantly, as she told me she was sure that in all his travels the Bishop had never met with such a character as I was. She was certain that neither of us would be gratified. "You remarked," she said, "his humble bearing; but you did not perceive those piercing eyes, so deeply hidden in their sockets." "Excuse me," said I, "I did notice them perfectly, and I am not afraid of them. I am in search of truth, and I know very well that a man with such a bearing and with two such eyes in his head is neither a fool nor a hypocrite. I want some one strong enough to master me. I cannot talk to the nuns, for I think it would be wrong to repel their instructions by using my infidel batteries. But that man can defend himself, which I am not so sure that any one of your religious could, if I set myself zealously to work to attack them. The truth is I want to be convinced, but I don't think it is possible to convince me, and I cannot be convinced without telling my reasons for disbelieving, which I will not tell you or any of the religious." "I respect you the more for it," she answered, "for although we all believe ourselves invulnerable and inaccessible to a doubt, I would not like the religious, nor would I wish myself, to hear the pernicious teachings of infidels. You are right, my child, never to let us hear them, for, like poisoned arrows, they are dangerous even to play with.

"I will make known your wishes to Monseigneur Semeria. If he will consent to give you religious instructions you must consider it a very great favour, because his health is feeble and his mind and body require repose."

The following day the Superior brought the Bishop to the château. The moment he entered the room I felt the ascendency of a lofty and cultivated intellect, tempered by an humble but impassioned soul.

His manners were grave but perfectly simple, divested alike of familiarity or reserve.

We had hardly sat down and opened the conversation, before I became embarrassed, for he was a *good listener*, the first one I had met on the continent. His silence at last became so provokingly annoying that I stopped suddenly short and begged him to speak. "No," said he very gently, "I have come here to try to convert you, you are not going to convert me." "But, *mon Dieu!* Monseigneur," I exclaimed, "how do you expect to convert me unless you speak to me?" "Gently, gently, my child," he replied; "before I try to sow any seed I want you to permit me to examine the soil." He begged me to continue. I said that I would give worlds to believe that the Roman Catholic religion was true, but I knew that I never could believe it, because it was so contrary to reason and common sense. "Please," said he, "tell me what you know about the Catholic religion." Said I, "I know nothing in its favour; but I know everything against it." "You are like the majority of mankind," he replied.

I then quoted passages from Voltaire and Rousseau, and, to

my surprise, he did not attempt to refute them. I tried to draw
him into an argument, but he persistently avoided it. After I
had dwelt on the writings of Voltaire and the sayings of Jean
Jacques, he cast upon me a very significant glance, and mildly
asked me how I admired the lives of these two men, and if I
were a man would I like to live and die as they had lived and
died, and as a woman if I would like to have had Voltaire for
my husband, or Rousseau for my father. I reflected for a
moment, when my admiration for my two favourite philosophers
was instantly changed into horror, and I wondered that the facts
had never struck me before. "Monseigneur," I exclaimed,
"don't let us speak of them any more, for I am one of the most
jealous women on the face of the earth, and Voltaire would have
driven me mad. Why, he used to change his lady-loves as often
as he did his religion!"

The Bishop was unprepared for this outburst, and, in spite of
his gravity, he smiled. "Rousseau," said I, "the heartless
monster! the brute! Why he put his five children into the
Foundling Asylum as soon as they were born, and that was the
last he ever heard of them." This fact, for the first time, struck
a sensitive chord in my heart, and I buried my face in my
hands to conceal my emotions, as I thought of all that I had
suffered for having been called an illegitimate child. I thought
of the miserable existence of these five innocent beings, born
under the ban of society, and under the disgrace which is
naturally attached to the violation of her laws, remaining all
their lives with the stigma of such an origin, wandering and
proscribed, to languish in humiliation and vice: Said I: "I
hate Rousseau this moment more than you can ever know."

"If you can hate both these men, then you have suffered."

"*Suffered!*" I repeated after him: "I have been bred upon
suffering. I have hardly ever known anything else; and this
moment I would sooner die than to have such a husband as
Voltaire, or such a father as Rousseau." "You are right," said
the Bishop. "It is just as impossible for a bad tree to produce
good fruit as it is for a bad man to write good works. These
two writers are the most to be dreaded and feared, because they
are witty and subtle. Their style is brilliant and fascinating,
and without the assistance of supernatural light they would
seduce the saints themselves." I then asked him how was it
possible to disbelieve Renan? "The only time," said I, "I ever
wept over the sufferings of Jesus was when I read Renan's life
of Him." "Renan," said he, "has made a simple mockery of
Christ, for sensitive women to weep over. It requires very little

intelligence to see how this pantheistic novelist, by his sentimental phrases, ridicules Christ and everybody else."

"But," said I, "there is another evidence against your church. I have known the spirits themselves to declare that Catholicity is a lie. I believe in spiritualism, for I have seen it tested, and I know it to be a fact that some invisible and intelligent agency communicates with the visible world." Said he : "That is the devil." "Oh," said I, "I know very well 'that you Catholics try to put the thing down by calling it the devil ; but I don't believe that it is the devil." Said he: "I have given spiritualism a fair test, and I pronounce it nothing more nor less than the machinations of the devil." After a pause he contined : "You have read the Life of Jesus, by Renan? Did you ever read the Life of Satan, by Jesus?" "No," I answered ; and I looked at him to see if he was serious. "Well," said he, "I have. Jesus said that the devil was a liar, and the father of lies. Now tell me, do you believe our Lord spoke the truth when He called the devil a liar?" "Ah," said I, "everybody knows that the devil was a liar from the beginning." "Yes," continued the Bishop: "he was not only a liar from the beginning, but he is now, and ever will be. Knowing the character of the devil so well, I discovered that spiritualism was one of his powerful agencies in this century. He has tried it before. Read Josephus (and I think he told me that there were passages in the Bible that referred to these manifestations). He has tried it in different ages, but he never succeeded so well as he has in the nineteenth century, for the reason that the morality of the masses has never reached a lower ebb. I attended *séances*, and I discovered that the spirits would make frequent predictions that never came true; that what one circle would affirm another circle would contradict; that they inculcated the dissolubility of the marriage vow, free love, suicide, repudiated every tie, both social and divine, and attacked the very fundamental principles of every well-regulated society. They called our Lord a liar, for they deny His divinity, and they denounce His Church. Setting aside our Lord and His Church, I found that they lied about trivial things, therefore how can they be relied upon and believed in preference to our Lord Jesus Christ ? How can you, an apparently intelligent woman, risk the salvation of your soul by pinning your faith to any revelation coming from a source which is in constant contradiction with itself, which has never produced any good result, but whose adherents become morally and physically enervated and depraved ? Yet how many there are besides yourself who would sooner go to seek truth and light in such a maze of contradictions than in Christ's Church, where alone can be found that universal faith, which is all true, all life, all light, all union! which gathers together in one common fold all souls and hearts who adhere to its creed, adapted, as it is, to all ages, all peoples, and all degrees of civilisation. Yet how many thousands of souls close their ear to its teachings, while they are willing to listen with attention to every vain sophistry concocted by Satan and his followers.

CHAPTER L.

MORAL INDEPENDENCE — PRACTICAL ATHEISM.

No Morality without God—Moral obligations.

I TOLD the Bishop what had occurred on the day I had promised God that I would believe that Christ was His Son if he would take away the pain from my heart; the extraordinary light which I had received, and how changed I was: for I went at once and confessed to the Rev. Mother faults which my pride would not have permitted me to mention a few moments before.

"God granted you an extraordinary grace, my child, and believe me that God alone will be your Master; for your mind is so warped, and so distorted by bad associations and bad literature, that God alone will ever be able to straighten it. It would take a skilful psychologist at least ten years to undo your bad education; and I have not the time, for I must attend to the duties which brought me here."

"But," said I, "you will teach me something, will you not before you go?"

"I can teach you," he observed, "but I never could convince you of anything unless God Himself would come and verify it for me, as He did when He gave you that extraordinary light."

Said I: "I never could believe that it was necessary for a person to profess any religion in order to be saved. I believe in moral independence, and that if a man lives up to the dictates of his conscience he is just as pleasing to God as those who are always going to Church." "Moral independence, my child," replied the Bishop, "is nothing more nor less than practical atheism." Said I: "I beg your Lordship's pardon, but that is not true, for one can be morally independent and yet believe in God." "No," said the Bishop, "those who call themselves moral independents make use of God's name, but they discard God entirely; they would exclude Him from everything and put themselves in His place, if they could. What else is it but renouncing God to declare morality independent of Him? For by separating morality from God, we separate it from its root, which is God. If there is a God, He is our Creator; and if He is our Creator, He is our Supreme Legislator; and if He is our Supreme Legislator, He is our Supreme Judge. After you have done right, where do you find your sanction, and where do you seek for satisfaction?" Said I: "I seek it, and I find it in my self-respect." "Therefore you make your own self your judge and your God. There is just where your moral independent system leads to, and I now repeat that no one can be morally independent without being a practical atheist." Said I: "I have met many men who did not profess any religion, and I have found them more honourable and virtuous than I have half of the men I know who were canting Scripture to me from morning until night." "Well," said he, "when you meet any more of these upright men, without Faith and without Hope, say to yourself that these men are better than their principles; and when you meet bad men who profess to be Christians, believe me that their principles are better than they are. The Christian religion is not a mere matter of opinion. Religion commands—it obliges man—and that man who recognises no higher law than that which he finds within himself, what guarantee have you that, when he is tempted, he will not fall? Remember, I am comparing the moral practical atheist with the practical Christian." Said I: "I would trust one as far as I would the other."

"I would not," answered the Bishop, "and my long experience has often proved to me that I am right; for the Christian carries within his soul a law which God has placed there, and he recognises its author, and does not pretend that that law is independent of God. The moral independent, on the contrary, who recognises no higher law than his own sense of right and wrong, and seeks no higher satisfaction than his own self-respect, what has he to protect him against the two great enemies of all morality,—our interests and our passions? Do you suppose that the voice of duty, which becomes so cold and cheerless when it separates itself from God, is going to have sufficient control over him to make him resist the alluring voice of interest and passion? No, my child, that control cannot be maintained unless there is over man, over his interests and his passions an authority which commands the sacrifice."

"But has not the Church," said I, "always been accused of too much indulgence in regard to individual morality, so long as the individual submissively professes her doctrines?"

"That is another base calumny against the Church," replied the Bishop. "For the Church has never admitted, either in theory or practice, that faith exempts us from good morals—on the contrary, she teaches that the grace of faith augments our responsibility and increases our duty to be virtuous. She teaches that faith without works is dead; that he who does not believe will be condemned; and that he who believes and does not practise will be condemned also."

CHAPTER LI.

THE VAGARIES OF SCIENTISTS—THE WISDOM OF RELIGION.

Rome—Democracy—False Science—Divine permission.

THE next day when the Bishop came, I told him that some of my countrymen who had just returned from Rome had called on me that morning, and had decried the very thought of believing that the Catholic Church was the only true Church. They told me that I ought to go to Rome and see for myself; for " *Chi non vede non crede, e chi vede perde la fede.*" (Who sees not, believes not, and whoever sees loses his faith.)

"I have read Josephus's history of Jerusalem," said the Bishop, "and I have passed a greater part of my life in Rome, and I do not believe that Rome ever approximated to Jerusalem in corruption, discord, and filth; nor do I believe that the condition of Rome could ever be compared to the infamous practices, wanton crimes, and social depravity of the Jews during the reign of the Herods. Yet what did Jerusalem contain? THE ONLY TEMPLE OF THE LIVING GOD.

"But," said I, "the spirit of your Church and the spirit of the American people are directly antipodal. You know that the lower classes in my country are more enlightened than they are here, and they would not brook the restraint which the Church imposes upon the minds of her adherents. They look upon the spirit of the Church as oppressive and opposed to democracy."

"That entirely depends," said the Bishop, "upon the definition the American people give to the word democracy. If the Americans define democracy to be those principles which tend to improve the conditions of the lower classes, by aiding them to develop their moral being and assisting them to use *legitimate* influence in politics, the Church is not opposed to democracy. In this sense the Church has always been, and always will be, the firm advocate and supporter of democracy; but if the American people define democracy to be the tyranny of an ignorant, impious, bloodthirsty mob, who boldly proclaim the abolition of religion and of all civil authority, except that which is constituted by themselves—who believe that the proprietor is a thief and the servant is the lord—who congregate by stealth in hidden corners to concoct plans for the destruction and total extinction of all legitimate rules—if that is the kind of democracy they mean, they are right: the Church has always made war upon it, and always will."

"Yes," said I; "but the Church has its own despotism—of course, a little more refined than the democratic tyranny you have just described. It dictates to the colleges and universities what science, what philosophy, and what literature shall be taught. It even prohibits the laity from making a candid investigation into the researches of modern science, philosophy, and literature; and how, then, is anyone to know whether the old system of things is right and the new one is wrong unless he compares for himself the one with the other?"

"It is in view of the present and future happiness of her children," answered the Bishop, "that we look after their mental and moral training; and in doing so, we are actuated by the same feelings that prompts a fond parent to watch over his child. The Catholic Church has always honoured and encouraged those sciences which ravish from nature her secrets, in order to ameliorate and perfect the conditions of material and civil life, as well as those moral sciences which demonstrate that true happiness and prosperity, in order to be real, to be lasting, must be based on correct principles, acknowledging God for their Author and their aim. The Church has always rendered homage to those sciences, for she has always found them in harmony with revealed truth. But she will never willingly look on and suffer her children to pollute their minds by the so-called 'sciences' and philsophy of the eighteenth and nineteenth centuries; whose result is to extinguish the light of true faith in the minds of the people by their atheistic and materialistic suppositions, and whose propagandists call it progress, when, after laborious researches, they discover *man*, who was made after the image of his Creator, to be nothing more nor less than a mere animal—a perfected monkey, without a soul, there being no immaterial substance distinct from the body, since the soul is a mere function of his nervous system; who define conscience to be a piece of mechanism very simple in its kind, and, by analysis, they have discovered it to be a sort of mainspring of the nervous system, which they, no doubt, suppose can be wound up by an impression, and left to run down of itself, like the mainspring of a well-regulated piece of machinery, as a clock or a watch. And what do they proclaim to be the honourable aim of all their laborious researches? That they wish to ʻLIBERATE THE HUMAN MIND FROM HYPOTHESES AND SUPERSTITIONS,ʼ such as a belief in a God and in a soul; for they look upon the belief in God as tyranny upon *free thought*, and no slight impediment to the movement of that ʻmainspring,ʼ conscience.

"These pseudo-philosophers and their deluded followers call the Church despotic, tyrannical, and ANTI-PROGRESSIVE, when her clergy exclaim: ʻMay God deliver the rising and future generations from such sciences, such dogmas, and such philosophy!ʼ"

"They declare," said I, "that one reason which makes the Church prevent the people from investigating for themselves is, that modern science has proved the fallacy of miracles."

"Yes," answered the Bishop, "these harlequins of science deny a first cause because there is a second cause. They are not willing to admit that God has the power to do what man can do himself; for man, assisted by his knowledge of mechanics and chemistry, is constantly acting upon the laws of nature. He does not change them, though, any more than I do the law of attraction when I raise a stone from the ground. The law subsists the same as it did before—I only vary action under it. And just because the universe is governed by fixed natural laws, created by God, they dare to deny that God has the power of FREE ACTION. They deny that He who established these laws can suspend them."

Said I: "You Catholics attribute everything that happens to God." "Everything," said the Bishop, "but sin; for not a leaf moves nor a sparrow falls, except by His command." "Then," said I, "why should God permit the wicked to overpower and scourge the righteous?"

"God sometimes makes use of the wicked to chasten the just, in the same way as a father takes a rod and beats his son; but afterwards he breaks the rod and throws it into the fire. So God does with the wicked when they have served His purposes in chastening the righteous—He casts them into hell. But oftentimes God interferes, and will not permit the wicked to strike the righteous. We have thousands of proofs in cases where the righteous and just man has been shielded from the evil designs of the wicked; but that is what the modern scientists say God has not the power to do. They deny that God has anything to do with the universe, leaving it to be controlled and governed exclusively by natural laws. But we say that God does protect those who love and fear Him, and when He chasteneth the righteous man, he knows that it is for his good. Job is our great model, and shows us how God tries those He loves in the furnace of affliction." "Yes," said I ; " but Job had a good time at last—he was well rewarded for all he suffered, for he received tenfold more than he lost. But how many Jobs there are who die in their sores, without even a winding-sheet to wrap around them !"

" My child," said the Bishop, "virtue and faith would lose their merit if they were always sure to receive an earthly recompense. God has never made prosperity in this world depend on the practice of supernatural virtue. Christ would not have taught us to believe that the righteous should be rewarded after death and the wicked doomed to everlasting punishment, if punishments and recompenses were to be meted out to each one in this life in proportion to their merits or demerits. Such a view of the case would be unworthy of man's spiritual and immortal nature, and consequently unworthy of religion and of God, for it would reduce religion to mere worldly prudence, and the atheists and materialists would be so far right."

" But," said I, " if you tell the world that everything happens by the permission of God's will, it will ask you why you rush to the rescue and the relief of the afflicted, when calamities and misfortunes overtake them ; it will tell you that your conduct is a contradiction to your teaching ; for is it not thwarting God's designs when you interfere if He sends those calamities to punish the crimes of the wicked, or to give the righteous an opportunity of acquiring virtue ?"

" My child," said the Bishop, " when God imprinted on our minds a true knowledge of His justice, He told us not to forget His goodness, for we often can appease the one by imitating the other, and the affliction that may be sent by God to scourge the sinner, may also be intended to give the good an opportunity of sanctifying themselves by acts of charity. No one ever yet has escaped the goodness or the justice of God, although we often doubt them both when we see the prolonged prosperity of the wicked, and the continual oppression of the just. But because God is patient we should not complain. God can be patient, He can wait, because He is eternal."

Whenever the Bishop would cease speaking he always looked faint and weary. There were moments when a death-like pallor would steal over his face, but, as he never complained, I attributed that ghastly paleness and that contortion of his features, which he vainly tried to hide, to the emotions of his heart. I knew that he was wedded to God, and he suffered to see the greater portion of mankind living in open rebellion against the Creator.

I always dreaded the striking of the hour when he should have to leave, and always hailed with joy the hour appointed for him to return. One day he rose to go. "Good bye, my child," said he, "until we meet again. God has His designs upon you: continue always to pray and He will give you light." I knelt down to receive his blessing; he gave me his hand and I kissed his ring. When I arose my eyes were filled with tears, and yet I could not tell why. I knew that he was going to start that evening for Bordeaux, but in a few weeks he was expected to return. Still I dreaded to have him leave, for the convent seemed doubly sweet since he had been there. He too appeared sad at parting, and that evening I followed him out of the château and we parted at the garden gate, where he repeated: "May God bless you, my daughter," and then we bade each other a last good-bye. A few weeks passed away, but he did not come back. One afternoon I saw Sister Madeleine in the garden gathering fagots. She had a blue check apron on, and every now and then I noticed that she raised the corner of her apron to her face as though she were wiping away her tears. I ran out to her, and begged her to tell me why she wept. Said she: "Go and ask the Rev. Mother;" but I refused to leave her side, and kept close by her, and began helping her to gather the fagots. At last we reached a spot in the garden where poor Sister Madeleine gave way to all her filial tenderness, and stooping down, she kissed the ground beneath her feet as reverentially as though it had been her crucifix. My heart felt a pang, and I at once divined the secret: my reverend instructor was dead! I threw my arms around her neck, and began to weep as though she had told me all. It was on that spot of earth, which had become so sacred to Sister Madeleine, that the Bishop had stood when he last spoke to her, when he gave her his parting blessing. I knew it, for I saw them. "Oh, madam," she exclaimed, "he was a saint! He sanctified the ground he walked on, he was so much like our Lord."

We continued gathering fagots until we reached the Sister's little rustic oratory, which was only a statue of the Blessed Virgin placed on a heap of stones in one of the angles of the garden. But she had concealed the stones by evergreen and

moss. There we both knelt down, and I began to implore our
Lord to have mercy on me; but Sister Madeleine's guardian
angel must have told her that I was not praying as I should, for
she leaned towards me and softly said: " Pray for him, it will
make him happy, he took such an interest in your salvation, and
he will not forget you now."

The Sister's words filled my soul with joy, and the statue of
the Mother of God brought the good Bishop vividly before me.
I had already felt how sweet it was to pray for that mother I
had never loved; but in that garden, before that little rustic
altar, I felt, for the first time, how it is doubly sweet to pray for
those whose memory we revere and cherish; and Madame
Xavier's words seemed to fall once more on my ears: " It is a
good and wholesome thing to pray for the dead." I rose from
my knees consoled, and so did Sister Madeleine, for we both felt
that he was happy. We knew that he had sent in advance his
heart and his treasures there where stability reigns, and that
when Death came he must have welcomed it as he would a
sister upon waking; because for him it was sleep that ended, it
was life that began, and the eternal day that dawned.

CHAPTER LII.

MY NEW TEACHER—GOD'S INSTRUMENT—THE CHURCH OF ENGLAND.

A Scrupulous Monarch—An English Sanhedrim—Religion
by Statute—Board of Trade and Doctrine.

A FEW days after the Bishop left for Bordeaux the Rev.
Mother introduced me to Monseigneur Morrell the curé of St.
Mandé, who was to undertake the arduous task of teaching me the
Catholic doctrine. He explained to me all the essential dogmas
of the Church, those which embarrass Protestants and infidels,
and which they find most difficult to understand. He also spoke
to me a great deal about the English Church and its constitution,
because he saw that I was inclined to believe that that Church
was as much God's Church as was the Church of Rome.

I begged him to tell me what proofs he could give that Christ
gave to the Catholic hierarchy the power to govern His kingdom,
any more than He did the Episcopalian Church, or the Church of
England. Said he "I cannot make you understand that until I
shall have proved to you that ours is the only true Church; and I
can only do so by first convincing you of the divine authority of
the Church.

"Christ was sent by God: therefore He received His authority from God; and He transmitted His authority to His apostles. 'As the Father hath sent Me, so,' said He, 'I send you' (John xx. 21). He was speaking to His apostles, and He gave that power *to them*— which was not giving it to every man throughout Judea, —and they transmitted the authority they received from Christ to their successors by ordination as well as by election. He also gave His apostles the power to remit sin; for, after His resurrection, He breathed on them saying, 'Whose sins you shall forgive, they are forgiven; and whose sins you shall retain, they are retained' (John xx. 23). No one has the right to remit sins unless he receive that power from the successors of the apostles, and we know by history and tradition that we Catholic priests alone are the rightful successors."

"Tell me," said I, "how it is done." "Why, God makes man the instrument of His power, as He did Moses and Aaron: the absolution is given by the priest, but the grace that justifies the sinner is given by God."

"But," said I, "we dissenters look upon the power that man has to forgive sins as a very convenient thing. We can sin as much as we please: all we have to do is to go and confess it, and then we are absolved."

"How little " he replied, "you understand our religion. A priest cannot absolve a penitent, unless the penitent, having confessed all the sins he is conscious of, has a sincere contrition and a determination to sin no more. Whenever the penitent brings to the confessional these conditions, the priest grants him absolution. If, however, the penitent has not these conditions, his confession and the absolution of the priest, instead of benefiting him, redound to his greater condemnation. Even the most ignorant Catholic knows that he may, indeed, deceive the priest, but he cannot deceive God."

"How " said I, "can a bad priest remit sin ? "

"If a sovereign state," replied the curé, "give to a bad man the power to forgive certain delinquents their misdeeds, on condition that they make a stipulated reparation, and the delinquents comply with the terms, the pardon they receive from the bad man is just as effectual as though they received it from a good man ; for this agent does not pardon in virtue of a power derived from himself, depending on his own individual merits, but he receives that power from the state. So in the case of the priest: although he be a bad man, the power he has to pardon sins is given to him by the Church, and it was given to the Church by God. The Church gives this power to forgive sinners, after they make a proper reparation, and the spiritual reparation consists in contrition, confession, and, if possible, a satisfaction for the offence, and a sincere determination to do right in future. If a dishonest judge has the power to pardon a malefactor, what difference does it make to that malefactor whether the judge be an honest man or not? Therefore all sacraments which are administered by bad priests who are invested with authority, are just as efficacious as though they were administered by saints. It does not concern the sinner what the priest is : the sinner must look to his own case, and let the priest attend to his."

"But " said I, "the Episcopalians are a branch of the Catholic Church, are they not ? Their litany and creed are the same, and they have many things in common with you." "What of that ? " he replied. "They have plucked off a few stray leaves from the tree, but what are they good for? The moment they are detached from the parent stem which gave them life, they can bear no fruit. Now the history of the English Church can be told in a very few words, for it dates only a few centuries back.

"The Church of England took its birth from Henry VIII whom all history proclaims to have been a most licentious and unscrupulous monarch.

"At the beginning of his reign Henry was the strong ally and devoted friend of the Pope. He rendered such service to the Church, by his zeal in opposing Lutheranism, that Pope Julius II. gave him the title of *Defender of the Faith*, which is still one of the proudest titles of the English sovereigns, and appears on the coins of the realm. But Henry wanted the Pope to grant him a bill of divorce, alleging that as Katharine of Arragon was his brother's widow his conscience troubled him for being wedded to one in such close affinity, and he felt that it was unlawful and sinful. The Pope tried to quiet the conscience of his royal ally. But this irascible monarch's conscience refused to be comforted, and he at last demanded a writ of divorce, which the Pope peremptorily refused. Henry then declared that he would make himself Pope, and he actually did proclaim himself head of of the Church as well as of the State. He sacrilegiously invaded the spiritual domain of Christ's Church, and dared to confer, limit, and withdraw spiritual jurisdiction.

"In the reign of his virgin daughter, Elizabeth, who was the worthy daughter of such a father, the people began to murmur about the encroachments of the temporal on the spiritual power. In order to stop their murmurings, Parliament passed an Act conferring on Elizabeth the same right of spiritual supremacy which Henry had usurped. Their *reason* for passing such an Act was that ' Henry VIII. had had the supreme power, jurisdiction, order, rule and authority of the estate ecclesiastical.' Thus was that treason against high heaven,—the robbery of the spiritual power,—apparently legalised by Elizabeth's time-serving parliament. They did not bring forward any witnesses, nor permit any discussion. They did not change the nature of the crime. It remained stained with the same irregularities which it can be charged with from the beginning."

I cannot help calling the reader's attention to the remarkable resemblance there is between the history of the usurpation of the spiritual power by the English crown, and the trial and sentence of death of our Lord. Our Lord had been unjustly seized, and dragged to the house of Annas, and from thence to Caiaphas, where he was condemned to death. They were fully determined to put this sentence into execution, but they feared lest the people might murmur and raise an insurrection.

In order to give their proceedings a show of justice, they bring the matter before the Sanhedrim, where they make no investigation into the case, to see if the former proceedings had been legal and just; but they merely confirm what had already been determined; and when the grand Sanhedrim had confirmed the sentence, the people were *silenced*: they were *overawed*. Now it was but a repetition of the same thing in England. The crown had already unjustly seized the spiritual power, and was determined to keep it; but the people became perplexed and doubtful. To silence their murmurings, it was necessary to give a show of justice to the crime. The crown lays it before Parliament (which can be compared to the grand Sanhedrim), which, without investigating the legality or justice of Henry's assumption of spiritual power, merely confirms that right of spiritual jurisdiction in the throne, just because it descended to it from Henry VIII. This act of Parliament overawed and silenced the English people, just as the sentence of the grand Sanhedrim had the Jewish people. It is very noteworthy that these two acts of the the civil authority bearing so closely upon Christ and his Church, should present so striking a resemblance. It is an illustration of the truth, " *History repeats itself.*"

"Many of the English people believe," continued the curé, " that the English Church derives its power from their Bishops. But they can appeal from their Bishops to the Crown, which shows that the Crown is their head and source of spiritual jurisdiction. Of course they are not willing to admit the real state of things as existing among them, viz.: that the civil power is made the root and source of spiritual jurisdiction ; but all lawyers are agreed that such, as far as law goes, is the actual constitution of the Church of England. When doctrines are disputed within the English Church, the same authority which sits as a Board of Trade will pronounce as a' Board of Doctrine; for what is the supreme tribunal in the affairs of the Church of England? The Privy Council. And what is this tribunal? This court is in its constitution in exact accordance with the original statute, 25th Henry VIII., c. 19, which consummated the schism, and by which the ecclesiastical causes of the Church and the realm of England were governed and decided from the days of King Henry (except that it was repealed in 1554, and revived in 1559) to those of William the Fourth. It runs thus: ' IV. And for lack of justice at or in any of the courts of the Archbishops of this realm, or in any of the King's dominions, it shall be lawful for the parties grieved to appeal to the King's majesty in the King's Court of Chancery; and that upon every such appeal a commission shall be directed under the Great Seal to such persons as shall be named by the King's highness, his heirs, or successors, like as in case of appeal from the Admiral's Court, to hear and definitely determine such appeals, and the causes concerning the same·; which commissioners, so by the King's highness, his heirs or successors, to be named or appointed, shall have full power and authority to hear and definitely determine every such appeal, with the causes and all circumstances concerning the same. And that such judgment or sentence as the said commissioners shall make and decree in and upon any such appeal shall be good and effectual and also definite; and no further appeals to be had or made from the said commissioners for the same.'

" The utter absence of all title to apostolicity must be fatal to any claim of the Church of England to be considered a part or branch of the true Church of Christ. The links in the chain of succession to Peter and the apostles have been broken, as may easily be proved by radical defects of form and intention in the conferring of orders. But even if the consecration of those bishops were valid, still they could have no jurisdiction after denying the authority of the Chief Pastor, the successor of Peter. By separating from the centre of unity those unfortunate men lost all right and power to watch over or guide any portion of the flock which Christ bade Peter to feed."

CHAPTER LIII.

THE MIRACLE OF MIRACLES.

The Mystery of Love—Christ's own Memorial.

THE dogma of Catholic faith which, in those days, appeared to me most absurd and superstitious, was the doctrine of the real presence of Jesus Christ in the Eucharist. I asked the curé to give me some explanation of that mystery. His proofs and arguments made me see with a new light that incomprehensible miracle of Christ's love. "In fact," said he, "there is no dogma taught in clearer or more unmistakable words.*

"Non-Catholics say they cannot understand the real presence, and therefore will not believe it. Now, it is the height of foolishness to pretend that everything must be reduced to the proportions of our narrow understanding. It is silly to have so much confidence in ourselves and so little in God. It is as easy for God to conceal His sacred flesh and blood under the forms or appearances of bread and wine, as it is for Him to conceal His glorious divinity, although everywhere present, from our eyes. Christ came to instruct us and not to deceive us. When He saw that the Jews were shocked, and asked, 'How can this man give us his flesh to eat?' was not this the opportunity to undeceive them, and then to explain, if He did not mean what He said? Instead of this, we find Jesus, after a double amen, which means TRULY, insisting no less than six times, in the most unequivocal manner, upon the necessity of receiving His flesh and blood. We find St. Paul (1 Cor. xi. 29) condemning the unworthy receiver for not discerning the Lord's body. Surely we could not be required to discern the body of Christ were it not in the Eucharist.

"The Church does not teach that that which strikes the senses changes: on the contrary, she says that the exterior form, the appearance of the bread and wine, are preserved after the words of consecration, that the substance alone is changed. The senses can only conceive its qualities, its attributes, and its accidents, but not the substance. Non-Catholics admit the existence of God, yet they have never seen Him; and they disbelieve the mystery of the Eucharist just because they cannot see with their eyes the substance of the body of Jesus Christ, when everybody knows that substances are invisible.

"The Catholic Church affirms that when Jesus said, 'This is my body, this is my blood,' He meant just what He said. And

* John vi. 35, 48, 51, 52, 54, 55, 58.

He pronounced those words on the vigil of His death, making His testamentary dispositions, He bequeathed to us a treasure worthy of a God."

THE MASS.

I asked him to fully explain to me the Mass, and how it originated, for I had always heard the sacrifice of the Mass ridiculed and scoffed at in my country. It appeared to the Protestants, and so it did to myself, like mummery to see so much parade at the altar, and when watching the different movements and gestures of the priest we looked upon the whole ceremony as savouring of superstition.

Said he: "It appears like mummery and superstition only to those who are totally ignorant of the Bible and its teachings. The Mass is a sacrifice, or offering of the body and blood of Christ, under the species of bread and wine. It was instituted by Christ at His last supper, and its end was that the sacrifice of the cross might be daily represented before our eyes, and the memory of it ever continue, so that the blessed fruits thereof might be continually imparted to us.

"This adorable mystery is a sacrament and a sacrifice. It is a sacrifice inasmuch as it is offered up to God by the priest. Yea, it is the very sacrifice foretold by the prophet Malachi: 'From the rising of the sun to the going down thereof my name is great among the Gentiles, and in every place there is offered up in my name a clean oblation.' (Malachi. i. 11.) After the consecration, and as long as the consecrated particles exist, they constitute the sacrament of the Eucharist.

"As a sacrament, the Eucharist is salutary to him who receives it; it confers on him sanctifying grace and the other advantages which are specially attached to this sacrament; while, as a sacrifice, it is not only salutary to the priest who receives it, but also to all those for whom it is offered. And as the priest, in saying mass, offers up this sacrifice for himself and others, in the same way may those present offer it up for themselves and for others. As, when a city sends a present to a prince by deputies, all the inhabitants have a share in the offering, although there is but one among them who speaks; so, in the sacrifice of the mass, although there is only the priest who speaks, and who offers the sacrifice, all those who assist have a share in the offering.

"The mass is a propitiatory sacrifice. It is the only form of worship on earth in which all hearts and souls can join. God is all justice, all goodness, all mercy! He forsaw the wants and needs of every soul, no matter how abject the body which contained it might be ; and He instituted a mode of worship in which the learned, the unlearned, the deaf, the dumb, and the blind could join, when they meet together in His sanctuary to offer to Him acceptable worship.　The deaf, the dumb, and the blind can take part in it, just as well as the most perfect and learned and enlightened.　The mass, as a sacrifice and a devotion, has all that can satisfy every heart, and can give peace to every soul.

"There is not a word, an action, or a ceremony at the mass which does not signify some holy and mysterious thing.　The vestments in which the priest is robed, and the ornaments that cover the altar, have all a mysterious signification.　The vestments worn at mass are to-day substantially the same as those worn by the people eighteen hundred years ago.　The Church desires to assimilate the sameness of her customs to the unchangeableness of her doctrines."

I asked the curé how it were possible for any rational being to believe that the Pope was infallible, when I had read from Catholic authors that some of them were ambitious, licentious, dishonest, and perjurers.　"The Popes," he replied, "have not been worse than other men, and, notwithstanding their failings, God has never failed in His promises to His Church and to Peter.　Christ promised to pray for Peter, that his faith might not fail; but He did not promise Peter that He would never fall; but He did promise that He Himself would ever be with Peter, and his successors, and the Church to the consummation of ages. If a Pope were perverse enough to try to impose false doctrines upon the faithful, he could not, for God would not permit him."

"Can you believe that ?" said I.　"Believe it," answered he; "certainly I believe it.　Eighteen centuries have passed, and, notwithstanding the many vicissitudes through which the Church has passed, the doctrine that we profess to-day is the very same that Christ handed down to His apostles.　When we say that the Pope is infallible, we do not mean that he cannot sin.　But when he speaks as head of the Church, we assert he is infallible." "But if God is always with the Church, why does He allow bad men to rise to the Papacy ?"　"To prove that it is His own power, and not man's, that guides the bark of St. Peter.　The glory and the power of the infallible word of Christ shine forth with greater lustre when the faithful see a miserable, weak, and imperfect man at the head of the Church.　It proves to us that God is there to watch over her, and will not permit the faithful to be led astray by human weakness.　If all the Popes were saints, the vitality of the Church would not be so striking a miracle of the Holy Ghost. This preservation of the Church, in spite of the weakness and blindness of her chiefs, is a perpetual miracle which non-Catholics cannot help admiring, even though they do not understand it."

CHAPTER LIV.

I AM BORN AGAIN.

My first Communion.

AFTER the curé of St. Mandé had finished his instructions I asked to be baptised.

The Christmas of 1867 found me before the little altar in that self-same chapel where, but a few months before, I had sat pitying Madame Xavier for the untiring efforts she was making for me with our Lord, that He might make me one of His rightful heirs by the gift of faith. The chapel was filled with my devoted friends who had first known me in Paris and who had always clung to me. The Prince Czartoryski and his sister, the Princess Iza, were my sponsors. The Princess placed upon my finger a beautiful ring—an oriental pearl set in diamonds, rubies, and sapphires, to each of which gems she attached beautiful symbolical meanings of purity, hope, fidelity, and suffering, while the ring itself was the token of my alliance with Heaven.

Madame Xavier told me that our Lord would grant me whatever I asked of Him immediately after baptism; and she begged me to ask something of the Blessed Virgin, just to try her; for I had not yet learned to feel much confidence in the prayers of the Mother of God.

Immediately after I was baptised I asked God for six favours:

1st. For my sister's conversion;

2nd. For my brother's conversion;

3rd. That Mrs. Dix might be my friend;

4th. That Mrs. R—— might stop abusing me;

5th. For future happiness; and

6th. That I might have it in my power to help the poor.

That evening, as I was speaking to Madame Xavier, I chanced to take up the little book called *Words of Jesus*. I opened it, and my eyes fell on these words: "Daughter, be of good cheer; thy sins which were many are all forgiven thee." I was so struck with the appropriateness of the words that I translated them to Madame Xavier, who emphatically declared that God intended to speak to me then. I felt that it was true, for I had hardly finished the verse before I felt a sweet peace fill my soul.

On the morning of the 27th of December, 1867, Feast of St. John the Evangelist, I was kneeling once more near that little altar in that same chapel, waiting to receive our Lord. My mind was calm and peaceful; but around my heart I felt a lurking pain like that of a wound which had just been cleansed, but which time alone could heal. The curé of St. Mandé, who offered up the Holy Sacrifice, addressed a few words to me before I approached the altar. After speaking to me of our Lord's tenderness and love, he stepped aside, and, pointing to the statue of the Blessed Virgin, he exclaimed : " My child, you will soon receive your Father and your God ; but 'behold thy mother !' I give you to her ; and remember, from this day forth, you are no longer an orphan ; for God is your father, Mary is your mother, and Jesus is your spouse. You cannot be united to Jesus unless you are to Mary, His mother ; for His body was formed of her immaculate flesh and blood. Be a faithful child to God and a loving spouse to Jesus, and Mary will ever be to you a fond, devoted mother. Come, come, my child, and receive that God whom we all adore."

As he pronounced these words, "Come, come," my soul panted to taste of that living bread, and, as I advanced towards the altar, I inwardly exclaimed : " O beloved Jesus, heal my heart." I knelt ; the priest placed on my tongue the sacred Host. Again I implored Jesus to relieve me of that lurking pain. Instantly I felt the sacred wafer dissolve, and my whole heart was bathed, as it were, in a most delicious balm.

To be united to our Lord, it is not enough to offer Him our conscience, our comforts, and our wealth ; He demands all we have to offer, our will, our hope, and all our heart. That morning I received Him in my bosom, but He did not enter into the sanctuary of my heart, for all its avenues were closed against Him, my heart was still another's ; even at that altar I was thinking of Laferrière, and it was his *souvenir* that brought back the lurking pain. But our Lord took pity on my wretched state, and did not refuse me a drop of the solace of His divine love, so that I might know henceforth where to go and seek relief.

From that day forth I loved the Blessed Virgin ; for when the curé said to me : " Behold thy mother," I looked up at the statue, and perceived, for the first time, that on its pedestal was written in large letters of gold, " *Voilà ta mère,*"—" Behold

thy mother," and I felt that the Blessed Virgin had said to me:
" Yes, I am thy mother." I smiled and thanked her. All my
prejudices were swept away, and I felt a sweet sympathy kindle
in my heart for Mary.

CHAPTER LV.

CORRECTING THE INCORRIGIBLE—MY HOME DEVIL.

A Treasure gone—Cure for a Spinster's Spleen—Confusion in the Convent—
A Sleeping Witness.

WHEN I left the chapel and entered the château, I found that
my maid had swept the rooms but had not dusted them, and
she was sitting leisurely at work on a piece of tapestry that she
was making for herself. I asked her in a gentle tone why she
had not dusted my rooms, for there was no place for me to sit
down without ruining my white silk dress. She tartly replied:
" That is the way you come home from your first communion!"
The tone and look which accompanied these words meant to
imply that I had come home in a bad humour. Said I: " You
will leave my service on the 7th of next month." I then
turned away, and seeing a picture of the Blessed Virgin which
the nuns had hung over my bed, I spoke to it and said: " I
promise you, Mother, that I will send her away on the 7th, for
she is too wicked to live with any longer."

On New Year's Day, 1868, I went to Paris and remained a
few days with my sister. While there I got the Viscount to send
for his old servant, Madame Daujat, to come and replace my
maid.

On the 2nd of January, as I was passing through the Passage
de Choiseul, I bought a beautiful little ivory statue of the
Blessed Virgin, and an ivory crucifix. When I returned to the
convent I found that my maid had been behaving unusually
well, and was doing all she could to induce me to keep her. My
heart relented, and I almost decided after all, that as she was
trying to do better, it would be wrong not to forgive her, and
perhaps that might be more pleasing to the Blessed Virgin than
if I kept my vow.

The next day the curé came and blessed my little statue and
crucifix. He had just left when I was standing by the window
holding the little ivory statue of the Blessed Virgin in my hand,
admiring its beauty and exquisite workmanship, when my attention was called to something which showed a marked improvement in my maid. I turned to her and told her that I was sorry

she had not always done so well, but that I could not keep her,
that I had already sent for Madame Daujat.

"*Madame Daujat!*" she repeated after me with emphasised
contempt. "Madame Daujat! I pity you, for she is the most
disorderly woman that ever was; you should have seen your
wardrobe how it was packed. I even found one of your child's
old shoes in your jewellery box."

"Well," said I, "supposing you did, the best thing for you to
do is not to touch it."

"Not to touch it!" she exclaimed, straining her eyes to the
utmost. "I took it out at once and threw it into the fire."

"What!" said I, "do you mean to say that you burned up
that little shoe?"

"Of course I did," she replied.

Said I: "You brute, leave my presence at once."

For an instant I forgot everything else: I was beside myself
with grief, and the tears started into my eyes at the recollection
how that little shoe had been to me during my late visit to
America, a monitor and a solace.

After weeping for a few moments I looked at the little ivory
statue of the Virgin that I held in my hand, and was suddenly
consoled for the loss of the little old shoe. I thought to myself
perhaps God had intended that it should be so, and that it was
all for the best. I had ceased to be a pagan, and was now a
Christian ; the little old shoe had done its mission, and must now
be set aside for the statue of the Blessed Virgin, which would
take its place. I knelt down and placed the statue on my desk,
and covering it with my hands, I renewed the same vow that I
had made about three years before, that I would ever be a good
mother ; and I implored the Blessed Virgin to pray for me that
I might ever keep my vow. I arose from my knees with a light
and joyful heart, went and found my maid, and excused myself
for my rudeness. She appeared quite overcome with such an
act of humility on my part, and begged my pardon for all her
misdoing during her stay with me. I concluded that I would
keep her.

The 7th of January came. It was a mild genial morning for
that season of the year. I was walking in the garden, and every
step I took I thanked God for the peace of mind He had
given me. I thought it would always last. I entered the
château. My maid was arranging the fire, and I mildly asked
her where she had put the patterns she had cut from my dresses
made at Worth's. Said she: "I burnt them the day you told
me that I must leave your service on the 7th." I felt the blood

rush to my face, and had an impulse to thrust her head into the fire; but I instantly controlled my temper, and felt humiliated that such a trifle should be capable of disturbing my peace of mind, and I said to myself: "There is no virtue in you if you are not capable of standing more than that."

When my mind was perfectly composed I said to the girl, in one of the mildest and blandest tones, in order to soften the effect of my words: "I have just as much right, Josephine, to burn up one of your aprons as you have to destroy my patterns."

She was on her knees before the fire. In her right hand she held a huge pair of tongs, which clenched a lighted stick; her left hand was placed on a pail of water that she had brought in to wipe up the hearth. In this position she turned her head, and looked me full in the face, and, in one of the most provoking tones, and with the most disdainfully spiteful expression, she replied: "*That is the way you understand our religion; for that is the way these ladies teach it to you.*"

The expression of her face and the emphasis she put on her last words were too much for me. The blood rushed through my veins like hot lava. "I won't get angry," I exclaimed, "for burnt patterns, but I will fight for those nuns;" and I sprang upon her. I caught her by the waterfall, seized a candlestick from the chimney-piece, and I pounded her with it until she got out of my way.

A few moments afterwards the Superior and Madame Xavier came rushing into the room, for Josephine had run out into the garden, and told them that I had nearly battered her to death with a candlestick. I was so exhausted and so frightened at what I had done that I could not articulate a word. In Josephine's efforts to get away from me she had upset the pail of water, and the burning stick which she held in the tongs was out in the middle of the room, blazing in the centre of a Turkish rug. Madame Xavier without speaking, quietly looked for the tongs, took up the burning stick, and placed it in the fire-place. She then returned to see if there was any more fire about the room, and seizing hold of something with the tongs that she found lying near the door, and quite mystified as to what it was, she held it up in the air, looking at it intently and exclaiming: "*Qu'est-ce que c'est? qu'est-ce que c'est?*" (What is it? what is it?) Said the Rev. Mother: "I should think you would recognise it, for it is Josephine's waterfall." "Yes," said I, "that is what I held her by;" and they both burst out laughing; but when I told them the whole story they laughed still more.

The Rev. Mother told me to go over into her parlour until one of the Sisters had arranged my room, for it was flooded with the water.   She told me that the girl must leave the convent at once.

As I was crossing the street I began to reflect on the trouble the girl might give me, for in France it is a very serious affair to strike any one.   When I entered the Rev. Mother's parlour I saw on her desk " 7me *Janvier*," and then I recollected the promise I had made to the Blessed Virgin on the morning of my first communion that I would send Josephine away on the 7th. The thought struck me that it was the Blessed Virgin's wish that I should not break my promise to her, and this had all happened that I might fulfil it.   I rushed into the chapel to implore her protection, and I said to her just as confidently as though I was speaking to some one by my side whom I could see and who could hear me:

" Blessed Virgin! I am sure you have got me into this scrape; now I shall look to you to get me out of it!"   I felt that she answered me, and said she would.   I thanked her, and left the chapel perfectly composed, for the moment I had made that speech I felt that all was right.   Not so with Laferrière, who called that day to see me.   He thought that my quick temper had more to do with it than the Mother of our Lord, and he scolded me, for he was sure that the girl would drag me before the magistrate of St. Mandé, and that if he attempted to interfere the whole opposition press would cry out against the Court for trying to interrupt the course of justice.   But in spite of all he said to me I did not feel the slightest fear or regret.   I felt that it was all right, and that the Blessed Virgin would protect me.

About a week passed away and still no news from Josephine, until the curé called on me one morning to say that he had just been speaking to the magistrate of St. Mandé, who had asked him if it was really true that there was a lady residing in the convent who had beaten her maid.   The curé avoided answering him directly, but he learned from the judge that Josephine had called on him, and had made a complaint against me; but they refused to summon me because they doubted the girl's veracity, and they believed her to be crazy.   She said that there was no witness but herself, and when the magistrate asked her to show him the marks she refused, assuring him that *modesty forbade it*; and that is the last I ever heard of the incorrigible Josephine.

As I have said a great deal about what I have been taught by the priests, I will say one word of their behaviour, or better, I will not say the word, but let the reader judge for himself.

One day after the curé of St. Mandé had been giving me an instruction I went to open the door to Josephine's bedroom, when I was startled by her coming in with the door, and falling with a heavy bound at my feet. She had fallen asleep with her ear against the keyhole. I helped her up, and asked her what was the matter, for the truth did not flash at once across my mind. She had hardly recovered from her nap and her fall, when she replied, " that she could not help it, it was so lonely to be always by herself with no one to talk to," from which I concluded that she had been a vigilant sentinel at the keyhole ever since my instructions began ; and the reader, if he has any appreciation of such a character, will easily believe that there never could have been any mischief going on, for if there had been *Josephine never would have fallen asleep.*

CHAPTER LVI.

A TRUCE WITH MY ARCH ENEMY.

A Parley and a Treaty—The Enemy's Pity.

ON a blustering winter's day, towards the middle of January, the snow was falling thick and fast. It was nearly sunset. The thoroughfares of St. Mandé are usually still at that hour ; but this evening I was startled by the noise of a carriage, which came rolling rapidly down the street, and made a sudden halt before the convent door. Who could be coming to see me at such an untimely hour, and in such a dreadful storm? I ran to the parlour window: the sister had already opened the massive gate. In a second it was closed, and a lithe female figure, closely wrapped in velvet and furs, tripped lightly after the sister, as she mounted the old stone steps. I opened the door to receive my visitor. In an instant more she was in my arms, and we were fondly embracing each other. It was Mrs. R——, a well-known American belle, who never lost an opportunity of creating prejudice against me, and was the one who had worked, through the Viscount's daughter, to prevent my marriage with him. She had come to beg a truce of hostilities.

We sat down, and after asking mutual forgiveness for all the wrongs we had inflicted on each other, we began to compare notes to see which of us had been the victor. It was difficult for either of us to decide. She awarded the palm to me, inasmuch as I had actually annihilated her good name in many circles, and all her enemies put together had never been able to deal her such a deathly blow as I had by a certain *bon-mot* that had fallen from my lips. But I repelled her generosity, for I was not willing that she should yield to me a triumph of which I felt that she was too deserving herself; and I told her that I thought her intrigues to break off my marriage with the Viscount surpassed all the humiliations I had ever inflicted on her. After we had conversed and come to a perfect understanding, that neither of us in future would ever breathe aught but good concerning the other, she rose and began to look about her. Having caught a glimpse of the high walls through the falling snow, a tremor passed over her and her face became deathly pale. With a deep sigh she exclaimed: "Dear, dear, what a horrid place this is! I heard that it was so beautiful. It would kill me to stay here: I should jump out of the window." Said I: "That would not do you any good, for you would light in the garden without being able to get into the street."

"Then," said she, "I would dash my brains against the wall, for I would die if I were forced to remain here twenty-four hours. They all say that you are playing the hypocrite, so as to have royal sponsors, and gain favour with the old nobility. But I don't believe it *now*. I am sure you are in earnest; for a king-dom itself would not compensate for the sacrifice of remaining in such a place as this is for a week,—and here you have been nearly six months! How I pity you!"

She begged my pardon for all the mischief she had done me; for she felt that she perhaps had been, in a measure, the cause of condemning me to such a gloomy existence. Gloomy indeed it appeared to her, compared to what my life might have been in the brilliant saloons of the château of Fléchères,— where she had lived for several months with the Viscount's daughter. As soon as Mrs. R. left me, I recollected that this was one of the things I had prayed for on the day of my baptism.

CHAPTER LVII.

SIMPLICITY THE TEST OF TRUE NOBILITY—JEAN JACQUES TO THE RESCUE.

Proud Humility—My Patience tested—An Old Story adapted—Jean Jacques' Mistake—I gain my Point.

AFTER I was converted and received into the Church, I found that the Mother Superior had a much better opinion of me than I deserved. I wished to undeceive her, but was perplexed how to go about doing so without letting her discover my bad breeding. I feared, on the other hand, that she might suspect, with my American friends, that I was not sincere, which would have been unjust; for I was sincere as far as I went, only I had not imbibed the self-sacrificing spirit of Catholicity as much as she and her community were charitable enough to believe.

I admired and could applaud the self-sacrificing Christian, but I had not the slightest intention of imitating that kind of Catholics. Even while saying my chaplet I never once meditated on the dolorous mysteries. I meditated on the joyful and glorious ones, always leaving out humility and obedience, and substituting charity and the gifts of the Holy Ghost in their place. I thought that, to be perfect, God only required of me to be chaste, truthful, and charitable: which last virtue I confounded, in a great measure, with benevolence or rather liberality, for I had not seized it as the Bishop had tried to make me understand it. I had often asked the curé of St. Mandé if that was not enough, and he would invariably reply, " It is enough for you to *begin on*."

In spite of my strong and sanguine determination to always speak the truth, I found that I was continually misrepresenting things; so that I imagined that I was every day growing worse than I had ever been before in my life.

I began to be discouraged, and complained bitterly of myself to my director. But he cheered me up, and told me that if I appeared so much worse now in my own eyes it was because I had never paid any attention to my faults before. " As we grow better," he remarked, " we always appear worse to ourselves, because, the nearer we approach God, the light we receive from Him enables us better to see ourselves as we are." That encouraged me. But I, who had always endeavoured to conceal my bad breeding, found that it required an almost superhuman effort not to quarrel with the Superior, a temptation I had never had before my conversion.

The Superior was a lady of noble origin, and extremely well bred; but, in spite of her vast experience and her wonderful gift of reading character, she actually believed that I was a thoroughbred lady, and had been reared so from my cradle; and this is the way I imposed upon her;—*I never complained, never boasted, and always gave the preference to others over myself, and I was always self-possessed.* I had picked up this piece of knowledge, or rather tact, by mixing with a few families in the Faubourg St. Germain.

From the moment I was introduced among the old nobility,

I detected at once the true mark of distinction, by which they could be invariably distinguished from an upstart. This invariable mark was SIMPLICITY.

I discovered that those who were the *frankest*, the most *ingenuous*, the most *modest* and *simple* in their address, were those who were the most accomplished, the most refined, and who were of the best descent. From a lesson the Viscount de Laferrière taught me one day, I have defined in my own mind good breeding to be nothing more nor less than " affected humility." I was one day at the palace, waiting for the Viscount. Near me sat a priest, talking with one of the generals of the imperial staff. The manners of the general were intensely vulgar, while those of the priest were refined ; not a gesture nor an expression of his face escaped me, and I concluded that he was some generous soul who had *sacrificed* himself to become a servant of Christ. When the Viscount entered, he at once addressed a few words to me, and told me to wait until he could despatch his guests. After their departure, alluding to the priest, I said to Laferrière that I did not see how such a nobleman could embrace such a life of abnegation. The Viscount smiled, and said to me, " You are mistaken this time, for *your nobleman* descends from a peasant near Fléchères. But he is an humble man and a good Christian, and this is my instruction to you for to-day : that humility often takes the place of good breeding, and is much *preferred to it by the theocratical aristocracy.*" From this observation I have since concluded that good breeding was nothing but *affected humility.* Therefore if people are not really humble, let them appear so at least, if they wish to pass for well bred.

But there is something I have remarked myself, and I hold it to be true—for I have found it to be so in all circles that I have lived in, both at home and abroad—it is this, and the reader may set it down as a rule :—Whenever you see persons constantly complaining that this or that thing is not good enough for them, hinting that they are better than their neighbours, presuming on the opinion they have of their own superiority, showing it by trying to thrust themselves between you and your friends, delighting to intrude on other people's *tête-à-tête*, or ever watching for an occasion to " snub " someone, who is not as well-off in the world as themselves—you may depend upon it they have sprung from a sewer, or if they did not themselves their grandfather did.

To return to my subject : I always strained every nerve to conceal my early education, and I not only never complained,

but I went still farther. I *never* wondered. I learned that
"*Nil admirari*" was the motto on the arms of Lord Bolingbroke. I did not fully comprehend its signification until I had
for a long while practised it. But one day I was at Lord Here-
ford's, and there the signification of *nil admirari* came across
my mind like a flash. The first lesson the English nobility
teach their children is self-possession. If they are angry, envious, jealous; if they love or hate—they must conceal it; good
breeding demands it. In the convents we are taught to disclose
those feelings to the Superior or our confessor, so that they may
assist us to root them out and destroy them, for Christianity *demands it*. But I preferred the English way as yet, as I had
always been accustomed to it.

The moment I became a professed Catholic the Superior put
my frail Christian patience and my sham good breeding to a
fearful test. Formerly she refused me nothing that was consistent with the rules; but now I noticed a general falling off in
little things. No doubt the Rev. Mother thought that I wanted
to suffer a little too in order to enter into the Kingdom of
Heaven. But I became a Christian out of love for myself, and
not for the love of Christ. I wanted to be happy: for I was
devoured with *ennui*, remorse, and disappointed love. I was
seeking for relief; Christianity presented itself, and I accepted
it, after despairing of finding anything better, and I was determined to give it a good *fair trial*. But I had no idea of suffering. If I had thought that *that* was included in the bargain,
I never could have been induced to embrace the Christian religion. I became a Christian to be happy, and after all that I had
gone through, how would it have been possible to convince me
that true happiness was to be found in suffering?

I called myself a Christian because I had been baptised; and
I tried to practise three or four Christian virtues, which I believed to be the only ones of importance. I thought I was good
enough then: yet to my surprise I was anything but happy.
The unaccustomed rebuffs I was receiving in the convent made
me suffer keenly. I would have found them trifling in themselves (as they really were), had not my pride made me morbidly
sensitive. But I never admitted to my confessor how dreadfully
angry I would get at times, for I did not consider that that was
my fault. I looked upon it as a part of the Rev. Mother's sins,
which she would have to answer for.

One day I wanted to go out skating in the park of Vincennes,
and I had sent word to the Superior that I wished a Sister to
accompany me, without whom I could not go out; I was all

dressed, in my skating costume, ready to go, and was already impatient to be obliged to wait for the Sister. At last, when my impatience had reached its height, Madame Xavier came with a message from the Superior, to tell me that all the Sisters were engaged, and there was no one to accompany me, so that I would be obliged to defer my skating.

I knew very well that the Rev. Mother was aware that her refusal' would be superlatively disagreeable to me, or she would not have called Madame Xavier from the schoolroom to bring me the message. Madame Xavier simply delivered the message as graciously as she could, then remained silent, expecting a reply. I could feel that she was looking intently at me, although I fixed my eyes on the floor; for I was afraid that if she could see me full in the face she would detect there something besides Christian resignation, or the expression of a well-bred person who was *always* self-possessed. After we had remained in this awkward position for a few seconds, Madame Xavier gently inquired if I had any answer that I wished her to take back to the Rev. Mother.

She had hardly spoken when a thought struck me, and I replied to her: "Yes, I will tell you a story, and my story is the answer you will take back to your *Reverend Superior;*" and emphasising the last words, I burst out laughing. She was horrified at my tone and my laughter; but that soon passed off, for in a moment afterwards she thought that I was in the best possible humour.

I told the story without any regard to the way Jean Jacques related it. But as I was sure that no one in the convent would ever read *his* confessions, I knew there was no danger of my ever being found out; so I related it to suit myself, hoping that my interpolations and deviations might help me to carry my point.

Said I: "Tell your Rev. Superior that once upon a time Jean Jacques Rousseau, when he was a lad, went to Turin, where he found himself without any money or friends, not knowing where he was going to sup or to sleep. As he had excellent letters he applied to the Hospital of the Catechumens in that city, where he was kindly received; and he entered there at once as a Catechumen. They all went assiduously to work to try to convert him. But he was well versed in Protestant controversy, which he had learned at Geneva, and, while they were trying to convert him he was doing his best to convert them, thinking it was the same with the Catholics as it was with the Protestants, that it was only necessary to beat them in an argument in order to reason them out of their faith. He pretends that he came off at first victorious, and those who had first undertaken to instruct him retreated, to give place to a master who was as disputatious as himself, but who possessed far more learning, experience, and skill.

" Whenever Jean Jacques would assert anything in opposition to what his new instructor said, and would name his authority, the other would deny that such an author had ever said any such thing, and he would hand him a large Latin folio, and defy him to find any passage of the kind in the book ; and thereby the master would beat him, because Jean Jacques was a poor Latin scholar, and it might have been in the book twenty times without his being able to find it, and if he had found it his instructor would have been sure to translate it to suit his own theory. This master was as tenacious and as persevering as Jean Jacques was obstinate and conceited, and they continued to dispute week after week and month after month without success. In the meanwhile they coaxed him, they petted him, they gave him bon-bons and tarts, to try to induce him to become a real Christian and be baptised in the Catholic faith, but Jean Jacques was inexorable.

"At last an archbishop came to pass a few days at the hospital, and Jean Jacques who, by this time, had become tired of his pauper existence, and filled with ambitious aspirations, thought that it would be a splendid thing after all for him to become a Catholic. He imagined that the whole institution must be in admiration of his talents and address, and that they would not fail to recommend him to the archbishop, who might probably make him one of his secretaries. This consideration decided his conversion, and he announced his desire to be baptised. The next day his indefatigable instructor, to whom he had given so much trouble, washed him and combed his hair, dressed him up in a grey suit, and placing in his hand a lighted taper, led him to the altar. Immediately after he was baptised the same person led him back into the sacristy, made him take off his grey dress and put on his old clothes, then, placing a few francs in his hand, he conducted him to the door and kicked him into the street, cursing him for having given him so much trouble, and for having held out so long.

" Jean Jacques hastened away as fast as he could, reflecting as he did so that he little thought that morning when he was meditating what palace he should live in, that in the evening he should find himself in the street; and as the shadows of night came on, he began to sigh for his comfortable quarters, his

wonted caresses, his bon-bons and tarts, and he at last thought
to himself what a big fool he had been not to *hold out longer.*"

Said I to Madame Xavier : "After you have told this story to
Rev. Mother, please tell her that I think Jean Jacques was right,
that he was a fool, for he should have *held out longer.*"

Madame Xavier left me at once. In about half an hour a
Sister came and told me that the Rev. Mother had sent her to
accompany me to the park. Returning, I saw Madame Xavier,
and I asked her if she had delivered my message. " Yes," she
replied, " but I did not wait for a reply for the Superior-General
was with Rev. Mother, and as soon as I finished your story I left
the room. But I could hear them laughing until I reached the
study-hall."

The next morning I saw the Superior, who received me more
affectionately than usual. We both laughed heartily, but we
never once referred to the story. It had the desired effect however, for it brought back all my former privileges, and I never
had reason afterwards to complain of the Superior. She was no
doubt convinced that if ever I became a saint it would only be
by slow degrees, and that it would require the hand of time.

<hr>

CHAPTER LVIII.

GENERAL ROLLIN'S IDEA OF A "RETREAT"—MADAME XAVIER'S ANTIDOTE
FOR SORROW.

A Hallowed Scene—The Abbaye aux Bois—The General charges again—
Reposing One's Hair—Farewell to St. Mandé.

FROM that day I became more and more contented with my
convent home. I continued my studies, but my history lesson
was replaced by a religious coming in every afternoon at three
o'clock, and reading to me until dark. She read to me the Life
of Jesus. It was beautifully written. I fear I have forgotten
the author's name, but I think it was the Abbé Borrasseau.

I remember, during one of these readings, having horrified
the religious by asking her how many brothers our Lord had ;
for I remembered that Renan had stated that Christ had several
brothers. When she got over her astonishment she said to me
that *my historian, Mr. Renan,* was probably not a Hebrew
scholar, and if he was he must have been a very poor one if he
quoted the New Testament to verify such an assertion, for the
word *brothers,* according to the custom of the Hebrews, was used
indiscriminately for brothers or relatives, because in that

language the same word signified either; and then, if our Lord had brothers in the sense that Renan gives to that word, why did He confide the care of His mother to John His disciple? The moments I passed at this reading lesson were among the happiest I ever knew, for, even then, the whole scene in the life of our Lord, to the description of which I listened, would appear to me like a beautiful living tableau.

The nun used to seat herself near the window, and the last rays of a winter's sunset would peer through the branches of the cedar of Lebanon, and fall on the form of that pure and lovely creature, who, in soft and gentle accents, read to me the life and words of Him to whom she had given her all.

I could feel by every word, look, tone, and gesture, that in that body dwelt a soul that was most pleasing to the God-made Man. I would sit, listening attentively to every word she uttered, but ever regretting the declining day, whose last twilight glimmers fell, like a mysterious curtain, upon a hallowed scene.

Spring came, and one bright afternoon Madame Xavier came to give me my lesson. We were very happy, and were laying out plans for the summer, when we happened to look out of the window, and saw two men standing on the lawn in close conversation, who every now and then would point towards the château.

Madame Xavier turned pale. I asked her what was the matter. She told me that these men were the Father-General of their Order and their architect, and she feared they were deciding to build on that side of the street, and not purchase the property where the convent actually stood, as had been once determined.

In the evening the Superior came and told me that they owned the property which was attached to the château; but the grounds and buildings on the other side of the street, which joined on the Park of Vincennes, were only leased. As the lease would expire in three years the Superior-General had decided to repair the château and build an addition to it, and thus convert it into a convent.

Of course the château could not be inhabited from the moment they began the repairs. I secured apartments at the Abbaye aux Bois, an ancient monastery situated in the Rue de Sèvres, about ten minutes' walk from the Tuileries. It is an immense building, whose walls enclose large, spacious gardens.

The object to which this place is dedicated is twofold, each being entirely distinct from the other. The interior of the

Abbey is devoted to the education of children, while the exterior is let out to widows or ladies of the nobility who wish to lead a life of seclusion and retirement, without being obliged to enter a convent.

The religious who have the superintendence of the institution are cloistered, and always converse with the outside world from behind a grating, while their faces remained concealed beneath a black serge veil. Those who hire apartments at the Abbey are perfectly independent of the institution. It is considered a great privilege for a lady to be received there, and objections were made at first about receiving me, on account of my youth and because I was an American. Their apartments were seldom let, except to ladies who were well known to the nuns and their society.

I set right to work to furnish my apartments, which consisted of two suites of rooms. In a few weeks I had them arranged in almost regal style.

I was delighted with the change which apparently forced me back into the world, and which made my reappearance in society appear a necessity, not a choice.

It was soon noised about that the château was going to be repaired, and how much the nuns regretted to have me leave them, and how dejected I was to go. I pretended to be sorry too, while I was in heart delighted to get away, for the restraint became galling the moment I saw my chance of escape. I loved the nuns, but I loved the world and Laferrière more. His devotion to me, from the day I entered the convent until the moment I left, had been untiring, and he became dearer to me than ever; I also knew that, under the circumstances, my return to Paris would be a perfect triumph. I was so full of joy that it seemed to me that the gates of Heaven itself were opening to receive me, every time I turned my thoughts towards the beautiful city. From the depths of my heart I intoned continual chants of praise to God, for I attributed all my happiness to Him as I formerly had all my sorrows, and I thought that this was to be my reward for having been good. I felt that the sacrifices I had made and intended to make, merited a glorious return, and my approaching triumph redoubled my faith; I believed that God was treating me like a pet child, in giving me at once all that I could desire. And to complete my happiness, I was sure that my nuptials with Laferrière would soon follow, because his daughter was then lying dangerously ill. I became more devout and fervent than ever, and every morning I would rise and gather a bunch of violets, which I placed on the little rustic altar in the garden, at the feet of the statue of the Blessed Virgin.   I did everything that I thought would be most agreeable to God, to show Him my gratitude for His goodness.

General Rollin was among the first to drive out to congratulate me on the prospect of my return.   He expressed himself as though I ought to be canonized for not letting myself "be caught;" for he had given me up, until Laferrière came and announced to him that I was coming back once more to reside in the gay city.   I said to the General, and he frowned as I spoke, that I could not understand his aversion to such holy souls, for I truly admired them and sincerely loved them, but I had not the virtue to imitate them.

He smiled and said to me, "Now you speak like a little saint. Admire them and love them as much as you please, but never be one of them, for I would like to know what a woman is good for the moment she takes a mania for the cap and veil?"   "Well," said I, "General, you will not deny that they do a great deal of good."   "Yes," replied the General, "and that is just the reason we will never be able to get rid of them, for they always have some friend at Court to throw up their good works into everybody's face.   I believe a woman's mission is to get married and have children.   Where would you and I have been if our parents had taken it into their heads to make monks and nuns of themselves?"

"They say here," said I, "that there will always be plenty of women in the world to have children, and there will never be enough who will devote themselves to save them.   They say that their mission is to save souls, and not to bring them into the world ; that if a child is born and goes to hell, it would have been better for that child had it never been born."

"Yes, but for myself," replied the General, "I prefer being born, and to run the risk, and you will think so too the moment you get out of here.   They have killed more men than they have ever saved : for it seems to me that it is just when a man has fallen in love with a woman, she chooses that moment to shut herself up in one of those places.   I never will forgive them for seducing my beautiful friend, whom I have never seen nor heard of since."   I began to inquire about some of my acquaintances whom I had not seen for months, and I expressed my joy at seeing once more Madame "du Monde," a lady wholly devoted to the world.   The General quickly replied, "You will not see her for a few weeks to come, for she has gone into *retreat*."   I expressed my surprise, and told the General that I never suspected her of being so devout.

"Devout!" said the General, "I don't see what devotion has to do with it. She has simply retired to the château *pour reposer ses cheveux*." I thought surely he meant horses (*chevaux*) and I said to him, "Why does she not keep two span?" "*Cheveux, cheveux, enfant;* these women have made you forget your French." "What," said I with an outburst of laughter, "she has gone into retreat (as you call it) to rest her hair? I suppose her director then is her *coiffeur* (hair-dresser)." "Yes," replied the General, seriously, "and a very honest one at that; for he loses by her going into retreat. But you know that Madame "du Monde" has not missed a ball, soirée, concert, matinée, or fête this winter; and it appears that her hair is so fatigued after so much dyeing, puffing, curling, crimping, braiding, banging, etc., that her *coiffeur* says she must rest it, or she will lose every bit of it."

The general made me a present of a magnificent crucifix, which he had made to order expressly for me at Barbédienne's. He also gave me beautiful ornaments for my new home in porcelain of Sèvres for my dining-room, and paintings for my parlours, and had Asiatic plants arranged in front of the mirrors, which gave my apartment an Oriental appearance.

As the time approached to leave the convent my impatience grew greater and greater. My heart was light and gay; I had entirely forgotten all about my former *ennui* and satiety, and I began once more to build castles higher than ever. I consented to leave my child at St. Mandé another year. Madame Xavier was the one who regretted my departure most, for she was the most attached to me. She advised me like a fond sister, and tried to tear the illusion from my heart that I would one day espouse Laferrière. She assured me that something told her that God never intended I should be his wife. I laughed at her predictions, but she would take every opportunity to say to me that I would never be happy until I had detached myself from him. On the eve of my departure she taught me in Spanish the following prayer, and told me that I would find in it an antidote to sorrow and care:

> Let nothing trouble thee;
> Let nothing terrify thee;
> All passes away;
> God never changes.
> Patience obtains everything.
> Who possesses God
> Lacks nothing;
> God alone suffices.

I told her I was sure that all my sorrows were at an end, for

I could not see any cloud on my horizon; that my sojourn in the convent had just the effect I had anticipated and hoped for: it had either killed my enemies or taken the venom out of their shafts. But she shook her head doubtingly, and told me that she did not believe that God would exempt me from trial and sufferings, as they are the common lot of all. She made me promise that whenever I was sad I would say her little prayer and meditate on it, for it contained a great truth; and whenever I did repeat it, I was to think of her and the happy days I had passed at St. Mandé.

CHAPTER LIX.

MY ENEMIES VANQUISHED—PLEASURE PALLS—I ENVY THE LOWLY.

Worldly Success—Fond Memory—*Le laid Beau-monde.*

I HAD calculated well, for my return to Paris was like a triumph. I believed that I had at last conquered every obstacle and misfortune which had beset my path since the hour I was born.

I had not been residing long at the Abbey before I received an invitation from Mrs. Dix to come to her daughter's wedding. I went, and was most cordially received, not only by the family, but by all those who had formerly been my persecutors. Mrs. Dix called soon afterwards to see me at the Abbey, the interior of which she desired to see, because it had once been the residence of the famous French beauty, Madame Récamier. Mrs. Dix was charmed with my apartments, which had at one time been the home of Madame de Genlis. She was delighted with her visit, and from that day she became a sincere friend to me.

Mrs. Dix afterwards told me of all the influences which had been brought to bear to prejudice her against me. In fact, she said some Americans almost went on their knees to implore her not to receive me. But the moment she heard that I was received by the Czartoryskis, and that the Princess Iza was my godmother, she began to suspect that envy and jealousy had had their part in prejudicing others against me, and she resolved to make my acquaintance and judge for herself. I felt that I owed Mrs. Dix's friendship to the prayer which I had made at the altar on the day I was baptised.

The moment Mrs. Dix declared herself my friend my position in Paris was secure. People seemed to get tired of fighting me; they gave it up and I had no further difficulty. My residence at the Abbey was a great source of protection.

Laferrière and Rollin were so delighted to have me once more near them, that they became to me like two devoted slaves. They refused me nothing that it was in their power to bestow ; so that my rooms were crowded with people who· sought my patronage and influence. Besides, there were half-a-dozen other dignitaries who called on me occasionally who were as influential as Laferrière. I seldom undertook to obtain anything but what I was sure to succeed. The consequence was that I was not only sought after by the rich, but my antechamber was sometimes thronged with the poor.

This excitement delighted me at first. It was what I had often craved during my cloistered life at St. Mandé, and every night I would retire wondering how I could have ever stood it there so long. But my vanity was soon surfeited ; I began to long for the quiet and peace of the convent, and two months had not passed before I would steal away to St. Mandé, sometimes two or three times a week.

I went to St. Mandé to be confirmed. I was at the altar waiting for the archbishop to confirm me, when the curé of St. Mandé said : "What name will you take? Choose one that you have not been baptised by." And without giving me a chance to speak, he added : "Take the name of Geneviève," which I did.

Meanwhile I went regularly every morning to Mass, and would receive holy communion once or twice a week. I went usually to St. Sulpice, after which I would take a stroll up to the Pantheon to say a little prayer before the altar of St. Geneviève : and I imagined, whenever I failed to go there, that everything went wrong the rest of the day. At that time I thought I had religion, whereas I had only the phantom of it. Religion had triumphed over me; it had seized hold of my conscience; but Laferrière had my heart, and I found that I could no more wrest my conscience from God than I could my heart from Laferrière. The training I had received at the convent had made a lasting impression on my soul. It had enlightened me. In vain I tried to close my eyes to the light, or to turn a deaf ear to remorse : the instant I committed the slightest offence against God, I was miserable until I had obtained absolution.

When I first came to the Abbey to reside, I did not go out on evenings, as the doors closed at eleven o'clock. At first I was contented to lead this semi-cloistered life ; but I soon found it excessively stupid, and I began to grow low-spirited, just because I could not get into the abbey after eleven o'clock at night.

I soon discovered that the old man who had charge of the

gate, and who had been the porter of the Abbey for over twenty years, was as easily bribed as the parish bell-ringer at St. Mandé. He was suffering with the liver complaint, and I began by giving him bottles of Vichy water. One day I put a Napoleon on the cork, which made the old man's eyes sparkle, as he gratefully exclaimed: " *Merci, merci, madame ;* "—and he told me that it was more than all the old women in the convent had given him for the past six months,—they always gave him a few francs every Christmas, but that was the last until Christmas again. " Oh," said I, " you know this has nothing to do with Christmas, for at Christmas I intend to make you a handsome present for having let me out; but I think that it is worth four bottles of Vichy water a month, with a Napoleon besides, to be *always let in.*" The old man thought so too, and he told me that whenever I came home after the hour, I must not let the coachman drive up to the convent-gate, but walk a few steps and then rap on his window with my fan, and if he saw there was no danger of being caught, he would let me in. As this was too great a risk always to run I engaged a room next door to the Abbey, so that in case the old man dared not open the gate, I could go there and sleep; and this system we kept up until the old man died.

His successor was a hale, hearty youth who served at the altar. I never attempted to bribe him, for I was sure he would refuse : so, whenever I remained out late at night, I would sleep in the room outside the gate. The religious murmured ; but I told them it was not against their rules, for they had told me that the gate closed at eleven, but they did not tell me that I should be inside of it.

But I soon got tired of operas, theatres, and *soirées*, and preferred one hour passed at St. Mandé to them all. One evening I was at the opera with some friends. Laferrière joined us after the first act. I became so exhausted that I begged him to take me home. " Why, child ?" he replied, " do listen to the music." " Oh," said I, " I am so weary—it sickens me : I am not made for this."

" Tell me," he said, " what you are made for ; nothing seems to amuse you. You must break yourself of this restlessness. Tell me, were you ever satisfied to keep still five minutes in your life ?"

I begged him to come with me, and I forced him back into the saloon attached to the box. He began to scold, and declared that everybody in the house would think that we had gone into the saloon to talk sentiment and love. " Well," said

I, "leave me.   If one of us is condemned to listen to the play,
let it be you."

He left me at once.   I began to weep and muse on the past,
and I recalled a time that I *once* sat still.   It was when I used
to sit on the door-sill of my uncle's cottage, listening to the
cricket which sang under the stone step ; and whenever that
moral nausea which a surfeit of pleasure gives would seize me, I
would willingly give all the pleasures in Paris if I could have
been carried back to listen to that cricket's song again.

How often, when I have been sitting in one of the imperial
boxes, ensconed in satin cushions and damask drapery adorned
with tinsel hangings, over which were embroidered the insignia
of Royalty, and surrounded by hearts to which I felt coldly
indifferent, have I been seized by such a spell of *ennui* that I
turned my eyes from the stage and looked at the third tier, to
watch and to envy some young peasant whom I chanced to see
there sitting beside his intended or his youthful bride.

I have often watched them during the whole play.   Even now
I have only to close my eyes and I can see them still.

How naturally, and at the same instant, they turn towards
each other to read mutual joy and satisfaction in each other's
eyes.   They are constantly doing so at the same time that they
are all attention to the play.   The curtain falls, the play is over,
everybody hastens away; but my charming couple linger.   Every
back is turned towards them (just what the swain is waiting
for).   The gas in the third tier is suddenly extinguished, yet I
can see the outlines of their forms as the young peasant quickly
bows his head close to hers.   She starts back affrighted; but is
instantly assured by him that the danger is over, and they joy-
fully hasten out hand in hand to join the rest.   The young
rogue stole a kiss ; it was for that he lay in wait.   I mistrusted
him, and I waited to see it out.

But how I envied them when I saw him take her hand, and
they tripped away gaily side by side.   I envied them their
independence ; and my soul would sicken when it fell back
again once more upon myself, and that dread feeling of isolation of the heart would come over me.   In such moments I
hated fortune, titles, honours, and distinction, and I looked upon
them as the enemies of my repose; for every day they seemed
to separate me more and more from the one I loved.

One day I opened my heart to Laferrière and told him that
there were moments when I felt like flying from Paris, so sick
was I of this kind of life.   He replied : "Did I not tell you so ?
I knew how it would be—I foresaw all this ; but I did not

expect it would come so soon. I knew I could place you in a position that the world would be at your feet, and that the day would come when you would loathe it as you would a nauseous drink. I can sympathise with you; for it is a penalty that I have had to submit to ever since the Emperor gave me my appointment. But I have this to console me, whereas you have not that consolation: I did not seek my position—it was thrust upon me; whereas you made every effort to attain yours. I much preferred the solitude of Fléchères to this Babylonian life at court. I shrank from it; but, from devotion to the cause that my father had made such bitter sacrifices in espousing, I accepted it as a burden, not as a means to happiness. I am so disgusted with court life and the flattery of sycophants that I often envy my valet, and wish I could exchange positions with him. But you deserve to be punished; for this is only what you sought for. Now that you have attained it, you find yourself miserable. I can do nothing more. But I knew just how it would be; and I always told you so that the day would come when you would sigh for your former quiet and unassuming home, and would care little who despised you, so long as they would leave you alone."

"No," said I; "that is not so. I have never once sighed after the little apartment, because some people turned their backs on me there for living in it. They thought I deserved it to be so treated."

Laferrière's face assumed a bitter smile as he replied, "You will never be convinced of the truth of anything I tell you. Do you suppose that the world crowds around you now because men think that you are more deserving than you were then? My dear child, I am sure they have a worse opinion of you now than they had then. I thought you could read people; but how vanity and pride do blind us! You will find that they will press your hand so long as they can find something in it; but believe me, the moment you cease to amuse them, or to be of any service to them, you might be an angel, and they would not know you if they met you in the street."

———

CHAPTER LX.

MY SOUL IN DARKNESS—THE COUNTESS DE MONTALEMBERT BRINGS
BACK THE LIGHT.

A New Departure—The Old and the New Régime.

I HAD not led this life three months when I awoke one morning, and it appeared to me that I was as much an infidel as ever.

It was one of the most dreadful moments I ever knew. I was so distracted that I had an impulse to run down the street and throw myself into the Seine,—I had lost my Faith. I looked upon the Catholics as so many fiends incarnate who had succeeded in entrapping me, and I began asking myself: How are you going to get out of this? how are you going to get out of this? It would be contrary to my nature to keep up the disguise, and make believe that I was a Christian when I was not. I felt that I was fitted for any other *rôle* in duplicity but that, and *that I would not play*. I preferred being shunned by the whole world as an infidel to being honoured while knowing myself to be a hypocrite. I had always sincerely hated hypocrites, and to be forced to be one myself, in order to keep up my position, I felt was more than the whole thing was worth. But I was sad, very sad. What a scandal it would make! and how it would grieve my friends! my godmother whom I so much loved! and when I thought of Madame Xavier I wept like a child. But what could I do? and, every moment becoming more and more distracted, hardly knowing what I was about, I sank down on my knees, and began to implore God to help me.

That day I refused to see anyone, locked myself up in my room, and raved like one who had been following an *ignis fatuus*, until it had led him to a precipice, and who had not discovered the cheat until he found himself dashing headlong down. In this miserable state I remained until three o'clock in the afternoon, praying fervently to God all the while to inspire me what to do in order to get out of my embarrassment. Finally the thought struck me that I would say nothing about it for the present. I should first study the question, master it, and would not declare myself an infidel until I was strong enough to defend myself. I recollected that the Catholics had been too much for Jean Jacques, but then he was only a boy, and they never succeeded in making such a fool of him as they did of me, for he knew better all the time, whereas I was in downright earnest.

I then recalled how well they had refuted everything that I had said against them. But my resolution was taken, and I was determined to carry it through,—this time I should master both sides of the question, so as not to be taken by surprise at anything that could be said in their favour, as I had been at St. Mandé. How many people had called me a fool! I now felt that they were the only ones who knew me.

My maid came and told me that the carriage was waiting. I then remembered having ordered it for three o'clock, to go to the Princess Sulkowska's. It was her reception-day.

As soon as I entered the saloon the Princess came to me and said : " I am so glad you have come to-day, for I want you to renew your acquaintance with the Countess de Montalembert, who is your neighbour.   She resides in the Rue de Bac, very near the Abbey.   I have just been telling her of your extraordinary conversion, and she desires very much to see you."

The Countess could not recall me, and had lost all remembrance of our former acquaintance.   She began to congratulate me, and to say many edifying things, which fearfully embarrassed me, as the Princess Iza joined in the conversation, at a moment when all my doubts and the despair of the morning came back upon me. I did not know what to do or to say, but I concluded it would be wise to keep silent for the present.

Madame de Montalembert introduced me to her daughter, the Countess de Meaux.   In a few moments I was surrounded by half-a-dozen, all congratulating me, among the rest Monsignor Bauer, afterwards chaplain to the Empress, whom I had always disliked.   While he was running off a few silvery phrases I was seized with an almost irresistible desire to tell him to hold his tongue, that I believed his religion was all a humbug, and that he was one of the chief charlatans who were running it.

Whenever my impatience reached its pitch it had become a habit with me to say, *Je ne suis pas faite pour cela* (I am not made for this) : then I would give up and leave, no matter where I was or what I was doing.   It was in the middle of one of Monsignor's sentences that this thought struck me, and I tried to make my escape, but I had hardly advanced three steps before I found myself face to face again with Madame de Montalembert, who with her hand motioned me to a seat by her side.

The conversation took a general turn, and for the first time in my life I was captivated by a woman.   I was charmed with her, she was so frank, so ingenuous, so witty, so thoroughly devoid of affectation. I remembered how uncomfortable she and her society had made me feel when I visited her three years before; I was then so afraid that they would find out how little I knew.   But now I had made up my mind to take the other tack, and pretend not to know anything at all.

In a few moments it seemed as though we had known each other all our lives.   I described to her the kind of life I was leading, and told her that I was dying with *ennui*.   She replied : " I am not at all surprised, for such a life would kill anyone who had any good sense."   I told her that I feared it was because I was entirely devoid of it that everything bored me.   She would not admit that, but said, on the contrary, she was sure that my head was full of it. I smiled, for I thought what would Laferrière say had he heard her pay me such a compliment.

She spoke of her husband's illness, and said it was the only thing that would prevent her seeing me as often as she felt she would like to, and then she named an hour, and told me that if I would call on her any day at that time she would receive me.

She said: "You interest me; I want to know you more. But I will tell you at once a good thing for you to do: instruct yourself in our religion, that is good food for your mind, and the most essential aliment too."

I told her that I had that very morning resolved to do it. She was delighted with my reply, and offered at once to be my teacher, which offer I readily accepted. She said: "You will read only such books as I recommend," to which I agreed.

When I told her that I had resolved that morning to instruct myself in the Catholic religion, I told the truth; for I was determined to study both sides, and I thought it would be as well to learn one side thoroughly first before I undertook the other. Now as Providence had been good enough to throw a teacher of Catholicity at once in my path, I accepted it the same as I would have done had a teacher of infidelity first presented himself.

Madame de Montalembert presented me to many ladies of rank in the Faubourg, who were mostly her own relatives, and when she told them what a warm attachment she had for me, they all received me as if I were one of her family. I wrote their names in my book of addresses. Laferrière's eyes happened to fall on them one day. I noticed his countenance change. He let the book fall from his hand, sank back in his chair, closed his eyes, and knit his brows. I asked him if he had seen any new name there that he objected to. Said he: "Those families to whom Madame de Montalembert has introduced you are my relations." "Then," said I, "you know them?" "No," he sadly replied, "I only know them by name. They have always adhered faithfully to the old *régime*, and consequently we have never met; the breach took place between my father and his family before I was born."

This at once gave me something to do, for I instantly resolved that he should know his relations, and in less than two months I succeeded in introducing him to several members of his family.

One evening, after my guests had left and I was alone with Laferrière, he remarked: "Perhaps it was to render me this service that Providence sent you to me. How singularly the wheel of fortune turns!   Just think that *you*, a homeless, friendless waif, whom I have always considered that Providence wafted over the sea for me to protect and cherish, should be the only one who could introduce me to my family, whom I might have never known had I never met you!"

CHAPTER LXI.

THE LADIES OF THE RETREAT—A HOME OF TRUE CHRISTIAN CHARITY.

Another Sanctuary.

THE Marquise de Ferrière le Vayer, who was one of the Viscount's cousins, introduced me to the "Ladies of the Retreat," a religious community whose convent was situated in the Rue de Regard, a short distance only from the Abbey. The special aim of this community is to instruct ladies in the world in their religion and give them opportunities of making spiritual retreats. She recommended me particularly to one of the religious, Madame de la Chapelle, who was also a distant relative of Laferrière's, whom he had never seen.

From the day I made the acquaintance of the "Ladies of the Retreat" their convent became a second St. Mandé to me.

I was seriously studying my religion, and would frequently go for explanations to the "Ladies of the Retreat," who could teach like theologians.   They appeared specially gifted for giving instructions and advice.   If the one you addressed was not capable of solving your difficulties she would introduce you to one of her sisters in religion who was better informed.

Everything about this convent breathed peace and heavenly rest.   There was something in the very gait and manner and expression of these religious that drew you to them, and from them to God.   One thing about them was irresistibly sweet, which I often remarked, it was their relations with each other.

It could be easily seen by their intercourse that they were united by mutual love.   There was no affectation, everything was candour and simplicity.   Whenever they addressed each other it was always with an accent of the most tender and sisterly regard.   I never left their abode without feeling what a Heaven in itself each home might be if all families were united and would live together, as do the "Ladies of the Retreat." There was no strife, no ambition, no envy among them, for these things can easily be detected however well they may be disguised.   There is a nervous, unquiet, oftentimes rigid and always shrinking, motion of the eyes that cannot be controlled, when envy, jealousy, and distrust lurk in the heart. With the " LADIES OF THE RETREAT " everything was peaceful and joyful, as only those homes can be which are filled with hearts united by Christian Faith, Hope, and Charity.

CHAPTER LXII.

MADAME XAVIER BRAVES THE SPANISH COMMUNE—A WOUNDED HEART REFUSES TO BE HEALED.

The Heroic Nun.

WHEN the heat of the summer set in I went to Mont Doré, chaperoned by some ladies of the Faubourg St. Germain. These ladies were pious, cultivated, and refined, and possessed every moral quality that makes social intercourse something more elevating than idle pastime. For a few weeks I was happy and contented: my health improved; the past seemed entirely effaced from my mind. I was happy in the present, and felt no anxiety about the future.

A letter from my sister changed the whole current of my thoughts, and set me to brooding once more over the past, and dreading some fearful scandal in the future. She had separated from her husband, and said that she would begin a suit of divorce if he did not consent to comply with certain conditions that she exacted of him. It was a long letter, every sentence of which was in such discord with my present associations and habits, that it brought before my eyes vividly the degradation out of which Providence had raised me.

The publications in the newspapers of such a trial would expose my origin, and hurl me from the proud social eminence which I had attained. I was crushed at the very thought of the Princess Iza ever knowing anything about my past, and the remainder of my stay at Mont Doré was as painful as the first few weeks had been happy and contented. This new and unexpected anxiety wore so upon me that I returned to Paris little benefited in health by my sojourn among the mountains.

As soon as I returned to Paris I went to St. Mandé. The Superior had left to take charge of one of their houses at Bayonne, and Madame Xavier had been sent to a house of the Order in the interior of Spain. I then placed my child at the Abbaye aux Bois, for when Madame Xavier left there was nothing to draw me to St. Mandé.

At a time when Spain was in the height of revolution, when Spanish communists robbed the churches and invaded the convents, and were committing every species of sacrilege in different parts of the country, they made a raid one morning on the very convent to which Madame Xavier had been transferred. All the religious fled except Madame Xavier, who fled to the chapel and placed herself between the railing of the sanctuary and the tabernacle.

The miscreants first plundered the cellars, and secured all the provisions they could find; after which they rushed to the chapel to make booty of its sacred vessels. They supposed the convent was deserted, and were surprised when they reached the chapel and found a nun standing before them in an attitude of defiance, with a crucifix in her hand. They instantly halted, when she cried out to them and ordered them to kneel down and ask God's forgiveness for daring to desecrate His sanctuary.

They began parleying among themselves as to what they should do. Some cried out : "Let us seize her !" while others said : "No ; let us wait for the captain ;" and these kept the others at bay until the captain arrived. When the captain came, he was so struck by the bravery and courage of the nun that he promised her that their convent should never be molested by one of his band, nor would they carry off any booty if she would go and breakfast with them. She agreed to the stipulation, and the last I have ever heard of Madame Xavier, she had breakfasted .with a band of Spanish communists.

CHAPTER LXIII.

A SISTER OF CHARITY IN THE MORNING; A WOMAN OF THE WORLD IN THE AFTERNOON.

Lessons to Misery—A Light to my Conscience.

ON my return from Mont Doré I received a letter from the Baron de Toucy, requesting me to do him the favour of calling at the Neckar Hospital to visit a patient.

When I arrived at the hospital it was about half-past six in the morning. The portress treated me uncivilly and refused absolutely to let me in, on account of the earliness of the hour ; but, as I persisted, she told me to pass through the lodge, and she would search my pockets and a little satchel I had in my hand, and then *perhaps* she would let me in. She made the perquisition, and concluded to let me pass. At that instant I saw

a door on which was written *Bureau du directeur*, and before
the man in blouse could stop me I was in there. Here I found
a gentleman writing, who appeared very much surprised to see
me. Before he had a chance to speak and order me out, I told
him what I came for, and desired to be conducted to bed No. 10.
"Why, Mademoiselle," he replied, "no one ever comes here at
this hour." Said I : "It appears they do, *for I am here !*"

He replied : "It is against the rules ; no one can visit a sick
person at this time of day. You must call a few hours later."

"I have not come here," said I, "to receive your orders ;"
saying which I pulled out the Baron's letter, and handed it to
him. After he had read the letter he ordered the servant to
conduct me to bed No. 10.

This hospital is in charge of the Sisters of Charity. It receives
first-class poor, for not every person they pick up in the street is
allowed to come there. They only receive that class which does
not come under the common appellation of paupers ; and many
of its inmates belong to the respectable labouring people,
whom penury obliges to seek assistance when they are unable to
work.

This morning I must have remained there three or four hours,
conversing with the Sisters and consoling the sick. One of the
Sisters conducted me to the door, and begged me to call often.
I told her of the search that the portress had subjected me to.
The Sister instantly descended the stairs, went to the director,
and asked him to give me a ticket which would admit me any
time I chose to call.

From the time I entered the hospital until I reached home it
seemed to me that ten years had passed over my head. A new
phase of life had just been opened to me, and as I entered my
luxuriously furnished apartment the very sight of my own wanton
extravagance sickened me.

That same afternoon Laferrière arrived, and I related to him
my morning visit to the hospital, and how wretched it made me
to see so much suffering that I was unable to relieve. I had
emptied my purse there : it was but as a drop in the ocean.

I had seen mothers lying there with their newly-born babies,
without any clothing to put on them excepting a few bandages
and pieces of muslin that the Sisters had with difficulty been
able to procure for them. I happened to remark that I wished
I could go there and pass a few hours every day. Laferrière
replied : "I do not see what there is to prevent you." I began
to enumerate the many things I had to take up my time ; and
when I mentioned the hours I devoted to the study of the

Catholic religion, he caught that up and said : " The best lesson that you can take in our religion is to go to the hospitals, where you will see the fruits of it ; for there is no book that can instruct you like the daily examples of the " Sisters of Charity." So saying, he handed me a few hundred-franc bills to give to the sick poor for him.

General Rollin came in. He followed Laferrière's example, and said that I could count on him for a remittance for my poor every month, as he took good care never to be seen giving away money himself, for fear his doors would be besieged by paupers and impostors.

From that day I rose an hour earlier, and devoted a part of every morning to visiting the sick and the poor. I visited the hospital three or four times a week, and it was by the bedsides of its unfortunate inmates, listening to their simple stories, and often catching with difficulty their dying words, in which were frequently summed up the deceptions of a whole life, that I learned to reflect seriously.

It was there I received my daily instructions ; it was there that my mind received lights to which I could not close my eyes. In the histories of these poor creatures I could find some analogy with my own. They had been brought down to that wretched state through the faults of their parents, through the injustice, ingratitude, and cruelty of others, and frequently by their own faults. By their bedsides I would make my own examination of conscience, and would lift my heart to God, and ask Him why He had allowed me to escape their lot, for I felt that I had often been exposed to it, and was much more deserving of it than they.

I never descended the hospital stairs without making a firm resolve never to wilfully offend God, who had shown me so much mercy, and I never left the sick there without remorse for having squandered so much money in luxuries that only gave me a momentary satisfaction, and which might have relieved the necessities and made the happiness of many a miserable being. I would then resolve to convert my past folly to some good account. I passed my mornings like a Sister of Charity, and my afternoons like a woman of the world, intriguing to get influence, power, and money, just in order to help the poor.

One afternoon a lady from the Faubourg St. Germain, who had only known me in my morning character as lady of charity, called on me, and was scandalised to find me surrounded by half a dozen of the *beau monde*, to whom I was playing the agreeable. As soon as we were alone, she was candid enough to tell me how much I disedified her. I threw open a large pantry, and showed her the piles of clothes, &c., stored in it for distribution among the poor, telling her that I got them out of just such people as those who had left me, and from charitable Americans, like Mr. Warden, head of the French house of A. T. Stewart.

As my motive was good this lady encouraged me to go on. Not so the Countess de Montalembert, who was at her château. She was called about this time unexpectedly to Paris to pass a few days. When I told her how I was passing my time, without exaggerating at all on my coquetries, she was too smart to be so easily deceived by the good results of the sacrifices I made to mammon in order to be benevolent, and she slyly remarked on my manœuvring: " It seems to me that it is something like trying to lead God and the Devil in the same harness."

— — —

CHAPTER LXIV.

THE GIUSTINIS.

A Syrian Mother—A Mute Appeal—An Irate Landlady—Evening Meditations—A Bedroom Sanctuary—Children in the Abbey.

To give an account of all that I went through during the months that immediately followed my sojourn at St. Mandé would take too much space. I will here give the history of a single week. In the Rue des St. Pères lived a poor statuary named Caussinus. Caussinus and his wife were always speaking to me of a poor family named Giustini, who had come all the way from Syria to collect a claim they had against the French Government. They had been already six or seven months in Paris. The Caussinuses never ceased to importune me to help Giustini to collect his claim. I met this man one day in the statuary's shop. He implored me. for the love of God to help him. Mrs. Caussinus had told him about my influence at Court, and it appears he had been coming there daily for weeks in hopes of meeting me. I gave him a few francs; but his woe-begone face and look of despair haunted me wherever I went.

The next day I sent for Caussinus and asked him to explain what Giustini's claim against the Government was. He told me that the Count de Bentivoglio, who was French Consul at Aleppo, had been authorised by the Government to appoint a consular agent at Aintab. Giustini, an Italian, was appointed. He married into one of the best families of the East. His wife became a Catholic. Her conversion caused a rupture between Giustini and

his father-in-law's family. Giustini had acted as consular agent for France for eleven years, but had never received any salary. He had lately been removed by order of the Chief of the Consulate Department in France. He had come to Paris to collect eleven years' salary.

The French Government denied his claim *in toto*. It was said that he had never been legally appointed consular agent, and even had he been legally commissioned there was no other emolument attached to that consulate than the perquisites. The Government also declared that Giustini had never rendered any service to it, and had only made use of his position to obtain illegitimate gains, borrowing money which he never returned, forcing the Cawas to pay him, and, far from remunerating them, he sold his influence, &c. It was for these causes, and for others still greater, that he had been removed.

The Count Charles de Lesseps, Monsieur Chatry de la Fosse, and other influential men who knew Giustini in Syria, had tried to enforce his claim; but the only answer they received from the Government was a list of the charges that I have mentioned.

I did not wish to engage in such a hopeless case, and told Caussinus never to mention it again, as I could do nothing for them.

Caussinus undertook to describe their misery; but I would not listen to him. Yet the moment he left I found it impossible to drive the affair out of my mind. That day during dinner the sorrowful countenance of Giustini haunted me. After dinner I called my maid and told her to put a bottle of wine and some food in a basket for the starving family.

It was the last of October; the evenings had begun to be chilly. My maid threw a shawl over my shoulders, which I objected to wear; but she insisted that it was cold, and that I would need it before I got home. We called at the hotel where they lived. Instead of conducting me to them the landlady began to tell me how many months they had occupied her rooms without paying her a cent. She had endeavoured by every means to put them out, but the very *gendarme* who had come to put them into the street had been seduced by Giustini, the silvery-tongued scoundrel, and instead of putting them out, as he had a commission to do, he gave him five francs and reported the case to his captain, who begged her to keep them a little longer. She begged me, if I had any influence with them, to induce them to leave. My maid uncovered the basket and showed her our mission. The woman frowned, as though it were a charity ill placed. She reluctantly conducted us up two flights of stairs, pointed to a room and left us.

We knocked at the door, but receiving no answer, my maid shouted to those inside that we were not the police, and begged them to open the door. At last I put my mouth to the keyhole and calling Giustini by name, I told him that I was the lady he had met in Caussinus's shop. He immediately unlocked, unbolted, and unbarricaded the door; for he had pushed up his trunks, and all the furniture in the room against it.

When the door opened, it was impossible for us to distinguish anything in the dark, except the figure of a man. I told him to strike a light; that there was no one there to molest him. He feebly answered that he had no light, not even a match.

At these words my maid seized hold of my hand: she was trembling with fear. "Oh! madam," she exclaimed, "let us go: I am afraid to stay here." I too felt timid about going into a dark room with a starving man, and we both retreated into the corridor. The man who fully recognised me, followed us and begged us to come in, so that he could fasten the door. "*Oh, Dieu!* no, thank you!" we both simultaneously exclaimed, and my maid made a dash for the stairs, and almost reached the first flight before I could stop her. I gave her my purse, and told her to buy a candle and some matches.

When she returned I was already in the room, and never shall I forget the scene that burst upon me, when she brought in the light. Before me was a woman, sitting up in bed, with beads in her hands, saying her rosary, while her eyes were fixed on three long glossy strands of hair spread across her lap. By her side lay a boy of at least twelve years. Presently the woman raised her eyes, looked at me a moment, and smiled; then fixing her gaze once more on the strands of hair, she continued her prayer as devoutly as though she had been alone.

Her husband said to me: "She smiled to thank you for the light; for she always weeps when it grows so dark that she can no longer see those strands of hair." I asked him whose they were.
. He replied: "My wife is an Eastern lady, and it is customary in her country, when a mother leaves her children, to take with her a strand of hair from the head of each; and those belong to our three daughters whom we left in Syria, and we fear we shall never see them again."

He was so overcome when he spoke those last words, that he sank down on his knees, and began to weep and to implore God to have pity on them. The wife having finished her prayer, wound the chaplet around her wrist, clasped her hands together, and addressed a few words in Arabic to her husband. Her husband then said to me: "She has just told me that she knew that the

Mother of God would not abandon us, for she had been praying to her the whole day long."

I approached the bed and asked her if she was ill. Instead of answering me she looked towards her husband to have him interpret my words, for she only spoke her native tongue. He told me that she was exhausted for want of food, that she was so cold that she and her child were in bed to keep warm, for their clothing had been made for a much more genial clime.

My maid had taken the provisions from the basket. They saturated the bread with wine and ate sparingly of it. The husband told me how often they had suffered with hunger. I sat on the side of the bed listening to his story. He opened a trunk half full of papers. These documents, he said, could prove his innocence ; but, as he had no money, no lawyer would take an interest in his case. The Government officials were prejudiced against him, he said, and would not even give him an audience. He had come thousands of miles, all the way from Syria, and had never been able to speak to anyone connected with the Foreign Department, except the sentry at the gate of the ministerial mansion, or the valet in the ante-chamber, and now that he was known to the sentry he would not even be permitted to pass. He had lost all hopes of ever returning to Syria, and was afraid that he and his family would die of starvation.

I asked him to show me the list of accusations that the Government had sent him. He handed me a paper, which bore the ministerial seal, in which were over thirty serious charges against him, signed by Meurand, who had been Chief of the Consulate Department for thirty years.

Meurand was a man noted for his accurate decisions. If a person appealed to the Emperor he would refer him to the Minister of Foreign Affairs, and the minister would be obliged to refer the matter back to Meurand. Meurand was the real head and labouring man of his department : he knew everything that concerned it, and was a man of acknowledged ability, strict integrity, and unerring judgment.

I looked over a few of the papers, but none of those which he handed me had any bearing on the case.

After cross-questioning Giustini I was forced to the conclusion that he was a scoundrel.

While we were talking, his wife, who could not understand a word we said, had resumed her prayer with the chaplet in her hand, while her large oval eyes were fixed on the strands of hair.

I saw her shiver, and the whole expression of her face instantly changed, yet she still continued to say her beads. Her husband also noticed the tremulous change that passed like a congealing breath over her, and he said to me: " She is cold."   I instantly took up my shawl, which lay at the foot of the bed, and wrapped it around her.   As I did so she looked up into my face and gratefully smiled.

As I folded the shawl across her bosom I came so close to her that I touched her.   She smiled again, and instantly I felt something strike my arm.   I looked down to see what it was, and placing my hand upon her I felt it again.   I looked into her face inquiringly wondering what it could be.   She blushed, slightly inclined her head as she spoke a few words to her husband, who then told me that she was again to be a mother and for that reason she so longed for home.

My whole soul was so moved with compassion that I began talking to her, forgetting that she could not understand me. But her heart was her interpreter; for true sympathy needs not words to express it.   She burst into tears, seized my hand, and held it with a steel-like grasp, and as she drew me to her and gently kissed my forehead, the beads of the chaplet were deeply embedded in the back of my hand, and in that same instant the little unborn leaped again.   This time it had a magic touch, which thrilled me through and through, and it seemed as though my very heart, instead of my lips, spoke, as I exclaimed, while I felt the beads of the chaplet kneading deeper and deeper into my hand: "*In the name of the Blessed Virgin I promise never to abandon you until the Government sends you home!* "

The husband threw himself on his knees and kissed my feet, he then arose and interpreted to his wife what I had said.   A deathlike pallor overspread her countenance as she replied.   At her words the husband too turned pale, and began wringing his hands in despair.

I begged him to speak and tell me what she had said.   " Ah!" he wildly exclaimed, " she is right.   I forgot for an instant when you breathed those words of hope, but, ah! she is right.   The Government! the Government! what does the Government care for us or our miseries?   One might die here with hunger and it would never give us a thought.   We have been here seven months, and the only reply that it has ever given us is that list of accusations."

" Do not be discouraged," said I.   " Give me a few months, and I will surely succeed."   My words, instead of reviving his hopes, seemed to ring in his ears like the last knell of despair. He replied, " That is just what my wife said, that it would be *months,* and we have only one month more ; that gone, and the ·

season will be too far advanced to travel in Syria. My wife and child would perish here from hunger and cold before then." He showed me their scanty wardrobe, among which was some covering that they had obtained from the Sisters of Charity.

He told me that he had applied to many convents, and that several religious had called, but only one had ascended the stairs and had seen his wife, the others had been frightened away by the woman in the lodge, who was determined to harass him in every way in order to force him to leave her house. It was only people who came to dun him and torment him that the landlady would encourage to call on him.

He gave me the names of some prominent men whom he knew in Paris, and showed me letters from them. It was these very gentlemen who had encouraged him to come and demand his pay. They had formerly been his friends and his guests, but they now refused to give him a cent, or even to recognise him, since they found him penniless and in disgrace with the executive. I took their addresses. He told me that all these gentlemen had called on the minister to promote his claim, but had all signally failed, so that there was no hope from them from the Government; that his wife had been constantly praying that God would send them some generous soul who would give them the means to return to Syria.

Said I, "You do not imagine that anybody will give you money enough to take you back to Syria? It would cost thousands and thousands of francs to pay for three persons." I saw that he hoped and expected that I would give him the money. But since I had witnessed so much poverty and distress, I had learned too well the value of a few thousand francs, to even think of lavishing such a sum on one family, when I knew that the same amount would relieve the miseries of fifty.

He implored me until I got provoked at his assurance. My maid joined in my displeasure, and finally, with an impatient gesture, she seized the basket, and said we should hurry home or we would be locked out, as the half-past ten o'clock bell had just rung.

I told Giustini to throw all his papers into the basket, which he instantly did, all but the list of accusations. Said I, "I must have that too," for it was the paper that I intended to read first. He reluctantly handed it to me, declaring that he was innocent of every one of the charges made against him. I took the paper and put it in my bosom. Turning to bid his wife good night, I saw her sitting in the same position in which I had found her, saying her beads, with her eye steadfastly fixed on the locks of hair. I told her husband not to disturb her, and I hurried out of the room.

We had just time to reach the Abbey when the clock struck eleven. My maid was furious at the presumption of the man, but his wife she thought was a saint. She would scold when she spoke of the man, and weep when she spoke of his wife.

For years I had a habit of sitting before the glass just before going to bed, to make a sort of meditation on what I had passed through during the day, and at the same time prepare my programme for the morrow.

In the Abbaye aux Bois this looking-glass meditation took place in my toilet room, out of which was a long narrow corridor which led to my bedroom.

My bedroom resembled an oratory more than a sleeping-room. I had arranged it in light-blue silk and gold. On a pedestal in front of a mirror was a beautiful statuette of the Immaculate Virgin and an hour-glass, opposite which hung a portrait of our Lord. The window opened on a small court-yard in the interior of the Abbey, near a little chapel, where the children were wont to meet for their devotions, sometimes early in the morning, but oftener late in the afternoon.

One afternoon I was in this room, deliberating what use I should make of it, intending to make of it a store-room, when I was surprised by hearing strains of music sung by infant voices. I opened the window and found that it was the children in the Abbey singing the "AVE MARIA." I got on my knees and joined them in spirit. We were separated by thick walls, and as the deadened tones reached me they had the same effect as music heard from a distance.

The window of this little room looked out on dingy moss-covered walls. I glanced upward: the sky that day, which was blue and serene, spread itself like a celestial canopy over their tops; and while watching the motions of some swallows that were fluttering around the eaves over the chapel, as though they too were drawn by the music, I decided to make it my sleeping-room. I had tried to arrange it so as to reflect the impression that the old walls, the blue sky, the Ave Maria, and the swallows twittering about the eaves, had made on my mind. I had the ceiling tinted a delicate blue, and studded with stars, with a cornice of dark mazarine blue and gold. I looked on this room as a hallowed spot, and never entered except to sleep or to listen to the children singing, or to pray.

If I chanced to hear a strain of music from that side of the Abbey I would leave everything—company—all— no matter who

was with me, to fly to this little room to hear the children sing
the vesper hymns. If I happened to be alone I would turn over
the hour-glass, and would oftentimes pray and meditate there
until its sands had run through, and never could I pray anywhere else as well as I could pray there.

The last thing my maid did every night before leaving me
was to light a candle in this little chamber. As soon as I had
finished making my midnight meditation before the glass I
would put out the light, and then grope my way through the
narrow corridor to my bedroom. The moment I entered it,
coming suddenly out of the dark, and finding myself in this
subdued blue light, I had always a feeling that the Blessed
Virgin and God were there,—the Blessed Virgin to intercede for
me, and God to answer her prayers.

The evening that I passed with the Giustinis, as soon as I
was alone, I could only think of the man and his daring to hope
that I might give him money enough to return to Syria. My
maid, too, had excited me more against him than I otherwise
would have been, for she had remarked all his gestures and his
insinuations, many of which had escaped me on account of the
close attention I paid to his wife, for whom alone I felt any
sympathy.

Just as I was in the act of extinguishing the light I saw a
paper lying on the floor ; I stooped in the dark, and felt for it
until I found it. I then groped my way through the narrow
corridor into my bedroom. The moment I entered it I forgot
all about the paper I had in my hand, and instantly dropped on
my knees, and offered up my wonted ejaculations : " O, Saviour,
may I love Thee more ? and wilt Thou love me more ? May I
love Laferrière less ? but make him love me more !"

I continued to pray for several minutes. As I was about to
put out the light, I recollected the paper I had in my hand,
which I at once recognised as the one containing the charges
against Giustini. I opened it and read it through, and when I
came to the last words: "It is for these offences, and still
greater, that you have been recalled," &c., I looked up at the
statue of the Blessed Virgin and began talking to her as though
she were really present.

Said I : "I believe he is guilty of every one of the charges,
and yet he dares to imagine that I will pay for his misdeeds,
and give him money enough to go back to Syria !" and I continued to abuse him as hard as I could, until I happened to
notice the red marks on the back of my left hand which his
wife's chaplet had made.

R

I at once recollected my vow, and the whole scene came vividly before me. I was so moved that I threw my arms around the statue of the Blessed Virgin, kissed her feet, and the tears gushed from my eyes while I repeated my vow. "Yes, mother, I do promise you that I will never abandon that Syrian mother and her unborn babe. I will make the Government send them home;" and as I renewed my vow, I felt that the Blessed Virgin demanded it of me.

I had scarcely renewed it when my eyes fell again on the paper which contained those fatal accusations which seemed to instantly bury all my hopes of success. But the moment my eyes fell again on the marks on my hand, all my courage returned; I felt that the Blessed Virgin had written there, with this sorrowful mother's chaplet a promise to assist me.

The thought filled me with joy. I reached out my left hand towards the statue, while in my right I held up the paper, and shook it with a triumphant air as I spoke to it: "We shall see who is the stronger, the inflexible, unerring Meurand, old head of the Consulate Department, or the Blessed Virgin!"

I then threw the paper on the floor, stamped on it with my foot, and continued talking to the Blessed Virgin, as though she were actually present. I was as happy as I could be, for every time I looked at my hand it seemed as though I saw the promise of the Blessed Virgin written there. I then turned lovingly towards the portrait of our Lord, and said to Him: "I know Thou canst not refuse Thy mother anything: I pray Thee listen to her when she intercedes for that afflicted mother and her unborn babe."

That night I slept peacefully, until I was awakened by the children in the Abbey singing a morning hymn to the Blessed Virgin, for it was Saturday. I was so happy that I repeated over again and again to myself, "How sweet it is to be a Christian!" and as my eyes chanced to fall on the portrait of our Lord, I said: "Oh, I hope it is all true! I hope it is not all an illusion." The tears started to my eyes at the thought of this illusion vanishing like the rest with which my life had been filled, and I wept at the dread of ever being thrown again on myself, as I was before I used to invoke the names of Jesus and Mary.

While I lay there weeping, I recollected that I had promised to go to the hospital that morning, to visit a sick English girl. I instantly arose, kissed the feet of the statue of the Blessed Virgin, and implored her not to forget her promise. I looked at my hand, but the marks had disappeared. I was disappointed in not seeing them, but I instantly took hope and said : " They have left my hand, mother, mother, but I feel that thou hast written them in my heart. I will not forget my vow, neither will I shrink from any obstacle that may come in the way of my keeping it."

CHAPTER LXV.

CALLED TO TASK BY COMMON SENSE.

My Client's Character—Faith in Bureaucracy—The Words of my Master—Advice thrown away.

As soon as I reached the hospital, I heard that the English girl in whom I took an interest had just given premature birth to a child, and the doctors told me that in about ten days she would be able to take possession of an attic room I had succeeded in obtaining for her.

This young Englishwoman was about twenty-six years old, and highly accomplished. She spoke several languages, played the organ, and could design. She told me that her husband had joined the troops in Spain and had been killed. She gave her name as Eliza Amore. She had fallen crossing a street; a carriage had run over her right hand and had completely crushed it, and she had been brought to the hospital for treatment. I used to bring her books, and would spend much of the time I passed at the hospital with her; for she appeared to be in every respect a perfect lady, and I pitied her.

This morning I remained with her only a short time. I hastened back to the Abbey, went to the chapel, and laid the Giustini case before our Lady of all Help, *Notre Dame de tout aide.* From there I made my usual visit to the Pantheon, and as I crossed the Luxemburg Garden I lingered longer than usual round St. Geneviève's statue, which is of colossal size, and is placed near the road which leads directly to the Pantheon. I fervently implored her to intercede for me, and to inspire me what to do. On my way I bought some flowers, and when I reached the Pantheon, I laid them at the foot of St. Genevieve's altar. While invoking the Saint to pray for me, I felt inspired as to the course I ought to pursue. As soon as the idea struck me, I thanked the Saint and hastened back to the Abbey.

When I reached home, I ordered the carriage and started out to see the gentlemen who Giustini told me had been formerly his friends and his guests. I took the basket of papers with me in the carriage, and in order not to lose any time, I examined

as many of them as I could on the way. I found every gentleman I called on at home, and they all gave the same account of
Giustini.   That he was a generous-hearted, reckless, extravagant
fellow, who only cared for money to spend ; one of that kind of
men who take more pleasure in giving entertainments and alms
than in paying their debts.   That he was unscrupulous in his
dealings, but the very sum which he might have wrenched from
some miserable being who had been so unfortunate as to fall into
his power, he would give away an hour afterwards to the first
one who happened to call on him in distress ; and he was deluded
enough to believe that he would always find plenty of men in the
world like himself, who would as readily help him out of his
troubles as he had always helped others.   But they all spoke
well of his wife, called her an angel of goodness and devotion,
who was incapable of seeing any fault in her husband.

These gentlemen had done all they could to influence the
Government in Giustini's favour, and had only abandoned him
when they saw that his case was entirely hopeless, which was
easy indeed to see from the first; for even had no charges
been made against him, Meurand declared that he had never
been properly delegated, for he had never received an exequatur.

I told them all that I had a hope the Government would be
induced to send him and his to Syria, on account of his family,
who were in a most pitiable state.   They smiled when I spoke,
as though they were listening to some charitable enthusiast
who was incapable of understanding how affairs of State were
conducted in France.   Only one of them spoke plainly to me,
for the others seemed loth to undeceive me.   They admired my
generous efforts, and preferred that some one else besides themselves should strip me of my illusions.   But one of them was a
plain, blunt man, who thought the best kindness he could do
me was to tell me the truth.   He enumerated a dozen infallible
reasons why the Government would not act, and to do it out of
charity was impossible, as they were foreigners, and there were
so many disabled French soldiers who were in need of the charity
of the State.   When he saw that his words did not discourage
me in the least, but on the contrary, the more desperate he
represented my case to be, the more hopeful I became, he grew
impatient, and said that I ought to have sense enough to abide
by his long experience, and not to discredit everything he said.

"Oh," I replied, "who would use his good sense in such a
case ? You have to rely on something better than that."
"Well," he responded, "I don't know of anything better,"
" I do," I replied, "and that is Faith. I am going to persevere

through Faith. I pray to God to assist me, sir, and I believe that He will take pity on this poor family, and make the Government send them home."

With upraised hands and eyes, he said : " My dear good lady, it is no use to pray to God to grant you anything that Meurand has set his signature against. God can do nothing for you."

" What ? " said I, " do you think Meurand is more powerful than God Almighty ? " " Yes," he replied, " in the Consulate Department, I do : they have order there."

Said I : " God has order too ; and one infallible order of His divine providence is that He will never abandon those who put their trust in Him. Madame Giustini relies on God alone : she prays to Him from morning until night, and from night till morning. Do you mean to say that God is going to abandon her ? "

" *Mon Dieu*, Madam ! " he replied, more impatiently than ever. I see it is of no use to try to advise a woman ; for you can never convince her of anything when she has once made up her mind. I assure you that you will never obtain anything from the Government, and that you need not expect that God will interfere and upset the natural order of things, just to oblige Madame Giustini."

" *Nous verrons*," said I, " *nous verrons* (we shall see, we shall see). I once knew a good old bishop, who taught me that God, who created all things, was the Master of all things, and that all natural order was controlled by His divine will. I believed the bishop, and I could not adore the Supreme Being unless I believed He was all-powerful. Now do you blame me for believing the bishop in preference to you ? "

He laughed, and then replied : " I cannot blame you for that ; but it is a pity that he did not teach you at the same time to listen to reason." " He did," I replied, " but only to that reason which is guided by Faith." " That is right," said he ; " let Faith guide reason, but not make reason her slave as you are doing."

" But," said I, " the bishop told me too that reason must be subservient to Faith as well as guided by it." " Yes, my dear lady," he replied: "but did he not tell you that it required a well-balanced mind to find the just medium, without which reason and Faith would both suffer an overthrow ? " " No, sir, he did not ; he taught me that Faith was adapted to all minds, no matter how stupid, and that there never could be an overthrow so long as we inclined towards Faith; for it was the hand of God that held that side of the balance, and no one was ever lost who ventured into it."

" But don't you suppose he meant that you should understand that God held equally the other side ? "   " No, sir, he did not : on the contrary, the bishop taught me that man, through ignorance and pride, had wrested it out of God's hands, pretending that he knew more about managing it than God; but that God only took care of those in it who submitted to Faith, the rest were at the mercy of pride. He left to every man his free will, and the fact that the majority of mankind preferred to lean upon pride rather than to trust in God, explained why so many were lost."

Said he : " I am sure that this good bishop was a very sensible man ; but did he not find it difficult to convince you of anything ? " Said I: " He told me that my mind was twisted, or was turned upside down, he could not decide which, but he was sure that it was either one or the other." Then the old man laughed more heartily than ever, while I continued : " But if he heard me talking to you in this way, he would have said that it had got straightened out."

" You talk well enough," said he, " and I am astonished that you will not act as wisely as you speak ; but I believe that is the common defect of your sex. Still, you should try and raise yourself above their defects, as God has gifted you with a capacity of comprehending and appreciating truths that very few women ever take an interest in."

The old man saw that I was true to the instincts of my sex ; for the moment he paid me such a compliment I did not attempt to conceal the pleasure it gave me ; and he at once turned the conversation on the object of my visit, thinking, perhaps, a little flattery would do more than the soundest reasoning, to induce me to follow his advice. So he continued, " I hope you will abandon your intention of soliciting the Government for a thing when you are sure to meet with a dead failure. I tell you this for your good, so that you will not pass weeks and weeks in useless efforts, which will be sure to end in disappointment, and that you may at once resort to some other means to try to raise the money to send them back, if you are determined to do so."

" No," I replied, " the Government must do it, for if I exhaust the benevolence of my friends for the Giustinis, it will be taking away just so much from other poor people, in whom I am equally interested. It will cost a large sum to send them home, and I will make the Government pay it. I am obliged to, I made a vow to that effect, and I know that God expects me to keep it. I dare not try to shift out of it, when I know that God and the Blessed Virgin will assist me in all my efforts to aid this poor woman."

This time he vainly tried to conceal his impatience, as he replied, " Now you show your want of sense again. Do not think that God is going to help you to do impossibilities."

Said I, " There is no impossibility about it. The Government has *got to do it!* If I am a Christian I am going to be a Christian, and I am going to give religion a good fair trial. I do not believe in doing things by halves. If the Bible is the Word of God, whatever we undertake for His glory becomes possible, when we have His word to sustain us; for He has promised never to abandon those who put their trust in Him. I feel that He sent me to that woman in answer to her prayers. I made a vow, in the name of His Mother, never to abandon them, until the Government sends them home; and I never intend to, and if I do, you may conclude that I have become a pagan."

" Well," said he, " I am afraid you will become one, if your faith as a Christian depends upon the Government sending the Giustinis back to Syria." Said I, " If I succeed, will you give Giustini as much as his other friends will? for they have all promised me that, if I made the Government send him home, they would give him something, so that he would not arrive there destitute."

" Certainly, certainly I will," he jocosely replied; " they would promise you anything too; for they all know, as well as I do, that if their charity depends on that, you will never be able to make a claim upon it." " We shall see," said I, " and I will not say *adieu*, but *au revoir, et à bientôt.*"

———

CHAPTER LXVI.

THE MAN WHO ENVIED HIS VALET.

I Invoke the Viscount's Aid—An Official Snubbing—Regrets—Regrets regretted.

I THEN drove to the Tuileries, and as I entered I saw Laferrière's carriage waiting for him at his door. I could not help exclaiming, " Surely God is with me!" for in a moment more he might have been gone. I told him my adventure of the preceding night, which deeply interested him, and he volunteered to drive over at once to the Minister of Foreign Affairs, and make them take some action in the matter. I spurred him to it, by telling him it would be a pretty thing for the hostile press to get hold of, that a man who had been acting as Consul for eleven years for the Empire had been permitted to die of starvation within gunshot of the Tuileries.

I was not frank with Laferrière. I merely told him that the man was very *distingué* in appearance, that was all I said about *him;* but I dwelt long on the piety and angelic sweetness of his wife, and told him of the scene when I had made my vow. I also repeated to him all that the notable men I had just seen had said about the lady. He hurried off to the Department. It was agreed between us when we separated that he would come and dine with me and let me know the result.

As soon as I got home I gave instructions that I would receive only my particular friends until I got this affair off my mind. I locked myself up in the library, and passed the rest of the day carefully examining every paper, but discovered nothing that could serve me in the least.

I was aroused from my occupation, by hearing Laferrière enter the ante-chamber, and ask for me in a most excited tone. I ran to unlock the door, for I was dying with impatience to know the result. He pushed by me without saying a word, pretending not to see me. His face was livid with rage. He threw himself into an arm-chair, and exclaimed; " This is just what every man deserves who allows himself to be governed by a woman ! "

It was the first time I had ever seen him angry, and I did not for an instant suppose that he could be angry with me: I approached him as I was wont to do, but he motioned me from him by a gesture of his hand. That frightened me so that I forgot all about the Giustinis. He continued to scold me for several minutes, before he made the slightest explanation. At last he told me what had happened since we parted.

He had called at the Minister's, and had seen Meurand. That worthy official had given the dark side of the Giustini case, for he only spoke about the husband. Laferrière, not accustomed to be refused, told him that something *must* be done. Meurand, as little accustomed to hear such a word as Laferrière was to be denied, haughtily asked him to explain to him the reason why the Consulate Department *must* do something for a foreign family, which had no claims upon it.

Laferrière then began relating to him the miseries I had just described, when Meurand interrupted him in the most abrupt manner, and told him that that did not concern his department, and referred him to the *Bureau of Public Charity*, after which he bowed him most unceremoniously out of the room.

Laferrière loaded Meurand with abuse for having dared to treat him so uncivilly. He knew that if it had been the Minister himself, he would have been received like a prince ; for Laferrière saw the Emperor every morning at eleven o'clock, and

he had it often in his power to crush a man or to make him,
with a single word. After I found out the cause of his displeasure, I felt indignant that he should scold me, just because
Meurand had treated him in an off-hand way. He finally wound
up by saying, that Meurand had treated him as though he were
his valet. Said I: "That is just what you wanted : you are
always envying your valet, because you are so bored with attentions. Hereafter perhaps you will be more satisfied with your
lot, and stop sighing to exchange places with your servants, as
Meurand has just proved to you that you have no taste for
being treated like one."

I expected a retort ; but he closed his eyes as though he had
not heard me, and remained perfectly silent for about fifteen
minutes. I thought he was angry, and I was determined to be
as angry as he was ; but, to my surprise, when he opened his
eyes, he offered me his hand, and in one of the gentlest tones
that I had ever heard him speak in, he said to me: "You are
right, your lesson is a good one : we ought not to wish to descend
to positions that we have not the virtues to fill."

I would have given anything then to have recalled my words.
I implored his forgiveness. "No, no," he replied, "I must ask
yours : for I can never forgive myself for having spoken to you
in this way, when you came to me, in the simplicity of your
heart, to implore my protection for that poor woman. But your
story moved me so. I did wrong and was wholly to blame. I
should have informed myself about the antecedents of the man
before I went to the Department ; for you could only see his
distress. How could I expect you to have known the man's
transgressions ? Meurand was right after all. I was too hasty.
He is independent ; he knows that he will never be removed : he
does not fear or care for anybody when he knows that he does his
duty. I wish the empire was made up of such men ; the Government would be a little more secure. But tell me, did I not hear
you say that Monsieur Chatry de la Fosse and others who knew
Giustini in Syria spoke well of him ?" Said I: "I said they
spoke well of his wife." I began to feel uneasy, for I felt that I
was all to blame, but I did not have the courage to confess it.

We sat down to dine. Whenever the valet left the room
Laferrière would beg me to forgive him, and expressed the greatest
contrition for having spoken to me so rudely. After dinner,
I told my maid to take a bundle of clothes around to the
Giustinis. Laferrière pulled a fifty-franc bill from his vest-
pocket, handed it to her, and she supposed for a second that it
was for herself ; she smiled, and thanked him most graciously as

she took it from his hand. But when he added: "Give it to the poor family," she expressed her disappointment by giving me a look of regret, and saying : "*C'est presque dommage donc d'encourager ce filou* (it is almost a pity to thus encourage the scamp)," filled with vexation, she hurried out of the room.

Laferrière started up and threw me a furious glance. I turned scarlet, which made him still more indignant, for he judged by my confusion the depth of my guilt. "What," said he, "you knew that the man was a rogue, and you have never acknowledged a word! You are incorrigible! and I take the liberty of withdrawing all my excuses, for I only said to you just what you deserved!" His indignation only increased when I tried to excuse myself by saying that he started off so quickly that he did not give me a chance to tell him what I thought of the man. He told me that he was deeply wounded, that I should have treated him with more confidence ; and he begged of me never to mention the affair to him again, he wanted to forget it.

CHAPTER LXVII.

General Dix—An Ambassador's Sympathy—The Minister won over.

THAT night the moment I entered my room, I recollected my vow, and instantly fell on my knees and began to weep; for I felt that I merited every reproach which Laferrière had given me, and by my want of sincerity I had lost his powerful aid. I begged God to forgive me, and I excused myself to our Lord for my want of sincerity by alleging that I had always been deceived by the men, and as I had never been able to succeed with them unless I deceived them too, I begged him not to abandon me, just because I had lost Laferrière's help in this affair, but to forgive me, and to send me some one else in his place.

The next morning was Sunday, and it was hardly daybreak when I started to the church to hear Mass. From the church I went to the hospital, where I was met by one of the Sisters. As I was entering the large hall, she told me that the young Englishwoman had puerperal fever, and could live but a few days. I went to her bedside. She knew that she was going to die. How that knowledge changes us ! *Now* she spoke the truth. She told me that she had never been married, but was the victim of her own waywardness and the cruel treatment of her relatives. She attributed all her perversity to her mania for novel-reading.

She had been addicted to it from childhood, and had grown up under its influence. It had given her a taste for adventure. Her parents, who were rigid Protestants, had sent her to a Protestant boarding-school in Brussels, to give her greater facilities for learning German. She had there formed an intimacy with one of the young ladies, to whose house she went every Saturday night to remain until Monday. This young lady had several brothers, and it was one of these brothers who had introduced her to a young Brazilian named Amore. She eloped with this fellow, who abandoned her two years afterwards. She then returned to her home in England; but her parents and her younger sisters never forgave her fault, and were constantly reproaching her with it. One night, in a fit of despair, she robbed her mother of all her jewellery, even to the diamond engagement-ring given to her by her father, and came to Paris, where she led an abandoned life. She was intoxicated the day she had fallen in the street, and had her hand injured.

The Sister handed me some letters which belonged to the poor victim of her own folly and man's licentiousness. The dying girl implored me to write to her parents, and tell them to come to her. She wanted to hear them say that they forgave her, before she died. She would constantly exclaim: "Oh, my mother! I have killed my mother! I have broken her heart!" The Sister who attended her, although long accustomed to harrowing scenes, could not restrain her tears. She knelt down beside her and said a prayer aloud, which the girl repeated after her. That made me weep, for it brought back a similar scene in my life. The Sister then began another prayer with which I was not familiar. The dying girl repeated it after her. The Sister stopped for a moment, for she was choked with tears, and to our surprise the girl continued, and finished the prayer alone.

The Sister and I looked at each other in astonishment, without saying a word. As soon as she could control her feelings, the Sister asked the girl if she had ever been a Catholic. She shook her head, and said: "No; but my lover was; he with whom I eloped, taught me that prayer." She then began to reproach herself for not having listened to him, for he had only abandoned her on account of her viciousness. She had taken to drink, to gambling, and was unfaithful to him.

She implored me to bury her, in case her parents failed to come and claim her body: for in a pauper's hospital a dread thought hangs over all who have no friends to bury them, that their bodies will come under the medical students' dissecting-knife.

The Sister had sent for a priest, for the girl wished to be baptised; and as I left her bedside, the last words I heard her say were—"O God, have mercy on my soul! forgive me my sins, forgive me my sins, for Jesus' sake."

Whenever she addressed those who were lying around her, she would say to them: "It is the reading of bad books that brought me here. Oh, never read them, or let your children read them."

I promised the Sister, as she accompanied me to the door, that I would call again in the afternoon. When I got to the Abbey, my maid met me and told me that there was a gentleman waiting for me in the library. I scolded her for having let any one in; for I wanted the whole day to myself. When I entered the library, I found General Dix.

He made an apology for having called on Sunday, and so early in the day; but he said that whenever he had visited me he had always found me run down with visitors, that he had never had an opportunity to speak to me, and he wanted to become better acquainted with a lady whom half of the world was praising and the other half abusing. I told him that he had chosen a bad moment to judge me, for I was not myself that morning, I was so oppressed with grief; and I related to him the scene I had just witnessed at Neckar Hospital. While I was speaking, I recollected the letters I had in my pocket belonging to the dying girl. I took them, and making two piles of them; I handed one to the General, and the other I kept myself, and we both began perusing them. We had not read over two or three, before I observed that the General was deeply moved. The letters read nearly all alike; they were either from her father or her sisters, who had sent her remittances from time to time. They were all filled with reproaches for her dissolute conduct.

The last one she had received was from her father; it was in answer to one she had written him with her left hand, telling him of her accident, and giving her address at the hospital. The father's answer to this letter was, that he hoped it would be a good lesson to her. There was not one pitying word in it; but he said that he would write to Mr. Blount the banker, to provide her with means. He did write to Mr. Blount; but he failed to say anything about his daughter's accident, or even that she was in a hospital. She wrote to Mr. Blount with her left hand, and sent the doorkeeper of the hospital to get the money. But the teller refused to believe the messenger's story, and paid no attention to it, as he suspected it was a fraud.

I learned all this when it was too late! for the girl had wished to conceal from me her history, and she had feared to send me to Mr. Blount's lest they should tell me all about her: for they had got her out of several scrapes, and she was afraid that, if I knew that she was a disreputable woman, I would abandon her.

I was surprised to see General Dix so deeply affected at what I had told him. I was so accustomed to deal with bronzed hearts that I could not help saying to him: "Why, General, what a tender-hearted man you are!" "Oh," said he, "I think this is dreadful. It is evident from these letters, that the girl belongs to a cultivated and respectable family." He continued to remark how much suffering and misery there is in the world, of which those who live in their comfortable homes have no knowledge or conception.

General Dix was the last man in the world that I suspected to be capable of expressing so much real feeling. As he handed me back the letters, he remarked that he did not wonder there were plenty of good people ready to defend me, if that was the way I passed my time. As he spoke, he looked me full in the face, and I saw that his eyes were moistened, this poor girl's story had so affected him. I knew then that he really was in earnest, and not making believe, that he had felt every word he expressed; and instantly the thought struck me, that I would make use of him to help me out of the Giustini affair.

As he rose to leave, I begged him to remain a little longer, and listen to the misfortunes of a poor family, who resided only a few doors from the Abbey, and in whom I was deeply interested. I told him all about the *woman*, showed him some letters from prominent men, which had been addressed to her husband, and I soon saw that my second story was affecting him as much as the first. At last I asked him abruptly if his relations were good with the Marquis de Moustier, Minister of Foreign Affairs.

He replied that he was on excellent terms with the Foreign Department. "Then," said I, "you must give me a letter to him, and request him to give me an audience." The General quickly retorted: "Why, you are in with all that class: you don't need a letter from me. I only know him officially; get some of your friends to put you in relation with him."

I pretended to be piqued and wounded that he should refer me to them, and told him that it placed an American lady in a much better position to be recommended by the representative of her country than by foreigners, and that the Marquis would pay much more attention to a letter of introduction from him than he would to one from any one else.

The General said that I was right, and I then gently referred

to the trouble I had had, to conquer the prejudices of his own
family. He excused himself for having hesitated; for I
insinuated perhaps that that was his reason for having refused;
but he assured me that it was not, for both he and Mrs. Dix were
convinced that the world did me great injustice, and they both
felt the highest esteem and regard for me. Said I: "I will
measure yours by the strength of your letter to Moustier." He
laughed, as he bade me good-bye, and told me that he would
write a good strong one, and that I should receive it the following day.

The moment the General left, I rushed into my bed-room, and
threw myself on my knees before the statue of the Blessed
Virgin, and said to her: "I know that you must have brought
General Dix here this morning, I am sure of it;" and I thanked
her with all my heart. Having written to the mother of the
dying girl, and told her to come on at once, if she wished to see
her alive, I started for the hospital, and found that the girl was
dead, and that her body was already removed to the amphi-
theatre. I made arrangements with the director in regard to
the body. He promised that it should be kept in the amphi-
theatre until Thursday morning, which was a great favour, but
he granted it to me, as I wished to give her family time to arrive. I made every arrangement for the burial, in case none of
her family should come.

CHAPTER LXVII.

CHURCH MICE—HOW THEY NIBBLE AT THEIR NEIGHBOURS' CHARACTERS—
IS THERE ANY HOPE FOR THEM?

A Minister always "out"—The Minister's Merits—The humility of Charity
—A Lady Preacher and Confessor—Self-satisfied Virtue.

MONDAY morning, the first thing I did was to buy some
flowers to place on St. Geneviève's altar. In the vestibule of the
Pantheon I met a lady acquaintance who devoted nearly all her
time to good works. I told her that I had come to implore the
Blessed Virgin and St. Geneviève to intercede in favour of a
destitute family. While I was speaking she was looking at the
flowers, and at last said to me: "Did you just buy them?"
"Yes," I answered, "as an offering to St. Geneviève, who is so
good to me; she obtains for me whatever I ask." She continued: "Do you not think it would be more pleasing to God,
to give the money that you paid for those flowers to the poor to
buy bread?"

I was confounded for a moment at such an unexpected rebuke, and felt that I had done wrong. The lady kept on talking and sermonising to me. While she was speaking, instead of listening to what she said, I fell to thinking how I had fallen into such a foolish habit. I was so blind to my own defects, and so puffed up with self-conceit, that whenever I committed a fault I always sought to excuse myself by throwing the blame either on God Himself or on some one else. I soon recollected that it was from Madame Xavier that I had got my devotion of making sacrifices to decorate the altars of our Lord. But I loved Madame Xavier too much to be easily persuaded that she could ever have taught me to do wrong, and I was determined to defend her.

After my friend had finished, I said to her: "Have you not heard it said, that the Lord rewards you a hundredfold for everything you give Him?" She readily nodded an assent. "Well," I replied, "I have a desperate case on hand. Ten francs is what I paid for these flowers, and it is not a fraction compared to the sum I am obliged to have in order to succeed. I am doing all I can to induce God to help me, and every flower I buy for His altars I charge to His account, and beg Him to pay it as soon as possible to this poor family whom I am trying to serve."

"Indeed," replied the woman, "you have more faith than I." "Well," I answered, "it is a virtue, is it not?" "Certainly," she answered. "Who is your director?" "Oh," said I, "director to the dogs! You don't suppose that I am going to let a priest rule over me? I change about every week. I learned all I know about religion at St. Mandé." The woman was so shocked that she fairly shrank from me. At last she said: "Your faith is beautiful: it is a precious gift; but you will soon lose it if you go on this way." "What!" I exclaimed, "offering flowers to our Lord!" "No, no," replied the woman; "but changing your director every week." "Oh," said I, "that means once a month perhaps,—every time he refuses to absolve me. I direct myself, I confess my sins, and am always praying to God to watch over me and direct me." She replied: "That is right to pray always to Him; but we should be guided by Him, through the successors of His apostles." We then separated. I could not forget her last words. I thought they were well spoken; but I did not believe her.

When I got home I found General Dix's letter on my table. It was a splendid one. I had just time to read it when Laferrière came. He was kind to me and regretted his irritability of Saturday evening. I was nervous, because I did not dare to make use of General Dix's letter, without asking his permission.

For it would have been a bold thing for me to go to make the acquaintance of the Marquis de Moustier without the Viscount's knowledge. I disliked, too, to bring up the Giustini affair, as it would remind him of our quarrel of Saturday.

I began to relate to him the conversation that had taken place that morning between the pious lady and myself. He interrupted me before I finished, and said: "You are ruined if you get one of those women against you." "Why?" said I; "they are saints, they give all their money and time to the poor." "Yes," he replied: "but these women know not how to forgive. The majority of them are so puffed up with their good works, that to see them and to hear them you can readily believe that they feel they are honouring God by serving Him. I do not like the idea of your becoming so intimate with these devotees of the Faubourg. Everything will go on well so long as you consent to contract yourself to the narrow gauge of their minds, and you are willing to let yourself be ruled by them. But undertake to resist them, and show your native independence by daring to innovate upon their ideas of orthodoxy, and you might as well have so many harpies let loose upon you; they will tear you to pieces, and will at once ostracise you."

"How you frighten me!" I exclaimed. "Why, they are all so pious and charitable!" He interrupted me again: "Not a bit of it; they are pious and benevolent, but they have not one particle of charity. You will find it out if you happen once to incur their censure. They are as intolerant as so many mongrel tyrants, and particularly towards their own sex, if they happen to be younger and more prepossessing than themselves." I got a little footstool and sat down on it close to him. Said he: "I know, *chère enfant*, that you have got some favour to ask of me. Why are you afraid to speak? All I ask of you is to be frank and ingenuous, and never conceal anything from me. Why do you hesitate?" "Oh," said I, "that poor family! And there is only one month more."

He frowned, but I continued, "What I wish is your permission to advocate their cause myself before the Government." "My goodness!" he replied, "if that is all you want I grant you it with all my heart; but if you appeal to the Emperor he will refer you to the Minister, who is never at home; and if you succeed in passing the antechamber of the ministerial mansion you will find yourself in the presence of His Impertinence Monsieur Meurand. I ought to encourage you to try it, out of revenge for the scrape you got me into. After you have had one short interview with Meurand you will be willing, I think, to drop the Syrian scamp, and consign him and his family to the care of Divine Providence." Said I, "I feel that Providence led me to their door, and calls upon me to protect them, and all I ask of you is to give me full liberty to act." "My gracious, child! do whatever you can ; don't think because I happened to speak roughly to you that I am suddenly transformed into a brute." "But," said I, "I shall not go near Meurand. I am not such a fool as that. I shall *go* directly to the Minister." "Why," he replied, " *c'est le ministre introuvable* (he is the Minister that can never be found), that is his cognomen all over France. He is always out to everybody. He has never done an hour's work since he has been in office. A gentleman told me that he was closeted with him one morning in regard to a personal matter, that they conversed in the Minister's private office. This gentleman wished to make a note of their agreement, when, lo and behold! there was not an inkstand or a pen to be found !"

" Nevertheless," said I, " I think I shall be able to find him;" and I then ventured to pull out General Dix's letter. "Well, well!" he exclaimed, " you are a true daughter of Eve ; for it is only when a woman has decided to do a thing, and has got all the preliminaries prepared to put it into execution, that she ever comes and asks permission." It was easy enough to see that he was anything but pleased. But all was right the moment I told him that I had not seen him since I had seen General Dix, and that I had not the slightest intention of making use of the letter without his consent.

I translated to him the General's letter. As soon as I had finished he remarked, "I suppose you told the General the woman's side of the story, as you did me." " Oh," said I, " you know you are always scolding me for talking too much ; so I was discreet when I spoke to him of the man." " Ah!" he exclaimed, "we poor men ! But it is a wonder to me that you did not induce the General to go and ask the Minister to send this family back to Syria, as a national favour to the American Republic. For they have just as much claim on the United States as they have upon France."

After having a good laugh he told me that there was not the slightest danger of my ever seeing Moustier; that I would probably receive an answer that the Minister had gone to his château, and if the matter was urgent to please make it known to his secretary. He then threw out a few hints in regard to Moustier : that the Emperor had nominated him just because he belonged to the old nobility, as he desired to conciliate them as much as he could, but that Moustier liked to enjoy himself; and he began relating to me his gallantries. Thought I to myself, I am glad to be aware of all this, as it gives me an idea how to manage him.

Laferrière wished me to send the letter at once, but I told him that I had not my case prepared yet, and I pointed to a file of papers that I was going to examine before I could decide what tactics to adopt in order to succeed. "What!" said he, " do you condemn yourself to wade through all those?" I then showed him another pile, which I had already finished. "Well," he said, "this is real charity." I had refused to go to the opera, as I wished to employ the evening examining the papers.

I worked Monday evening until midnight. The next morning I started early for the Pantheon, more from a spirit of independence and opposition than from devotion. I bought a beautiful bouquet, hoping to meet my lady friend, and show her that I felt perfectly independent of her, and was going to do as I pleased, and was not going to be ruled by a priest, much less by a woman.

I reached the Pantheon without seeing her; but as soon as I got close to the altar what did I behold? A beautiful bouquet of fresh flowers, much handsomer than those I held in my hand. The whole sanctuary was filled with their fragrance. Instead of being rejoiced to see such a beautiful offering, which graced the altar and perfumed the air, the sight made me sad; for I felt that I had a rival, and I was ready to weep.

When I rose from my knees, and was ready to go, I saw the lady I had hoped to meet on my way, and I instantly suspected that it was she who had bought the flowers, which suspicion, as it crossed my mind, pleased and provoked me at the same time.

She rose and came towards me, as though she had been waiting to speak to me. I asked her at once if she had not placed the flowers there. "Yes," she replied, as we descended the steps of the Pantheon; "for you gave me a light, and I have been meditating on it ever since. We rely too much upon ourselves and upon our own efforts; and I believe we would be able to do much more good if we depended less upon ourselves and more upon God." I was so delighted that I embraced her right in the street.

During our conversation, she spoke in such a holy manner of the necessity of suffering, the goodness of God, and the consolation derived from frequenting the sacraments, that I was edified and charmed with her, while I was angry with Laferrière for trying to prejudice me against that class of women.

That afternoon I repeated to Laferrière what the lady had said, and told him that he was mistaken this time, for this lady was a saint; that she not only forgave me for not agreeing with her but actually followed my example. In fact she had advised me like the Bishop.

"Well," said he, "she must be one of the rare exceptions in that class. I have heard that there were exceptions, but I never had the good luck to meet with one of them yet. The most disagreeable, uncharitable and gossipping women I have ever known are those very ladies in the Faubourg, who devote their time and fortune to good works. You will do well to be on your guard, and not judge them all by this good woman. Take my advice and do not permit them to become so familiar as to let them think that they can direct you; for if they once assume that position, you must never venture to go beyond the circle of their restrained ideas of propriety or decorum. If you do, you will soon see that charity is not a part of their profession, for it is a well-known fact that these women do not know how to pardon. And as they live, so they die; for no confessor ever reached their conscience. The reason is, that they believe themselves perfect; and very few priests have the courage to attempt to undeceive them, for they know them too well to risk the danger of incurring their ill-will. The priests are too happy to make use of them, for the benefit of the poor, without daring to go further.

"When you are more enlightened yourself, and have had more experience, you will see that pride and vain-glory are the weapons the devil makes use of, that we may not reap the benefit of our good works. It is easier to root out all our evil passions put together than it is to prevent pride and self-complacency from creeping into our hearts, when we hear ourselves applauded for our virtues. It is not by giving our time and our money alone that we will ever effect the amelioration of the sufferings of mankind; it is by practising humility and charity; and I beg you will pray for me, that I may have a little of both." Said I: "I think you need them a little more than those devotees."

"No," he replied, "I will not admit that: for I do not make a profession of being perfect, and present myself and my ideas as models for others. But when I see a woman holding herself up as a model of Christian piety, who has no humility and less charity, I look upon her as a monstrous abortion, conceived by ignorance, and nourished by pride and self-conceit. I would very much prefer to be condemned to live with a courtesan that flaunts through the streets, rather than with one of them ; for in these two classes of women you will find the two extremes : one does not go farther than the other from the centre of Christian perfection.   And there are more hopes of the latter than the former, because an abandoned woman is often reclaimed, but a false devotee—*Never !* Read Boileau, and he will tell you that, if he should marry a covetous woman, she would not ruin him ; a gambler, she might enrich him ; a blue-stocking, she might instruct him ; a prude, she would not disgrace him ; a shrew, she would exercise his patience ; a coquette, she might wish to please him ; a woman of gallantry, she might go so far as to love him ;—*but a devotee!* What could he expect of a woman who wishes to deceive God and who only deceives herself ? "

Said I : " Under which category of women do you place *me?*"

He replied : " You have the imperfections of the whole eight ; but what redeems you is, that you never try to conceal them." " What !" I exclaimed, " how dare you tell me that I have the imperfections of a false devotee ? " " Why, my child," he replied, " you have pride and self-conceit enough in you to damn two of them."

This repartee, instead of making me laugh as I was wont, struck me to the heart.   I turned pale.   He noticed the change and said : " What is the matter ? I only said it for fun."   " No," I replied, " you did not : for I believe that you spoke the truth ; and perhaps God may refuse to listen to my prayers, and I may never be able to get that family back to Syria.   But I am really in earnest when I pray to God."   " Of course you are," he replied ; " but if I talk to you this way, it is because I am afraid you may be tempted to fall into the extreme I deprecate."

He tried to take back what he said ; but my conscience told me that he had spoken the truth ; for in all my good works I had always felt that my merit, before God and man, ought to increase in proportion as I multiplied them ; and this I acknowledged to him.

Said he : " Do you not suppose that I take interest enough in you, to be able to detect everything that concerns you ? If I have exaggerated in speaking of the defects of these good women, it was only to put you on your guard, that you might avoid the faults of the worst of them ; for I know as well as you do, that there are among them a great many holy souls.   But it requires a solid and long-tried virtue to resist being puffed up with our own self-sufficiency when we see to what an extent the happiness and miseries of others lie in our hands.   I know it by examining my own conscience ; and if I have set you to examining yours to-day, you rendered me the same service a few days ago, when I came to this conclusion, that it was better for me not to long to be a servant until I had the virtues of one."

He took my hand, and, after a pause, continued: "My dear child, I do not say this to wound you; but I have observed with regret the change that has taken place in your character since your conversion." "What!" I replied, "don't you want me to be good? why are you moralising at me all the time unless you want me to practise religion as well as listen to you?"—I suspected that he wanted me to give less of my time and sympathies to the poor.

"You might better ask me," he replied, "why I give you so many good precepts, and at the same time set you such bad example; for I took upon myself as a refutation of that old saying, *C'est dèjà être vertueux que d'aimer la vertu.* (To love virtue is to be already virtuous.) But set me aside, and look to yourself. I do not find that you are half as deserving in the sight of God since you profess to honour and serve Him, as you were before when you declared yourself His enemy, by professing to be an infidel. I looked upon you as more of a Christian then than I ever have since."

I was horrified at this assertion, and tried to withdraw my hand. But he held it in spite of me and said I was not going to get away from him until I had heard him through. Said he: "I suppose this is just the way you do when you go to confession. You bolt the moment the priests begin to expose to you your faults. But I have the advantage of them; for I shall hold on to you until you have heard me through."

I began to laugh and to look upon the whole thing as a farce, and replied that it was a pity the priests had not the same privilege. He too began laughing, and retorted that they would never be able to get a woman to come to confession if they had. "But," he continued, "I am serious. Since your conversion I have noticed that you are not half as charitable and forgiving as you were before."

"Oh," said I; "then it was because I used to feel so wicked myself that I never dared to retaliate on others for offending me, lest God should retaliate on me for my offences against Him; and I never dared to judge others, when I felt that a severer judgment should be passed on myself."

"There," he replied, "by your own words I condemn you: for that inward sense of your own unworthiness was more pleasing to God than all your good works and actions are now, accompanied as they are by the spirit of self-complacency and

pride. I hardly ever knew you, before you professed to be a
Christian, to say an unkind word against anyone, or to attempt
to avenge an injury, and that to me was your greatest charm :
you subdued me by it, and I used to give myself up entirely to
your influence. But now I have to be on my guard against
you, for fear you will lead me to commit some injustice, just
to gratify your wounded pride."

I did not deny the truth of what he said to me, but tried to
justify myself, by telling him that I could not forgive people
their selfishness, since I saw how much good could be done by
giving more of our time and means to others.

"Yes," said he, "that is just it ; you set yourself up as the
arbitress of other people's actions, instead of humbly thanking
God for having given you a natural disposition to sympathise
with sufferers, which it is impossible for you to restrain. He
may have denied the same blessing to others, and He will only
exact of them a return in proportion to the talents He has given
them."

Said I, "It is true, for when I used to do wrong I felt that I
merited reproach, and I used to forgive everybody, whatever
they might do or say against me ; but now that I am trying to
do right, I hate everybody who dares to attack me."

"Well," he replied, "that is not being a Christian. When
you were an infidel you practised the most essential Christian
virtues ; but now that you are a professed Christian you do just
the contrary ; whereas it is more your duty now to love those
who hate you than it was then. You had much more humility
and charity then than you have now; and charity is all God asks
of us. If you continue to retrograde for the next six months,
as you have during the six past, the result will be that you will
become one of the worst of those disagreeable devotees who
change their adoration from God to themselves, and their hatred
of sin to the hatred of those who refuse to acknowledge their
sanctity. Now I would rather see you a Magdalen, with all her
sins, than one of these ; and I will give you six months more
to become one of them, unless you stop seeking yourself in God
instead of seeking God in yourself."

"You do me more good," I remarked, "when you talk to me,
than any confessor I ever had yet."

"I don't suppose," he answered, "that there was ever one yet
who was able to keep you long enough for you to hear him
through."

"That," said I, "is just what the good lady declared ; so you
see that you and she are alike "

"Alike? No," he replied: "that would be paying her a poor compliment to compare her with me; for by what you tell me, I should judge that she practises what she preaches."

CHAPTER LXVIII.

A GLEAM OF HOPE.

A Discovery—Confidence Rewarded—I write to the Minister—The Answer.

As soon as Laferrière left me I went into my bedroom to pray. In a few seconds I heard the children's voices, and as the strains of the melody which pealed forth the AVE MARIA, reached me, they seemed to awaken my soul to a more steadfast faith than I had ever before experienced. When the music ceased I arose, turned over the hour-glass, and prayed until its sands had run through. I lighted my votive lamp to the Blessed Virgin, which I never lit except on Saturdays. Then I went to work examining Giustini's papers, and worked assiduously until dinner-time. I took a few of them to the table with me, and looked at them during the interval when the waiter was changing the courses, so as not to lose a minute's time.

After dinner I locked myself in, with a prohibition that any one should come near me unless I rang. The clock struck eight. My head ached; I had worked so steadily that I was sure I must have mistaken the number of strokes. I was certain that it must be nine. I looked, but it was only eight. I then turned wearily to resume my task. The clock struck nine. I again rose, feeling so discouraged that I was ready to weep. Again I sat down, took up a paper, opened it, and nearly swooned away with joy. I could not be mistaken, for it resembled a paper that the Executive in Washington had once given to my husband, and which was still in my possession; the paper that I now grasped was Giustini's *exequatur*.

I did not wait to read it. I merely recognised the French official seal and the signature of the Count de Bentivoglio. I rushed into my bedroom, threw myself at the foot of the statue of the Blessed Virgin, and began embracing the very pedestal on which it stood; and by the dim light of my votive lamp I read that paper, which my heart told me was to be the saviour of that wretched family.

I picked up the list of accusations which I had thrown on the floor, and had afterwards kicked under the bed, so as to be perfectly sure that I could not be mistaken. There it was, in black and white, that he had never had an *exequatur* and had never been officially delegated.

The whole truth flashed over me at once how it had been possible for Meurand to make such a mistake. The paper had been issued twelve years previous by the Count de Bentivoglio, who was then Consul at Aleppo, and who had been authorized by the Minister to appoint a consular agent at Aintab. The probability was that Bentivoglio had never made a note of it in his official report, Aintab having no commercial importance to France, with no salary attached to the office there, and, for that reason, Giustini's name had never appeared on the files at the Consulate Department in France, and when Giustini arrived he was so confounded by his reception, no one deigning to give him even a hearing, that he entirely lost his wits, and had not had sense enough to produce the only paper among the hundreds he handed to me that was of any importance.

I never had such faith in a Divine Providence as was given me at that moment, for I felt that it had led me to his door, and was sure that that was done in reward for that wife's steadfast faith and confidence in the intercession of the Mother of God. No one could have doubted it could he have seen that mother at prayer ; and I felt from the beginning that there could not be a God in heaven if He refused to assist me in my efforts to restore that unfortunate mother to her children.

Having read once more the accusations, I began to calculate how I should catch Meurand so as to make the most of the *exequatur ;* and I began to pray God to inspire me what to do, for I could not at once decide the best use to make of so slight an advantage in answer to such a catalogue of charges.

The next morning I went to the Pantheon, as usual, to make my offering. But as soon as I started I began thinking of what the lady of charity had said to me, and my conscience began to smite me for changing my confessors so often. I had sense enough to know that it was not from virtue that I had ever changed them, and that the only fault I had to find with them was that they found so much fault with me. When I reached the Pantheon I went immediately to St. Geneviève's altar, and thanked God that I had escaped the woman that morning, for I did not wish to see her. In my outburst of gratitude I promised our Lord that when he would make me a better woman I would stop changing my confessors.

When I returned home, I was disappointed in not receiving a letter from England, from the English girl's family, but I still hoped that the afternoon's mail would bring me some intelligence from them, for I dreaded being obliged to have the girl buried in the potter's field.

I wrote a few lines to the Marquis de Moustier which were to accompany General Dix's letter. I was afraid that the fact of living in the Abbaye aux Bois would prevent him giving me an audience, as he might suspect that it was some pious old woman after a subscription, and refer me to his secretary. In order to prevent any possibility of being refused, I wrote him to send an immediate answer to my residence at the Abbaye aux Bois so that I might not be delayed in receiving it, as I otherwise would be if he sent it to the American Legation, and I hoped that the fact of residing at the Abbey would not prejudice my request to such an extent that I would receive the customary unvarying ministerial reply, that "*His Excellence was out,* or *His Excellence had gone to his château,*" when it was well known that his Excellence was at home; but, to allay any prejudice that my pious asylum might raise in his mind, I thought it prudent to add that I was not residing at the Abbey for *seclusion,* but for *protection.* That it would be useless to refer me or my case to his secretary, for neither of us would go to him; that I wished to see himself, *only himself,* and if he would *give me an audience, and immediately grant my request,* if ever he built a temple to Gratitude I would volunteer to serve in it, as high-priestess, for the rest of my life.

I then took what I had written and wrapped it around General Dix's letter, and enclosed the whole in a white perfumed envelope with rose-tinted lining, upon which my initials were neatly stamped in lilac and gold.

I knew that if he was as gallant as Laferrière represented him to be he would not fail to reply. I had hardly finished my letter when Laferrière's carriage drove into the yard. I thrust the letter quickly into my pocket, for I did not intend that Laferrière should see the appendix to General Dix's letter of introduction, as he might prevent me sending it, out of respect to the General. I went to the window and saw that his footman who was with him, went into the kitchen to chat with the cook.

The moment Laferrière entered, he remarked that he had brought Louis along to go on an errand for him, and he was afraid that it was all over now that he got with the cook. I proposed that he should take General Dix's letter to the Minister's. Laferrière went towards the bell. I understood his movement but pretended not to notice it. Before he had time to speak and tell me to stop I was out of the room into the kitchen, where I quickly thrust the letter into his valet's coat pocket, telling him not to touch it for fear he might soil it. I then gave him the order and begged him to go at once, telling him to be sure and leave my letter, no matter if they told him the Minister was dead, for I was afraid he might be stupid enough to bring back the letter and that Laferrière would see into the manœuvre.

"Well," exclaimed Laferrière, as soon as I came into the room, "there is an end now to the Giustini affair for the present; for goodness knows when you will ever hear from the Minister, and when you do, he will refer you to Meurand or his private secretary. I would just like to witness an interview between you and Meurand, to see which of you got the advantage in the dispute. Of course he would get it *de facto*; for he never would yield so far as to grant anything that he had once set his seal against."

I said nothing to him about the important paper that I had found, for I was not decided what use to make of it. Laferrière threw himself back in an arm-chair and closed his eyes, as though he was half dozing. He must have remained in that position for at least twenty-five minutes, when we were startled by a loud ring at the bell.

"Oh," said Laferrière, "that rings like Louis. But it does not seem as though he had had time to do both of our errands." The door opened, and the waiter handed me a letter, which Laferrière immediately took and opened, while I signed the receipt for it.

"Well," said Laferrière, greatly surprised, "what does this mean? I cannot believe my eyes. The Minister writes you, appointing an audience for to-morrow morning, at eleven o'clock. Well, he must be courting favour with the United States, to give such prompt attention to a letter of introduction from the American Minister.

I was imprudent enough to say, "That depends." "Ah," said he, "perhaps you have met the Marquis at Court, and you know each other already by sight."

I saw at once there was a tempest brewing for me if I excited his jealousy, and I quickly assured him that I had never seen nor heard anything about him, except what he had told me himself.

He scanned me closely for a few moments, and then said:

"Don't go to dressing up much. Dress simply: wear your neat little grey costume, your plain hat, and your little black lace veil, and be very reserved; because these noblemen have a light opinion of the American women in general."

I could see that he regretted having consented to let me make use of General Dix's letter. He never would have done so had he thought it would ever come to this. While he was advising me to dress very simply, I decided upon wearing the richest and most becoming costume I had.

The bell rang again. This time it was Louis who presented himself at the door and said: "I gave Monsieur le Vicomte's message. I called first at the Minister's, but his Excellence was *out*. I left the letter as Madame ordered me to do." That set us both laughing, and instantly all suspicions and jealousy vanished, and he passed the rest of his time preparing my mind for a disappointment, and hoping that, after I had seen the Minister, I would be satisfied with my efforts, and leave the Giustinis in the hands of God.

CHAPTER LXIX.

SAD MEMORIES NEARLY THWART MY MISSION OF CHARITY—THE MARQUIS DE MOUSTIER.

"Only a Pauper"—"O ye Tears!"—The Mother—At the Minister's—
Pleading the Case—The Minister Confesses—The Suit Won—
A Confidential Talk.

THE next morning I rose early and repaired to the hospital. I found the body of the poor girl laid in the coffin I had ordered, and placed in the chapel before the altar. I ordered a cross to be made, and marked with her name, and placed over her grave, for I could not give up the hope that the parents would come to claim the body of their deceased child.

I was the only one in the chapel, besides the priest and the boy who served at Mass. As I knelt there alone, praying for the soul of this poor girl, I recollected that my mother had died in an insane retreat, and that there was no one near her to follow her to the grave, or to mark the spot where she lay. I thought, too, of her sufferings and her remorse, and compared them with those of the poor girl whose corpse was within the shadow of God's altar. I was so overcome by those thoughts that I gave vent to my feelings and wept bitterly. The priest, when he approached the coffin and had sprinkled it, handed me the aspergillus and as he did so, he threw me a pitiful glance, for he doubtless mistook me for a relative of the deceased. His look only made me weep the more, for my heart instantly filled with memories of my mother, and I thought how little the priest knew what was passing in my mind.

After I had sprinkled the coffin, I knelt down again and continued to weep. When the service was ended and the corpse placed on the hearse, a Sister joined me and said that the cross had been attended to, that she had written the name, and that the boy said it was ready. As the hearse moved off, the priest asked me if I was not going to follow my friend to the grave. I told him that I had no time. He showed his surprise. When I told him that the girl was no connection of mine—that I was merely a lady of charity who had promised to bury her, he asked me to excuse him, saying that he had judged from my tears that I was a relative.

"Oh," said I, interrupting him, "I am not weeping for her, but for another. The soul that I am weeping for, father, needs our prayers more than she;" and I pointed towards the hearse, which was just moving out of sight. I asked him to pray for the soul that I was weeping for.

He then said a few words to console me, and I instantly recollected my engagement with the Minister at eleven o'clock. All my grief instantly fled, and I was as furious as I could be with myself for having wept. If I had committed a crime I could not have been more provoked. I abruptly left the priest, flew to a water-spout and washed my eyes, then rushed into the porter's lodge to look into the glass to see if my face was red and my eyes swollen.

"Yes," thought I to myself, "you will stand a pretty chance with such a man as the Marquis de Moustier if he sees you with a face like a lobster." I was annoyed with my discomposed looks, and felt that my foolishness would be the ruin of the Giustinis; for I reckoned my chances of success more on the impression I would make on his imagination and his heart, than I did upon the justice of my cause or any sympathy I might awaken in him for the family.

When I got to the Abbey I noticed a cab standing at the gate, on which was a little trunk. My maid met me at the door and told me that there was a lady upstairs waiting for me, who could not speak a word of French. The thought did not instantly occur to me who it might be; but the moment I saw her I knew that it was the mother of the deceased girl.

She had written to her daughter as soon as she had received my letter, that she would leave for Paris the next day; but a raging storm had set in, which made it dangerous to cross the Channel, and she was detained twenty-four hours on the English side. When she arrived in Paris she drove at once to the hospital; but it being very early, and she not being able to make herself understood, the portress would not permit her to pass the lodge. She then drove to the Abbey, where she had been waiting for me ever since.

She apologised for her impatience, and begged me to have the kindness to take her at once to her daughter, for every moment seemed an eternity, so great was her anxiety and her impatience to be with her child. I felt dreadfully when I found that she was at the hospital door while the services were being said over her daughter, and the portress would not let her in. My heart was filled with grief. I was so choked with my efforts to control my feelings that I could not speak, and I feared I should again burst into tears.

The mirror showed me that the redness of my face had disappeared, and was succeeded by a death-like pallor; and I was determined not to weep again. My maid was astonished to see me look into the glass instead of answering the woman. She asked me if I could understand her. Said I: "Too well. Leave me alone and get my things ready; I am in a hurry to go to the Minister's."

By this time the English lady had nearly fainted. She was looking at me as if to see whether she was speaking to a woman in her right mind or not, for I seemed to be more intent upon admiring myself in the glass than in listening to what she said.

An instant more and it was all over. I had conquered myself, and was as cold and as rigid as marble. My whole soul was bent on sending the Giustinis back to Syria, and I would not let my pity interfere with the execution of this object.

I told the woman that I had just returned from her daughter's funeral, and would have followed her to the grave, but was prevented by an important engagement that I had at eleven o'clock, and it was already half-past nine.

The woman, instead of going into a paroxysm of grief, as I expected, clasped her hands together, and, raising her eyes, she asked me: "Is she really dead?"

"Yes," said I.

"Thank Heaven!" she exclaimed. But in a few moments afterwards she began to weep—all her sympathies for her erring child had come back.

We breakfasted together, and she related to me the same story that her daughter had told before she died; and she added as she finished: "I am glad that she is dead, for it is a relief to my heart, and it will also relieve the hearts of my husband and children."

She told me that she left them in the greatest affliction at the very thought of bringing her home, for they all feared that she would bring upon them some terrible disgrace. They had already reported her as dead in order to silence the suspicions and inquiries of the society in which they moved.

I explained that it was impossible for me to accompany her that morning to her daughter's grave, nor could I that afternoon, as it was my reception-day. We deferred it until the following morning.

As I drove to the ministerial mansion of the Marquis de Moustier my bosom was filled as much with hatred for Meurand as with compassion for the Giustinis. I was determined to have revenge for his insolence to Laferrière, and I began to devise how I might manage to torture his pride, for I knew that a man whose decisions had always been above reproach, and from which scarcely an appeal had been made during thirty years, must be on pretty good terms with himself, and would be keenly sensitive to any rebuke, particularly from the Minister himself, *and from such a Minister!*

As soon as I gave my card I was ushered into the presence of the Minister, who rose as I entered, and received me in a courtly manner. For a second I was abashed by the grandeur and magnificence of the apartment, and the graceful and indescribable dignity of the Marquis. He was a man of about forty, of most prepossessing exterior and charming address.

I began the conversation by remarking that I had applied to my Minister for the interview, because I thought it was more *en règle;* but perhaps it would have aided my cause if I had made his acquaintance through his cousin, the Countess de Montalembert, who was my intimate friend. At the mere mention of the Countess's name the whole expression of his countenance and his manner changed, and I saw that he hoped that it was in his power to oblige me, for, after speaking admiringly of her talents and her wit, he remarked that she had treated him coolly since he had accepted a position under the Empire, which treatment he deeply regretted.

Presently our conversation became animated and extremely amusing. All at once he recollected himself, and said: "But you came to ask a favour of me?" I laughed as I replied: "And you have just reminded me of it."

He was not insensible to the compliment; and we must have continued to chat at least twenty minutes longer, when he reminded me that I should not go without telling him what he could do to serve me.

I then pulled two papers out of my pocket. One was the list of accusations, and the other was the *exequatur*. And I related to him the scene of last Friday evening, when I visited the Giustinis. I began with the doorkeeper, and ended with the vow I had made in the name of the Blessed Virgin, never to abandon them until the Government sent them home.

The Marquis was deeply moved and exceedingly interested. As soon as I ceased speaking he said with earnestness: " I will attend to it at once, and see that justice is done."

I replied: " I have not come for justice, but for mercy and revenge, and I instantly handed him the list of accusations. He began reading them attentively, but had not read far when he turned over the leaf to glance at the signature, and the moment he perceived Meurand's name, with his official seal, he said : " This man must be an arrant knave and impostor." Said I : " Which of them do you mean, Meurand or Giustini ?"

He replied : " Why, your *protégé*, of course." Said I : " It will take a good deal to convince me that Meurand is not a greater one." Which reply made the Marquis smile. After he finished reading the paper, and was going to hand it back to me, I said : " But those accusations are all lies." " That is impossible," he answered; "for here is Meurand's name, with his official seal. Whatever he endorses can be relied upon." " Yet," said I, "take my word for it, they are all false." The Minister then undertook to explain to me who Mr. Meurand was, and what were his responsibilities.

I impatiently interrupted him and said : " You cannot tell me anything about Meurand, for I know more about him than you do, and I have come here to expose him. A foreign family have served the French Government eleven years, and are induced to come on here by such men as the Mayor of St. Germain, Chatry de Lafosse, the Count de Lesseps, and other diplomatists, to demand remuneration. They came all the way from Syria, and have been here seven months, without being permitted to speak to anyone but your valets."

" But," said the Minister," " look at these accusations. The chiefs of the departments have too much business to attend to to be able to receive every impostor and knave who dares to set up a claim against the Government."

" Oh," said I, " that is just what I expected, that you would side with Meurand. He appears to have deluded the whole Empire into a belief in his infallibility." "My dear madam," replied the Marquis, "you would not wish me to side against truth and justice ?"

I replied, " I do not wish you to; but it appears you are determined, whether I will or not. And I assure you that if Giustini is a scoundrel, Meurand is not much better, and very impertinent at that, to make up such a list of accusations, and not permit a man to come forward and defend himself. Why, he even presumes to insult one of his Majesty's officials, who comes and demands that something shall be done for this man. It would be a nice bone for the hostile press to pick at, to be able to say that one of the Emperor's Consuls, who had been in office eleven years, was permitted to die of starvation right in sight of the Tuileries !"

The blood mounted to the Marquis's face as I spoke. I did not give him a chance to reply, but took advantage of his emotion to add : " And that is just the way business is conducted in this department. Everybody knows that you pass most of your time at the chase, in boudoirs, or at the races, and that it is impossible for you to surmise all this unless somebody has the charity to come and tell you of it."

M. de Moustier tried to suppress his smiles, leaned over, and striking his breast three times, exclaimed, " *Mea culpa, mea culpa, mea maxima culpa.*" He then added, " I confess that I am more deserving of your censure than the chief of the Consulate Department." " Yes," said I ; " but you will reform, and put order up there now ; for it stands in great need of it, when Meurand will boldly declare that a man has received no *exequatur* when he has one."

" Why," exclaimed the Minister, " that is the most important accusation of all ; and therein Meurand cannot be mistaken." " But," said I, " he has an *exequatur*." The minister continued to deny it, and I continued to affirm it, until I saw that his patience was at an end. I then drew my chair towards him, and looking him straight in the face, I said to him, " I will make you a wager that he has an *exequatur*. If I can produce it you must promise me to send him and his family back to Syria, and if I fail I promise you never to mention the subject again."

" I agree to it, madam, most willingly," the Marquis exclaimed ; for his patience was thoroughly exhausted. " What !" said I, " do you promise me to send them back at once, if I can produce his *exequatur ?*" " Certainly, madam, *parole de ministre.*" Said I : " That is sufficient ;" and throwing the paper to him with a triumphant air, I exclaimed, " LE VOILA. (There it is.)"

He opened it, and instantly rose to his feet, and advanced

towards the table, then hesitated, looked over the list of accusations to see that he had read aright, and was just going to ring, when I begged him to wait a moment. Said he: "I am in no hurry; I was only anxious to serve you." "Yes," said I, "but I have my confession to make. I have been trifling with you all the while. I ask your pardon, and hope you will be my friend."

He smiled, and inclined as graciously as when I first entered the room. Said I: "I believe this man Giustini is guilty of every charge made against him. But for his wife and children's sake, I am determined to have them sent back to Syria. That affair is settled, as your Excellence has just given me you word." He nodded an assent. "But now," I continued, "I have another favour to ask, which I have still deeper at heart. I love Laferrière, and I hate Meurand for the unceremonious way he received him. I was the cause, because it was out of devotion to me that the Viscount interested himself in the family, and I look to you to avenge me; for we have caught Meurand."

I then told him how I suspected the mistake had been made. He agreed with me. I then begged him to take advantage of it, so as to give Meurand a pretty sound humiliation, before he gave him a chance of throwing the blame on Bentivoglio. The Minister's face lighted up, and I suspected that he was not displeased with the opportunity I had given him to say that he was the only minister that had ever been able to show Meurand that he could make a mistake.

"It will be satisfaction enough for the Viscount," said he, "when he sees that I will oblige Meurand to send them home."

"No, no, no," said I; "that may be enough to gratify Laferrière, but nothing less than a good rebuke will ever satisfy me. The Marquis began to laugh, and said that he might have suspected that there was love and revenge mixed up in the matter. I replied that I was actuated by the best of motives, when I started out to assist this family, that I did it from pure love of God and my neighbour; but that the devil had mixed himself in the business the moment Laferrière complained that Meurand had treated him uncivilly. "Well," replied the Minister, "I promise you that you shall have full satisfaction."

As I felt that I had accomplished everything I came for I rose to go, but he detained me, and all at once our conversation took a confidential turn in regard to the Government and some of its officials, so much so that he lowered his voice, although we were sitting near a table in the centre of a spacious room.

"Why," said I, "there is no danger of anyone listening, is there?" "No," he replied, "but it is better to speak low."

Said I : "I am not going to open my lips, until you look behind the *portières ;* "—and we both of us rose. He went to one side of the room, and I to the other, and looked behind the drapery that hung before the doors.

When we resumed our seats, I laughed and exclaimed, "I know more about those fellows than you think I do." "What fellows ?" said he. "Ah," said I, "don't you suppose I know what you are afraid of? And you have reason to be. But I did not suppose that they would dare to insinuate themselves into the interior of this palace. You must go to America to breathe freely. I sometimes feel that my very breath is chained here." "In fact," he replied, in an under tone, "we never can tell whether our servants are enrolled among them or not." "You are talking to no novice," said I. "If you only knew my experience."

This excited his curiosity, and he insisted upon my telling him my experience, promising on the honour of a gentleman, never to betray me. I had said so much, that I was afraid, if I did not tell him, he might suspect that I was among them my-self; and as there is no character that I look upon as more hatefully despicable than that of a spy, I was determined to rid his mind of any such suspicion,—although some persons of rank did not disdain to occupy that position, not only for the Emperor, but even for Bismarck.

CHAPTER LXX.

The Prefect of Police—The Prefect's Valet—A "Watchful" Servant— Braving a Spy—The Spy made useful—"Choice of Directors"—Self- reproach.

I WAS in splendid humour, for I felt that I had just tri-umphed over the lower regions in securing Giustini's return ; and I kept the Marquis laughing the whole time I was relating to him what I knew about the Secret Police :—

"Last summer, when I was at Mont Doré, I had my rooms in the centre building on the rear. Piétri, the Prefect of Police, arrives and takes two rooms opposite mine, and one on each side. There I was, as it were, actually hemmed into my apart-ment by the cuirass of the French Government.

"I did not suppose that I was of sufficient importance to be placed under the surveillance of the police, except from the fact that I was intimate with ladies from the Faubourg St. Germain, who were bitterly opposed to the Empire.

"These ladies I never invited to my rooms, lest they should say something derogatory to the Government; and I did not wish to have my name mixed up with anything of the sort.

"Whenever I give dinners I always require an extra valet. I had returned but a few days from Mont Doré, when a young man presented himself, and offered to come and serve me at my extra dinners for half the price I was accustomed to pay. He showed me excellent references from the best families, and I took him. He gave me his address in an obscure part of Paris, which was situated several miles from the Abbaye aux Bois, and told me that he had a friend residing near the Abbey, and whenever I needed him to address him in care of his friend. I found him very efficient—far more so than any other servant I had ever had; but, from the moment my maid laid eyes upon him, she declared that this man had been Piétri's valet at Mont Doré, and that she noticed that he was always watching me there; that when I was on the promenade she had seen him looking at me from the top of the house, and had once caught him following us up the mountain. I told her that she must be mistaken; for Piétri's valet had a moustache, and did not resemble this man in the least.

"My maid replied, 'I will admit that he does not resemble him much. But every time I caught him watching you, he would dodge out of sight so quickly, that I could almost imagine no one was there. And this fellow resembles him in his ways, for when you were in your bedroom the other day I caught him in the narrow corridor that leads to it, and he made the same exit, and goodness knows where he disappeared to.'

"She told me that she had accused him of being Piétri's valet, but that he had denied his master, and declared that he never heard his name before; and the more she accused him the more vehemently he denied it.

"As my maid, however, had more perseverance than the one who accused St. Peter, she one night borrowed a bonnet, a pair of spectacles, and a veil, and dogged his steps till they led her directly to the Prefect's door. I rewarded her for her curiosity and perseverance, and told her not to intimate to him that we knew his true character. I suspected that she was trying to make me her dupe, and had trumped up this story to get rid of the young man, so as to bring back the valet I had discharged.

"I determined to watch the fellow myself, and to play police on the police, so as to be fully satisfied before I discharged him.

When I engaged him for a dinner he would always come in the
morning and pass the day doing extra work about the apartments.   The next time he came, whenever I went into a room,
no matter if there was anyone with me or not, I would wait
until I thought that it was time for him to be listening, when I
would spring out of the room with the rapidity of a hare, and
I invariably caught him escaping with the movements of a
Thug.

   "One day I went into my bedroom, and knelt down and
prayed: 'O God, help me to catch him!' and with that I made
a spring, and I saw him vanish through a door that led into the
main corridor.   I tried the door and found that its hinges had
been oiled.   I then went into the antechamber, and looking
through the grating in the door I distinctly saw him dodge back
into the narrow corridor, and, as he swept by me, he put a paper
into his coat-pocket.   I was afraid that it was one of my letters
which he had stolen, and I began to think how I should get this
paper.

   "I was furiously excited, and it was as much as I could do to
restrain myself from going up to him and snatching the paper
out of his pocket.   I first secured the door of the narrow corridor by bolting it on the inside.   I told him to bring me the
step-ladder and a brush.

   "'Now,' said I, 'dust the cornices.   But you had better take
off your coat or you will get it covered with dust.'   He instantly
obeyed, took off his coat, and as he mounted the ladder I opened
the windows.   After I did so I leaned over the railing, pulled
out one of my earrings and screamed out; 'Oh, Leon! one of my
earrings has fallen!   Run and get it for me as quick as you can.'

   "In an instant he was out and down the stairs.   But this
time I was as quick as he was.   I flew to the door, sprung the
latch, and bolted myself in.   I then ran and secured all the
windows.   By this time he was back again, trying to get in.   I
carefully took the paper from his coat-pocket and began to read
it,—and what do you think I saw?"

   The Marquis replied: "I suppose you saw your own confession,
written out better than you could have made it yourself."
Said I: "Precisely; and it made every hair of my head stand
on end; for before my eyes I saw a long file and a correct
inventory of everything I had been doing for the past week,
—how often I had been to church,—how long I had stood
before the glass,—who supped with me,—what they had talked
about,—the hour they came, and the hour they left,—whom
I had written to, and what I had written about, and who had

written to me, &c. I knew by that that he must be in collusion with my cook, the porter, or some one else in my service, and I felt the most uncomfortable sensation pass over me that I ever experienced in my life.

"While I was reading this document you would have thought that the Abbey was bombarded, by his efforts to get in. After I had read the paper I put it back into the coat-pocket, just as I had found it, and then went softly through the narrow corridor into my bedroom and began singing. I continued singing until I reached the little door, which I opened, and he instantly darted by me into the library. By the time I got in he was hugging his coat. I went into the antechamber and quickly turned back the latch, then came back and asked him what they were doing to the Abbey; if they were tearing down a partition, for I had gone into my bedroom and it was impossible to pray on account of the noise.

"'Why, madam,' he exclaimed, 'it was I trying to get in.' I looked at him, apparently surprised. Big drops of perspiration were standing on his face. Said I : 'Why did you not open the door with your key?' 'Because,' said he, 'you bolted them both.' 'What,' said I, '*I bolted them?* as though I ever turned a key or shoved a bolt in my life.' I smiled, and began to saunter down the room.

"But before I could think he rushed to the door and came back looking as white as a ghost. 'But,' said he, 'there must have been *someone* else in here for the latch is all right now.' 'Oh,' said I, 'what nonsense! You only imagined it was down.'

"He was out of my sight again in an instant, rushed into the kitchen to ask the girls if they had seen a man go out; then to the janitor. He came back, looked behind every door, into every closet, under the sofas, into boxes that a cat could hardly have crawled into, and not finding *his man* he began to examine the carpets to see if they were all tacked down, then the wainscoting. I pretended to pay no attention to him.

"I treated the valet-detective with greater confidence than ever, for I felt it would be a sorry day for me if I made an enemy of one of those fellows, and Machiavelli taught me, years before, never to make a man an enemy unless I had the power to crush him, or had no reason to fear him. I knew that it was of no use to discharge him for I should be sure to have another in his place, and I felt that I had another already in the house.

"One day your cousin, the Countess de Montalembert, came to dine with me. I told her to be careful what she said for my house was full of *mouchards*. The moment we sat down to dine, she commenced to abuse the Empire and everybody connected with it.

"It frightened me to hear her speak so unreservedly. She made me feel as though the guillotine were looming up in the distance, waiting for one of our heads. I interrupted her in the midst of her invectives, hoping to put a stop to them, and asked her if it was consistent with Christian charity to speak that way. 'Certainly,' she replied. 'IL FAUT TRANCHER LE MAL' (*we must strike at evil*).

"As soon as I thought we were alone I asked her how she dared to speak in that way of the Emperor and Empress after I had put her on her guard. 'Oh,' she replied, 'I should be rejoiced to have them both know my sentiments, and I could not allow so good an opportunity to pass of letting them know what I thought of them.'

"Her audacity and cleverness amused me, and I thought it was so worthy of imitation that I was inspired to do likewise. So I instantly converted this terrible grievance into an instrument to avenge old wrongs and new ones as fast as they came.

"All the maids of honour are against me. Two of them are Laferrière's cousins, and they have taken to hating me, through fear that I may one day become his wife. I have often tried to get some of the chamberlains to repeat to the Emperor and Empress remarks that the maids of honour had made about them; for they are always attacking me, and saying that I assume a position which I have no right to. But now let me hear one word from them, and I cannot sleep until I get satisfaction. I give a dinner, but instead of inviting ladies of the Faubourg, I bring together a lot of gossipping, disappointed chevaliers, and unfold to them, in the presence of Piétri's valet, what I have heard, and it goes straight to their Majesties.

"I keep the thing up, and I am playing the very devil among them. Laferrière, Rollin, and other *habitués* of the Palace come to see me and talk over everything that occurs: who is in favour and who is in disgrace, and they are all mystified as to the person who strikes these blows; for things are told in the Palace that they thought that none but they knew."

The Marquis laughed heartily, for in relating this to him I told him the names of the persons whose heads I had taken off, what they had done to me, and what I had said they had done to their Majesties; and I admitted that I had never been over-scrupulous about speaking the truth, particularly whenever it concerned Laferrière's daughter or the rest of his connections, who were all at war with me.

"But," said I, "this is the point for you to meditate on. If you had refused my request, I should have given a dinner in a day or two, and in the presence of my indefatigable Léon, I should have read Meurand's accusations, and then produced the *exequatur*, to show how business was done at the Ministry of Foreign Affairs; and it would have beeen easy enough for me to persuade Laferrière, after the reception Meurand gave him, that it was his duty to take them and show them to the Emperor. But I should have first let the intelligence reach his Majesty through his spies, and would have taken pains to add that if we went to Syria the probability was we would be able to disprove the other charges." I again rose to go, when the Marquis detained me once more by asking me: "But how is it, madam, that you can be a Sister of Charity in the morning and a Nemesis in the afternoon? I should think that two such opposite characters would breed serious discord in the same bosom." "Oh," I replied, "they agree admirably in me; but I never avenged wrongs until I became a Christian." This made him laugh still more. "Why," said he, "that does not seem evangelical." "Well," I said, "I wish I had only the mischief I do my enemies to reproach myself with."

Said he: "I would like to be your director." "Oh, no," I replied, laughing; "we would quarrel if you were. But you don't suppose that I ever confess those things, do you? I lay them all to the Government, for what business has it dogging me like a felon, when I am leading the life of a saint?"

"I always admired an enlightened piety," said he, "and I really think that you ought to choose me for your director." "If all I have heard about you," I answered, "be true, I am afraid that your direction would lead me the contrary road to that which goes to Heaven. The Viscount de Laferrière is my director. He makes me listen to him. But I never do as he tells me; if I did I should have presented myself before your Excellency attired in a neat little grey costume, a plain hat, and a little black lace veil, and should have been very reserved, for such were his directions."

"*Mon Dieu, madame!*" exclaimed the Marquis, "the Viscount is jealous, and it is he who is watching you." Here we both looked at the clock. It was just half-past one. "Goodness, madam!" he continued, "we are both lost, if he ever knows that we have been conversing two hours and a half. Tell him I told you I was engaged in council, and that I kept you waiting two hours." With those words he conducted me to the door of the ante-chamber, and, holding up the papers, he said: "*Au*

revoir, and I hope the next time we meet I shall have fully
satisfied your pity and your revenge."

When Laferrière called on me that afternoon my conscience
smote me for having disregarded his counsels. He noticed my
dejected appearance and attributed it at once to my ill-success
at the Minister's. I repeated the Marquis's lesson, that he had
kept me waiting two hours, but had taken the papers which I
had submitted to him, and said that he would give them his
immediate attention. Said Laferrière: "That is the last you
will ever hear from him ; but you will probably receive a line from
Meurand, that the Consulate Department respectfully declines to
convert its calling to that of office of Public Charity."

I told him that I had not been thinking of the Giustinis, but
of him, because I did not treat him as well as he deserved, for
all his kindness.

"What have you been doing now, that you reproach yourself
with?" he inquired. Said I: "You are always giving me
advice which I never follow."

"Why," he replied, "you would not be a woman if you did.
They are all alike ; they never begin to speak the truth or to
listen to others until just about eight days before they die.
Don't reproach yourself for anything you have ever done to me.
I don't hold you responsible for your faults. Come, cheer up,
and let me see you smile again." But instead of smiling, I wept
at my own perversity. He could not believe that I was reproaching myself in earnest, but attributed all my sadness to
my failure in not being able to assist the Giustinis.

———

CHAPTER LXXI.

ELIZA AMORE

The English Girl's Grave—The hated Name—One of the "Fortunate"—
A Grave-digger's Sympathy.

THE next morning I went to the Pantheon and made my usual
offering. When I returned I found the mother of the English
girl waiting for me to take her to her daughter's grave. We
first went to the hospital, as she wished to thank the Sisters and
remunerate the convalescent patients, who had assisted her
child during her last hours.

The Sister then gave me an account of the girl's last
moments. She died soon after she was baptised, blessing the

Catholics, and after having several times exclaimed, " Oh, if my family only knew what the Catholics really are ! What would have become of me, Sister, had it not been for you ? But I die happy now : I feel that peace and joy await me. A few moments more and I shall be at rest."

After hearing the Sister's story, I went to the mother, who was standing by the bed where her daughter had died ; and, thinking to console her, I repeated to her what the Sister had just said to me. " What," she exclaimed, "my daughter died a Roman Catholic ! O mercy ! " and, for a moment, she appeared more distracted and distressed than I had yet seen her.

" Well," she continued, " I would never dare to tell her father that, or he would curse her, even in her grave." Then recollecting that I was a Roman Catholic, she became more distracted than ever : but, this time, her face reddened with confusion, and, not knowing what else to say, she remarked ; " I know that they are *not all bad.*', It could easily be seen that the thought of her daughter dying a Roman Catholic, distressed her, perhaps, more than did her sinful life' and that she looked upon her dying in that faith as the climax of the infamy which her waywardness had heaped upon her family.

One of the hospital attendants conducted us to the cemetery. The girl was buried in the cemetery Mont Parnasse. · He left us at the graveyard gate, in care of the keeper, who promised to conduct us to the spot where the bodies had been interred that came from the hospitals the previous morning. The price for burying a body at the hospital is thirty francs. The Sister told me that that would cover all expenses ; it would pay for the coffin, shroud, grave, hearse, and services.

I supposed that this meant one single grave, and I expected that the man would lead us to a newly-made grave marked by a black wooden cross with white lettering. We passed by a line of what appeared to me to be a wide, low, black hedge-fence. I did not pay attention to it, for I was engaged in earnest conversation with my companion.

At last the man stopped, and said : " Here it is, madam." I looked down, and seeing myself standing close to one of these extraordinary looking fences, I called out to the man, who had already taken his departure : " You are mistaken; there is no grave here." Then throwing a glance about me, I nearly fainted. I had mistaken for a broad, low, black fence, innumerable little black crosses, about two feet high, which were closely knitted together, each one bearing a different name. There were at least twenty clustered around the one I was looking for.

The English lady, not understanding French, was not yet conscious that her daughter lay beneath her feet, and seeing me turn pale, and looking wildly about me, at the same time that I addressed the man, she impatiently asked me: "Can he not find the grave? It ought to be easily found, as she was only buried yesterday morning."

I told the man I would give him a franc if he would push the crosses away from the one bearing the name of Eliza Amore; and I told him to do so, while I attracted the lady's attention in another direction. I called her aside. Her back was turned to the grave. I began talking to her, while I kept my eyes on the movements of the man, who easily thrust aside the crosses in the newly-made earth, and arranged them so that this cross stood alone in the centre, while the others interlaced around it had the appearance of an impenetrable hedge. I then went and stood before it, and asked the man if he could not remove them a little farther, so that the lady might think that her daughter was buried by herself. The man shook his head and said he could not do so without violating the rules; that he had already pushed them to the very edge of the trench to which they belonged.

The lady, who was all this time impatiently waiting for the man to proceed, approached us, and was going to speak, when her eyes accidently fell on the cross bearing her daughter's first name by the side of the name of the man who had ruined her. Nothing could equal her emotion as her eyes fell on that name. All strength seemed to forsake her for an instant, and it was with the greatest effort that I could support her until the man came to my assistance. Presently her strength returned, and starting from us and speaking like a maniac who had just come out of a swoon, she exclaimed:

"Why did you bury her by that name? Let me bury it with her." So saying, she sprang towards the cross as though she would have seized it and have hidden it in the earth. But she was prevented from reaching it by the other crosses, which seemed to bid her defiance. Then, as if maddened by her fruitless efforts to grasp it, she turned upon me and, with a defiant look, pointing to the cross exclaimed: "That man was a Roman Catholic!"

"If he sinned," I replied, "he may have repented; for your daughter told us before she died that he taught her to pray." "Ah," answered the mother, with an angered look of horror and disgust, "she told us the same story, that he taught her to say the Catholic prayers. After enticing her away from school and ruining her, he tried to make her a Roman Catholic, so that she could do what she liked without fear of God ; for all she would have to do then would be to go to a priest, a man, and be forgiven."

The very blood boiled in my veins as she made this assertion, but I pitied her so much that I made no reply. She continued: "We caught her once with a string of Catholic beads, with a cross at the end. He gave it to her. She used to wear it around her neck under her dress."

Here, turning to the grave, the mother exclaimed : "What a strange-looking grave ! how large and disproportioned ! Why did they fence it in with these clumsy black sticks ? " As she said these words, her eyes fell on the names that were written on them, and as the truth flashed over her mind, she uttered a shriek.

"What !" she exclaimed ; "is she buried here with so many others ; " and throwing upon me a reproachful look, she said : " You told me that you had paid for a grave." Said I : " I did ; and I supposed that she would be buried by herself. All this appears as horrible to me as it does to you."

I then questioned the grave-digger, who had already begun to dig another trench. He told me that that was the way they always buried those who were brought from the hospitals, and had been baptised ; that they dug a deep ditch and buried them altogether. Said I : " How many are there here ? " and I began counting the crosses. "Hump !" said the man ; " you cannnot calculate by them ; for there are a great many buried there who had not money enough to pay for a cross."

I was chilled with horror when I reflected that, at the hospital, those who had money enough to bury them, or who had found some sympathising soul that would promise to fulfil for them this last office, were called the *fortunate ones ;* and the unfortunates were those who had not one single dime or a friend, and whose bodies were destined to pass through the dissecting-rooms. I then remembered that I had not had any particular mark put on the coffin, as I supposed that the cross would be sufficient to find the body any time it might be called for.

As I was making this reflection the mother began to consult with me about the means to be taken to obtain the body. I was obliged to tell her the truth, that all the coffins were alike, and that there might be thirty bodies buried in the same grave ; so that they might be obliged to open most of the coffins before they could find the right one. This difficulty did not seem to deter her from persisting in the intention of having her daughter disinterred. But in the midst of our deliberations the expression of her face suddenly changed, as though a thought had occurred to her which settled everything in her mind; she shook her head, and then said, "No, no;" let her rest where she is; our family would never permit a Roman Catholic. to be buried in our burial ground. I will not have her removed." And she instantly withdrew from the spot, as though the very thought of her daughter having died a Roman Catholic made her shrink from the grave.

Instead of stopping to pass judgment on this woman's prejudices, let this be a lesson to those who profess to be Roman Catholics, that their sins may not bring down such odium and hatred upon their religion as to make those who are ignorant of its truths shudder at its very name.

CHAPTER LXXII.

THE TRIUMPH OF A MOTHER'S FAITH.

Sturdy Beggars—The Viscount Avenged—Faith and Gallantry—My
Director's Approval.

THAT same Friday afternoon General Rollin and Laferrière called. Laferrière told Rollin of the Giustini affair.

"Well," said Rollin, "she will have this satisfaction if she does get them home, that they will not be able to return and ask her to do the same favour again."

"Ah," answered Laferrière, "that is the plague of obliging anyone."

Laferrière had a fund attached to his appointment, which he had the privilege of distributing among the poor, in the name of the Emperor, as he saw fit. Said the General, "I would not accept your position for all France, unless the Emperor would transfer that fund to somebody else. If I were in your place I would keep a garrison at the door to fire on everyone who came, saying, 'Monsieur, you assisted me 'on a former occasion, and I take the liberty to apply to you again.' Assist them twice, and this time they leave their address, and if they need you again they present themselves with a haughty air of command and ask you to serve them in a tone which is as much as a reproach for having given them the trouble to call. Whenever I want to relieve the poor," continued the General, "I do it so that they will never find out where it comes from; it is one of the precepts of the Gospel that I most adhere to. Our Lord must have understood that kind of fellows pretty well, when He put us on our guard against them, in that passage of the Gospel where He says, ' Never let your right hand know what your left hand does.' "

The General's remark created no little amusement and laughter, in the midst of which an attaché of the Consular Department entered, and said : " Madam, his Excellence Monsieur le Marquis de Moustier has ordered me to say to you that he has granted your request, and has given orders that Mons. Giustini and his family should be sent back to Syria at the expense of the Government."

Laferrière could not conceal his astonishment and delight at the discomfiture of Meurand, and exclaimed: "And that *cretin*, Meurand : what has he to say ?"

" I left him foaming with rage," replied the young man; "for the Minister had made him affirm several times an accusation against Giustini ; and after he had done so, his Excellence, in the presence of several gentlemen, handed him a paper to prove that he had made a mistake, and had accused the Syrian ex-Consul unjustly."

" His Excellence," I remarked, " stole that from me ; for that is the way I caught *him*." And then I related part of my interview with the Marquis.

The young man then took his departure, and the Viscount and the General loaded me down with praises and compliments for my perseverance and tact. When they rose to leave, and had already reached the door, the Viscount turned towards me, and, making me a most courteous bow, said : " If ever I need an appointment, madam, I shall apply to you."

The Viscount let the General pass before him and descend the stairs while he lingered behind to speak a few words to me at the door of the antechamber. His face assumed a serious expression, as he said to me, in an affectionate but earnest tone: " My dear child, promise me, in the name of the love I bear you, that you will never return to the Minister of Foreign Affairs to thank him for his kindness. You only need to write him a formal note. I will dictate it for you." " Oh, no, no," I quickly replied ; " I prefer dictating my own notes." " Well," said he, " write whatever you choose ; but never call on him, and never receive him if he calls on you. I fear the perils of gratitude "—or, to put the words in his spicy French—"*je crains la reconnaissance*." He then said : "*A bientot ;*" and quickly descended the stairs. But I called him back and said to him : "Well, you and the General are moralists worthy of attention. The first thing you did when you came was to rail and abuse the poor for their pride and ingratitude, and the last thing you enjoin upon me when you leave is to appear proud and ungrateful." "Precisely," he quickly rejoined ; "because I wish to be always consistent : for all virtues must be practised with discretion, otherwise they degenerate into vices."

As soon as I entered my library I wrote a note to the Giustinis, announcing my success with the Minister of Foreign Affairs, and then went to the Pantheon. When I reached St. Geneviève's altar I began talking to our Lord, the Blessed Virgin, and St. Geneviève, as though I were speaking to them face to face.

Since my conversion there have been intervals when my mind is so freed from doubt that the objects of faith are to it a living reality. In such moments I will converse with God, the Blessed Virgin, and the Saints, in the same way as I used to talk with the chairs, the footstools, and the table-legs when I was called "Tick," and with the shrubs, the rocks, the trees, and the sun when I lived in the Highlands of Dutchess.

That evening I went to the Opera Comique. Laferrière smiled when he saw me, and said : "We did not expect you at all : we expected that you would stay with the Syrians all night." I replied : "Why should they thank me ? I did nothing for them. I left it all to God, and He did it." His face brightened as he said : "That is the true spirit—that is the spirit of God. Always render the glory and success to Him. It is the first time I ever heard you speak like a Christian."

The next day I called to see those gentlemen who had promised to give me something for Guistini if the Government agreed to send him home.

I called on the old man of reason and good sense first, and related to him the whole affair. In the midst of my narration he interrupted me, and said : "That is a fact. I forgot to reckon in the gallantry of the Marquis." "Oh," I replied, "you forgot to reckon on more than that ; for you did not give Faith its full value." "Well," he added, "I will rectify my mistake by adding what I subtracted from it to the Marquis's gallantry, and reason will deduce from it that you owe more to the Marquis than you do to God."

"I ask you, sir," I replied, "who made the gallant Marquis?" He answered : "God made him ; but I think you will admit that you owe more to the devil for the Marquis's training than you do to God." "The devil," said I, "can do nothing without God's permission. If you are a Roman Catholic, you should believe the same; but you see that reason and good sense are leading you astray."

He then sighed, and pretended to be very serious, by trying to assume an earnest expression, as he continued: "The Marquis will never know how much he is responsible for, for your success will make you more crazy than ever." I replied: "If you call an increase of faith, and putting all my trust in God, getting more crazy, I will confess that I am more demented than ever. Besides, my director, for the first time, sanctioned my conduct. He told me that I was right, that I should always render all the glory to God." "Oh," exclaimed the old man, "Priest-cant!" Said I: "There was no priest about it, for the first chamberlain of the Emperor is my director." "What!" he exclaimed with astonishment, "the Viscount de Laferrière! that you are sure to meet every night in the *coulisses* of the Opera?" "Precisely," said I; "and he is better than all the priests; for he knows as much as they do, although he has not the strength of will nor the courage to practise what he preaches. Therefore he is modest about it, and will point out to you your defects, and tell you their remedies without scolding and frowning like a Pharisee; for he knows how it is himself." "Well, well," cried out the old man, "I will congratulate the Viscount upon his fair penitent." "The Viscount," I replied, "will tell you that you have not much to congratulate him for on that score: he finds me furiously unmanageable." "Madam," said he very seriously, "I shall not accuse reason or good sense for leading you astray." Said I: "Laferrière would tell you that it would be a libel on both if you did, for I have neither; but that those are your defects, and that *mine* are a fondness for pleasure and for having my own way." "Madam," he replied, "I easily divined them, since you have been taught by a Bishop our religion so thoroughly, and you afterwards chose a courtier instead of a priest to be your director."

CHAPTER LXXIII.

REMORSE OF RENEGADE NUNS—THE HEARTLESSNESS OF THE POOR FOR THEIR FALLEN SISTERS.

Clinical Studies—The " Virtues " of Paupers—Comparisons—Heartsick.

MY rescue of the Giustini family and victory over Meurand were bruited about, and gave me that importance which I had so long coveted; but I now found it a never-ending cause of weariness and annoyance. I never let anything interfere with my morning visits to the hospitals. I went there to study and reflect. I would learn more at the hospital in one hour, listening to the simple stories of its unfortunate inmates, than I could in a whole year in the flash of the world. Standing by the bedsides of suffering souls, whose life was stripped of all illusions, I learned the value of a sympathising look, of an encouraging word, and the untold value of a slight caress. Patients would implore me with streaming eyes to come and stand by them when they were about to undergo some painful operation. A slight pressure of the hand, a sympathising look, a fond word, or a hand gently passed over their foreheads, seemed to take away half their agony.

From the Sisters of Charity I learned to control myself in these scenes. At first I would become faint with pity, but they taught me to master my feelings in the presence of suffering. One day I was standing by the sick-bed of a young woman who could not have been thirty. She noticed a little medal of St. Benedict, which I wore around my neck, and reaching out her hand towards it, she begged of me to let her kiss it. She then asked me how I came by it. I told her that the Mother-General of the Ladies of the Holy Family had given it to me. I had hardly spoken those words when she buried her face in her pillow, and fell to sobbing and weeping. I asked her to tell me what there was about that medal, and the name of the Holy Family, that affected her. I remained beside her at least half-an-hour, imploring her to speak; but the only reply that I could obtain, through her sobbing, was, " Don't ask me." I was most curious to know her secret, and the next morning I repaired at once to her bed.

She at first refused to answer my question, and said : " You are so intimate with the Sisters here that I am afraid to tell you lest you should betray me, because they all love me, and are so good to me, and they would have a horror of me if they knew what I have done."

I promised her faithfully that I would be a true friend to her, if she would only tell me the truth, and what there was between her and the Ladies of the Holy Family.

She then told me that she had been a religious in that society for four years, at their Novitiate in Bordeaux; that her mother was opposed to her entering, and was constantly coming to the convent and importuning her to leave. During the four years she had been ill a part of the time, and the nuns took the tenderest care of her. But her mother at last triumphed over her resistance, and she resolved to leave. No sooner was she out of the convent than she became intensely miserable. Her mother died in less than a year. She applied to be received by the religious again, but they refused to take her back. One misfortune succeeded another, until she was reduced to beggary, and her health being poor, she had been staying at the hospital, off and on now for over a year.

I listened to her story with the deepest interest, and was delighted that Providence should have thrown the poor creature in my path: for since I had left St. Mandé, many and many a hater of Catholicity had said to me, "They took care to hide their devilry from you;" and as I had always been deceived and was easily given to suspect, I would have to struggle with myself not to be influenced by these foes of the conventual life. I was determined to be convinced of the truth, if there was anything wrong about the nuns, or to silence for ever any suspicions that ignorant, prejudiced souls might henceforth try to resuscitate in my mind. I began questioning this lady in a way that would induce her to speak ill of the religious, if any ill could be said. But whenever I insinuated the slightest thing against them, it would wound her as though I were abusing a beloved spouse whom she had abandoned, and who now refused to take her back to his bosom. She reproached only herself, and saw the smiting hand of God in all that she had suffered and still suffered. I asked why she dreaded to have the Sisters know her story. "Oh," she replied, "I never want them to know what brought me to this. I committed a serious offence in giving up my vocation." Her heart was rent with remorse; but at that time I could not appreciate her scruples.

I met two other religious, who had made their novitiate in other convents. One of them had been sent away, and the other had left of her own accord. One's account was that a relative came and incited her to rebel against the rules, and she was

·dismissed.   The other had been enticed to leave.   The manifestations of remorse and repentance were exactly alike.

I was present at the death of one of these.   Her last words :
" Forgive me, beloved Jesus, for having abandoned Thy house,"
rang through my heart.   As I heard those words, I sank on my
knees, and asked God to forgive me for ever having doubted the
holiness that existed in religious life.

I have often felt since then that God had His designs in
throwing these three repenting souls in my path, for they have
armed my weakness for ever against any suspicions in regard to
cloister-life.

Listening to the regrets and prayers of these repentant souls
I felt the full enormity of my mother's fault, and I often knelt
at their bedsides, and implored God to inspire me what to do,
that I might atone for her sin.   I prayed Him to let me undo
the wrongs that my mother had done and I would offer myself
up to God and implore Him to do with me what He would.
These offerings always brought peace to my soul—I felt that
God was there to answer my prayer and to accept my sacrifice.

Not only did I learn in the hospital to feel the enormity of
my mother's fault but also to have charity and compassion for
her.   It was then, and only then, that I could feel how much
more deserving of pity than of reproach she was.

If the world wants to see the culmination of pride, intolerance,
disdain, and hate, let it mingle with the paupers who frequent
the first-class public hospitals and poor-houses.   I have seen
them torture the very life out of poor girls whom they suspected
of having been the victims of some libertine.

I knew one unfortunate creature who left the hospital so ill
that she could hardly drag herself away, choosing to risk dying
alone in the streets rather than endure any longer the disdainful
looks and contemptuous smiles of those around her.   No one
would speak to her, except to insult her.   She dared not
approach anyone, but they would all abuse her among themselves, and not fail to let her know it by their side glances and
leers.

It was while studying the characters and manners of these
paupers that I conceived how my mother sought by every means
to excuse herself, and to throw the blame of her own conduct on
others.   Because females who have erred and who cannot conceal
their guilt, and are possessed of one grain of sensibility, can
suffer no greater martyrdom than to fall beneath the censure of
this class, which, for intolerance, ill-breeding, insolence, and
pride, far surpasses even a first-class " shoddy " aristocracy.

But those whom " shoddy " singles out as targets for its abuse and scorn are more fortunate than their penniless rivals, since they have the means to fly, and to conceal themselves from the darts of their Pharisaical persecutors. But for the pauper there is no escape; his indigence dooms him to stand face to face with his tormentors and receive their blows.

And what blows can strike deeper, and inflict greater pain on an erring soul, possessed of a proud and sensitive nature, than to be obliged to live in the midst of human beings, whose looks, words, and gestures are filled with scorn and disdain ?

Many erring and unfortunate females are willing to resort to any crime in order to escape falling under such a ban. They know full well the trials that await them if they do.

By mingling with this class I learned to have feelings of compassion and sympathy for my mother, and to pity while I condemned her. She was proud and sensitive. She wished to make herself appear the helpless victim of priestly crime, and in order to enlist the sympathy of the hospital attendants, she invented her improbable story.

All these scenes would bring back to my mind my own erring days; and my heart would rise in gratitude to God, for having spared me what seemed to be the common lot of all those who began life in the same way that I did. And often I would mentally exclaim, when I witnessed scenes that would make my blood run cold; "Oh God, why didst Thou spare me ? "—and then and there I would make a firm resolve that the future should atone for the past.

After having passed the morning trying to console the poor, I would return to the Abbey, loathing the *rôle* that I was to play in the afternoon ; for those morning scenes would fill my mind with such serious thoughts and generous resolves, that they tended every day to disgust me more and more with my worldly life.

I would often resolve to abandon society altogether, and devote all my time to good works; for it was in them alone that I found any satisfaction. But instantly my attachment for the world's opinion would deter me from executing my resolution ; I was so afraid that the world would say that my reason for not appearing at such and such receptions was that I was not invited; and I was too much the slave of opinion to endure that thought.

But even when I sought to fly from the world the more the world seemed willing to throw itself at my feet. This but surfeited my vanity and my pride, while it left my heart empty. I

would often ask myself, when I was making such sacrifices to
opinion, what I was living for, any way ; and my heart always
had its answer ready, which was too distinct to ever deceive me:
it was to marry Laferrière. To marry Laferrière! it was for that
alone that I lived! I was even more attached to him than I had
ever been before, and that dolorous feeling of disappointed affection increased with my love.

No matter whether I stood by the bedside of some penniless
outcast, or was kneeling before God's altar, imploring His mercy
and protection, or in a palace surrounded by courtiers, who vied
in showing me attention, that feeling of disappointed love, like
a cancer, was eating into my heart; and, to aggravate it, Laferrière treated me every day more and more as if I were his
child.

CHAPTER LXXIV.

THE DREAM—THE WARNING—WAS IT THE VOICE OF GOD?

A Prayer and a Vision—A Frenchwoman on Divorce—The Plea of the
Children—A Letter which is a Sermon—Modesty.

IT was the 1st of December, 1868. Laferrière had gone to
Compiègne. I gave myself up entirely to visiting the sick,
helping the poor, and prayer. This kind of life I continued
for seven days. I had only intended to prolong it three days at
farthest, but I pleaded with God, just as though I were going to
excess ; and the last four mornings I would say to Him, as I left
the altar, " Only one day more, and then I will stop."

I believe it was the seventh evening, on the seventh day of
the month, that I entered my bedroom, and knelt down to say
my usual night-prayer.

I had laboured hard during the week, and had passed that
whole day in prayer. I was so exhausted that I leaned on an
ottoman for support, and looking up at the statue of the Blessed
Virgin, I said to her, " You ought to be pleased with me to-
night, for you know that I am only weary because I have been
working so hard for the poor. I think you owe me something.
Now, I want you to tell me what to do to get rid of this aching
about my heart. I wish you would take it away. Give me a
good dream to-night and a *true* one. Show me what I ought
to do; and I will do just as you tell me."

Towards five o'clock in the morning I awoke. I had just seen
myself in a dream, standing on the deck of the French steamer
Pereire. I dreamed that it was just leaving Havre for New

York, and that as I was standing on its deck, weeping and bidding France a long and a sad farewell, I saw my harp lying on the French shore, with all its strings broken. I burst into tears and then awoke, as the ship, I thought, moved off without it.

I instantly recollected the request I had made on going to bed. I rose at once, fell down on my knees before the statue of the Blessed Virgin, and screamed out, "Oh, anything but that! anything but that!" For the recollection of all I had suffered in America came up vividly before me, and to my mind the saddest scene that could be predicted in my future, was to see myself bidding a long farewell to France, and returning to America to make it my home. I implored the Blessed Virgin that that dream might never come true, and I lay down again, after making the same request that I did on going to bed.

I soon fell asleep, and the same vision came to me again, but more distinctly than before. When I awoke I wept bitterly, and began to implore the Blessed Virgin to take pity on me. She ought to know, I said, what those Americans were, and how they would treat me if they got a chance; and I pleaded harder than before that that dream might never come true, and lay down again, making the same request, that she would tell me what to do in future to take away that aching from my heart.

This time I fell, as it were, into a swoon; for I was conscious, but I could not move; and the same vision appeared before me, more distinct than ever. It vanished, and I awoke. But this time I was calm and resigned, and offered myself up to God, and said: "Do with me as Thou wilt, Lord: not my will, but Thine, be done. I will put my trust in Thee. I know that Thou art strong enough to protect me, even against the Americans. But tell me when I must go."

I passed the whole morning at the Church of our Lady of Victories, imploring God to inspire me when to go.

At noon I went to Munroe's, my banker's, 7, Rue Scribe. Mr. Stone handed me a letter from my brother-in-law, which stated that my sister had commenced a suit of divorce against him, and begged me to come on and try to induce her to withdraw it; for if she persisted in her proceedings against him it would bring ruin on us all, as he was determined to have the custody of his children, and would disclose his wife's parentage, thinking it would have some bearing in his favour.

The moment that I read the letter I decided to go to New York, as I felt that God had sent me those visions to decide me. As I had resolved to go, even before I got the letter, I returned to our Our Lady of Victories to thank God for having sent me such a good excuse to get off.

I did not dare to speak of my vision to anyone, for fear of being laughed at; and I knew that it would raise me in the estimation of all my friends to see me leave my child, my beautiful home, and all the advantages I had in Paris, to cross the Atlantic, in order to make peace between my sister and her husband. Everybody was startled at my determination, and none more so than Laferrière; for he knew my repugnance to America, and it was a sacrifice he thought me incapable of making to a sentiment of duty.

I studiously concealed from everyone, without exception, the motive that prompted me to make such a sacrifice. I was thoroughly convinced that God had made His designs known to me. I was so well satisfied of it that I was willing to risk all, in order to obey Him.

The steamer *Europe* was to sail on the 17th, and the *Pereire* two weeks later. I decided at once to take the *Pereire*.

One evening I was sitting by my window, facing the apartment which was once occupied by Madame Récamier. Over a terrace underneath the saloon windows is a colossal statue of the Blessed Virgin. The twilight in Paris is of much longer duration than in New York, and whenever I was alone I would always pass that hour saying my beads with my eyes fixed on the statue. I was always sad at that hour, and used to try to avoid passing it alone; for if I was alone I was sure to weep. That evening I was saying my beads, and at the same time invoking the intercession of St. Joseph, when I felt that God spoke to me, and told me not to go in the *Pereire*, but to take the *Europe*. I was as much convinced that God told me to take the steamship *Europe* as I was that He had told me that I must go to America. The next day I engaged my passage in that steamer.

The moment it was known that I was to sail in the *Europe* my bankers, and even the officers of the Steamship Company, tried to dissuade me from it, as the *Europe* had met with several accidents during her last trip. She had lost one of her paddles, and this was to be her last voyage. She was only going to take over a cargo of merchandise, and was then to be repaired. Only three or four passengers were going in her, because she would be at least twenty days crossing the ocean; and, finally, as December was one of the worst months in the year to cross the Atlantic, they all said that by all means I should take the *Pereire*, which was the safest and the fastest steamer of the line; besides, Captain Duchesne and myself were great friends. I pretended to my bankers that I had a superstition about sailing on the 17th—that it was a lucky number for me, and I would risk all, and nothing could induce me to sail on the 2nd; for the twos had always brought me bad luck. That was the only reason I gave for sailing in the *Europe*.

Laferrière, when he heard these reports against the *Europe*, insisted that I should take the *Pereire*. He said that he was willing to let me have my own way in everthing else; but it seemed to him madness on my part to take a steamer that was pronounced unsafe by everybody, even by the officers themselves. But nothing that he could say or do could dissuade me from taking the *Europe*, because I was sure that God had told me to take it.

The following letter I received from the Countess de Montalembert just before I sailed :—

"CHATEAU DE LA ROCHE EN BRUNY,
" (Côte d'Or.)
"13 December, 1868.

" MY VERY DEAR FRIEND:

" If my poor husband had not been seized with another painful attack of sickness you would certainly have had tidings of me. He charges me to say (for I have told him so much about you) that he, like myself, is very much moved by the sad news of your departure for America.

" I wished for some time past to write and ask you if you went to Rome (as you talked of doing, provided Mme. de Ferrière went) to come this way—the place in which I live is on the road to Marseilles—but I was so occupied in a correspondence with my husband's physicians that I had not time, and so, alas! the whole project failed.

" I should have taken so much pleasure in receiving you and talking with you. Truly Fr. Gratry was right when he said a few days ago: ' If everyone did his duty in his own sphere the morals of the world would be perfect, and everyone would be happy.' The motive of your departure, which you confided, dear Madam, to my friendly heart, has filled me with sadness—an unhappy lawsuit between a husband and wife—and to obtain what ?—the absolute rupture of the sacred tie of marriage. Ah! what a misfortune! what a scandal! what a lamentable situation for the poor children, whose father will not be any the less their father, although separated, divorced from his wife!

Yes, I sympathise with you with all my heart, and I admire the
task you have so generously imposed upon yourself, of going in
spite of the severity of the season, in spite of the terrible sorrow
of placing the ocean between yourself and your sweet little girl,
to try to put a stop to this unfortunate trial.

"When I used to meet in the world women who were made
unhappy by their husbands, and who sought to console themselves by doing wrong in their turn, how many times, when I
was young, ardent, impassioned, have I thought : ' Yes, if they
had no children, I should know how to understand such revenge,
and such crimes !' Still I would think them guilty, for our conscience tells us that we have not the right to become wicked
because others are, or appear to be so.   Without children these
revenges, these shortcomings, could be understood, though not
excused.   But with children—*mon Dieu !* how could a truly
maternal heart inflict upon these poor, little, weak, defenceless
creatures such disgrace, such irreparable dishonour ?

"When we love, we know how to suffer everything : yes,
everything, for those we love ; a mother ought to suffer everything, rather than diminish in any way the reputation, the joy,
the peace, of those who depend on her to the extent in which
poor children depend on their mother, on her reputation, her
sentiments, her conduct, her goodness, her love, or her hatred !

"Dear Madam, I hear the rain falling, and I think of your
voyage.   But God will protect you against all accidents ; for you
venture to endure storms, and even shipwrecks, to protect, if you
can, all these great moral and even temporal interests.   For the
honour of a family is a reward in this world.

"I will pray for you with all my soul—I did so to-day at
vespers.   I, who am always so sea-sick on the water, so afraid
when the wind blows—I cannot tell you how I admire your
sisterly devotion.   I recollect the portrait that you showed me
of your sister, and which was so beautiful : God could not permit so beautiful an exterior to enclose a soul without tenderness
for her children, and pity for her husband.   You told me that
she was travelling in Europe, and meanwhile her husband had
fallen sick in America.   I cannot help thinking that the world
will ask, why your sister should put such a distance between herself
and him.   With us a woman would never travel alone in this way
for pleasure, unless it were to alleviate griefs that she might have
at home.   And then, these poor little children !   I do not know
them, but you have so often told me how charming they are—
how can she help thinking of them, help pitying them, when
they open their eyes to what is going on between their father

and mother'? I know a little girl who *died* of grief, after witnessing the separation of her parents. She was the child of a distant relation of mine.

"May God then grant you the extreme joy of succeeding in the admirable mission that you so generously attempt to fulfil. I will beg it often of Him until you return to the charming appartments that you have arranged in the Abbaye aux Bois, where I was going to give myself a treat by visiting you in February, on my return to Paris.

"When I pass your gate, I shall see with a sad heart your *closed* windows. If you authorise me, I will go to see your dear little girl from time to time during your absence. Mention me to the religious, so that they may know that I come by your permission.

"I am so hurried that I write as fast as as my pen can run. Excuse me for doing so. Allow me to embrace you with greatest tenderness, my dear excellent friend,

"MÉRODE DE MONTALEMBERT."

When I arrived at Brest I received the following letter from Laferrière:—

"PALACE OF THE TUILERIES, PARIS,
"*December* 18, 1868.

"MY DEAR CHILD,

"My thoughts are always with you, they accompany you in your painful voyage, they follow you across the wide ocean which separates us, but which in spite of all its power cannot efface your memory from my soul, or destroy my hope of soon seeing you again.

"I hid my feelings when we parted, to render the separation less painful, and to leave you the courage you will need so much in executing the difficult mission that you have imposed upon yourself.

"In spite of the grief I feel I cannot blame your determination: it raises you in my eyes as it will in those of all who know you. I love you too much not to be proud of your conduct; it proves how worthy you are of my affection.

"You will undoubtedly succeed; and the consciousness of having fulfilled so great a duty will assuage your grief.

"I regret that I cannot share your hardships and your weariness; my advice and my experience would be of great service to you in these difficult circumstances. Still I am convinced that you will act with wisdom.

"You have become a fervent Christian, and your religion

will give you strength; it will help you to endure injustice and
wrong.   It has already taught you that the miseries of this
world are the trials that lead the way to a better life, and that to
suffer with resignation is most meritorious in the eyes of God.
Be strong and patient, therefore, my dear child; do not give
way to your first impulses; ask yourself what I would advise
under all circumstances.

'" You have grown much more prudent and reserved, but you
still have too much *abandon* with strangers.   This is because of
your excellent disposition ; you think everyone sincere and true,
because you are so yourself.   You do not remember that men
can act a part.   Dear child: time and experience should have
taught you that great and small are all actors; that everyone
here below wears a mask to hide their features.   To distrust
everyone is sad, but it is better than to confide in them.

" Women generally will be jealous of you; they will try to
find out your secrets in order to do you some ill turn.   Men
will pay homage to you, and if you give them the *least hope*,
they will become your bitter enemies, as soon as they find that
they cannot possess you.   All this is not encouraging, but it is
better to know the danger than to walk blindly along a way
bordered with precipices.

" You are warned; you are wise and strong ; so, God helping,
you will escape all danger.

" Be careful of your health, my poor child! your body is too
weak for the ardour and fire of your soul—it is a covering
wearied by the strength of the passions it encloses.   Try to be
more calm; it is necessary for the success of your enterprise,
and indispensable for your health.   When you find yourself
troubled and agitated take the 'Imitation of Jesus Christ,'
you will always find words of consolation there which will bring
peace to your soul.

" You have had, dear child, a life full of crosses, deception,
and griefs ;—undoubtedly you have not deserved so much misfortune.   But you have never had any rule of conduct ; you
have allowed yourself to be too much carried away by your
passions : to-day you have some experience, but more than that
you have religion, that solid foundation on which you can lean
without fear.   Therefore I hope that you will triumph over all
difficulties.   Do not forget what I have told you so many times
—that modesty is one of the surest means of success ; and that
it consists in speaking *as little as possible of one's self, and of
what one has done.*

" In America you are all rather boastful.   You love to tell of your life, your relations, your friendships; this is a defect not known in France among well-bred people; they have others quite as serious, but not this.

"Now I have given you a great deal of good advice, dictated as you must know by my profound affection and my desire to see you perfect. You will receive it then, dear child, with the certainty that I have only had your welfare and happiness in view.

"While your are working so courageously for others, you may be sure that I will watch over your child as if she were my own. I will give her toys, bonbons, caresses; I will try to take your place.

"I hope, my dear child, that my letter will find you at Brest in tolerable health and in a courageous frame of mind. I do not speak of your heart; I know it is torn, and I can give you no other consolation than to say that I pity you, and I share your sorrow.

"You have grown much in my esteem; I respect you now as well as love you. You were my good and loving child; now you have become a strong and courageous woman, and my confidence in you is deeply rooted. I pray God to watch over and protect you, and to sustain you in your trials. Do not forget me in your prayers; and be assured that my thoughts and my love will be ever faithful to you.

"Ever yours,
" LAFERRIÈRE "

CHAPTER LXXV.

GENERAL DIX ON DIVORCE.

Accident to the *Pereire*—A Truce between Husband and Wife.

I SAILED in the French steamship *Europe*, and after a voyage of twelve days arrived in New York, Jan. 5th, 1869.

Mrs. General Dix and several other ladies gave me a cordial welcome. Mrs. Dix fully coincided in the opinions expressed by her husband, General Dix, in the following letter to me.

"AMERICAN LEGATION, PARIS,
December 17th, 1868.

"MY DEAR MRS. ECKEL,

"I have received your letter informing me of your sudden departure for the United States, and the cause. I need not say that I deeply regret it. Your sister came to the Legation in the summer of 1867. I remember her very distinctly, and I was most favourably impressed with her personal appearance and her conversation, as well as her lady-like manners. Nothing could be more unfortunate for her than to have her domestic relations made the subject of a public investigation ; for, admitting that she is entirely faultless in the unhappy difference between her and her husband, it will be a perpetual stain on the reputation of her children if she succeeds in making out such a case against him as to justify a judicial decree of separation. It is far better to submit to the deepest of conjugal wrongs than to send innocent children through life with such a burden of reproach upon them. Even when the error is on the part of the wife, whom the world always judges more severely than the husband, it had better be covered up, and the family shame averted by a quiet separation. If the true friends of your sister present these considerations in such a manner as to assure her that they are actuated by a sincere interest in her welfare and that of her children, she will not, I am sure, refuse to listen to them.

" To you any public exposure would be most unfortunate, by prejudicing your social position at Court, and in the society of Paris. Divorces here are not allowed, either by the civil or the ecclesiastical law. They are a badge of dishonour, and so strong is the prejudice against them that it extends, in some degree, to the other branches of a family. That a divorce in your sister's case would injure you very seriously there is no doubt.

" On her account, on that of her children, and on yours, I earnestly hope that such a calamity (I do not use too strong a term) may be averted. If she and her husband cannot live together let them separate quietly. Life is full of changes, and time often brings troubles to an end much more satisfactorily than our own action, even when it is guided by the greatest prudence.

" If there is anything which I can do for you to aid you please advise me, and it shall be done promptly.

" Very truly yours,

"JOHN A. DIX."

I had only been in New York a few days before the news came that the *Pereire* had met with a dreadful accident, and was obliged to return to Havre after losing several passengers. That occurrence redoubled my faith in prayer, and strengthened my convictions that God was watching over me.

My sister withdrew her suit for divorce and shortly afterwards returned to her husband.

During my stay in New York, in the parlours I frequented,

most of the people were well bred: yet occasionally, here and there, could be seen some figures whose manners and accent would betray their origin and training. In vain they tried to conceal it by gewgaws, and a feigned air of haughty reserve. It was just as impossible to mistake one of these people for a a gentleman or lady as it would be to take a genuine African for a pure Caucasian.

CHAPTER LXXVI.

MIDNIGHT REFLECTIONS BEFORE THE LOOKING-GLASS.
Shoddy—Why Donkeys eat Thistles.

I HAD just returned from a first-class New York sociable, which reminded me of a field of full-blown clover interspersed with thistles. The clover, with its gracefully drooping blossoms, has an aspect of instinctive ease and modesty, which seems to be innate in persons of good breeding, while the thistle stiffly shoots itself above the clover with that air of impertinent presumption which so readily distinguishes the upstart. Yet the blossom of the thistle and the clover have the same violet hue; and the thistle even outvies the clover in the downy texture of its flower, which shoots itself up boldly, as though, like an aigrette of gems on the head of a haughty, ill-bred woman, it sought to attract the gaze of all. The thistle too can outdo the clover in bustle and show; but just watch the cattle, and you will see that none but the jackasses like it and eat it.

I once asked my husband why the donkeys ate thistles. "Because, darling," he replied, "they are jackasses, and they don't know any better." During the winter I passed in New York, 1869, I never went into society without thinking how many men there were in the world who resembled the jackasses in this respect.

CHAPTER LXXVII.

BACK IN THE HIGHLANDS—AUNT HULDAH ON INFALLIBILITY.
My Brother—Was Noah a Catholic?—A Retrospect of Betsy Dot—I buy the little Cottage.

GETTING weary of New York, my thoughts turned once more to the Highlands of Dutchess. I had never heard from the place since I left it ten years before.

I wrote to one of my cousins, asking if it were possible for me to obtain board for a few weeks, with anyone residing on the hills.

Shortly afterwards I received an answer to my letter saying that my uncle Horace was dead, that my aunt Mercy had moved and was living down in the village—that I could obtain board with a family who lived in the little cottage near the pond.

This was one of the spots I most cherished. It was the same little cottage, that I had looked upon in my childhood, and longed to possess, and the very same pond on whose brink I used to stand, and watch the waves as they seemed to whisper to me my father's name; and it was on a ledge of rocks near that pond that I used to sit for hours, looking at the far-off hills, whose outlines could be but dimly seen, on account of the blue haze, which always seemed to envelop them, as it were, in a mysterious shade. I now longed again to see the beloved spot, and I replied by return of mail, appointing the day to meet me at the train.

I left New York for Amenia in the latter part of June. I got off at Wassaic station, and at the moment I alighted from the train, and saw the old depôt once more, I recollected that it was just ten years since I had stood there and bade my Aunt Mercy good-bye, and had said to her that it would be ten years before she would ever see me again.

As we pressed through the little village on our way to the hills, I found everything just as I had left it, and even as I had found it twenty years before, when my father brought me there a child.

We stopped at Aunt Huldah's, and I found the old lady looking just the same, excepting that her step was not quite as quick. She did not recognise me; no one had told her that I was coming. The moment I made myself known to her, she stepped back, so as to take a good look at me, and then said, in a sort of exclamatory tone: "Lord sakes! where did you get all those fine clothes from?" Said I: "Never mind my clothes, aunty, but tell me how my brother is." "Your brother," she replied, "has gone and made a fool of himself, and thrown himself away. He has gone and got married to a Catholic girl, and she got around him and made him jine her church before she would have him; and that is just how it is."

"What!" I exclaimed, "my brother a Roman Catholic!" and I immediately recollected that this was one of the things I had asked for at the altar, immediately after I was baptised. "I am rejoiced," said I, "to hear that my brother is a Catholic; for I am a Catholic myself." "What!" she replied, "you don't mean to say that they have got around you too? Well, I hope they

will not make such a fool of you as they have of him. Their
meeting-house is six miles off, and your brother walks it sometimes, for his wife won't let him go to our meeting any more.
Humph! the Catholics say that God takes care of their Church!
and they will never come down, for God will never let them.
Well, He did not prevent them all going under once."   "When
was that?" I asked. "If you ever read your Bible you would
know," answered Aunt Huldah; "at the time of Noah's ark.
Noah and his family were the only ones that were saved, and
they were not Catholics."

I burst out laughing, and said: "There were no Catholics
then, aunty; if there had been, Noah would have been one."
"Don't think," she replied, "that you are coming back here to
teach me Scripture, for I read it before you were born." Said
I: "Let us talk about something else. I have come here to
stay a few weeks. I am rich." At that she opened her eyes,
and asked me to sit down. I continued: "I expect the people
around here will tear me to pieces. But I have come back to
see the country, and not the folks, and I hope you will not join
in with the rest." Said she: "I will stand by you; for I like
people who know how to get along in the world. But tell me
where you got your money from. We saw in the papers that
you went to Court, and that you had on diamonds and pearls:
and they all say around here that the Emperor gave them to
you; how did you manage to get in with such a big man?"

"Those are all lies," said I: "I made my money by specula-
ting; but just because I am a woman, people are envious of my
success, and they will not give me credit for knowing more than
themselves. But you know how it is with the St. Johns, they
are all enterprising."

"Yes," she replied, "all but your father; and I always
thought that you would make another spendthrift, just like him,
and give your last cent away to the first trooper that came along.
Well, now, if you have got money, keep it, and don't go to fool-
ing it away. I always said that you were a St. John, and you
have proved it by your smartness." "Don't you think I look
like them?" I asked. "Well, I kinder think you do, but anybody can see that you have been steady, for you look as young
as you ever did."

I returned her the compliment, and after making her reiterate
her promise to defend me whenever she heard me abused, I
jumped into the waggon and we drove towards the hills. The
moment that I got a sight of the old big hill was one of the
happiest moments that I had known for years, and the pure

fresh air that I inhaled seemed to infuse into me a new life. We passed my uncle's cottage, which was now occupied by strangers. I threw it a hasty glance but had no desire to go in. Betsy Dot was sitting with her back towards the window; she was at her loom, in the same position in which I had left her ten years before.

We then passed the spring, and when just a little beyond it my eyes happened to fall on a little thick white marble stone, about six inches square, which was planted in the earth by the side of the road, and on its top were cut out two letters—N. Y. Thought I to myself: "This is something new;" and I began to wonder if they had buried a dog there and had given him a monument. The thought had hardly occurred to me, when the man said: "Now we are *across the line*." "What does that mean?" said I. "Why," said he, "have you been in France so long that you have forgotten your English? 'Across the line' means that we are out of York State into Connecticut." I never knew before that the whole country did not lie in "York" State.

We had not yet reached the cottage when I missed the large chestnut-tree, under which I sat the day that I was on my way to the shoemaker's, the afternoon that my aunt refused to let me come into the house unless I would consent to be whipped. The tree had been cut down even with the fence, and formed a part of it. The trees had grown up around the little cottage and gave it an air of modest reserve which lent it an additional charm.

The moment I entered my whole soul was filled with those same buoyant feelings that I had felt in my youth, and I raised my heart to God and thanked Him for having inspired me to come and visit this place again.

One morning I was sitting on the trunk of the old chestnut-tree, and I began thinking about the troubles in Paris, and thought how nice it would be to fly to such a spot as this, if there was ever another reign of terror in France.

The more I thought it over, the more probable it appeared to me that it might really come to pass, and I wished that I owned the place, so as to be prepared for such an emergency. The very thoughts of flying there, and hiding myself with Laferrière in those wild woods, appeared to me like a vision of terrestrial bliss.

These thoughts rushed through my mind quicker than I can relate them, and, last of all, came the recollection of the time that I sat under the old tree, when I was a penniless child, and how I had coveted the possession of such a home as that little white cottage. As soon as that recollection came back, I ran into the house and asked the man how much he would take for his farm. He told me his price, and I at once agreed to purchase it.

The moment I bought the place, I began to feel that my mission to America was ended, and that it was in order to buy that spot of ground that God had inspired me to return to the United States.

CHAPTER LXXVII.

RESTITUTION AND RETRIBUTION.

A Receipt in full.

I CALLED once to see Aunt Mercy. So many things were repeated to me which Aunt Mercy had said against me, that I never cared to call on her. Among other things, when she heard that I had paid Betsy Dot five dollars for bewitching her loom, Aunt Mercy declared that if I gave Betsy a thousand dollars it would never pay her for all the sighs and tears that I had caused her to heave and shed.

When this remark was repeated to me I protested that Aunt Mercy placed too high a value on Betsy's sighs and tears. "For," said I, "I'll bet that she will take twenty-five cents for them, and consider herself well paid too." So the next day the man with whose family I boarded went with me to see Mrs. Dot, and we found her in the loom. I read to her a paper I had brought with me and told her that if she would sign it I would give her twenty-five cents. She readily agreed to do so. The paper ran thus :—"Received from Mrs. L. St. John Eckel twenty-five cents in full payment for all the sighs and tears that she has ever caused me to heave or shed." She signed it, the man endorsed it, and I sent the paper to Aunt Mercy to show her that she placed a much higher value on Betsy Dot's sighs and tears than Betsy Dot did herself.

But a very little while after my uncle Horace's death, Aunt Mercy had been married to a man who had no religious convictions. I was told that my aunt confided to some of her friends that she suffered intensely around the heart, and it was all caused by trouble ; that she was jealous of her husband, and that no tongue could tell how wretched at times she was and how her heart pained her.

When this was told to me I looked upon it as retribution, that God had permitted that feeling to be excited in her bosom, as a punishment for all the sorrow she had given my husband; for few were the happy days he ever knew, from the hour she awakened the demon of jealousy in his breast.

CHAPTER LXXIX.

THE SACRIFICE.

Our Lady of Victories—" I will, Lord "—I keep my Word—
Obedience and Sacrifice.

I RETURNED to France in the latter part of September. When I arrived in Paris I found it almost deserted. Laferrière was at his château. Rollin and other friends whom I had left in good health were dead. I became low-spirited; and for the first two weeks I passed nearly all my time at St. Geneviève's altar or at Our Lady of Victoires.

Notre Dame des Victoires is situated in the vicinity of the theatres and opera-houses. There are evening services in that church every night in the year. It was seldom that I ever arrived at the opera or the theatre until after nine o'clock; for I almost invariably attended the services at Notre Dame des Victoires first.

I would leave my opera-cloak in the carriage, and put on a large waterproof with a hood, which I would throw over my head. Thus my hair, which was usually sparkling with gems, my bare neck and white dress were entirely concealed, and I would pass among the crowd unobserved.

About ten days after my arrival in Paris Laferrière returned from his château. He was overjoyed to see me, and showered upon me every attention and kindness; but nothing that he could do for me could make me happy. The only consolation— the only real happiness I found, even then, was in prayer. I was always sad when I thought of him; was sadder, too, when I was with him, because I loved him every day more and more.

One evening as I was praying before the altar of Our Lady of Victories I made a firm resolve to live a more perfect life. My heart was wrung with repentance. I rose and went into the first confessional I came to, and made a humble, sincere confession of all my sins. I told the priest of my deep remorse, and my firm resolve to lead a more perfect life. After I had made my confession the priest gave me his blessing and told me to come back again. This drove me nearly wild. I went home, and was so ill that I was obliged to keep my bed. Laferrière implored me not to conceal from him what it was that preyed so much upon my mind; but I did not like to tell him that a priest had refused me absolution. One evening, just to change the conversation, I told him that I had purchased a little home among the beloved hills where I passed my childhood. If I had announced to him my future husband he could not have been more surprised. "Then," said he, "you intend to leave me, and abandon me for those woodlands that you are always raving about." "Oh," I replied, "I intend one day that you and I shall go and live there together." Said he: "I am almost inclined to think that you have lost your mind." "But," said I, "if there is a revolution, and the Emperor is dethroned, and the whole of you are exiled, how sweet it would be to fly with you there!"

"Ah," he answered, "*pauvre Empereur!* do you think that I would ever abandon him? His fortune is my fortune. If ever, for the misfortune of France and the world, he should fall before a revolution, I would fall with him. My destiny is linked with his; the servant of his happy days will be his devoted servant still in the days of misfortune. It is not then that I would abandon him. Would you abandon me in the hour of adversity?" My answer was a flood of tears, which spoke the devotedness of my heart.

"Well," he continued, "no sooner would I abandon him than you would me. But why should you have bought a home in America? You certainly intend to go there to live." "Oh," said I, "I bought it under an inspiration. I cannot tell why I bought it; but I felt that I was doing right."

He left me that evening feeling so sad that he could hardly restrain his tears when he bade me good-night. The next day I grew more despondent, and each succeeding day only increased my depression. At the end of the week I rose from my bed and drove to Our Lady of Victories. This time the priest gave me absolution; but he refused to let me receive holy communion, and told me to come again in another week. I wept and implored him to have mercy on me, told him how ill I was, and that he was killing me; but he remained inexorable.

The next morning I had a raging fever. Laferrière came. He had seen my physician, who told him it was nothing but grief that made me so ill. He did nothing but scold me for being so sad and discontented when I had everything to make me happy. All that he said only served to exasperate me and make me worse. I prayed constantly that God would inspire me what to do in order to bring peace again to my soul.

One evening I was kneeling in my bed making that same request, and continued repeating it for hours. The clock struck one. I threw myself back upon my pillow and tried to sleep, but I was seized again with such feelings of despair that I instantly arose, and kneeling again in my bed, I recommenced praying and imploring God more fervently than ever to have mercy on me.

At last I exclaimed: "O beloved Jesus, have mercy on me and inspire me what to do that I may be happy once more!" I repeated those same words aloud twice, and as I was about to utter them for the third time I heard a voice within me distinctly say: "Give up Laferrière." I instantly replied: "I will, Lord!" and immediately my soul was calmed, and I experienced that same joy and that same peace which I had felt at the moment of my conversion. I was sure that God had spoken to me and told me to give up Laferrière.

I instantly got out of bed, lit the lamp, and wrote until morning.

I made a brief sketch of my acquaintance with Laferrière, and how wretched I had been since he had told me that I could not be his wife while his daughter lived, that I had never known a really happy hour since. After writing a long letter in a cool, determined, deliberate style, I forbade him ever coming to see me again unless I wrote to him to come.

I knew that God had spoken to me, and that He had told me to give him up. I instantly consented, for I thought that He meant that I was to give him up *only for a while*, and I believe that if I obeyed God He would finally unite us before His altar. I could not imagine any other happiness on earth than to be wedded to Laferrière.

Laferrière wrote me a kind and affectionate letter in reply, attributing all that I had written to him to a state of nervous excitement. He hoped that his few words would find me peaceful and calm, and that I would send a message by the bearer of this note appointing an hour for him to call.

There was a great struggle then between nature and the fear of God. But I dared not disobey the voice that I had heard speak within me that night, for I firmly believed that it was the voice of God, and I feared to disobey it, lest God would never permit me to marry Laferrière. I believed that of myself I could do nothing, but that the destiny of all mankind was in His hand. Thus I succeeded in overcoming nature, and I

answered Laferrière's letter, telling him that I was fully resolved not to see him, and I begged him not to call at the
Abbey, for I *would not* receive him.

No sooner had his messenger left than I shed a flood of tears.
Yet I did not regret what I had written, I only deplored that I
was forced to do it. I knew I had done right, for my conscience
approved of my action, but I was miserable that God should
exact of me such a sacrifice before He would let me reach the
goal of earthly happiness.

In a few days I was well enough to leave my room, and I
repaired to Our Lady of Victories. The priest still refused to let
me receive holy communion, and told me to return again in
another week. This was too much for my feeble condition to
bear, and I nearly fainted in the confessional. For an instant
all my strength failed me. He closed the grating of the confessional, and heard a confession on the other side; then opening on the side where I was, he became extremely abusive, when
he found that I was still kneeling there, for he thought that I
remained from obstinacy. When I tried to assure him that I had
not the strength to leave, that he had nearly killed me by refusing
me this time, he roughly replied that he did not wish to see any
such affectation in the confessional; that he doubted my sincerity, for if I was as anxious to do right as I pretended to be,
God would give me the strength to obey; that my obedience
would be as acceptable to God as if I received holy communion; "but so long as I see you hesitate to be obedient,"
said he, "just so long will I doubt that you are worthy of
receiving holy communion." I instantly rose and left the
church.

When I reached the Abbey I found Laferrière's valet waiting
for me with a note, in which he begged me to name an hour for
him to call.

I wrote on the back of the envelope "*Never!*" and told the
valet to take it to his master.

CHAPTER LXXX.

MONTESQUIEU AND THE JESUITF.

St. Augustine's Confessions.

THE next morning the Count de Clésieux called on me. He
had not seen me since I returned, and was struck with the great
change in me. The Count was a fervent Catholic. He had

founded an agricultural school at St. Ilan, Brittany, where he supported several hundred orphan boys at his own expense or through his own exertions. I told him that I had broken off with Laferrière, and he congratulated me with all his heart. I then told him the reason I was so sad, because a priest refused to let me receive holy communion; and I related to him the whole affair. He was indignant at the severity of the priest, and begged me never to return to him again, but to let him introduce me to his director, Father Bazin, a Jesuit, who lived in the Rue de Sèvres, a few doors from the Abbaye aux Bois.

I told him frankly that I never wanted to have anything to do with the Jesuits—that I never forgot a maxim I learned once in Montesquieu. "What," he asked, "did that blabber say that could prejudice you against one of the best societies that ever existed for the propagation of the Faith?" "That may be," said I; "but I like to be let alone; and it appears that the Jesuits are bad fellows to get into a quarrel with, for there is no escaping them. Montesquieu says: 'I am afraid of the Jesuits. If I offend a nobleman he will forget me—I will forget him. I can go into another province—into another kingdom. But if I offend the Jesuits at Rome I am sure to meet them at Paris. I am surrounded by them wherever I go. Their incessant correspondence with one another keeps alive their enmities.'"

"I would pay no more attention," answered the Count, "to what Montesquieu might say about religion or its propagators, than I would to the braying of an ass; for an ass understands the Jesuits and the Christian tenets just about as well as a sceptic who only admits the immortality of the soul just because it happens to suit his humours and self-conceit to believe himself immortal, like God: and such was the illustrious writer Montesquieu."

After much persuasion I promised him that I would permit him to introduce Father Bazin to me. The day following I went to Father Bazin and made my confession, and he gave me permission to receive holy communion. Father Bazin was an elderly priest, most high-bred and agreeable; but the fact of his being a Jesuit I was suspicious of him, and told him so, which only made him laugh.

He told me I ought to read the life of Father de Ravignan. Said I: "Was he a Jesuit?" "Yes," he replied, "and a very holy one." "I'll wager," said I, "that a Jesuit wrote his life too." "That is very true," he replied. "Well," I said, "if I wanted to find out the truth about your people I would never read the life of a Jesuit written by a Jesuit."

I received the congratulations of all my friends in the Faubourg for having given up Laferrière. He sent his valet as usual every morning to receive my orders. He entreated me to receive him, but I was inflexible. I concealed all the pain and suffering of my heart, even from Father Bazin, to whom I now went regularly to confession. I also went regularly to receive instructions from the "Ladies of the Retreat," to whom I became every day more and more attached. I kept myself constantly employed, and began to study Latin, the same as I would have taken a narcotic to lull my senses to sleep in order to forget Laferrière.

I made everybody my teacher. Father Bazin, Madame de la Chapelle, and every gentleman who called on me I would require to teach me something in Latin. Father Bazin told me to get St. Augustine's Confessions to read. I deferred getting them, supposing it was some stupid pious book, being the confessions of a saint. Every time he saw me he asked me if I had got them.

One day, as I was passing through the *quartier Latin* on my way to the Pantheon, to satisfy the Father I bought the book, brought it home with me, and it lay several days on my table untouched, The Marquise de Ferrière le Vayer saw it lying there. She took it up and said: "I don't think that you ought to read this book, you are too young." I replied: "My director told me to read it." "Then," said she, "you are right; for you should always do what he tells you. But who is your director?" —and she gave me a quizzical glance, as though she suspected that it would be difficult for me to name a particular one out of the many I went to. But I answered very gravely: "He is a Jesuit, and a very holy man." She replied: "They are all holy men, and I am glad that you have put yourself under their guidance. Of course *if he* told you to read it you ought to read it." "Well," I answered, "*he certainly did*." I could see by the way she emphasised *if* that she doubted that he had told me to do any such thing.

As soon as this lady left, my curiosity was excited to see what there was in the book that she thought I was not old enough to read, and I began at once to make a habit of reading a few chapters of it every night before going to bed.

CHAPTER LXXXI.

INCONSISTENCY OF THE HEART—I SEEK GOD'S WILL IN HIS WORD.
MY DIRECTOR DISAPPROVES.

I BEGAN to loathe what the world calls society, and would
only frequent those houses where, had I not gone, I was afraid
the world would think that I was not invited. I became less
fastidious about my dress, and instead of appearing always in a
new costume, I would say to our Lord: "I will wear the old
dress, and give the price of a new one to the poor for Thy sake."
Whenever I made that sacrifice I was sure to pass a happy
evening.

One evening I returned from one of the Empress's private
balls. That night I refused Laferrière's arm when he offered to
take me into the supper-room. I did it from pride, just to show
others that I was determined not to encourage him to think
that I cared anything for him. It wounded him. I was
rejoiced at the moment, for I felt that I wanted him too to know
what it was to suffer, forgetting that his heart had been in
mourning for years.

I was rejoiced to see the expression of interior agony that
passed over his countenance, and which he vainly tried to conceal. A few moments afterwards he spoke to me, and remarked
how well I was looking. I was flushed with excitement, and rejoiced that I had at last made his heart feel for an instant what
mine had suffered for so long a time.

He observed that my health appeared to be entirely restored.
I told him that I was perfectly well, and began talking to him
in the most recklessly, giddy style, telling him how happy I
was, how I was enjoying myself; and I named over the list of
my new acquaintances, taking pains to single out those who
were as influential as himself. I saw how every word I uttered
wounded him, yet I delighted in it, at the same moment that I
could have laid down my life for him. So inconsistent is the
heart when filled with pride, human attachment, and disappointed love.

The moment I entered my room I broke out into a hysterical
laugh. I felt that for once, at least, I was gratified. I knew
that he was wretched, and, in his misery, I seemed to find satisfaction for all the humiliations that his delaying our marriage
had heaped upon me. My soul gloated over its revenge. I
tried to convince myself that I had done well. Even when I

knelt down to pray I endeavoured to draw some response from God, some consolation to justify me for the way in which I had acted. My spirits were elated, but my heart soon became true to itself again, and I was troubled in spite of the efforts I made to deceive myself with the thought that I was happy. Morning dawned before I fell asleep.

The following night I was reading St. Augustine's Confessions at the place where he speaks of his return to faith. After I finished reading I began to review the past, to see if I could draw any conclusion from it, that I should one day be Laferrière's wife. I thought of the many different fortune-tellers who had all predicted that I would marry him. Even the famous Edmond had told me so. But the last fortune-teller I had consulted had told me that I would not marry him.

That night I felt inclined to give her credence over the rest. I also recollected that on the night that Laferrière told me that our marriage must be deferred until after his daughter's death, I had as plainly seen written on a scroll in my dream: " You will *never* marry Laferrière."

, This dream and the prediction of the last fortune-teller were uppermost in my mind, and my heart became deathly sad. I began to feel that there was no use of hoping against hope, and I would say to myself: " What is the use of all this sacrifice if I am never to marry him ?"

In my agony I exclaimed : " O God, why didst Thou create me, and why dost Thou delight in torturing me ?" And I began to implore God to speak to me and to give me hope, or to let me die ; for I was weary of such a life.

I reproached Him for being kinder to St. Augustine than He was to me. I did not believe that I had ever been worse than St. Augustine : besides, He had given St. Augustine a good mother. At last I exclaimed, with indignation : " Just look at the kind of a mother you gave me ! How could you have ever expected me to become a Christian ? The least you can do is to let me marry Laferrière. Yes," I continued, " how good you were to St. Augustine to speak to him in the Bible." I then recollected the time that I had opened the two Bibles in Brooklyn before the birth of my child, and I fairly screamed at the very recollection of the dreadful words I had found there.

I had never read but one chapter in the Bible since. I took out my Bible and began to kiss it and talk to it, and implore it to tell me the truth and give me hope, and to let me know if the old fortune-teller and the dream spoke the truth or not when they told me that I was never to marry Laferrière.

Then, raising my heart to God, I opened the book, and my eyes instantly fell on these words of Jeremias: (Chap. xxix.)

." 8. For thus saith the Lord of hosts, the God of Israel: Let not your prophets and your diviners that be in the midst of you deceive you; neither hearken to your dreams which ye cause to be dreamed.

" 9. For they prophesy falsely unto you in my name: I have not sent them, saith the Lord.

" 10. For thus saith the Lord: That after seventy years be accomplished at Babylon I will visit you and perform my good word toward you, in causing you to return to this place.

" 11. For I know the thoughts that I think toward you, saith the Lord—thoughts of peace, and not of evil, to give you an expected end.

" 12. Then shall ye call upon me, and ye shall go and pray unto me, and I will hearken unto you.

" 13. And ye shall seek me and find me, when ye shall search for me with all your heart.

" 14. And I will be found of you, saith the Lord; and I will turn away your captivity, and I will gather you from all the nations and from all the places whither I have driven you, saith the Lord; and I will bring you again into the place whence I caused you to be carried away captive."

I had no sooner finished reading those verses of Jeremias than my whole soul was filled with peace, hope, and joy. I interpreted them in this manner: That the fortune-teller had told me a lie, and that the dream came from the devil. As Paris is called the Modern Babylon, and as it was then the beginning of the year 1870, I was sure that our Lord promised me that in a year all my troubles would be at an end.

I soon fell asleep, and awoke the next morning as happy and as refreshed as though I had not been shedding a single tear.

As soon as I rose I went to see Father Bazin, and told him how miserable I had been, but how happy I was now; and I related to him that all my joy came from having opened the Bible, and having read certain words therein.

" My child," replied the father, " that is all wrong; you must never do such things as that. It is presumption and superstition. Supposing you had happened to open at something that was just the reverse. Instead of being peaceful and happy, you would have come to me with your heart wrung with despair. You must never do that again."

Said I: " I don't care what you may think or say about it,

father ; but God spoke to me then, and I know it." The good father tried in vain to convince me that I was wrong.

From the time I had opened at those words in the Bible—for weeks and weeks afterwards I would read them over regularly two or three times a day. In them I now found all my hopes of happiness : nothing troubled me. I was firm in the belief that God had spoken to me, and that He had promised to give me peace. I was passing the time as best I could, waiting for the year 1870 to roll round, at the end of which I believed the time was fixed for the consummation of all my hopes.

CHAPTER LXXXII.

DEATH OF THE COUNT DE MONTALEMBERT.

My First " Retreat "—A Supernatural Command.

MARCH came, and my director and some ladies in the Faubourg tried to persuade me to make a Retreat, which was to be given in the Chapel of the Ladies of the Retreat by Rev. Father Ducoudray, Superior of the Jesuits in the Rue de la Poste. I hesitated about going ; but one morning at Mass I determined to give a whole week entirely to God.

On Sunday morning, March 13th, the Count de Montalembert breathed his last. I went to see Madame de la Chapelle, to express my regrets for not being able to attend the Retreat ; for I wanted to be at the de Montalemberts. She replied that that need not interfere with my Retreat ; that I could come to the instructions, and then go and make my meditations in his death-chamber. I could not choose a more fitting place.

Monday morning, after the instruction, I called at the de Montalemberts'. There was a constant flow of callers ; yet none but the clergy were permitted to go in. The others left their cards.

I bribed the portress, and she allowed me to go up by the servants' staircase.

Never can I forget the impression that the solemnity which reigned in that room where the body of the great Christian orator lay made on my mind as I approached his corpse and knelt beside it.

The Count de Montalembert was beautiful as he lay there in death. His countenance bore an expression of manly virtue and of true nobility. At his feet lay a cross of Parma violets, in the centre of which was arranged, with white flowers, the initial of his last name. The whole room was impregnated with the odour of the violets, which stole upon the senses like incense lighted by friendship's hand around a hallowed bier.

I never prayed as fervently as I prayed there, and my constant prayer was : "Lord, have mercy on his soul and mine. Inspire me, beloved Jesus, what to do. May I do a great deal of good before I die ; and may I make Thee and Thy Church beloved !"

I did nothing but repeat that prayer, and it seemed as though my soul could pour forth no other.

Madeleine, the daughter of the deceased count, knelt silently at the bedside. As she rose to leave she saw me, and threw her arms around me. We tenderly embraced. and then kneeling down together, our arms entwined around each other, she wept, while I continued to pray, ever repeating the same prayer.

Tuesday morning I went there again, and also in the afternoon. It was but a repetition of the day before—only new faces ; yet none but the clergy entered the room. I offered up the same prayer. Wednesday I attended his funeral, and made my meditation there. Thursday was the 17th, and my birthday. I went to see Madame de Montalembert during the interval of the instructions. Friday I remained the whole day at the Retreat. Saturday morning, which was the Feast of St. Joseph, I prayed with great fervour and faith, and implored St. Joseph to intercede for me that God would inspire me what to do.

Just before I rose to go to receive holy communion, my heart began to burn. I could not remember ever having experienced such peace and joy. As soon as I had received communion, as I was about to rise from the altar, I cried out, from the innermost depths of my soul : " O beloved Saviour, do not refuse to answer my prayer. St. Joseph, pray for me that God will inspire me what to do." Instantly I heard a voice clearly say : "Go HOME AND WORK FOR GOD." I replied, "I will." I went back to my seat : and my whole bosom was aglow, and I could have swooned away with delight. I at once began to make preparations in my mind to leave, and resolved to reduce my expenses, that I might have more money to employ in God's service, when I reached America.

That day we finished the Retreat at St. Geneviève's tomb, in the church of St. Etienne du Mont (St. Stephen of the Mount), which is situated near the Pantheon.

While I was there I could think of nothing but returning to

America; and it was there that the thought occurred to me, that I would build a little church among my much-beloved hills. I had no sooner decided upon it, than it seemed as though God Himself sanctioned it: I was perfectly at peace and at rest.   I felt that that was the work God required of me, and all the way going home I kept mentally exclaiming: " I will go to America, and will build Thee a church; and then I know that Thou wilt bring me back again to France, and let me marry Laferrière."

My friends, and even my new director, Father Bazin, tried to dissuade me from leaving; and when I persisted in my resolution, they said I was crazy.

I wrote to Laferrière. He replied that he would not try to deter me from my resolution, but begged of me to consider it, at least two months, before I engaged my passage or made any alterations in my apartments.

On the 16th of May, the two months had nearly expired, and I was more sanguine than ever that God had called me to go to America and build Him a church.

CHAPTER LXXXIII.

REASON AND LOVE—PEACE TO BE FOUND NOT IN MAN, BUT IN GOD.

Human Love—True Rest.

THE two months having expired, I wrote to Laferrière that my mind was still unchanged, and that I was firmly resolved to leave France.

He came the day after he received my letter. Nearly seven months had passed since he had crossed my threshold. As soon as I told him where I was going, and my plans, he set before me all the difficulties of such a position, among people who were already predisposed against me.

I told him that I could not suffer more there than I did in Paris; for to live so near to him, and not to see him, was a continual martyrdom. Said he: "It was your own wish." "I wished it," said I, "because I believed God demanded it of me, and I believe so still. But whether that was an hallucination or not, it would be impossible for us to renew our former relations, because I have gone so far that all my friends would despise me and turn their backs on me, if I did. If I were your wife, I would not care; but situated as I am, and on account of my child "—

He interrupted me—"It is true; and it would be wrong for

me to permit you to make such a sacrifice on account of your
child.   Her future depends on the esteem others have for you.
But because you would not be willing this moment to sacrifice
the consideration of others for me, on account of your child, do
I reproach you for it ? and do I love you less because I do not
try and persuade you from doing your duty ?   The happiness of
my child is just as dear to me as yours should be to you   Religion should teach you to bear your cross, instead of seeking to
fly from it as you are doing.   In trying to evade one cross we
often encounter heavier ones; and I hope you may never have
cause to regret having placed the ocean between us.

"When you are in America, you say, you are going to give up
the world.   If you do, you will then have time to reflect; for
the world soon forgets us, when we no longer stand in its way,
or it can no longer make use of us.   Wait until you find yourself abandoned and alone : you will then reflect, and you will do
me justice.   But I pity you, and wish to spare you that.   I do
not consider that you are conscious of what you are doing.   I
look upon your imagination as diseased.   I would that my words
might have some effect upon you, and you would change your
mind, and try to be satisfied to live here ; for certainly if we
could not see each other frequently, we could occasionally, at
least, without the slightest impropriety.   I am willing to make
my share of the sacrifice, for I see that my doing so increases
the esteem that others have for you.   And if I have remained
away from you so patiently, and have not persisted in seeing
you, I made the sacrifice knowing that it would be for your
good.   My sentiments for you may not be as ardent and as de-
monstrative as yours are for me: *mais, croyez moi, que les
miens valent bien les vôtres* (but believe me, they are none the
less real and enduring)."

"All very well," said I.   "It is easy enough to talk about a
diseased imagination, and to make light of a sensitive and impassioned heart.   That heart may not have the sterling value of
your own ; but I am as God made me.   I can only love as I do
love.   I cannot command my heart to love you in a mathe-
matical avoirdupois way, as you can, and say I will love you just
so far, and no farther, submitting every pulsation within me to
the voice of reason.   I lose my reason when I think of you."

"Cold and passionless as my heart may seem to you," he replied, "I sometimes believe that my love for you will outlive
yours for me.   I have always had a presentiment of it.   I have a
deep and tender affection for you, and you know you can always
look up to me as you would to a father; and the time may come

when my words may come back to you, and you will wish that you had some one to love you and care for you, even as a father, much as the word may displease you now.

"For we are not always young, and the heart is not always warm and passionate. Age, sorrows, and disappointments often chill it. They have chilled mine, and you should not reproach me when I give you all the warmth that still remains in it."

Said I: "I have implored God to inspire me what to do that will bring peace to my soul. He has made His will known to me, and I shall do it, for I believe that as a reward for my obedience He will give me rest and we shall yet both be happy."

After he became convinced that nothing he could do or say would deter me, he said: "If you will go, go, and may God give you that peace and rest of mind you so eagerly seek! But you are seeking that which you will never find, until you seek it in God alone, for God has reserved that power to Himself, of giving peace and rest to the souls of His creatures. When you ask it of me you are asking of me what I ask for myself. We should not ask it of each other, for we have it not to give. And that peace, even then, which God alone can give, does not exempt us from suffering, for peace consists only in doing our duty, and being resigned to the will of God.

CHAPTER LXXXIV.

Vacillation—A Bugbear from Montesquieu—Indecision—The Bible decides—
The Broken Harp.

WHILE Laferrière was with me that afternoon it seemed as though I could think of nothing but the recompense that God would give me if I should obey Him; and it was my faith and hope in Him which sustained me, and made me insensible to everything that Laferrière could say to try to induce me to abandon my project. But as soon as I was alone I was beside myself with grief, all my courage and hope forsook me. That evening I was tempted to write to him that I would remain, but I began to pray, and then I dared not write.

The next morning I repaired early to the church of Our Lady of Victories, and, while praying at the foot of her altar, all my courage and hope returned. I became incensed with myself for having even hesitated, and to prevent any further vacillations, after I left the church I went to the office of the Transatlantic

Steamship Co. and secured a passage for myself and child in the *Pereire*, which was to sail on the 17th of June.

But I was no sooner back in the Abbey than all my strength and resolution failed me again, for my apartment was beautiful, and was most richly and artistically arrayed. I cast my eyes around it, and exclaimed: "How can I leave thee, and all my friends, and Laferrière?"

After my return to France a young woman of about thirty had applied to me for a situation. She was very *distingué* and prepossessing. I hesitated for a moment, then thought: "Well, I will run the risk, and see how a pretty maid can work, for, with all my precaution in singling out homely ones, they have all turned out to be rogues."

I engaged Françoise on trial, and soon found her a most excellent, trustworthy, and serious person. My motto now is, that a pretty maid is the best to have after all, but you must be sure and see that she is pious as well as pretty.

Françoise did all she could to cheer and encourage me, and offered to accompany me. "Ah, Françoise," said I, "you don't know the country I am going to." "Oh," she quickly replied, "I fear nothing; because my director this morning advised me to go with you."

I instantly recollected that her director was a Jesuit. The moment she pronounced those words I did not deliberate a second, but told her that I would not permit her to accompany me. My only reason for refusing her was on account of her intimacy with the Jesuits. I was resolved not to hold any relations with them in New York for fear they might find out things about me, and write back to their house in Paris.

I could not divest myself of the prejudices I had conceived against those priests, particularly the one that Montesquieu had put into my head. It was a great sacrifice I made to fear; for Françoise would have been a great consolation to me.

In spite of my refusal to let her accompany me she encouraged me to keep my resolution, and told me that it was too late to give it up now; that everybody in the Abbey had seen Monsieur de Laferrière's carriage standing for hours before my door, and it was already whispered through the Abbey that he would persuade me to remain; and she advised me to go, if I returned in the next steamer.

The next day I left the Abbey for good, and went to board at a house recommended to me by the Ladies of the Retreat.

For three weeks I did nothing but while away the time in the salons of my friends. My favourite resort was the *salon* of the

Marquise de Blocqueville, in which I had the happiness to meet the most distinguished men in the world of letters. The Marquise's apartments were the most elegant and sumptuous in Paris. They were fitted up in genuine Oriental style, under the immediate supervision of the Marquise, who is gifted with extraordinary natural abilities, which have been nurtured and developed by education, study, and association with the most refined minds in French society. This lady was among my dearest and most charming friends. Looking back on my chequered career, I cannot remember any period when I was so happy, in the worldly sense of that word, as in those three weeks, during which I communed with the highest order of minds.

As soon as I had decided to leave I wrote to Mrs. Dix of my intended departure, and a few days before I sailed received the following reply:—

"NEW YORK, *May 21st*, 1870.

"MY DEAR MRS. ECKEL,

"I am glad to hear that you are well after so long a silence, and not surprised to know that you are coming home; although I hoped that your anxieties and troubles, whatever they may be or have been, had come to an end, and that you were happy and at peace again. But if this is not to be in France, you are quite right to break away from everything that holds you there, and try, amid other scenes, to forget the past, and begin upon a new, and, I trust, brighter and happier page of your life's history.

"Bring your child with you too, and be contented here. The change may be hard at first; but if it is a sacrifice that is worthy, it will in the end bring its full reward. You know that you have never confided to me your history. I have only surmised many things, and I cannot advise you as if I had your entire confidence.

"Present us with pleasant remembrances to Monsieur de Laferrière.

"Their Majesties' names are often upon our lips, and are always cherished with grateful remembrance in our hearts. The Imperial vases are the pride of our home, and are the admiration of all who see them.

"I only wish I could express to their Majesties how honoured we feel in the possession of such a souvenir of our happy residence in Paris, the finest city in the world.

"Very truly your friend,

"CATHERINE M. DIX."

As soon as I read this letter I exclaimed: "Thank God, I have one faithful friend! that is enough." I was really attached to Mrs. Dix, and did not care if all New York went against me, so long as I felt that I could go to her for sympathy and encouragement.

Madame de Montalembert in the meanwhile had put me in relation with the Ladies of the Sacred Heart. She introduced me to the Assistant Superior-General, Madame Dessoudin, a middle-aged lady, and one of the most charmingly-sympathetic persons I had ever met. This lady gave me an excellent letter to their house in New York, in which she begged of them to do for me all that they could to assist me and encourage me in my undertaking.

No sooner were all my things packed—except my harp and some statuary—than all that consolation and hope which had buoyed me up during the past three weeks left me, and I began to dread returning again to the United States. All that Laferrière had said to me came back to me, and I felt that he was right and that I was really deluded.

From the moment I had announced my intention of returning to America to build a church, nearly everybody I knew had said to me: "Why, you have gone crazy." I had had nothing, it seemed to me, but that poured into my ears since the moment I had made my designs known; and I began to think that they were right and that I was crazy; and I wondered how I could have been drawn into such folly simply by imagining that I heard an interior voice on the 19th of March say to me: "Go home and work for God"—as if God would ever send me to America, after all my effort to do right and to please Him. "Oh," thought I, "it is too much. Rather will I go and confess to everybody that I was deluded—that I imagined I heard a voice, when I could have heard nothing." Yet all the while that I was trying to convince myself that I heard no voice I was sure that I had heard one.

I went to St. Sulpice and knelt before St. Joseph's altar. While on my way I was arranging in my mind how I could undo my folly. I would store my furniture away; and I made up my mind to suffer any humiliation among my friends rather than return to my native country.

As I prayed my faith increased, and I began conversing with God as I would with a fond and tender parent. I prayed there and wept until I was so exhausted that I had hardly strength enough to walk back to my home. When I got to my apartment I sank on the bed and continued to pray and to weep until nearly midnight, ever vacillating as to what I should do.

At last I thought of my Bible. It lay on a table, at the head of my bed. I rose, struck a light, took the Bible and pressed it to my bosom, and began to implore it not to forsake me this time. I knelt down by the side of my bed and said to our Lord: "I want to do right. Thou knowest I do. If I have done wrong forgive me. But Thou knowest that I was sincere. I thought that Thou didst speak to me. Oh, inspire me, Lord, what to do. Speak to me now, and whatever Thou tellest me to do I will do it, whether it be to go or to stay; but let Thy words be clear."

So saying, I opened the book, and my eyes fell on these words in the 26th chapter of Ezekiel, beginning at the 24th verse:—

"24. For I will take you from among the heathen and gather you out of all countries, and will bring you into your own land.

"25. Then will I sprinkle clean water upon you, and ye shall be clean from all your filthiness, and from all your idols will I cleanse you.

"26. A new heart also will I give you, and a new spirit will I put within you: and I will take away the stony heart out of your flesh, and I will give you an heart of flesh.

"27. And I will put my spirit within you, and cause you to walk in my statutes, and ye shall keep my judgments and do *them*.

"28. And ye shall dwell in the land that I gave to your fathers; and ye shall be my people, and I will be your God.

"29. I will also save you from all your uncleannesses; and I will call for the corn and will increase it, and lay no famine upon you.

"30. And I will multiply the fruit of the tree and the increase of the field, that ye shall receive no more reproach of famine among the heathen.

"31. Then shall ye remember your own evil ways and your doings that *were* not good, and shall loathe yourselves in your own sight for your iniquities and for your abominations."

I instantly rose and said: "Lord, I will go: I know Thou speakest to me now." My eyes had no sooner fallen on those words than all my doubts left me, and I received the same light, the same peace, and the same courage to make the sacrifice that I had felt at the altar when I heard that voice say to me: "Go home and work for God!"

The next morning I went to the Abbey. I was no longer afraid to look on its bare floors and unornamented walls. The moment I entered my room I saw that my harp was still unpacked. I took off the cover to loosen the strings, when, to my surprise, I saw it was broken. Who broke it? That I never knew. I suppose that some of the workmen must have let something fall on it or have knocked it over. While I was examining it the door-bell rang. I made a quick motion to go and open the door, for I was there all alone. The bottom of my dress caught in one of the pedals of the harp; I pulled it over, the top of it broke, and all its strings were loosened.

This made a fearful impression on me for a moment. I looked upon it as a bad omen. But I immediately recollected the vision or dream which had repeated itself three times, wherein I had seen myself on board the *Pereire* and my harp lying on the shore with all its strings broken, and the vessel moving off without it.

I had engaged my passage in the *Pereire* without any reference to the dream, and was only that instant reminded of it. As I looked at my harp all unstrung, I saw therein a fulfilment of the vision that I had had about eighteen months before, and I felt more satisfied than ever that it was the will of God that I should go.

I sent word to Erard, the harp-maker. He sent his foreman to examine the harp, who said that it would be several weeks before they could repair it; and they would ship it to me to New York as soon as it was finished.

CHAPTER LXXXV.

ADIEU, LA FRANCE—MY GOOD LITTLE ANGEL.

An Angel of Consolation—"My Normandy"—"The Good Shepherd"—A Vision verified—Last Glimpse of France—Words from Kind Hearts—Holy Words from a Statesman.

LAFERRIÈRE came to see me the day before I left. It was not to say good-bye, for he said that he would come to the station and see me off. I never saw him look so sad; he scarcely spoke—and I, too, could hardly speak; but I wept as though my heart would break. We were together over an hour, and to my sobbings he would say: " *Vous l'avez voulu— vous l'avez voulu.*" (You would have it so—you would have it so.)

As I expected he would be at the station to bid me a last

farewell, I had forbidden my other friends to come; for I wished to pass those few precious moments alone with him.

I arrived at the station with my child and Françoise. Laferrière's valet was there waiting for me, and as I descended from the carriage he handed me two letters. They were both from Laferrière : one was for me and the other was for Gen. Dix. I opened mine ; it ran thus :—

" MY DEAR CHILD,

" I have thought it better for you, as well as for me, to avoid a last interview, which the presence of others would render distressing. I send you a last and tender adieu, and my ardent wishes that your voyage may be calm and happy.

" May you find in your native land peace and repose, and forgetfulness of the past. When the immensity of the ocean is between us you will do me justice, and you will say that I have been a good and faithful friend.

" You may rely upon my attachment, it will always be a pleasure to me to give you proofs of it. Adieu, my dear child ! may God watch over you, and give you the happiness that you no longer find near me. I press you to my heart, and I embrace tenderly your child !

" I shall write to you at Brest. In the meanwhile receive the assurance of my sincere and devoted affection.

" LAFERRIÈRE."

I nearly fainted at the disappointment. His valet and Françoise supported me to the railway-carriage.

When the train started I threw myself back in my seat and gave full vent to my tears. It was the saddest disappointment I had ever met with, not to find him there to give me a parting farewell kiss. Every stride that the car made onward shook my frame as though an iron hand had grasped my heart, and was wrenching from it, root by root, the idol to which it clung, and to which it had given all its affections.

I must have remained there for over an hour, with my face buried in my hands, and my heart plunged in the direst agony, when I suddenly thought of my child, and looked up to see what had become of her. I had forgotten that she was with me, and that I was not alone. She had nestled herself up in a corner of a seat, and was praying with a little chaplet that Madame Dessoudin had given her. Her eyes were cast downward, and her infantine face wore an expression of peace and devotion, so sadly sweet that it seemed as though an angel of consolation had suddenly appeared before me.

As I gazed upon her my tears ceased to flow, and for a moment I forgot my sorrow. I looked silently upon her until she had told her last bead, then, raising her eyes, and seeing that I was no longer weeping, but looking at her, she sprang into my arms and cried out: " Oh, mamma! I knew that you would stop being sad, for I have said my chaplet for you three times through, and I knew that the Blessed Virgin would be good to you."

She covered my face with kisses, but instead of making me happy her sympathy only brought back to my heart its desolation, and I fell to weeping more bitterly than before.

" Mamma, tell me your sorrows!"

" You are not old enough, dear little one, to understand them."

" Oh, yes, I am, mamma," she answered. " You just tell them to me, and you will see that I am old enough. I can understand them. Do tell them to me."

She coaxed me so sweetly that at last I pretended to yield, and she got on my knee, and began to pass her little hand soothingly over my forehead.

" Then I said to her: " Mamma is alone in the world; she has no father nor mother to take care of her; she has no other father to look after her but God, and no other mother but the Blessed Virgin!"

The child quickly interrupted me, and in the most serious tone replied: " But they are the best of parents, mamma!"

Her pious and cheering remark drove away all my sadness, and I began to laugh at the serious expression of countenance the child had assumed, and the way she had uttered those words. She tried to stop my laughing, and begged me to continue and tell her my sorrows. " I have none now," said I. " Oh, yes, you have, mamma," she replied; " you had just began to tell them to me. Please go on."

" I was sad," I replied, " before I told you what was the matter with me, but since you have told me that God and the Blessed Virgin are the best of parents, I have no more reason to be sad, for I find that I am better off than I thought I was."

She was not satisfied with the abrupt termination of my story, and turning from me she began to look out of the window. In a few moments she turned towards me again, and said : " Tell me, mamma, all about our little mountain home, where you are going to take me." But before she gave me a chance to reply she called my attention to the view, and wanted to know if our little home looked like the one that she saw in the distance. At the same time she asked me if we passed through there when we came to France, when she was a little baby.

I looked out of the window. The country wore the same aspect as it did the first time I saw it. It seemed as though in a second my mind traversed all the varied scenes through which I had passed for the past seven years, back to the day that the train was bearing me towards Paris for the first time. Instantly I recalled the buoyant feelings of hope that had filled my breast as I entered for the first time that beautiful city. But now how changed was I! and how different, too, were the feelings that overflowed my heart!

I sank back again into my seat, closed my eyes, and tried in thought to live that day over again. Instantly that old French song, *Ma Normandie*, came to my mind, and I began humming it in thought. But this time instead of the first verse of the song, the words of the last rose in my mind—

> " Il est un âge dans la vie
>   Où chaque rêve doit finir;
> Un âge où l'âme recueillie
>   A besoin de se souvenir.
> Lorsque ma muse refroidie
>   Aura fini ses chants d'amour,
> J'irai revoir ma Normandie :
>   C'est le pays qui m'a donné le jour."

> " There comes an age in all our lives,
>   When ev'ry dream must have an end ;
> An age, when fond remembrance strives
>   To long-past scenes new charms to lend.
> When chilled by years my muse shall be,
>   Nor more to songs of love invite ;
> Then must I see my Normandy
>   Once more, where first I saw the light."

I had hardly uttered them in my mind before my child, turning to me again, asked why I did not want to tell her all about our little home among the hills. Said I, " Sweet child, that shall be our Normandie ; and when we get there you will pray for mamma, that God will help her to forget her sorrows."

She quickly remarked, " I am not going to wait until we get there for that, I am going to pray for that now, that God may make you forget them directly, for it would be a great deal better for us to enjoy ourselves going there. So don't look sad any more, mamma." She commenced talking to me and reasoning with me as a person of three times her years would have done ; and I soon actually began to confide in her, and said to her that I thought it was cruel in the Viscount not to come and see us off. " But, mamma," she replied, " you know how much he has to do, so you must not cry for that. And he told you once that you were always complaining of him, and he never deserved it."

I took the remark as a well-deserved reproach, and fell to weeping again. I longed to reach Havre to write to Laferrière, and tell him how much I loved him, and that I had faith and hope in God that all would yet be well.

As soon as I reached there I wrote him a long letter, in which I unburdened to him my soul. The next morning I arose early and went to Mass with my child, and received Holy Communion. We were just about to leave when I noticed that we were kneeling by St. Dominick's altar. This was Laferrière's patron saint, and Dominick was also one of the names given to my child. I was struck with the coincidence which had led me to that particular altar, and the fact that it should be the last shrine I was to kneel at before bidding a final adieu to France.

On leaving the church I felt strong and hopeful; and all the way back to the steamer I was joyful, because I had obeyed God. I felt that it was no illusion, but that He had called me, and that I was now doing His will; and I was certain that in return He would give me a rich reward.

On the morning of the 17th of June, 1870, the sun shone brightly on Havre, as the steamer *Pereire* moved off from the harbour. I was standing on her deck beside my child, watching the receding shore. My heart was raised to God in prayer, and I continued to implore Him to watch over me and to guard and protect me.

All at once I chanced to see that same old sign which had attracted my attention the first time I saw the shores of France. It was the clothier's sign, "*Au Bon Pasteur.*" "The Good Shepherd" was represented by a life-size figure of our Lord carrying in his arms a poor sheep which had wandered from the fold.

Instantly my heart overflowed with pious gratitude towards God. I found that picture symbolic of our Lord's ways with me, and was so moved by the just application of it to myself, that the tears streamed down my cheeks from a sense of God's goodness and my own waywardness, and I mentally exclaimed, "That represents you and me, Lord; for I have always gone astray, but you have never ceased to seek me and to follow me through all my sinful paths, and at last you overtake me and carry me in your arms. I am so glad that I obeyed Thee, Lord! I know that Thou wilt not abandon me, and wilt bring me back to these shores again. For I promise Thee that I will be good, and then I know that Thou wilt not refuse me anything."

The triple vision that I had received, eighteen months before in answer to my prayers was now realised. For I was standing on the deck of the *Pereire*, which was leaving the shores of Havre bound for America; and I was obliged to leave my harp in France with all its strings broken.

I now looked upon the vision as a happy omen, typical of my future. I firmly believed that all the chords of sorrow with which my heart from childhood had been strung were one day to be forever broken.

But how soon we turn from God to man! I had no sooner, entered my state-room than I began longing to reach Brest so as to receive Laferrière's letter; and my impatience increased as the steamer advanced. To wait so many hours seemed like being obliged to abide an endless eternity—especially to pass those hours at sea, where the moments were mostly counted in my berth by the motion of the ship, as it rocked to and fro on the water.

At last we came in sight of Brest, and the postmaster of the ship brought me a package of letters. I hastily ran my eyes over them. I recognised the handwriting of many of my friends, —but there was no letter from Laferrière.

This disappointment I felt far more keenly than the first; for my heart was worn out with expectation and impatience, and to reach the shore, and then to be disappointed, was too much! I went to the postmaster, and asked him if he had not made a mistake, and mixed one of my letters with somebody else's. He replied : " I handed you twelve ; that was all there was for you." I counted them, and would have willingly thrown them all into the sea without breaking their seals, in exchange for but one line from him.

For an instant my soul rebelled; but it soon submitted. A sense of fear came over me, and I felt that I was alone in God's Almighty hand, and I at once asked Him to forgive me, and give me His divine protection.

I went up again on the deck, and sat down on a bench, by the side of my child, and remained there with my eyes fixed on the shore, until it receded from my sight. When its last glimpse disappeared, and I could see nothing but the horizon's verge on the water, I was seized with that sickness of the soul, which spreads itself like a pall over the heart, as it sees all its bright hopes and visions of years vanish suddenly from view.

"O beloved France!" thought I, as I wept, "how could I leave thee? and when shall I ever see thy shores again? Will he live until then, and will he love me still ?"

My soul, buried in the deepest gloom, was awakened by a sweet, gentle voice, saying: "Mamma, mamma, Monsieur de Corcelles writes better than the rest, because I can read his writing." I looked at my child, and saw that she had been opening my letters, and was busy trying to read them. "Mamma," she continued, "let me keep Monsieur de Corcelles' letter, because I want that poetry that he has written to you; I will say it to my doll:"

She took up his letter, and read the words which pleased her so well, which were:

> "La toilette,
>   N'est pas l'esprit.
> On est belle,
> Sans dentelle,
>   Quand le cœur luit."

> "Oft rich dress
>   Small wit confines
> There's a grace,
> Without lace,
>   Where the heart shines."

I then read the following letter from my old and tried friend, the Princess Sulkowska.

"Paris, June 16th, 1870.

"8, Rue Fortin.

"MY DEAR FRIEND,

"You are now far from so many friends, who love, and who regret you sailing on the ocean, which puts space between us, but can never succeed in making us forget, because, for the heart and the mind, neither space nor separation exist.

"Happily so many souvenirs which bind our friendship, will render it enduring and unalterable among all the changes of life.

"I hope, dear friend, that you will write me a few words from Brest, and also as soon as you arrive in America, so that I shall not be left in suspense about you and your child. How M. de Laferrière must have suffered in seeing you start on so long a voyage,—poor wounded heart! But I can understand how yours is rent on leaving Paris, where you have passed so many happy hours, where the divine light shone upon your soul, and where you leave behind so many friends. May God conduct you both in safety to your journey's end. May He guide you, and order His angels to watch over you!

"I embrace you tenderly as well as my dear little godchild, who probably by this time has had enough of travelling by water.

"Your affectionately devoted friend,

"PRINCESS MARIE SULKOWSKA."

One was from Madame Mayaud, daughter of M. Louvet, then Minister of Agriculture and Commerce, in whose family I had been treated like a daughter:—

"SAUMUR (MAINE ET LOIRE),

"*June* 17, 1870.

"MY DEAR FRIEND,

"I hope these few words will reach you, and will give you a final evidence of the sympathies which you leave behind you.

"Your sacrifice then is made! You have withdrawn yourself from this intoxicating life of Paris to go where God calls you and where duty commands.

"Journey then in peace towards your new destiny, and love God above all things. He will give you, in proportion as you accomplish His divine will, secret joys and a delightful intimacy, which the world could never bring you. You will enjoy peace of soul in love—true, true!—because that is perfection itself.

"I shall await impatiently a line from you, to prove that I am not forgotten. My little Marie remembers her friend Geneviève.

"As for you, my dear friend, my prayers and thoughts will accompany you, and my affection will cross the sea with you.

"L. MAYAUD LOUVET."

The following is from M. Louvet, Madame Mayaud's father:—

OFFICE OF THE MINISTER OF AGRICULTURE AND COMMERCE,

"PARIS, *June* 16*th*, 1870.

"DEAR MADAM,

"At the moment of your departure from France, where we were so happy to have you, allow me to address to you a parting salutation in my own name and in that of my family. You carry with you the esteem and affection of all who have known you. Try and find in your native country that repose of mind and peace of heart without which there is no real happiness here below.

"Our prayers follow you. We ask God to take you under His protection. He will, I am sure, for He loves you, since He sought after, pursued, and led you back to Himself, like the Good Shepherd going after the loved and wandering sheep. Give Him, therefore, love for love, more and more.

" You will have, besides other heavenly assistance, the Blessed Virgin, who holds so exalted a place in our Catholic religion ; then the holy patroness under whose care your noble godmother placed you ; afterwards the guardian angel, who, according to the traditions of our faith, watches unceasingly at your side ; and, finally, the other guardian angel that God has given you on earth—I mean your charming little girl, whom you love more than yourself, and whose caresses are like a beneficent dew, calming and refreshing your poor heart. So you see, dear madam, you have a great many protectors ; if ever danger or trials overwhelm you, invoke them, and believe me they will preserve you.

"Adieu, dear madam ; when shall we meet again on this earth ? Never, perhaps. In any case, there is one place of meeting which will never fail—heaven ; where all pure sympathies and holy affection will be united, never to be separated any more.

" *A vous,* madam, cast a last look at the shores of our Brittany from your vessel as you depart !

" My highest expressions of tender and respectful attachment.

" LOUVET."

M. Louvet's letter brought back the bright hope and consolation that I had felt on leaving the shores of Havre, when I gazed upon that image of the Good Shepherd. It revived all my hopes and trust in God, and I felt that all would yet be well, as it was only from faith and confidence in God that I had made my sacrifice.

CHAPTER LXXXVI.

ESCAPE FROM THE JESUITS IMPOSSIBLE—MADAME HARDEY AGAIN.

Manhattanville—Discouragement—Mother Hardey.

I BEGAN to think seriously what I should do on arriving in New York, as I could not come into possession of my farm before spring. All my furniture was on board. If I should sell it at once, I should be forced to pay duty, which would cost me thousands of dollars.

I secured a large house on Fifth Avenue, which I rented until the first of May. Shortly after I arrived, I called on Madame Galway, who was then the Superior of the Convent of the Sacred

Heart at Manhattanville, to give her the letter that I had brought from their house in Paris.

She did not even read the letter, but begged me to explain what I desired. As soon as I told her my intention of building a church, and requested her to educate my child for less than their usual price, so as to leave me more money to devote to my work, she gave me a blank refusal; and said that I ought to use my money to educate my child, instead of building a church, if I could not afford to do both. I told her that I had come on to build a church and was going to build one, and gave her my reasons, none of which seemed to remove her impression that it was a foolish undertaking; and all that I could say to her did not seem to have the slightest effect in awakening her sympathies, either for me or my work.

She rose and was going to take leave of me; but I refused to take the hint, and persisted that she should read some of my letters. She replied: "They are all in French, and written by people that I know nothing about." "Then," I replied, "take them and give them to somebody to read who does know." She hesitated a moment, doubtless considering what she should do in order to get rid of me. While she was deliberating, I was beseeching her. I told her that Madame Dessoudin had assured me that I could count upon their protection. Said she: "Take your letters to Father Beaudevin. He resides at 49, West Fifteenth Street. He is a Jesuit. Show him your letters and tell him what you propose to do. I have a great confidence in his judgment: if he thinks that we will be doing a charity to assist you in your undertaking, we will do so." She then rose, handed me back the letters, and left the room.

I went into the chapel. I was so discouraged and so disappointed at my first step, that I burst into tears. I was provoked too that this lady obliged me to go to a Jesuit, when I had fully resolved not to have anything to do with them, and had even sacrificed Françoise, so as to get entirely rid of the order.

After earnestly recommending myself to God, and praying that He would protect me against the wiles of the Jesuits, and that I might never meet another Madame Galway, I took out of my pocket a little book that I had carried about me since the day I left Paris. I opened it and my eyes fell on these words: "*Le découragement seul a perdu plus d'âmes que toutes les passions réunies. Dans les causes du désordre, de la perversité même, il tient le premier rang.*" ("Discouragement alone has ruined more souls than all the passions together. It holds the first place among the causes which produce moral disorder and perversity.") Those words gave me peace. The following day I called to see Father Beaudevin.

The moment he entered the room, I mentally exclaimed: "Here is a mate to Mother Galway!" and I prepared myself for the worst.

He read my letters, among which was one from Father Bazin, which he had written to me from St. Malo. It was a brief note, which I will insert; for I believe that I am indebted to its few lines for my success with Father Beaudevin.

" HOSPITAL OF ST. MALO.

"June 13, 1870.

" MADAM,

" Your last letter from Paris reached me at St. Malo; I wish, but I scarcely dare to hope, that mine may arrive before your departure. I have placed with our janitor the little volume you were so kind as to accept.

" So, then, the sea, which I have here beneath my window, is going to carry you far from France, dear madam; but it will not carry away the souvenirs which you leave here in the hearts of your friends. May you be happy in your own land, to which you return with a heart renewed by religion, and may God bless your pious project! I promise to pray for you. I will not forget it, nor the hope I held out to you of sending a few ornaments for your chapel. You will write to me later, will you not, on this subject?

" I should have been happy to embrace your charming child a last time, and to make my adieux to you, but, unfortunately, I shall not return to Paris till after you have left. Pray for me sometimes when your thoughts traverse the space that separates us; in God there is no distance; He is the centre where we can always meet.

" Adieu again, dear madam; believe in my attachment, and my devout affection.

" Yours, &c.,

"BAZIN."

As soon as Father Beaudevin read Father Bazin's note, his manner changed, his face assumed a more cordial expression, as he asked me if there was anything he could do to serve me. I told him what I wanted, and that Madame Galway had referred me to him. "Why," said he, "this letter from their house in Paris is all-sufficient." "Madame Galway would not read it," said I. "I will attend to it," he replied. I then told Father Beaudevin what I had come for. He listened to me attentively. As soon as I had finished, he said to me : "You will succeed. I am sure you will." I asked him, "Will you be my friend?" "Yes," he replied; and the tone of sincere resolution in which he spoke gave me confidence in the goodness of my cause as well as in its ultimate success.

One Sunday I went out to Manhattanville, and I met Madame Hardey. We had hardly exchanged ten words before she knitted her brows, like a person who was trying to recall something in the past that time had nearly effaced from her mind, and asked me; "Have we never met before? It seems to me that I have met you before;" "Yes, good mother," I replied, "we have met before;" and I asked her if she remembered a poor young girl who had come to her, seventeen years previous, and begged her to educate her; how she had agreed to do so, and while this poor girl was speaking with her, a religious had come in, accompanied by a large dog, and asked her if the dog, should go too, and she had replied, "Certainly, for they will expect to see the dog as much as they will you."

"Yes," said Mother Hardey, with a smile, "I do recollect about the dog. But why did not this girl return?"

I told her that I was that poor girl; and I related to her what prevented me coming: how a lady had threatened to go and tell her that Maria Monk was my mother, and said that she would tear me limb from limb, if she knew who I was. "Oh" exclaimed Mother Hardey, with indignation, "*how foolish!*" When I told her that I had come on to build a church, she did not try to dissuade me from it, but gave me an encouraging look, as though she approved and admired my courage and zeal.

At parting she embraced me, and I left her that afternoon with the same sentiment of admiration and gratitude, that I experienced the first time I met her, seventeen years before. The only change that I could see in her was that her cheeks had grown pale. The first time I saw her, they were tinged with a deep roseate hue; yet the same sweet expression, and the same compassionate look and smile which animated them seventeen years ago still remained and seemed to defy the ravages of time.

CHAPTER LXXXVII.

AID FOR THE VICTIMS OF THE ANGLO-PRUSSIAN WAR.

Kind Words from France—A Cry for Help—Claims on our Gratitude—
The Cry Heeded.

MONTHS passed and I received no line from Laferrière, which silence was eating like a cancer in my heart, yet I never lost hope. From the moment the war broke out I believed more firmly than ever that God had inspired me to leave France in answer to my prayers. All my friends wrote to me, telling me how grateful I ought to be to Divine Providence for having inspired me, for they all now had faith in me, and Madame de Montalembert more than all the rest, from the service that Providence threw it in my way to render her.

In the early part of December, 1870, I received the following letter :—

> " RIXENSART PAR ATTIGNIES, BELGIUM,
> " *Nov. 25th*, 1870.

" MY DEAR AND EXCELLENT FRIEND,

" I have before me your charming letter of the 26th of July, containing the details of your new life, and your relations with the Sacred Heart, with the Jesuits, and with F. Beaudevin, of whom you have given me a description, which assures me that your soul is in good hands. This rejoices me greatly, for with the great ardour and frankness you have, and which I admire sincerely as one of the most powerful levers for good, it is necessary to have some counsel from time to time to moderate your ardour.

" I see, too, that your dear little girl is an inmate of the Sacred Heart, and that those ladies are very kind to her. Tell them that I thank them for it, because I love you *tenderly*, and more than that, that I have a true *esteem* for you, which, to my mind, is a sentiment very sweet, and very rarely met with. You seek God, His glory, the salvation of souls, and your own ; you desire to see Him one day, and you strive after all these ends (so forgotten by the most part of men and women too) with all the strength of your nature, and of your warm heart. What a foundation for *profound* sympathy ! One has so rarely the opportunity of working out these great things, and God has given you the signal grace of using, with reason and intelligent energy, the most practical means to attain these great designs with which you are inspired. Oh ! what cause for thanksgiving on your part, and of joy for your true friends! I feel that I am one of them when I think of the great pleasure I enjoyed the first time we met, and every time I have seen you since.

"I managed to put in order before the war all my affairs, and settle my children's, then arranged all my husband's treasured papers, so that I could bring them here, out of the way of all danger. I should have been heart-broken to have left them in the frightful position in which everything is among us on account of this horrible war, worthy of the Sioux, the Blackfeet, the redskins of America. Perhaps they are less barbarous than the Prussians. Is it not an unheard-of thing that Christians should practise such cruelties in this age of civilisation?

* * * * * *

"France in other times assisted America to gain her independence and her wealth. My grand-uncle, De Lafayette, went to her assistance: he expended, himself alone, 1,500,000 francs to equip a vessel.

"Many others among our gentry, M. de Rochambeau among the number, hurried to lend the assistance of their arms to your country at the risk of their lives.

"Can America forget all this? Can she rest, like England, in a state of cold and heartless non-intervention? Shall *we* always be the chivalrous nation *who aid all the world* in their distress, and to whom *no nation renders the like?* I often ask myself sorrowfully if such will really be the case with a nation so powerful, so rich and free as your own! I must at the same time, in order to be just and grateful, say that we have some warm friends in England, and that these neighbours have already sent us help in money, provisions, &c., for the plundered.

"I read in the papers that a few hundred American volunteers had landed at Brest, and were fighting for us. But what is this small number against 900,000 Germans? Shall we not at least have a large and general subscription for our burnt villages, which we reckon by hundreds? for our 300,000 unhappy prisoners, whose garments are in rags, and who, from the depth of Germany, ask pitifully for stockings, flannel, and shoes, to protect them against the rigours of winter? They would need 300,000 of each of these articles; and the Prussians are draining us by requisitions, not only in money, but of hundreds of dozens of all these articles of clothing for their own army. They empty all our warehouses, and leave us in many cities (as Rheims) only the empty shelves of the shops. Try, my dear friend, and organise a committee, which will occupy itself, quickly and generously, for the relief of our distress. We deserve this fraternal sympathy, these alms of affection and gratitude, since, *without us*, you Americans, so free, happy, and rich, would not, perhaps, have arrived so quickly at all that you possess, all which I congratulate you on from my heart, though not without a little sensitiveness at the indifference which you show to our actual suffering.

"The good king Louis XVI., who had not a very great mind, but whose heart was noble and generous, loved you: he compassionated your griefs, and he assisted your weakness. Then, let this great American nation in its turn pity our wrongs without number, in so unequal a struggle.

"But adieu, dear friend; may God inspire you ; and if you can create a movement in our behalf, you know well how good a work you will perform.—I embrace you tenderly.

"CTSSE. MÉRODE DE MONTALEMBERT."

"P. S.   "*November* 26th.

"I re-read my letter before sealing it, and I wish to add, as a postscript, that it will be a favour if you will send me some news of your church. It occurred to my mind to-night, that, if you need your influence among your acquaintance for the erection of this dear church, which determined you to quit Paris, you must not expend it in furthering those objects that I insisted upon with so much warmth in my letter.

"If, in order to succeed in building your church, dear friend, you must lead, like your patroness, a *laborious* and *hidden* life (such as you seem already to have imposed upon yourself), *do not leave it,* to devote yourself to other good works; one cannot do *all* kinds of good at a time.

"You know I never could bear (when we used to talk together in Paris) the devout ladies who sought to make use of you : our public calamities have given me neither the right, nor the wish, to do the like at present.

"If you could not do what I asked, without the inconvenience I have pointed out, be convinced I will never for an instant doubt your affection—(and I embrace you now again from the bottom of my heart, my very dear and tender friend, for such I know you to be)—do not then act as if it needed to be proved to me

"If you knew the horrors, the ruin skilfully planned, worthy of cannibals, that these Prussians (so cruel by nature) systematically commit everywhere!

"If you have the time, and are conversant with your political affairs, tell me if there is any truth in the rumour that America is, at this time, purchasing territory of Russia so as to help her indirectly to fortify herself, contrary to the treaty signed with France ; taking advantage of our misfortunes to rupture without good faith, this treaty relating to the Black Sea,—assisting the oppressor of Poland to become more powerful ! What a horror ! Would it be permitted for a country so far to forget all justice as to think only of its material profit ?   In this case republican egotism would be equal to monarchical !

"MÉRODE DE MONTALEMBERT."

I went assiduously to work to assist my friend.   I made the acquaintance of the vice-president of the Ladies' Fair for the Relief of the French Soldiers.   I read to her Madame de Montalembert's letter, and it was agreed that she should take the letter and read it to some of the ladies of the committee, and influence them to vote, at their next meeting, that a part of the money which still remained, should be sent to Madame de Montalembert.

These ladies immediately decided to send Madame de Montalembert twenty thousand dollars (20,000 dols.) to distribute among the poor and disabled soldiers.   The money was forwarded to her in due time, and later several thousand dollars more.

A few weeks afterwards I received from Madame de Montalembert a long letter of thanks.

"RIXENSART PAR ATTIGNIES, BELGIUM,
"February 12th, 1871.

"MY DEAR AND EXCELLENT FRIEND,

"How shall I express my gratitude for your incredible efforts and for the splendid success with which God has crowned them ! My cousin de Mérode was *wild* with joy at being able to relieve so many poor people in the environs of Paris, Ardennes, and other places, out of that magnificent sum of 93,000 francs which he received and at once made use of.   I would have liked to embrace you at once and express my gratitude, but I commenced by executing faithfully your instructions.

*   *   *   *   *

"How will you find time to read my letter with all that you have to do.   But I shall be satisfied if you can succeed in building your church.

"I press you to my heart.

"COMTSSF. MÉRODE DE MONTALEMBERT."

CHAPTER LXXXVIII.

CONFIRMATION OF MY MISSION TO BUILD A CHURCH.

Doubts Dispelled—Silenced if not Convinced.

JANUARY, 1871, came, and I tried to collect for my church. I had not yet seen any of those Americans who were indebted to me for favours I had done them in Paris. But, once I began my calls, I was soon undeceived in regard to their unselfishness, and whenever I descended their steps I thought of the old saying, "Gratitude is a lively sense of favours to come."

They nearly all laughed at me at the very idea that I should expect them to subscribe to a church.

Meeting with nothing but rude rebuffs or disappointments wherever I went I soon became discouraged, and was willing to believe that God had only induced me to leave France to escape the war, and that the thought of building a church was all a delusion; that He had not inspired me to build it.

I commenced deliberating what to do. I went and got my Bible, wishing in my heart that opening it I might find such words as would lead me to suppose that our Lord forbade me to build the church. I knelt down before my crucifix and holding up my Bible towards it, I exclaimed, "O beloved Saviour, speak to me, and let me know Thy will; and whatever it is I will try to do it."

I opened the Bible and my eyes fell on these words:—

"2. Thus speaketh the Lord of hosts, saying, This people say, The time is not come, the time that the Lord's house should be built." (Hagg. i. 2.)

I closed the book impatiently, saying: "I know, Lord, that the people say that the time is not come to build Thee a church. But tell me what *Thou sayest*; that is what I want to know. I implore Thee tell me what Thou sayest."

I then opened the Bible a second time and read:—

"7. Thus saith the Lord of hosts; Consider your ways.

"8. Go up to the mountain and bring wood and build the house, and I will take pleasure in it and I will be glorified, saith the Lord." (Hagg. i. 7.)

My heart palpitated with joy. I kissed the Bible and exclaimed: "How good Thou art, Lord, to give me such a proof that it is Thy will. I will now persevere; for I know that Thou wilt be with me and wilt surely help me." I began pacing the floor wild with delight, and had not put my Bible away when I heard a rap at my door. The door opened and the servant announced Father Beaudevin.

He noticed my astonishment at seeing him, and he began at once to explain the object of his visit. Said he, "I have come to try to persuade you to give up the idea of building that church, for I fear that"——"Father," said I, interrupting him, "you are just ten minutes too late. If you had come ten minutes sooner one word would have put a stop to it."

I confessed to him my despondency, and how I had doubted and had recourse to the Bible to know the will of God. I then showed him the two passages which I had successively opened at; his face lightened up, he slightly bowed his head, and said, "That is enough; continue; I shall not try to dissuade you-from it." From that afternoon the question of building the church was settled in my mind. I believed that God had inspired me to come to New York and build it. I now had but one thought, and that was to execute His commands, believing that my reward would be that He would unite me to the man I loved.

The latter part of January I wrote a long letter to Laferrière, telling him everything that had happened me since I left France; that I still believed that God had inspired me to come on here, and would yet reward me for all the sacrifices I was making, and the humiliations that I was suffering. I begged him to write me how he was situated, and if he needed a home to come to me; and I said that if he was poor I would willingly labour to support him.

I concluded by telling him how truly grateful I was for all that he had ever done for me, and that I even found a consolation in the misfortunes that had befallen him, believing that they would give me an opportunity of proving to him my devotion.

CHAPTER LXXXIX.

THE GOOD COUNTRY PEOPLE.

A House in the Country—" Rural Delights"—I engage a Rustic Swain—
With Wife and two Children—And Mother, Cousin, Cow, and Pig.

SPRING had come. I was in possession of my farm. After it was paid for, the cottage enlarged and repaired, and my stables mounted, I found that I had spent a great deal of money and had little to show for it compared to the expense.

On the 27th of June I left New York for my country home

For months I had been anxiously anticipating that happy day, for I longed to breathe again the free air of the mountains, and to have my little house in order, so that if ever Laferrière answered my letter about coming to America I should be prepared to receive him. Indeed I never could divest myself of the belief that we would pass many happy hours there together. Such were my dreams of living in the country; to have a little home daintily furnished, and have Laferrière come and reside with me until such time as we could both return to France. Those were my dreams; but the reality can only be told in "What I know about farming."

One of the religious of the Convent of the Sacred Heart had introduced me to a widow lady whom I will call Mrs. Voice. She was an accomplished musician, and sang divinely. She was to come and pass the summer with me. I thought I could build my church in a few months, and its success would be assured by having a choir.

I had engaged a young man and his wife to take care of my farm. He knew, and so did all my friends, of my inexpressible devotedness to my little daughter.

The evening before I expected Mrs. Voice to arrive, who was to bring my child, this man got beastly drunk, and I ordered him at once to leave the place, for it was one of the conditions I made when I engaged him, that if he ever became intoxicated he forfeited his place.

He was determined not to go, and begged and implored of me to let him remain only a few days—that was all that he asked—just a few days. That evening I surprised him in conversation with his wife. She was weeping, and looked idiotic from fright. I caught enough of their conversation to know that there was a question of my child, and I wondered what it could be, when I heard his wife exclaim : " That would be too cruel ; you could not treat her so l" The man answered her, with an oath, that she should see that he would.

I called the wife, and begged her to tell me what her husband had said. "Oh," she replied, "don't let him stay ; he has often threatened to steal your child, and now he declares that he will do it." Said I : " Steal my child ! What could he do with my child ?" The wife replied : "He would keep her until you gave him a large reward to bring her back." I could not believe that a devilish spirit like that could exist in a human heart, and particularly in the heart of this man, whom I had known for years, and whom I had always tried to help, and to whom I had even then advanced money.

I asked him if what his wife told me was true?

He did not deny having made the threat, but declared that he had said it in fun. I refused to accept his excuse, and insisted that he should leave; then he vented upon me the vilest abuse, and threatened me in every conceivable way.

Some of the neighbours were passing. I called them in to protect me. He then left, and shortly afterwards his wife followed him.

The next day Mrs. Voice came and brought me my child. Mrs. Voice's father accompanied her.

They were both afraid that they would not be able to remain: for, at that season of the year, it was next to impossible to hire a man, as everyone was engaged for miles around. I told him that I had placed my house under the protection of St. Joseph, and I had not the slightest doubt but what the saint would send me a man.

On the morning of the 5th of July I was in the kitchen with Mrs. Voice, who was expressing to me her doubts and fears about my being able to get a man-servant, and to whose anxieties I made but the one reply, "Oh, Saint Joseph will take care of me, never you fear. I have been praying hard this morning." These words had hardly escaped my lips when I heard some one spring over the fence with the agility of a hare, and, turning round, I saw a sprightly little Irishman, who without the least ceremony, came into the house. He wore a ruffled shirt, and a large red rose in his button-hole. The moment I saw him, I said to Mr. Voice: "There is the man!"

Without waiting to hear what he came for, I asked him: "What is your name?" He replied: "My name, madam, is Mr. Costello; but everybody around here calls me Mike." Said I: "You will permit me then to call you Mike, will you not?" "Certainly, madam." Said I: "Don't you want a job?" "Oh," said he, shaking his head, "I am dressed up too much to work." I began coaxing him. In a few minutes I made him forget his clothes, and he said that he would pitch right in and help me.

Mike was as ingenious and active an Irishman as one might wish to meet. He set to work, and did more in an hour than any other man I had had would do in a day. Towards night, when I offered to settle with him, he said to me: "Madam, I have taken a fancy to you, and I would like to hire out with you by the month. I think that you and I would get along first-rate together."

I answered: "I thought you were engaged to Deacon Reed?" He replied: "Oh, I'll quit the Deacon for you, if you will take me." Said I: "Would that be right?"

"The Deacon," he answered, "has lots of men working for him—you have nobody at all. I feel sorry for you, for everybody is trying to take advantage of you. You need a smart man to overlook things, someone who will take an interest in the house. Besides, I like the looks of that woman in black :" meaning Mrs. Voice—"I think she is a mighty pretty woman, and can't she *sing!*"

I was overjoyed that he was so anxious to come and live with me, and I engaged him on the spot. Mrs. Voice and her father congratulated me upon my *good luck.*

The next day, after he had worked until nearly noon, Mike came to me, with his eyes lowered on the ground. He appeared greatly embarrassed, and hesitated for a moment before he spoke. At last he caught hold of some high grass and began breaking it, while he stammered out: "I forgot to tell you, madam, when I engaged with you, that I had a wife. She lives down on the corner, and she doesn't like to have me stay up here nights, and leave her down there all alone." "Why," said I, "bring her up here : it is just what I want; she can cook and do the housework. I am very glad that you have a wife."

He thanked me, and went off to his work. A few hours later, he came to me again, appearing more embarrassed than before. Without raising his eyes, he said to me :—"Madam, I forgot to tell you that my wife has got a little baby, about seven months old. Her name is Delia, the cunningest little thing that you ever saw in your life. She never cries a whimper : all my wife does, after she nurses her, is to put her on the floor, and she will set there and amuse herself for hours ; so that my wife can do just as much work as though she had no baby at all. It won't cost anything extra to feed her. What am I going to do with the baby ?" "Why, Mike," said I, "you cannot separate the child from its mother : of course the baby is included : she must bring the baby along."

After he had finished his work and was ready to go home, he came to me again, and said he :—"Madam, I forgot to tell you that I had a little son, about three years old ; we call him Neillie. He is very delicate, never eats anything : it would cost nothing to keep him—never stays in the house with his mother, but is always hanging around me,—never speaks, and keeps so still that you would not imagine that there was a child on the place. What am I going to do with him ?" "Mike," said I, "how many more children have you ?" "Oh, madam," he replied, "I have no more : I have only two." "Well," said I, "you can bring them both along."

In a few days, Mike and his family were installed in my house.

The first day the "cunning little thing, whose name was Delia," screamed the whole time, in spite of the father's and mother's combined efforts to pacify her. The following morning I heard an infantine voice swearing like a corsair. I rushed down stairs to see what it meant, and I found "the delicate little Neillie, who never spoke a word," cursing my child, who was earnestly listening, trying to catch his words.

The instant I appeared Neillie scampered away, and my child ran up to me exclaiming: "Mamma, I cannot understand Neillie's English. Tell it to me in French." Said I: "It would be as difficult for me to put it into French, as it is for you to understand it in English;" I told the parents that they must prevent their boy from coming to the front part of the house; which prohibition the parents did not seem to like.

Things continued in this way for several days, until my ears were fairly stunned by the cries of the baby and the oaths of the boy.

Since they had moved in, I had noticed an old woman hanging round the gate, and I at last asked Mike who she was, and what she wanted. "Madam" he replied with a deep sigh, " it's my mother, and it is breaking the old woman's heart to be separated from the children. I am afraid it will kill her, if she cannot be with them; for she walks up the hill every day to see them. She is not very strong, and she doesn't eat much." "Mike," said I, " is she strong enough to keep those children quiet?" "Why, madam," he replied, "she has always taken care of them." "Thank goodness!" said I; "go and bring her in, and give them up to her; and I will consider that she well earns her living if she succeeds in keeping them still."

The house was in the greatest confusion. We were arranging and setting up the furniture, but the greatest disorder still reigned in the kitchen. The meals were served at all hours in the day: baking after baking was thrown into the swill: half of the time we were without bread; and a greater part of the time the meat had spoiled for want of care.

Mike came to me one day, and said he forgot to tell me that he had a cousin who lived under the hill who was a thrifty servant-girl, and asked me if I would be good enough to engage her, because his wife had too much to attend to. I engaged the cousin. The same afternoon he came to me again, and began as usual: "Madam, I forgot to tell you that I had a cow. She is worth a hundred dollars; but I will let you have her for seventy, and you can pay me for her whenever you choose."

Said I : "I will take her."

A few days afterwards he came to me again. Said he: " Madam, them two little pigs of yours don't eat up half the swill. I forgot to tell you that I have a fine pig. She is worth twenty-five dollars, but I will sell her to you for fifteen." Said I : "I will take her." A week rolled by, and he came to me again. " Madam," said he, " I forgot to tell you that I have a fine lot of hens and a potato-patch, and I would like to sell them to you cheap."

"Mike," said I, "stop! don't recollect anything else : you have remembered enough In order to get you, it seems that I must take all Ireland with you. " I began to count the things which he had added to himself since I bargained to take him. There was his wife, his baby, his boy, his mother, his cousin, his cow, and his pig, to which he wanted to add his hens and his potato-patch. I thought I had quite enough already, for I found that they made a large sum in addition. But soon the reader will see how I subtracted them by short division off of my place, all of them excepting the pig, which was the remainder.

CHAPTER XC.

A MEEK LAMB AND A LION-LIKE SHEPHERD.

Father Tandy—Paring the Lion's Claws—He Roars "Gently as a Dove."

As soon as I came to reside on my farm I tried to make·friends with the parish priest, Father Tandy, who resided in· Amenia. I was determined to conciliate him so that he would not be making complaints against me to the Archbishop; and, if possible, I was going to try to get him to go and speak a good word for me to His Grace.

The first Sunday I went to Mass in Amenia he made a short discourse. The moment he turned round to address the people I was quite taken aback, for I saw in him a formidable adversary. But instantly I decided on my mode of attack. I must be gentle with him, and kill him with kindness; for it was the only possible way that such a man could be caught. When Mass was over I went into the sacristy accompanied by Mrs. Voice and her father. The moment I addressed the Father I saw that his mind was already made up in regard to me. He received me very coldly and looked at me frowningly. Mrs. Voice and her father were received by him with a most gracious manner and complacent smile.

To appear very frank and ingenuous I launched out at once about my church. His first words were: "I would advise you to go and see the Archbishop before you begin it," "Oh," said I, "that will be all right, as I intend to deed it to the diocese it will give you a parish the more." He replied: "I have as many parishes now as I can attend to. But I understand that you are going to build it across the line. You take my advice and go and see the Archbishop."

I only spoke with him a few moments; but during that short interval he advised me three times to go and see the Archbishop. I begged him to call and see me and see what a lovely situation for a church it was, and what a beautiful little house I had; I was sure he would be pleased. I tried to appear as meek, as harmless, and as innocent as a lamb; and well I might, for I felt that I was stepping on the claws of a lion by putting up a church on the borders of his parish.

In a few days we all called on him at his house, when I renewed my gentle attacks. But his manner towards me as much as said: "I know very well what you want; but I am not to be caught that way." This day he advised me four times to go and see the Archbishop. Shortly afterwards he returned our call. The best things in the house were spread before him; if it had been the Archbishop himself there could not have been more fuss made; and if there had been a fatted calf on the farm I believe we would have killed it.

After a collation we all started out to climb the hill where the foundation of the church was already laid. While we were mounting it Father Tandy said to me again, but this time rather coaxingly, "Why don't you go and see the Archbishop?" "Oh," said I, "it is too late now, for I have already made the contract, and some of the money is already paid." "Well, then," he continued, "*put it over in New York State.*"

In a moment more we reached the top of the hill, where a magnificent view broke suddenly upon us. A beautiful valley lay at our feet, studded with villages, hillocks, and mounts. Directly in front of us, far in the distance, could be discerned the outlines of the Hoosack Mountains, whose peaks dimly rose above a circle of deep blue haze like a vision of peace.

Father Tandy was unprepared for the natural beauty of this rustic view, and he instantly fell a victim to its charms. For a moment his whole soul appeared enamoured with the scene, which seemed to render him oblivious of his parochial rights and sense of self-preservation. He stood erect, and stretching forth his hand as though he would bless the ground on which he stood, he exclaimed : "God created this spot for His church. If I were stationed here I would never leave it ; I would make everybody come up here and worship God."

This time it was our turn to be taken by surprise, for we were totally unprepared for the outburst of approbation, and his gesture, his words, and his looks, showed plainly that he sanctioned my work.

As we returned to descend the hill I threw a grateful look on the valley and over the hills. That spot became dearer to me than ever. I felt that it had rendered me a service; it had effected for me in an instant what I might not have been able to accomplish in years; it had ensnared Father Tandy, and made him forget himself so far as to be willing to have me build a church across the line. Never afterwards did he repeat that ominous advice, "Go and see the Archbishop." The lion was tamed, I had nothing more to fear from him, at least for the present, for from the moment he stood on the spot where the foundation of the church was laid, whenever I besought him to say "yes," that he would take charge of the little church after it was finished, he never said "*no;*" but, on the contrary, would smile as though he could not have refused to take charge of a dozen such churches, *even though they were built across the line.*

CHAPTER XCI.

LAFERRIÈRE'S LAST LETTER.

"Infandum renovare Dolorem"—The Emperor—Anguish: reassured by the Bible—A Day happily ended—"Our Father"—Submission to Fate.

THE position of the Imperialists was becoming worse and worse in France, and I lived in daily expectation of receiving a letter from Laferrière accepting my offer. I fancied that the misfortunes of the French would be the foundation of my own happiness, for I ever hoped that they would be the means of driving Laferrière to me to seek a home and consolation. I had arranged my house with the sole view of pleasing him, and there were moments that I would revel in advance at his joyful surprise, after crossing the ocean, to find in a wilderness a little home furnished with many things that were in his apartment when we first met. He had sent them to me when I went to St. Mandé to fill up those spacious rooms. There was his chair, his table, his lamp, and many little objects that would remind him of the past; and even some of his segars

were there until Father Tandy came, and then they were sacrificed to him.

It was the 13th or 14th of July. Nearly everything was
arranged: there was nothing left to be done but to hang a
picture or place an ornament here and there, when I received
a letter. It was from France, and was addressed to me in his
handwriting, and bore his seal. I had not received a line from
him since the morning that his valet brought me that note, and
handed it to me, just as I was going to take the train for Havre,
more than a year before; and not a day had dawned since I
placed my foot on the shores of America that I did not awake
thinking and hoping that the mail might bring me a letter
from him, perhaps stating the day, and even the hour, when I
should be his bride.

All these fond dreams, which had buoyed my spirits up
through so many trials, crowded upon me as I perused the
following pages:

"CHATEAU DE FLÉCHÈRES,

"*June* 28, 1871.

"MY DEAR CHILD,

"I was pleased and moved at the kind souvenir that you addressed to me from the other side of the Atlantic. Your letter
found me at Fléchères, where I had just returned, after an
absence of nine months.

"I passed all that time in foreign parts, not being able to
remain in France without being exposed to all kinds of annoyance and enmity. You will understand how much I suffered in
seeing my country ravaged, invaded, and not to be able to go to
her succour; it was one of the greatest griefs of my exile.

"Since you desire to know what I have done in the midst of
these great catastrophes, I will tell you in a few words all that
happened to me.

"The 4th of September I was, as was my duty, at my post in
the Tuileries, beside the *Régente,* who, badly counselled, did not
do all that was necessary in order to try to save the throne of
her son. The Empress left the Palace on the 4th of September,
at half-past three. I stayed in my apartment to put my papers
in order. For some days I was certain that the course taken
was leading to an abyss in which we should all be engulfed,
nevertheless I did not wish to have the least object removed
from the Tuileries. I thought it a more worthy course to remain
calm and regardless of one's personal interests in the midst of
the storm. So I left my apartment in its usual state.

" On the 4th of September, at six o'clock in the evening, the *Garde Nationale* having taken possession of the Palace, I went to my daughter's with my valise. The next day, the Government not allowing anything to leave the Tuileries, my property was sequestrated. So there I was at my daughter's with only four shirts and as many handkerchiefs! But the political situation was so grave that my personal losses gave me but little thought; I had enough of other cares.

" The 14th of last October I went to Geneva with my daughter, leaving all my affairs in disorder, but, what was much more distressing to me, leaving France invaded by enemies. From the time the Prussians had first put their foot upon our territory I had considered it a duty for all able-bodied Frenchmen to take arms. I asked and obtained the command of a regiment. My nomination was made the 2nd of September, the eve of the fall of the Empire, so my position was a difficult one: should I take the command which had been confided to me by the Emperor, or resign it? I went to see the Minister of War, who was one of my old comrades, and he thought that, in the state of public feeling at that time, the First Chamberlain would not be able to exercise the necessary authority over the Mobiles, so he decided to replace me by an officer whom I pointed out to him. It was on this account, and to my great regret, that I was deprived of the satisfaction and the honour of fighting in defence of my country. At Geneva I lived in profound seclusion, entirely outside of politics, communicating with no one, and wishing to meet no one. Nevertheless the police of the Republic took the trouble to busy themselves about me, and to publish me in the papers as one of the heads of a Bonapartist conspiracy. Several times I passed twenty-four hours at Fléchères, but they always hesitated about arresting me, though I was followed by agents who were robbing the Government and telling it a pack of lies.

" I believed it my duty, as long as the Emperor was at Wilhelmshöhe, to go to him and place myself at his disposal. I crossed the whole of Germany, which was then in arms, at that time when the Prussians were marching upon Paris, which, to a French heart, was a cruel spectacle. The Emperor was very much moved at seeing me. I passed two days with him, relating to him all that happened in his absence, and telling him the *truth* about men and things. The Emperor was not able to keep me, so I left him with a heavy heart. It is useless to attack, to insult, and calumniate him. I will declare, with my head on the scaffold, that he was the best of men, the mildest, and best-intentioned of the sovereigns of our times. This is the truth : the wretches who dishonour the French press, ambitious men who covet power, may insult this unfortunate monarch, but posterity will do him justice, and already our people express loudly their regrets at the fall of a power which gave them peace and prosperity.

" As for me, my dear child, arrived at the end of my career, disgusted with the men and things of this age, I intend to pass, in the strictest retreat, the time that remains for me to live. I do not wish to mix again in anything, no matter what it may be ; my age permits me to repose, and I desire to avail myself of this sad privilege.

" I hope, but I am not sure, that the frightful crimes that have dishonoured Paris will be followed by a time of calm ; there are so many causes of fermentation and discord in unhappy France that one cannot predict its future. If nothing prevents it I shall pass the most of my time at Fléchères ; but, in case France becomes again uninhabitable for those who have held any position under the Empire, I shall return to the mountains of Switzerland and buy a *châlet* there.

" I learned with great pleasure that you are contented and do not regret in any way having followed your fancies ; the thought that you are almost happy consoles me for many of my present griefs. We are separated by the ocean, and by unsurmountable difficulties, I do not see any possibility of our ever meeting again in this world ; it is a grief for me as well as for you, for your remembrance is very vivid to me. I often recall the past, and it is always with pleasure that I find the trace of so many happy hours passed beside you. *This sweet dream has vanished, never to return !*

" I beg you to embrace your charming little girl for me ; I shall remain for her a souvenir of that happy France where she passed many years. May the dear child be happy ! May you also find a peaceful life, and forget the pain I have caused you, to remember only the few good qualities which hide themselves behind my faults.

" I send the most tender farewell, and the assurance of an affection which will only terminate with my life.

" LAFERRIÈRE."

As my eyes ran over those lines, which I knew he intended me to consider as his last adieu, my courage forsook me,—but not the hope of seeing him again ; for love does not so easily abandon hope. But my courage left me,—the courage to persevere and

finish the work I had begun. I had an impulse to rush back to
New York, and take the next steamer that sailed for France. I
knew that he loved me, and he was only wounded because I had
left him, and that I had only to go back to him, and throw
myself at his feet, and all would be forgiven. There I was,
surrounded by everything and everybody that was most uncongenial to me; and Laferrière's letter brought back to me all that
I had lost; and I believed that I might regain it all again, if I
only went back to him.

I tried to conceal my anguish from those around me. The
more I suffered, and the more my courage and strength to persevere
failed me, the more I outwardly appeared contented, hopeful,
and happy.

On the 17th of July they raised the frame of the church, and
as the strokes resounded through the air, each stroke fell on my
ears like a demon's voice mocking and deriding me for my
obstinacy and folly. All the people around had predicted that
my much-talked-of-church would end in being made a barn.
"Well," thought I, "be it so. What do I care whether they
laugh at me or not? Let them laugh. I will place myself
beyond the reach of their deridings. I will go back to France,
for I cannot live any longer separated from Laferrière. I *will*
go back to him."

I went up stairs, into a little room that I had fitted up to
remind me of that little bedroom which I had dedicated to the
Blessed Virgin, in the Abbaye aux Bois. The walls were pale
blue, and on the ceiling were stars, and it was furnished with
light blue silk and gold. The same statue of the Blessed Virgin
too was there. I knelt before it, and there I began to pray,
and to ask our Lord to inspire me what to do. I never knew a
sadder hour. I could hear cheerful and merry voices everywhere
around me, but the heavy strokes of the workmen's axe jarred on
every fibre of my heart.

After praying a few moments, and fervently imploring our
Lord to let me know if it was His will that I should continue
to build that church before I returned to France, I got my
Bible, and kneeling down again before the statue, I said:
"Lord, Thou shalt decide for me now as Thou didst before;
and whatever Thou tellest me to do, I will do it."

As quick as thought I opened the Bible at these words—
(1 Chron. xxii. 11):

"The Lord be with thee; and prosper thou, and build the
house of the Lord thy God, as He hath said of thee.

"12. Only the Lord give thee wisdom and understanding,

and give thee charge concerning Israel, that thou mayest keep the law of the Lord thy God.

"13. Then shalt thou prosper, if thou takest heed to fulfil the statues and judgments which the Lord charged Moses with concerning Israel: be strong, and of good courage; dread not, nor be dismayed."

My soul was filled with the sweetest consolation as I read these lines. I felt just as though God were beside me, leading me by the hand.

"Dearest Saviour!" I exclaimed, "I will do as you tell me. I will build the church, and I will be good, and will never doubt again that Thou didst send me here. Laferrière can call it caprice, fancy, what he will; but I know now that Thou didst call me. I will trust in Thee, and I will ever keep Thy ' statutes,' and I know that Thou wilt not abandon me."

I was as happy and joyous the rest of that day as I had been sad and despondent in the early part of it.

As soon as the workmen had left, Mrs. Voice, her father, my child, and myself, went up to the church, where the old gentleman said the rosary, and the rest of us responded. The fiery rays of the setting sun were reflected on the eastern sky, so that the whole country appeared as though it were canopied by a radiant dome.

I left them and went down to the ledge of rocks, which lay by the roadside, opposite to the pond. My child came tripping after me, and, as we leaped from one stone to the other, she anxiously inquired at every jump, if I would have a "steeple to the church, a cross, and a bell." I replied: "I will put on it everything that the Lord will give me; but before we ask Him for a steeple, let us pray that He will give us the money to pay for the foundation."

"Oh, mamma!" she cried, "I am sure that He will do that; but I think we ought to ask for a steeple too. I am going to pray the Blessed Virgin for that." As we leaped from rock to rock my heart was burning with gratitude to God for all His goodness.

I stopped an instant to catch breath, and taking hold of my child's hand, I said to her: "Let us thank God, my child, for all that He has done for us." "Yes, mamma," she replied, "for God is such a *good Father!*"

I was looking down at the pond when the word "Father" escaped her lips. A slight tremour passed over the water, and those tiny waves seemed to whisper back to me the words my child had spoken: "*God is such a good Father!*"

I then recollected the day and the hour that I had once sat there alone, when a child, without a home or a friend; and when I saw the water move, how I rushed down the rocks, and knelt down by the edge of the pond, and called on the spirit of my dead father to look down from heaven and protect his child.

I then looked towards the cottage where the shoemaker lived. He had long since died; but his cottage was still there, the sight of which brought back a painful remembrance. I turned away from it, and said to my child: "Let us go home."

As I came in sight of the house my heart bounded with joy, for I then recollected that I had, that very same day to which I allude, sat by the roadside, under the chestnut-tree, and coveted that little home. I said to my child: "How true it is, dear one, that God is good, for He has given me everything that my heart once desired. He does not even forget the prayers I made when a child." ·

I could say no more, my soul was too full for utterance, for there, too, was the church already begun, which seemed to say that nothing was forgotten, and that our Lord had been watching over me when I stood there in years gone by, and had thought how beautiful it would be to go up on that hill to worship God!

In that moment I rejoiced, and was glad that I had left France, for I felt that by leaving it I had made God my Father and my Friend. But alas! for the inconstancy of the human heart; before another day had gone, I was asking Him with streaming eyes, how long I still must wait before I should see Laferrière again!

CHAPTER XCII.

SUBMISSION TO FAITH—AN EXODUS.

Patience ceases to be a Virtue—A Microcosm in a Waggon.

THE day after the frame of the church was raised, Mrs. Voice's father returned to New York, and we were left under the protection of Mike.

He, and his wife, and his mother, and his cousin were principally employed in trying to pacify, to feed, and to clean the two children, while I was constantly praying God to make me patient and resigned.

One day I called Mike to drive out a heifer I saw in my lot. "Why, madam," he exclaimed, "that is your own: it is the fine little cow that you bought of me." "I don't want any such looking cow as that," I returned, "and I will give you ten dollars, Mike, if you will take her back ; " to which Mike agreed.

As I never made any complaints, everybody took me to be either crazy or a fool.

I was a mystery to Mrs. Voice, who one day began telling me what her impressions were, whenever she chanced to go into the kitchen. Said I, "Do as I do. I close my eyes, and stop my ears, and hurry through it as quickly as I can; therefore I see nothing, I hear nothing." "Hear nothing !" she exclaimed; "why, you can hear the children crying all over the place." "*You* may," said I, "I do not; for when a child cries, I think of something else, and won't listen to it."

In a little while, Mike came to the conclusion that I was neither crazy nor a fool, but that I was afraid to speak, for fear of losing them ; and he doubtless said to himself: "The woman is right; for what could she do without a man to take care of her farm ? " The reason why I was so lenient with this gentle band was, that I had always made it a rule never to give an order unless I could enforce it, and whenever I gave one, I would be obeyed, or I would discharge the servant at once.

One evening Mrs. Voice was goading me more than ever, trying to open my eyes, when I said to her : "If I give an order, I will make them obey me, and if they refuse or are insolent, I will oblige them to leave."

"Goodness," she exclaimed, "let them go ! for what do they do but wait on themselves ? "

The next morning I found the boy Neillie on the piazza, where he had been creating a disturbance with Mrs. Voice's child and maid ; to avoid a repetition of the scene I took the gentle Neillie by the hand and led him to his mother. I had hardly left the kitchen when Mike came to me and said he wished I would settle with him at once that he did not care to stay where his child could not have the privilege of going on to the front steps ; that the mother would not stand it, and was so indignant that she had taken her hands out of the dough, and had gone to a neighbour's to hire a room.

Said I ; "Mike, you don't mean to say that you would leave me for such a trifle as that ? " Then he became bold. "Yes," he replied, with earnestness, "we will all of us leave, Maggie and all ; and I would like to have you settle with me on the spot." Said I : "Mike, whenever a servant comes to me, and tells me that he is going to leave, I have but one reply, and that is that he has *got* to go. So pack up your things."

Mike was taken aback, and made no reply. At that moment

his wife returned. I went into the kitchen and found her at
work. I begged her to stop, and give all her time to preparing
to leave. But they had changed their minds and had concluded
to stay.

Said I: " Mike, you must leave because you told me you would
go." He, then coaxingly requested me to let them remain. But
finding that he could not move me by kindness, he began to
threaten, which had no effect on me either. At last, drawing
himself up to his full height, which then did not make him appear
very tall, he exclaimed: " Then we will settle, and you will pay
me for my cow before I will leave."

Said I: " I bought your cow, and for ten dollars you agreed
to take it back, and I have given you time to go and sell it for
yourself. The cow is yours, not mine." He swore that he would
sue me. Said I: " You can sue me, but that will not make me
buy your cow."

The court-house was in Sharon village, which lay about seven
miles off. I thought it would be well for me to secure the
nearest lawyer to be had; so I told Mike to put the side-saddle
on the horse, and I started to consult Lawyer Swift, who lived
in the valley. Mike, suspecting where I was going, took a short
cut across the lots, and got there before me, and secured him for
himself.

As soon as I got home, we had another pitched battle, Mike
all the while threatening that he would sue me, to make me pay
him for his cow.

The next morning I gave them no peace, and kept right in the
midst of them, urging them to leave. Mike began threatening
again to sue me.

Said I: " Mike, you talk just as though you thought that it
would annoy me to go to court, whereas, I would love to go to
court with you. It would be such a luxurious change compared
to the monotonous life that I am leading on this hill." About
an hour afterwards Mike came to me as mild and as meek as a
lamb, and said: " Madam, I would prefer not going to court,
and I will settle with you for five dollars difference." To which
offer I agreed, thus annihilating all my prospects of having the
pleasure of going to court.

Mike had stored his furniture over the cow-house. In a few
hours it was piled up on a large lumber-waggon ready to leave.
The clock struck two; and I heard a voice cry out; " Well, we
are all ready now: let's go."

At that happy cry I rushed out of the house, and sat down on
the piazza to view the parting train, taking for subject of my

meditation the Exodus of the Israelites; and I wondered if there
ever was a widow throughout all Egypt, who needed the services
of a Jew as much as I did Mike's, and yet was as glad as I was to
see him go. I concluded that, in my joys as well as my sorrows,
I was destined ever to be alone, singled out by Providence as an
exception. to womankind; and my heart bounded with delight
at the strange sight of a waggon-load of furniture, with a kettle
hanging down from the axle-tree behind, with Mike, his wife,
the tender Neillie, the baby, the cousin, and the grandmother,
all driving out of sight, and leaving me utterly without "help."
A man soon afterwards came and drove away the cow, and then
might have been heard a squealing, down towards the barn; it
was Mike's pig, the only living thing which still remained to
remind me of *what had been!*

CHAPTER XCIII.

FATHER TANDY'S STORY.

A Chapter of Accidents—Enmeshing the Lion—He tells a Story—The
Moral of the Story—It fails to convert me.

IN a few days after Mike left I succeeded in getting two girls
and a boy about fourteen years old to do my work.

September had come and it was time to take my child back
to school.

One morning I started off very early on horseback to call on
Father Tandy. I was almost there when a terrible hail-storm
set in, which frightened my horse and he ran away. He clinched
the bit between his teeth so that I had no control over him, and
it was all that I could do to keep on his back. Just as I got in
sight of the parsonage the saddle turned, and I was thrown to
the ground without being injured; for as the saddle turned on
his back the horse instantly stopped. I had hardly time to open
the gate before two tremendous dogs sprang towards me, and
when I got into the yard one of them caught me by the heel.

I had had a narrow escape in being thrown from my horse,
and, before I had yet recovered from the shock, to be attacked
by two fierce dogs in a hail-storm, made me feel for a moment
as though the infernal powers had been let loose upon me.

I had no sooner got into the house than I looked on my
accidents as providential, as though the elements and the brute
creation had leagued together to forward my designs. Nothing
could have been more fortunate for me than to be caught there

in a storm, with a horse that had just run away with me. I felt that it insured me the Father's hospitality for an hour at least, and that was just what I wanted. I did not want him to suspect the motive that brought me to his house that morning, lest he might be on his guard and might refuse my request.

I knew that he was going to New York in a day or two, and I wanted him to speak a good word for me to Archbishop McCloskey.

I had done everything in my power to gain Father Tandy's good will. At first he was on his guard; but on further acquaintance I think that he began to consider me as a simple, good, honest-hearted woman who had little or no sense, and that there was no danger of my doing any harm as I was going to deed the church to the Bishop of Hartford, on condition that Father Tandy should take charge of it.

On a better acquaintance with him I concluded that I would rather not be subjected to him; I merely wanted his influence because I knew it was necessary in order to go on with my work.

As I had an idea that Imperial reverses would yet force Laferrière to seek a home on this side of the ocean, I was determined to be prepared for such an emergency; and in that case I should want to occupy the place myself as a country-seat. I knew well that if Father Tandy was once in possession of the edifice he would have Mass only when it suited himself, and that if I attempted to interfere he would lock up the church, put the keys in his pocket, and perhaps threaten me with the thunders of the church if I dared to murmur against his arbitrary rule.

To return to my morning call, when the very elements themselves seemed to favour my designs on this unsuspecting priest : —in spite of my endeavours to arrive before he had breakfasted, his housekeeper, who came to the door, said that he had already breakfasted, and had gone out.

On his return I related to him my adventures, and wound up my story by asking him if he would please to tell me at once at what hour Mass was to be in Dover on Sunday; for I ought to hurry home so as to get my breakfast. He instantly left me; but returned in a few moments, and said that it would not be safe for me to ride back on that horse ; he had ordered breakfast for me, and would send me home, in his carriage, as soon as it cleared off.

My breakfast was served in the library. Much time was consumed in talking, but saying nothing. I appeared all the while to be searching to find something to say; but at last the conversation came to a dead pause, and Father Tandy went to the window, and remarked that it rained harder than ever, and that there was no sign of it clearing off.

He resumed his seat again, which was right opposite mine, and he asked me if I would not give him a history of my conversion. I was delighted at the chance and instantly complied, making my story as pathetic and as interesting as I could.

As soon as my story was ended, he remarked: "After leading such a life, you will never be content to settle down here." "Oh," said I, "if I only had a little church, I think I could stay here and be happy;" and I began to tell him my troubles. One was, that I was going to New York, and was going to try to raise money to pay for what I had already contracted for, but that it would be difficult without His Grace's consent.

Said he: "Why do you not go to him and ask it?"

"Because," said I, "he would not pay any attention to me. You will not promise to take charge of the little church, and I do not believe that he would care to have me continue it, for fear that I would interfere with you. If you would only go and say a word for me yourself, it would all be right; but you would not like to do that, would you?" "Certainly, I will," he answered. "I will go and see the Archbishop, and I am sure that, after I have seen him, you will have no trouble." I thanked him with all my heart. I then wanted to go, and intimated that it was of no use for me to wait any longer for the weather to clear off.

"There is plenty of time," said he; "I will see that you get home before dark."

He was in no hurry to have me go, and seemed to think that it was his turn to talk; and he began to tell me a story, to which at first I did not listen, for I was so overjoyed with my good luck, that I could think of nothing else.

He noticed my inattention, and appeared displeased; for he bluntly remarked that I was not as good a listener as himself.

At that just reproach I sat still, and I listened to him more attentively than I ever listened to any man before. The instant that I paid attention, I saw that his story was intended for my instruction. I could see it in his face; for he looked at me as though he wished his every word would pierce the very marrow of my bones, that I might profit by another widow's sad experience, and never fall out with my parish priest. The moment that I seized the run of his theme, it filled me so with laughter that my whole body ached; for I did not dare to smile, but sat before him, looking vaguely, as though I little comprehended what he found in that story that could interest him, or that

could interest me.   By my gross inattention, I lost much of the
first part, but I am sure of the last, and can remember here and
there an outline of the first, just enough to give the reader an
idea of the whole plot.   It was the thrilling story of a widow,
who once upon a time determined to build a church, and her
first step towards the execution of her plans was to quarrel with
the parish priest, who declared that the remains of this widow's
deceased husband—he not having died in a canonical way—had
no right to repose beneath the altar of a Roman Catholic church,
in which spot his widow was resolved to place them.

The priest first requested her not to leave them there; but she
refused to comply with the request.   He then forbade it, and she
told him that she would do as she pleased.   He gave her then
to understand that he could not prevent her building a church,
or placing her husband's body wherever she chose; but that he
could prevent Mass ever being said there.   She laughed at his
pretensions, and went to work, disdaining the advice and warnings
of a simple parish priest.

In a short while she succeeded in erecting a beautiful little
church.   When it was completed she called on the priest, and
requested him to say Mass, which he refused to do.   She begged
him and implored him, but he was inexorable.   She went to the
Archbishop, who refused to interfere with his priest.   She went
to other priests, who would have willingly complied, but they
could not grant her request without the consent of the parish
priest.   She applied to him for that permission, which he
pertinaciously declined to give: and so it continued, and it was
TEN *years* before she succeeded in obtaining her request.   "What
do you think of that?"

I made no reply, pretending not to have seen the point; but I
felt very much like telling him that if I had been there I could
have taught that widow better.

Father Tandy did not appear satisfied when he saw that I did
not apply the important part to myself, and that perhaps his story
had not the desired effect.   He fell to commenting upon it and
said that if this woman had been clever she would have kept on
good terms with her parish priest, and then everything would
have gone on well.

Said I: "Perhaps she did not like him."   He answered:
"That had nothing to do with it; she should have studied her
interest, so as to have saved herself all that trouble."   "Trouble,"
said I, "who cares for the trouble?   If I did not like a priest
I would not be domineered over by him; but if I liked him, I
would do everything I could to please him."

Said he : " You mean to deed your chapel, after it is finished, to the Church, do you not.

" Of course I do," said I.   He continued : " And so did she. But it made no difference : she could do nothing without the consent of her parish priest ; " and he kept repeating it over until he was tired.   He then left me to order the horses.

I thought to myself, as soon as he left the room, how much I had heard people rant about wily priests ; but I did not consider the craftiest of them a match for the most stupid widow.

As soon as he returned, I wanted to remark : " But, Father, you know that I am out of your parish ; therefore this widow's case and my own are not parallel."   But I did not say it, thinking that it would be wiser to let him speak a good word for me to His Grace, before I should let him see that the widow to whom he had just given an instruction did not forget that she was building her church across the State line.

When I got into the carriage Father Tandy offered to give me one of his dogs.   He praised the dog's vigilance, of which I was easily convinced, as I still felt the prints of his teeth in my heel.

That night, after I retired, I began reflecting over my good luck, while my child, whose bed was near mine, was condoling with me for having been caught out in the rain, thrown by the horse, and bitten by the dog.   I was so absorbed in thought that I would answer her Yes and No, without listening to what she said.   But as my bad luck would have it, I happened to say Yes when I should have said No, at which she instantly sprang up, exclaiming : " Do get up, mamma ; strike a light, and show me."

" Show you what, child ?" said I.   " Why, where the horse kicked you."   " The horse did not kick me," I replied.   " Then, mamma, what made you say he did when I asked you ?"   I began laughing, and she wanted to know what there was to make me laugh.   Said I : " Don't ask me any more questions, child, for I can only think of Father Tandy's story."   " Oh, mamma," she cried, " you must tell it to me."   Said I : " Not now, for you will find it stupid ; but it will amuse you when you are older."   " No, no, mamma, you must tell it to me now, I know it will make me laugh."   I began to tell the story, but before I had finished it the child was sound asleep, and never since has she asked me to tell her Father Tandy's story.

CHAPTER XCIV.

ENCOURAGEMENT AND DESPONDENCY: THE BIBLE BIDS ME "NOT TO
FEAR."

I visit the Archbishop—His Grace is gracious—New Strength.

As soon as I returned in New York I went to the Archbishop's.

After passing the usual compliments His Grace stopped short, and waited for me to speak. That embarrassed me, for I expected that he would speak first, and I had prepared myself to be on the defensive. For a moment there was a dead pause. I apologised for my awkwardness, saying: "I am not accustomed to speak to archbishops, and I should only blunder if I tried to address you by your proper titles. Permit me to call you Father, and then I can put my whole mind on what I came to see you about." His Grace smiled, nodded an assent, and said he should be pleased to hear me call him Father.

"I suppose," said I, "you know what I came for?" "Yes," he replied, "but your business does not concern me, for you have built your church out of my diocese."

"That is the difficulty that I want you to get me out of. I could never raise money to build my church if it were known that it is out of your diocese."

I then showed him my list of subscribers, and told him that everybody I knew lived in New York State. Said he: "I cannot change the boundaries of the dioceses."

"Will you accept the jurisdiction of my church," said I, "if the Bishop of Hartford will cede it to you?" "Yes," he said ; "Father Tandy was here yesterday: he told me that the church is being built on a beautiful site, and he says that he is willing to take charge of it. I will see the Bishop of Hartford in a few days, and if he is willing I will accept it, and will write to you. I apprehend no difficulty." I thanked His Grace, but I could see that his mind had been already made up before I came, and that Father Tandy had paved the way for me.

I excused myself for not having called on him before. "It was very wise of you," said he, "to keep away, for I should have had to put a stop to the whole thing: it is a courtesy that one bishop always extends to another, never to build a church on the very border of his diocese in order not to interfere with the adjoining parishes."

"That is what I feared," said I, "and therefore I kept away from you, and I have been living in constant dread of receiving a line from you asking me to explain." "I never heard anything about your work," said His Grace, "until a week ago, when I heard at Manhattanville, from Mother Hardey, that you were building a church. I could not believe it, as I had not heard a word about it; and I assured her that she must have been misinformed. She insisted, however, that there was one building; but it was only when Father Tandy told me that he had seen it that I could believe it." "What must I do?" said I. "You must go ahead." He accompanied me to the door, gave me his blessing, bade me good-bye, and told me again to "go ahead."

I ran down the steps as happy as a child, for those words, "go ahead," coming from His Grace's lips, rung in my ears like the signal of success.

The last of September I received a letter from Mrs. Voice, saying that the carpenter had just finished his contract, and expected that I would come and give him my note payable in three months. I expected to remain during the winter in the country, supposing, of course, that Mrs. Voice would stay with me. But as soon as I returned I discovered that during my absence Father Tandy had digusted Mrs. Voice with the prospect of a winter's residence in my mountain home. The fact was, he wanted her to sing in his church; and I felt that taking Mrs. Voice from me would fully counterbalance all that he had done in my favour with the Archbishop. The morning after I returned to New York I received the following line from His Grace the Archbishop of New York :—

"Archbishop McCloskey presents his compliments to Mrs. Eckel, and begs to say that he has just received a letter from the Bishop of Hartford, granting all the permissions and privileges asked for.

"NEW YORK, *September 28th*, 1871."

I then went among Catholic gentlemen and tried to beg. But no one would give me anything, and many suspected me, seeing so many Protestant names on my list. I referred them to the Archbishop, but they would not take the trouble to go to see him. Not knowing what to do, I called on His Grace myself, who received me very kindly. I told him how others doubted me, and asked him if he would give me a line by which I could show that I was not an impostor. He replied: "I will sign your subscription-list, and give you a hundred dollars," which he did on the spot.

Having the Archbishop's signature on my list I thought that all my trouble was over.

I then called on several Catholic gentlemen, they received me kindly, but the most of them gave me nothing. In the meantime I had learned that my project of building a church had been discussed by some influential Catholics in New York; that the majority of them suspected my motives, and were doing all they could to thwart me. Several of these people I had known in France, and had rendered them services, for which they seemed now to owe me a grudge.

One evening I returned to the hotel more discouraged than I had ever been before. I had exhausted my list of Catholic names, of whom I had hardly been able to collect a cent. I fell to weeping, and I said to our Lord, " I do not wish to give up, but what can I do?" and I sat down on the floor, buried my face in my hands, and wept like a child.

I implored God to speak to me, and to tell me if He had abandoned me or not; and I implored Him, if He had not abandoned me, to inspire me what to do, and to let me know if I should continue as I was, blindly trusting in Him.

I got up from the floor to get my Bible, and a fresh gust of tears streamed from my eyes at the thought of being there all alone without friends, and surrounded by unknown enemies, who were doing all they could to injure me.

I opened the Bible and dashed away the tears that blinded me. My eyes fell on these words (Isa. xli.):—

" 10. Fear thou not, for I am with thee : be not dismayed, for I am thy God : I will strengthen thee; yea, I will help thee ; yea, I will uphold thee with the right hand of my righteousness.

" 11. Behold, all they that were incensed against thee shall be ashamed and confounded: they shall be as nothing ; and they that strive with thee shall perish.

" 12. Thou shalt seek them, and shalt not find them, even them that contended with thee: they that war against thee shall be as nothing, and as a thing of naught.

" 13. For I the Lord thy God will hold thy right hand, saying unto thee, Fear not, I will help thee."

I read and I re-read those four verses until my sorrow was turned into gladness ; and much as I wept an instant before from desolation and despair, I now wept as freely from joy. I wondered how I could have ever doubted, even how I could have mourned ; for after I opened at those words I felt as though there was no trial that I would not be willing to brave to show God that I would ever put my trust in Him.

The following day I went out, but met with no success; yet

I returned home hopeful and happy, and as soon as I entered my room I fell on my knees and renewed my vow to God that I would ever trust and hope in Him, even though He brought me to the direst woe, for I knew that His hand could raise me up and deliver me whenever He would.

CHAPTER XCV.

MY DRIVING LESSON.

A Race against Time—I put my Trust in Man—My confidence dashed.

FINDING it impossible to get any more subscriptions, on account of the Chicago fire, I resolved to go home and pass the winter on my farm.

Mrs. Voice had left me, and soon went to live in Amenia.

I was driving out one day, it was the 1st of November, and my horses ran away. I had hold of the reins and succeeded in managing them until they chose to stop. But I called on God to help me at every breath. I looked upon my escape as miraculous, and attributed it all to the hand of God.

That night I awoke shortly after midnight, and I immediately recollected that it was the 2nd of November, a memorable day for me. It was the fourth anniversary of the day that I had been able, by the grace of God, to forgive my mother, as the Angelus bell of St. Mandé ushered in All Souls' Day.

There would be Mass celebrated early the next morning in Amenia. But Amenia was seven miles away. Ever since my conversion I had always offered up my communion on that day for the repose of the soul of my mother, and I felt that to neglect it would be almost a crime. Yet I was afraid to go on account of the horses having run away; but a moment afterwards I was afraid to stay away for such a reason. I feared that God would punish me for my want of faith. I rose and told the boy to harness the horses, and we would go to Mass: but, before we started, we offered up a prayer that God would protect us.

Everything went on well until we came within two miles of the church, and then the horses started to run. The wheels almost ceased to turn, and would hardly touch the ground. The moment the horses ran I seized the reins in one hand and held the boy in with the other; he was determined to jump out for he was frightened. I was not; I felt that God was with me. They ran about two miles until they reached the village, where they were stopped by some men.

After I had received holy communion and was returning to my seat, I nearly fainted; but I never felt so happy and hopeful in my life. I felt that God would give me a rich reward for that morning's act of Faith. Father Tandy told his man John to get into the waggon and drive me home. But we had not gone far when the horses started to run again. John got afraid and I took the reins, and the horses stopped the instant that I began to pray.

The boy was standing up behind us holding on to the seat; but the moment the horses stopped he began to laugh. Said I: "What is there here to laugh about?" Said he: "I laugh to see how John turned pale; but if they start to run again I swear that I'll jump out, and I'll bet that both of you, if you tried, could not hold me in again." Said I: "We will let you go, for we shall have as much as we can attend to on this side of the seat."

We got home safely, and our miraculous escape was the talk of the town; for all those who saw the horses run expected we should all be killed; and they were still more amazed that we should always escape without the slightest injury to horses, waggon, harness, or ourselves.

I have said that *all* were amazed. But no! for there was neighbour White, who was the great horseman of the place. He laughed and made fun of me for "allowing those *ponies* to run away, and would often exclaim: "But what does a woman know about managing a team? You should take me along with you to teach you how to drive." Said I: "My friend, you shall have a chance any time you choose to go."

Shortly afterwards I told the boy to harness the horses and drive to Wassaic, to get a load of stove-pipe which I had bought for my church. He looked at me when I gave the order as though I were sending him to his grave. The boy begged me to go along with him for fear the horses might run away. It was getting late; there was no time to lose; to please him I got in. We had hardly got started before he declared that if the horses should begin to run he would surely jump out, and that it would be of no use for me to try to hold him in.

Just at that moment we passed a corn-field where I saw neighbour White at work. I called out to him, and asked him if he would not exchange, and drive the team, and let the boy husk the corn. "Certainly," he replied, "and *I will show you how to drive.*"

In an instant the boy was down out of the waggon into the field, and he threw after us a parting look, as though he never expected to see either of us alive again. Mr. White examined the harness and the waggon to see if everything was safe, and, as a double precaution, he buckled on an extra pair of reins. After he had pronounced everything safe and sound, he jumped buoyantly on the seat, snapped his whip, and said : " You must show them that you are not afraid of them—that's the way to drive."

I at once recollected that I had forgotten to pray ; " but," thought I, "there is no danger with neighbour White and an extra pair of reins !" The thought had hardly crossed my mind, when Mr. White spoke up in a bantering way, and said : " Before we go any further, you must promise to buy me a ticket for the next train for York if *these ponies* happen to get away." Said I : " We can keep on ; I will pay for your ticket, be not afraid ; but please don't flourish your whip so until we get down the hills on the plain." He laughed at me for being afraid when *he* was by my side. Said he ; " If you had the boy along, then you might be afraid ; " and he jerked the reins most daringly, and snapped his whip again. Thought I to myself : " I wish they would run away, and frighten him half to death."

We arrived at the depot perfectly safe ; but, long before we got there, Mr. White acknowledged that they were the fastest trotters in the place. " But you see it takes *a man* to manage a team. Why don't you get one to take care of *you* and your place ? " He loaded the waggon with pipe, and we started for home. All the while he kept running down my horsemanship and praising up his own.

We had gotten within a mile and a half of my home, when the horses started to run as they had done three different times with me. Neighbour White turned deathly pale, as he braced his feet against the board and pulled on the reins. The horses did not stop for that, but dashed along at lightning speed. I did not pray, nor even raise my heart to God, for I put my trust in neighbour White. But soon we came in sight of the turn—and that was all I saw ; for, in the same instant, I was thrown fifteen feet, with neighbour White by my side ; but " the ponies " still kept up their pace, leaving the stove-pipe, the waggon, neighbour White, and myself behind.

I was knocked senseless, and when I came to consciousness, I was in a one-horse waggon, leaning on neighbour White, who was driving with one hand, and sustaining me with the other. Said I : " Where are we, Mr. White ? " " Why," said he, "don't you know how the waggon upset, and the horses got away, and you and I were thrown close to the Dominie's fence ?—and it was a wonder that we were not killed. Miles Bump got the water to wash the blood from your face. This is Hen. Bird's waggon. Oh, my leg, how it aches!" As soon as I could re-collect myself, I exclaimed: " It serves me right, because I did not pray. If I had only prayed the horses never would have got away."

As soon as we were in the house I noticed that neighbour White would put his hand to his head, then to his elbow, and then to his knee, the same as I had seen the negro minstrels do when they finish playing the tambourine. I could not refrain from laughing, and I asked him how it happened that he was there, and why he had not taken the down express train? Said he: " I have ridden on the York Central lightning express ; but the fastest ride I ever took was the one I had to-night. All creation could not have held those brutes ; for, in trying to hold them, I pushed both heels off my boots ;" and he held up before me a pair of heelless boots ; the sight of which convinced me that it was better for me to put my trust in God, and hold the reins myself, than it was to take neighbour White along to teach me how to drive. From that day forth neighbour White never spoke about the *ponies*, but he has sometimes gently inquired how the *horses* were.

———

CHAPTER XCVI.

A CHILD OF MARY.

A False Light.

AFTER the accident of the horses running away, my servants wanted to leave me. The boy was even afraid to lead the horses to drink, and he left at once ; but the girl consented to remain another month. I began to then think that it was about time for me to leave too. So the 1st of December found me again in New York at the Westminster Hotel.

On the Feast of the Immaculate Conception, December 8th, I was enrolled among " The Children of Mary." The next day I tried in vain to get subscriptions.

The following morning I saw the Father in the confessional, and wept bitterly, as I related to him the humiliations I had been through the preceding day. He told me to try and bear up under them, by meditating on the Passion of our Lord. For a whole week I tried to do just as he had recommended ; but I was soon disheartened, and became a prey to the most violent temptations. I began to long once more to return to France. My director tried to incite me to work, but his efforts failed. Once he said to me: "I do not know what God intends to do with you; but I am sure that he wants us all to work as well as pray."

One evening I returned to the hotel sad and discouraged, with my mind fully determined to give up the life of retirement and devotion that I was leading. I took up my Bible and opened it, hoping it would sanction my determination, and my eyes fell on these words in Ecclesiastes x. 19 : "A feast is made for laughter, and wine maketh merry ; but money answereth *all things.*" As I read those words, I received with them a light ; but it was a sulphurous light compared to the lights I had always received when I had opened the Bible to know the will of God, with the intention of doing it whether it suited my will or not. I instantly rose to my feet, and stretching out my arms before me, as though I would seize the devil by the horns, and push him from me, I I exclaimed; "That was you, old devil, who opened at that place!"

My conscience told me it was a false light. I made a firm resolve to do right and to persevere ; and no sooner had I made that act of my will, which must have been pleasing to God, than I received another light, but this time a true one. My thoughts instantly reverted to Father Bazin, and his having told me that it was dangerous and wrong for me to seek to know the will of God by resorting to such extraordinary means. I saw that my revelations might come from the devil as well as from God ; for I was just as certain that the revelation I had just opened at came to me from the devil, as I was that the other ones had come from God. I sank on my knees, and thanked God, with fear and trembling, for having thus far escaped ; for I was sure that all my former revelations had come from him. But as I was now con- vinced that the devil could mix himself up with them, I asked myself: "How am I to know in future which is from God, and which from the devil ? I have had the grace this time, but will it always be so ?"

I felt drawn to tell my confessor about these things, and ask him how I should decide; but I was afraid that he would altogether forbid my consulting the Bible, as Father Bazin had done.

I now passed nearly all my time during the day, in St. Xavier's Chapel, before the altar of the Blessed Virgin. Thus I passed all the month of February. March came, but it did not bring the slightest change in my disposition or my situation, excepting that I was drawn more and more to prayer.

February 10th I drove to Manhattanville to see my child. L

saw Madam Hardey and confided to her my trials. I asked her what I should do, and she told me to say the thirty days' prayer.

I began to say it, and continued saying it every day.

CHAPTER XCVII.

TEMPTATION—SAVED BY THE BIBLE—MY FIRST GENERAL CONFESSION.

Misgivings—God is a jealous Lover—A Novena—Words of Mercy—
Their Application—Confession of a Lifetime.

ON the 11th of March I had finished the thirty days' prayer. I had written to a gentleman who resided out of town, to come and see me on the evening of that day; for I was determined that, if there was no change in my position by the time I had finished the thirty days' prayer, I would give up and go back to France. I felt that I had prayed long enough, and if God did not come to my assistance, it must be that I was labouring under a delusion.

I was sure the gentleman had arrived and would call on me, for in the afternoon I had sent around one of the hall-boys with a note to his hotel. He was a good man, who had always taken an interest in me; but he was sorry to see me such a "fervent Romanist," as he called it. I knew that the moment I should tell him that I was ready to give up my religious practices and my present mode of life, and that I wanted to return to France and marry Laferrière, he would give me the means to go, and would also settle up all my affairs.

I was very sad, and kept saying to myself: "If there is a God in heaven He cannot blame me for this step; for have I not prayed? have I not trusted in Him? and have I not made every sacrifice?" All these thoughts passed through my mind while I was dressing. I arranged myself with more than usual care. I painted my eyes, and decked myself with the few ornaments I had still retained. I hoped he would let me have the money to finish the church; for, although I doubted of everything now, yet I disliked to go back to Europe without being able to say that I had accomplished what I came for.

To while away the time until the gentleman came, I took up the Bible, and began reading over those passages which I now accused of having deluded me. I began with the first one I had opened at, in the 29th chapter of Jeremiah. I read them all through as thoughtlessly as I would have read an old letter that I knew by heart. After taking a long, admiring, look at myself in the mirror, I said: "Old Bible, I will open you once more to

see what you have to say; but I have been your dupe long
enough;" and, suiting the action to the word, I on the instant
opened the Bible, and was startled at seeing the following verse:

"And furthermore, that ye have sent for men to come from
far, unto whom a messenger was sent; and, lo, they came: for
whom thou didst wash thyself, paintedst thy eyes, and deckedst
thyself with ornaments." (Ezek. xxiii. 40.)

I restrained my tears, because I did not wish to wash off the
pencilling from my eyes. But the passage had wrought a
change in me, and I believed that God had ever been with me
and was with me still.

I really believed that He had just spoken to me, and that He
demanded of me to stop painting my eyes, before He would fulfil His promises, But I could not make my mind up to such a
sacrifice; for Laferrière had always admired my dark eyelids,
little suspecting that they were painted. And I said to our
Lord: "Now you are asking too much, for I will not stop painting my eyes."

I took the Bible and began reading those passages which had
presaged happiness for me. I read and re-read them with an
incredulous and almost despairing heart. In reading the first
passage which had consoled me so much in Paris, I was for the
first time struck with the condition which the Lord imposes in
the last verse, "And ye shall seek me and find me, when ye
shall search for me with all your heart." I repeated it several
times: "And ye shall seek me and find me, when ye shall search
for me with all your heart." I reproached myself, for the first
time, for not having sought God with all my heart,—in fact with
none of it; for all my sacrifices, had they not been made to
obtain Laferrière, and not for God Himself? Addressing God, I
exclaimed: "I have always heard it said that Thou art a jealous
God: is it true?" And distinctly I heard a voice within me
answer, "Yes." For the first time the thought occurred to me
that God might be jealous of Laferrière. The idea pleased me;
for, of all sentiments, jealousy was the one that I thought I
knew the most about, and I felt that if God was jealous of
Laferrière, He must love me,—and the thought delighted me that
·God could love me well enough to be jealous for me.

I fell on my knees while those words were still running in my
mind, "And ye shall seek me and find me, when ye shall search
for me with all your heart," and exclaimed aloud: "I will make
a novena to St. Joseph, and will try and seek Thee, Lord, and
not Laferrière; for if Thou art a jealous God, Thou couldst not
have been pleased with me. This time I will try to seek *Thee*;

but I implore Thee to give me the grace to do it."   I sat down
and wrote off the following prayer for my novena :—-

"11th March, 1872.

"*Novena Soliciting the Prayers and Protection of
St. Joseph.*

"May I have the grace to give my whole heart to God, and
may I love God with all my heart.   May I become patient and
resigned, and accept all past and future humiliations as coming
from His hand, and be persuaded that they are all for my eternal
good; and may God watch over me and inspire all my ways.
May He bless my little church; may I be able to finish it; and
may that little church be the means of saving millions of
souls.   May I become a true Christian at heart; may I have
more faith, and may I persevere unto the end."

I had not quite finished it, when the hall-boy brought me a
card.   The gentleman I expected had come, and I told the boy
to show him to my room.   He had not seen me for some time.
I related to him how I had. passed my time since we had met,
and I handed him the novena to read that was lying before him
on the table.   Said he: "How much in earnest you are!   I declare God ought to reward your faith."   Before leaving he asked
me if I had anything special to say to him.   I told him that I
did have, but that I would wait another week, for I was going to
let the result of that novena decide my future.

I would sometimes repeat my novena over twenty, sometimes
thirty times a day.   I would usually kneel down before the altar
of the Sacred Heart, and there I would implore our Lord to drive
Laferrière from my mind; for I was determined to fulfil this
condition, and seek Him with all my heart.

I would pray as though I were kneeling at the Saviour's feet
imploring Him to love me.   I would say: "O Lord Jesus, give
me the grace to want to love Thee: give me the desire to have
Thy love."   For I felt that the Lord could read my heart, and I
would acknowledge my own insincerity, that I did not desire it
as much as I pretended I did; but I wished, however, that I
could have the desire.

Friday, March 15th, my confessor asked me if it ever entered
into my mind to become a religious.   "NEVER," I replied; "I
would hang myself first."   "Well," said he, "I think your mind
has a tendency this way.   I cannot divest myself of the belief
that God intends to call you to be a religious."

I thought to myself: "What a wily set of fellows these Jesuits
are!   He really thinks that he will drag me into a convent"

(and a cloister, at that moment, appeared to me like a tomb).
I was then determined to leave him ; and I told him that I saw
through him; that he need not think he should ever draw me
into a convent. "It is God who will draw you there," he remarked, "not I. *I* could not remain in the chapel and pray for
hours consecutively, as you do : it would wear me out; but your
soul seems to delight in it."

That day I was fully resolved to change my confessor. The
idea of becoming a religious, which he had just put into my
head, kept running through my mind. The moment I entered
my room, I took my Bible, and fell on my knees, saying, " O
beloved Jesus, I implore Thee to have mercy on me ; do take
pity on me, and reveal to me my future, and let me know if I
am one day to marry Laferrière or not. But Thou knowest that
I could never be a nun." I arose, opened the Bible, and my eyes
fell on these words : (Isa. liv.)

" 4. Fear not ; for thou shalt not be ashamed : neither be
thou confounded ; for thou shalt not be put to shame : for thou
shalt forget the shame of thy youth, and shalt not remember the
reproach of thy widowhood any more.

" 5. For thy Maker is thine husband; The LORD of Hosts is
His name ; and thy Redeemer the Holy One of Israel ; the God
of the whole earth shall He be called.

" 6. For the Lord hath called thee as a woman forsaken and
grieved in spirit, and a wife of youth, when thou wast refused,
saith thy God.

" 7. For a small moment have I forsaken thee ; but with great
mercies will I gather thee.

" 8. In a little wrath I hid my face from thee for a moment ;
but with everlasting kindness will I have mercy on thee, saith
the LORD thy Redeemer.

" 9. For this is as the waters of Noah unto me : for as I have
sworn that the waters of Noah should no more go over the earth:
so have I sworn that I would not be wroth with thee, nor rebuke
thee.

" 10. For the mountains shall depart and the hills be removed ; but my kindness shall not depart from thee, neither
shall the covenant of my peace be removed, saith the LORD
that hath mercy on thee."

I was astounded at the wonderful application that the three
first verses had to myself ; but I did not receive a light and that
sensible grace which usually accompanied my former revelations,
and I said to myself : " This must be the devil, who is in league
with that priest that is trying to draw me into a convent ;" and I

said to our Lord : "This can never come true, I cannot be Thy spouse, for Thou knowest that I could never become a nun."

The next morning, Saturday, the 16th of March, the instant I awoke I heard an interior voice say, "Go and make a general confession." I was sure that God had spoken to me, and I instantly replied : "I will." At ten o'clock I went to see the Father, and I took the Bible with me. The moment he laid eyes on it he exclaimed : "What, a Protestant Bible !" Said I : "Not a word ; you and all the priests in creation could not separate me from that Bible, so don't you say one word." Said he : "I permit you to keep it for the present ; but whenever I tell you to give it up you will give it up." "Don't you be so sure of that," said I, "and take good care that you do not forbid it very soon, lest I prove to you that you are a false prophet." I then showed him what I had opened at the night before ; and when he read it he could hardly believe it possible. He doubted me, and it was with great difficulty I could persuade him to believe that I had never seen these words before. "Well," said he, "if you prayed with all your heart, and it pleased God to make His will known unto you that way, you will surely be a religious." I ridiculed his words in my heart, but was glad to see that he no longer doubted me.

One word brought on another until I showed him all the other passages, beginning at the first, and relating to him minutely all the circumstances under which I had opened at them. Said he : "All this gives me light, and I can now understand why you left Laferrière, and why you still persist in building that church. But why have you always kept these things to yourself ?"

I told him what Father Bazin had said to me, and that I was afraid to tell him lest he would put a stop to it. I finished by saying that I intended to make a general confession. Said he : "What has put that into your head ? How you do change !" Said I : "I believe God told me to make it this morning when I awoke." He told me to go down stairs and wait for him at his confessional, and, in the meanwhile, that I must pray God to give me grace to make a good confession. I obeyed him. I then began to make my confession from the time I was six years old up to the present moment. When I finished the priest gave me absolution, and said he felt that God was with me, and that He had aided me to make a good confession.

The next day was Sunday, the 17th, my birthday. That morning, after I received holy communion, my heart began to burn more sensibly than I had ever felt it burn before.

CHAPTER XCVIII.

THE EFFICACY OF PRAYER.—DETACHMENT OF THE HEART.

The Burden Removed—The Crucifix—Words of Mercy—Give Me thy Heart.

ON the following day I called on my confessor. In the course of conversation he remarked: "You have so much leisure time, I want you to promise me that you will devote a part of it to studying Latin." "Oh," said I, "I have studied Latin;" and I began to repeat to him my prayers in Latin. "Why," said he, "you know all that is necessary. But this is astonishing that you should have ever studied Latin: all this goes to show——;" he hesitated. But I knew what was running through his mind. When I passed out I slammed the door after me, and said: "It is the last time that I will ever cross this threshold. Good-bye, Mr. Jesuit; I have had enough of you."

I went into the chapel. There was no one there but a lame girl. I asked her to pray for me. I knelt down at the altar of the Sacred Heart, and I offered up my whole heart to God, and implored Him to take it, and to give me grace to love Him. At that instant Laferrière rose in my mind, but I inwardly exclaimed: "Not Laferrière, Lord, but Thee. I want to love Thee." I felt then that I was all alone with God, that I had no one to go to for consolation and pity but Him; for that Jesuit, on whom I had relied for months for consolation and sympathy, had the cruelty to try and immure me in a convent.

After I had prayed earnestly for a few minutes I became softened, and began to implore our Lord to come and help me. I forgot all about my anger and resentment in my longing desire to know and to possess the love of God. It was a feeling that I never had experienced before. Just as I was about to ·rise I mentally cried: "O dearest Jesus, do give me the grace to love Thee."

I then turned to leave the altar, and was embarrassed to see that the lame girl was still there; for in my fervour I had forgotten that she was beside me praying for me. I gave her my hand; but, instead of saying Good-night, I said Good-bye, meaning good-bye for ever to the world and its creatures, that I was from that hour to belong to God.

I then hurried out of the chapel. My step was once more as light and elastic as it was when a child I used to roam over the hills. I tripped across Union Square Park to the Hotel, as though I had just been relieved of a heavy burden, which I had been condemned to carry for years. I ran up to my room; the gas was lighted in the hall. As I opened my door, the light shone directly on my crucifix, which seemed to come forward to embrace me. I seized it in my hands, for my whole soul went out, as it were, to meet it. I sank upon my knees as I placed it to my lips. I covered it with kisses and drenched it with tears. For an instant I was speechless, my whole soul was so flooded with joy —a joy that no tongue can describe, for it was that joy which is unspeakable and full of glory.

As soon as I could give utterance to my thoughts, I exclaimed: " O beloved Jesus, how good Thou art ! How good Thou art ! for Thou hast answered my prayer." Laferrière's image then arose in my mind ; but I shrank from it, and I motioned it away with my hand. God had thoroughly detached me from him, and it seemed as though He permitted him to rise before me at that moment that I might see how poor and pitiable an object I had left for Him ; for such did Laferrière appear to me then, com- pared to the image of our Lord, which I felt was now impressed upon my soul.

I rose from my knees and lit the gas, and as I did so I caught a full view of my face in the glass. My tears had washed so effectually the pencilling from my eyes, that it seemed as though I had not really seen my face before for ten years ; and I recollected how, but a week ago, I refused to obey our Lord when He made His will known to me that He wished me to stop painting my eyes. As the thoughts of my obstinacy and vanity flashed over me, I exclaimed amid a renewed gush of tears : " I will scratch my eyes out, sooner than ever put a pencil to them again," and I took the whole apparatus, threw it into the grate, and set it on fire, and then returned to my crucifix, and recom- menced sobbing and covering it with kisses, saying to our Lord : " Thou hast kept Thy word ; for Thou hast taken from me that stony heart, and hast given me a heart of flesh."

I then took up my Bible and implored our Lord to speak to me, and to assure me that this happiness and joy which now flooded my soul was no illusion, and that it would never pass away ; and instantly, by chance, I opened again at the same words I had opened at on Friday :

" 4. Fear not; for thou shalt not be ashamed ; neither be thou confounded ; for thou shalt not be put to shame : for thou shalt forget the shame of thy youth, and shalt not remember the reproach of thy widowhood any more.

" 5.   For thy Maker is thine husband ; The Lord of Hosts is His name ; and the Redeemer the Holy One of Israel ; the God of the whole earth shall He be called.

" 6. For the Lord hath called Thee as a woman forsaken and grieved in spirit, and a wife of youth, when thou wast refused, saith thy God.

" 7. For a small moment have I forsaken thee; but with great mercies will I gather Thee.

" 8. In a little wrath I hid my face from thee for a moment; but with everlasting kindness will I have mercy on thee, saith the Lord thy Redeemer.

" 9. For this is as the waters of Noah unto me; for as I have sworn that the waters of Noah should no more go over the earth; so have I sworn that I would not be wroth with thee, nor rebuke thee.

" 10. For the mountains shall depart, and the hill be removed; but my kindness shall not depart from thee, neither shall the covenent of my peace be removed, saith the Lord, that hath mercy on thee."

Thought I : " Perhaps I opened this passage this time because I have already opened at it." I put down my own Bible and took up the one that lay on the bureau, which belonged to the hotel, and as I opened it, I closed my eyes and exclaimed : " O beloved Jesus, speak to me, and tell me it is not all an illusion! that I am Thine for ever; that I am Thy spouse; that Thou hast taken me for Thine own." I opened the Bible which I had never opened before, and I opened at the *very same chapter ;* and this extraordinary fact, instead of surprising me and filling me with greater joy, made my breast as calm and as peaceful as a troubled soul that had just found a shelter in the bosom of its God.

A myriad of thoughts crowded themselves upon me, but not confusedly; for now everything was clear that related to the past, and I could see that God had had His designs upon me from the hour of my birth, and that I now owed this moment of unspeakable joy to a life of suffering. I felt that each sorrow, each disgrace, each misfortune that I had writhed under from my infancy had been so many powerful levers to raise me to my God. All those trials which I had borne up under through faith appeared to me now like so many supernatural aids to conduct my exiled heart to its country; and as I knelt there enraptured, pressing my crucifix to my lips and then to my heart, the horizon of the supernatural world seemed for a moment to open before me, that I might view the perspectives of eternity.

I could then see and feel the fallacy and folly of all earthly attachments, and that nothing was worth seeking or loving but God. And as my earthly loves and my earthly hates came back to me, what a change! I shuddered at the very thought of ever becoming the Viscountess Laferrière, and I felt like throwing myself at my director's feet, and asking his pardon for my foolish anger, and begging him to accept my grateful and heartfelt thanks.

I realised in that moment that I had behaved towards God since He had chosen me just as Laferrière had done with me. He had given me everything but himself, and I preferred him to all his gifts. Nothing that he could offer me, except himself, could ever satify me. And so had I been with God. I had given Him everything but my heart; whereas, He preferred that to all my sacrifices and to all my gifts.

Much as I dreaded being a nun but an hour ago, it was now the only thought of my soul. I took up a handkerchief and bound it round my forehead, and then threw the double skirt of my dress over my head in the guise of a veil, to see what kind of a looking nun I would make; and I found it so comically unbecoming that it set me laughing.

A few days after I had been received as a Child of Mary, one of the Children of Mary introduced me to a Mr. Miller, who, she told me, would finish my church without asking any profit by it, and as he was rich, she was sure that he would wait until I could collect the money to pay him. The following day, which was the 19th of March, the Feast of St. Joseph, I went up to my farm with Mr. Miller, in order to make an agreement about the finishing of my church.

While at my house I invoked the prayers of the Blessed Virgin, that I might ever be faithful to the great grace I had just received, and that I might never doubt of my vocation. A little Bible lay on a prayer desk; I opened it without asking for anything, and I opened at the very same chapter in Isaiah that I had opened at twice the previous night.

CHAPTER XCIX.

HARD KNOCKS—THE BIBLE MY PHYSICIAN—"THE CHURCH-MICE" TRY
TO DRIVE ME FROM THE HOUSE OF GOD.

My Director Distrustful—Nibblings of Church Mice.

THE next morning I repaired early to the Convent of the Sacred Heart in Seventeenth Street, where my confessor had begun to give a Retreat to the Children of Mary. I was most anxious to see him, expecting that he would receive me most graciously when I told him that I felt sure that God had given me my vocation, and that I longed to be a nun, and would enter a convent the moment my church should be paid for. But to my astonishment he received me as though he had been impatiently awaiting a culprit who deserved to be chastised; and he asked me in the most brusque manner what I meant by trying to make a fool of him, and if I really thought I was going to make him my dupe. I undertook to relate to him all that had happened to me since I had last seen him. But he refused to listen to me, and began to relate to me the opinion others had of me, and said that my conduct justified it.

On the following day, he sent for me, and his treatment towards me was but a repetition of what it had been the day before, only if anything worse. This time he made me suffer; but I loved the suffering, and told him so.

Friday morning I began to dread a renewal of the scene and fell to weeping just as I was ready to go out. I fell on my knees and implored God to give my director light, so that he would see that I was sincere and was not trying to deceive him; and I implored God to tell me what to do if he still persisted in not believing me. I opened the Bible for my answer, and the following words gladdened my heart:—

"Thou shalt weep no more: He will be very gracious unto thee at the voice of thy cry; when He shall hear it, He will answer thee.

"And though the Lord give you the bread of adversity, and the water of affliction, yet shall not thy teachers be removed into a corner any more, but thine eyes shall see thy teachers:

"And thine ears shall hear a word behind thee, saying, This is the way, walk ye in it, when ye turn to the right hand, and when ye turn to the left." (Isa. xxv. 19, 21.)

I was immediately consoled. I marked the passage, and took the Bible with me to the church, where I found my confessor in his confessional. I told him that I knew he would be more gracious to me, for our Lord had just told me so. Before I read the words to him, he said to me: "What new invention is this? Let me hear it." I then read to him what I had opened at in the Bible. Said he: "I do not see anything very wonderful in that." "But I do," I replied; "and I know those verses refer particularly to you." Said he: "I am not convinced of it." "Because," said I, "you don't happen to see your name, age, and address there, you are not willing to believe that that first verse refers to you; but I am not afraid of you now, nor do I dread to come near you; for I know that you will be kind to me." Said he: "How do you know?" I replied: "I know it because

our Lord has just promised it to me ; and I know that He can
and will give you light." Said he: " I suppose you have told
Madame Hardey all about it ? "   " I saw her yesterday," said I ;
" I just approached her, knelt down and kissed her hand, and
then ran away from her as fast as I could, without saying a
single word, because you forbade me to tell her."

His manner at once changed towards me, as he asked if I
would obey him.   " Certainly," I replied, " for I believe you are
a good man."   He then told me to consult Madame Hardey, as
she was a lady of vast experience and of rare charity.

That same afternoon I was with Madame Hardey an hour and
a quarter.   I opened my heart to her with as much confidence
as I would to my director.   When I had finished, she gave me a
few encouraging words, told me not to pray so much now, but
to go to work, and advised me not to be seen so often at the
Jesuit church, as people were passing remarks about it.   That
made me sad ; for I felt that, if driven out of the basement of
that church, I would be obliged to remain shut up in my
room.

The next morning I wept as I told the Father what Madame
Hardey had said.   He consoled me by saying : " Madame Hardey
wishes you to avoid giving others the slightest occasion of
abusing you.".

" What can I do to stop them," said I, " if they will not permit me to come into the chapel and pray without abusing me ?"

" You are right ; they have no business to abuse you for that ;
and I give you permission to go into the chapel and pray whenever you like."   " It is but granting me, Father, a privilege
that is extended to every beggar that walks the streets."

God had thoroughly detached me from the world and Laferrière
on the vigil of St. Joseph's Feast ; and what could more fully
justify my indifference for the world's opinion than this: that,
since I was trying to lead a perfect life, it not only turned its
back upon me, but would not permit me to go by myself into a
chapel and pray without passing some uncharitable remark, such
as, " *We are sure she has a motive,*" or some other equivalent
reflection.

The same afternoon that I opened my heart to Madame Hardey,
I brought my ball-dresses to her, and she had them converted
into vestments for my church.

CHAPTER C.

"THE BOARD OF GRACE" SIT ON ME.—I AM TOLD TO WRITE A BOOK.

Father Bapst—I Shrink from Writing a Book—Easter Joys.

MY desire to enter a convent increased every day; but my director and Madame Hardey both said they did not see that I had the vocation, and neither of them would consent to it until they had stronger proofs.

But I thought that God had given me my vocation on the 18th, and I was so anxious to take the veil that my impatience would hardly brook waiting to finish my church; and I tried to persuade myself that my motives in erecting it had not been pure, and that I had always sought my own glory in its completion more than the glory of God.

I went to the French church to implore God to make His will known to me, whether I ought to finish the little church before I entered a convent or not. After praying for a long while, without being able to decide what I should do, I determined to go home and resort to the Bible; which I no sooner thought of than I went into the parsonage and borrowed a French Bible of Father Aubril. It was the first Catholic Bible I had ever had in my hands. I took it into the church and knelt down before the altar of the Blessed Virgin. When I was in the act of opening it I implored God to let me know if it was His will that I should keep on and finish my church, or go immediately into a convent. I then opened the Bible and read: (1 Paral. xxii.)

" 19. Now set your heart and your soul to seek the Lord your God; arise, therefore, and build ye a sanctuary of the Lord God, to bring the ark of the covenant of the Lord, and the holy vessels of God, into the house that is to be built to the name of the Lord."

I went immediately to my director to tell him how I had prayed, and for what I had prayed, and the answer God had given me.

He did not appear to pay the slightest attention to what I said, but rather seemed impatient for me to finish that I might hear what he had to say.

His impatience was caused by the officious interference of some of those devotees who form, as it were, a " Board of Grace," without whose permission it is not lawful for a poor soul even to aspire to Heaven, and who often deem it their duty " to sit " on a candidate for admission to the sacraments. When he discovered that the representations of "the Board of Grace" were false, he said :—

"How you are persecuted! I now believe that you are sincere, and that you have given your heart to God. At the same time I will not continue to direct you without the consent of my superior. To-morrow morning you must make a general confession to Father Bapst, and show him those passages of Scripture. If he says it is God's work, and tells me to continue to direct you, the whole world may go against you, but I will stand by you just as long as I am convinced that you are trying to do right. But I want to know whether I ought to continue to direct you or not. Whatever he decides will be for the best. And I want you to pay particular attention to what he says, for whatever he tells you to do will be for your eternal good. He is a holy man, and you must listen to him as though God Himself were speaking to you."

The next morning I came to see Father Bapst, and did as I had been told. He listened to me attentively. When I came to the evening of the 18th, when I entered my bedroom and felt as if my crucifix came towards me, his eyes filled with tears, and he said: "Poor child!" After I had finished I told him to decide and tell me what to do.

"I believe God has called you," said he, "to build that church. What His designs are I cannot tell, but the first thing that you must do is to finish it. I do not see that you have a vocation. You must not enter a convent yet, for you have not yet received a definite vocation. But you can serve God out of a convent just as well as you can in one. God has His designs upon you—I am convinced of that. He will make known to you what they are when the proper time comes. For the present go ahead and finish your church, and then we will see.

"In the meanwhile I know of no one who can direct you better than your present confessor. He has his defects: he is quick-tempered, easily roused; you will often have to bear with a great deal from him; but you will always find him *true.*" I went into church at three o'clock, and took the little Catholic Bible with me that I had borrowed of Father Aubril. While the Fathers recited the *Tenebræ* (for it was in Holy Week), I implored our Lord to settle my mind in respect to entering a convent, for I was not willing to abide either by the decision of Madame Hardey, Father Bapst, or my director. I was more satisfied that I had received my vocation than I was of anything else. I was so certain of it that no one on earth could have convinced me of the contrary. I implored God not to abandon me, but to tell me something that would give light to my director and to his superior.

I then knelt down and tried to completely annihilate my own will before the will of God. Although I felt that to live in the world now would be a continual martyrdom, yet I promised that, if it was His will, I would not murmur, but try in all things to submit my will to His. I opened the Bible at these words: " *Tant que tu vis et que tu respire, ne t'assujettis à personne* " (So long as thou livest and hast breath subject thyself to no one). (Eccles. xxxiii. 21.)

I closed the book, and said, "Then tell me, Lord, what I am to do?"

I opened the Bible again, and my eyes fell on these words: " *Conserve-toi l'autorité dans toutes tes œuvres. N'imprime point de tache à ta gloire! Au jour de la fin des jours de ta vie, et au temps de la mort distribue ton heritage* " (In all thy works keep to thyself authority. Let no stain sully thy glory. At the day when thou shalt end the days of thy life, and at the time of thy decease distribute thy property).

I then discovered that I had opened both times at the same chapter; and as soon as I had read those last words I received a light, and my mind was at rest; for it seemed that God had made known to me His will that I should found some work for His glory.

The next morning, as soon as I awoke, I began to speak to our Lord, and ask Him how I should raise the money to found my work, and how I should ever even get the money to pay my debts. I had hardly asked the question when I heard an interior voice say: "Write a book; write a history of your life; that will procure you money to pay your debts and to found your work." I buried my face in my pillow for shame, and inwardly cried out: "O beloved Saviour, do not ask that of me; for all would point their finger at me." Then I distinctly heard an interior voice speak to me reproachfully such words as these: "This is your detachment from the world; you see that you still love the world more than Me."

A fearful struggle took place within me between nature and grace. But grace at last triumphed, and I exclaimed: "I will, Lord, I will!" But I had no sooner consented than I instantly regretted it; and I began to excuse myself on account of my ignorance, and I said: "Thou knowest, Lord, that I have never studied, except to show off. How can I write a book?" The same interior voice replied: "You do not require to

be a scholar to speak the truth; and that is all God asks of
you."

I instantly arose, determined to make the sacrifice. I hastened
to the college to tell my confessor the new revelation God had
just made to me. He hesitated for a moment, and then replied:
"I never could tell you to do that. Do not ask me to sanction
your unfolding the story of your life to the whole world." Said
I: "You tell me that to spare myself I should disobey God?"
"I will call Father Bapst," said he, "for I shall not take upon
myself such responsibility." He called Father Bapst, who, the
moment I told him the revelation I had had that morning,
without the slightest hesitation replied: "Yes, write a book;
that is what you should do—write a book." I then told him
what my confessor had just said. "Never mind what the world
will say or do to you," he answered; "God will take care of all
that. It seems clear to me that it is your duty to write a book;
I tell you to write it." With those words he left me.

The next morning was Easter, and as I arose that Easter
morning I felt that "the heart too has its Easter when the stone
is rolled away," for no other words could express the joy and
peace of my soul. I was perfectly happy; for, in possessing
God, I felt that I possessed everything. I would not have exchanged the peace and joy which reigned in my soul that Easter
morning for the entire universe. The universe is after all but
a bubble compared with the priceless value of a soul filled with
God. I had often heard and read descriptions of happy death-
bed scenes when the soul longed to burst its earthly chains, and
I have ridiculed in my heart the transports of indescribable joy
which the author would fain depict. But now those very descriptions seemed to me but faint conceptions of the ecstatic
joy that a soul feels when it reposes in God.

CHAPTER CI.

THE BLACK VIRGIN OF POLAND.

The Bible changes Disappointment into Hope—No place for a Jesuit.

ON the first of April I returned to the country and began to
write this book, and to superintend the completion of my little
church. By this time I had very little money left. I had long
since parted with my diamonds, my laces, and most of my finery,
to raise money to go on with the church. I had an exquisite
Byzantine painting representing our Lady of Czenstochow (or

Loretto), of Poland, otherwise known as the Black Virgin, a present from the Prince Czartoryski.

Whenever I needed money I would be tempted to sell this picture; but those to whom I would apply would try to take advantage of my necessities, and would offer me for it much less than it was worth, and by the time they would agree to give me its value I had gotten out of my difficulties and would not sell it at any price. I was trying one day to raise five hundred dollars, and was met with rebuffs wherever I went. One Protestant gentleman, a hater of Catholics, ridiculed my faith that God would one day come to my help and would pay all my debts. Said he: "Where do you expect to find the key to the Lord's treasury? I would like to get hold of it myself." I replied: "You will find it in prayer, if you will perseveringly look for it there." "Madam," he replied, "you have answered well;" and with those words we parted. That day I exhausted every resource trying to raise the money, and concluded that I must part with the picture of the miraculous Virgin, Our Lady of Czenstochow.

The next morning I called a servant, told her to get ready and take it to Mr. ——. The tears started in my eyes, I hated so to part with it.

While I gazed upon it I fell upon my knees and implored the Blessed Virgin not to force me to part with that precious image of herself. Said I to her: "I know you can perform miracles—perform one now, and let me keep this picture. If you will help me out of this trouble I will never offer it for sale again; I promise you that I will never part with it if you will only get me the five hundred dollars." When the servant came to take it I said: "Wait until this afternoon, wait until the sun goes down; then come to me and I will tell you if you shall take it there or not." She left me and I still continued to pray, ever invoking the Black Virgin to inspire me where to go and ask for the money. I cannot tell how long I remained there, for my senses became lost as it were in prayer until I was startled as though awakened by the door-bell ringing, and its ring sent an electric thrill through my heart, and I rushed to the door to open it myself. It was the Protestant gentleman, the Catholic-hater, and these were his words:—

"Just as I was leaving the house to go down town you came into my head. I don't care a cent for your church, but I do admire your faith, and I think that it ought to be rewarded even on earth." "Why," said I, "it is rewarded on this earth. You don't suppose that God is going to keep us eternally waiting, do you?" "Well," he replied, "let me speak I have come to give you the five hundred dollars that you need on the day after to-morrow to pay tò the carpenter. Get your hat, come down with me to the bank, and you shall have it." Instead of thanking him, I at-once exclaimed, "The Black Virgin did it!—the Black Virgin did it !"—and in a second I was out of his sight in the parlour covering her picture with the most grateful kisses, forgetting all about the gentleman I had left in the hall. As soon as I recollected myself I returned to him and told him all about the picture, and that I believed that the Black Virgin had interceded for me, and God had inspired him to give me the money. He laughed at me, and declared that I was crazy. I accompanied the gentleman down town, and he made me a present of five one hundred dollar bills. To this day I pronounce it a miracle.

The church was now nearly completed.

Madame Hardey had made for me several sets of vestments, and presented me with several sets of altar linen. At Tiffany's I got a present of a beautiful chalice. But the most beautiful ornament that decorates the little church is the exquisite gift of Mr. D. M. Carter, the artist,—an original work made expressly for my church. It is a large oil painting, representing St. Geneviève at prayer in the open fields, in the garb of a shepherdess; and our Lord appears in the firmament with both hands extended, in the act of blessing her and the Pantheon, whose dome is dimly traced in the distance.

I had imported all the interior decorations, such as the colouring of the walls, the windows, the statuary, and the way of the cross.

The Archbishop had named Wednesday, the 17th of July, as the day that he thought he would be able to come and open my church.

A few days before the appointed time I received a letter from His Grace saying that he was obliged to leave home on affairs of his diocese on the 13th of July, to be absent until the middle of August, and referred me to Father Tandy to make arrangements for having the new church opened for the celebration of Mass.

I called on His Grace, and told him how impossible it was for me to treat with Father Tandy, for by this time he had become as incensed against me as I was against him. "Well," said the Archbishop, " as he does not wish to take charge of the new church, and you do not wish to have him, there is an end to the matter." His Grace afterwards gave permission to Father Bapst, the Superior of the Jesuits, to say the first Mass in it.

The Archbishop had named Wednesday, the 17th of July, to open the church, but as it was in the harvest time a great many labourers would be prevented from attending services, if it was on a week-day. Father Bapst preferred to have the church opened on Sunday. So he appointed Sunday, the 21st of July.

The next evening, after I returned home, I went up to the church, feeling disheartened and discouraged. Everything I saw reminded me how much I had set my heart on His Grace being there. I was so low-spirited at my disappointment that it seemed as though I carried an iron weight within me instead of a heart.

I began imploring our Lord to say something to me that would cheer and gladden me. I took my Bible, which lay in the sacristy, and knelt in front of the altar, and, as I opened it, I said: "Take pity on me, Lord." The first verse I saw was the following:—

"In the seventh month, in the one-and-twentieth day of the month, came the word of the Lord." (Haggai ii. I.)

I was transported with joy, not so much from having opened at those words, as from the effect of the light that accompanied them: for it was as though God had spoken to me and bade me be of good cheer, that it was His will that the first Mass should be said on the 21st and not on the 17th.

Saturday at noon found me at Wassaic station, with carriages awaiting the arrival of the train. The first person I saw alight was Bergé, the distinguished organist of St. Xavier's Church. Then came Father Bapst, who was followed by Father McDonnell and Brother Letique. Then I saw Bergé assist two ladies to get off the train; they were his sisters who were to assist in the singing.

After we had been a few minutes on the road, one of the ladies inquired if there was a village lying beyond those hills. "Oh no," I replied; "the higher you go up, the wilder it is." They all began to look at each other with a sort of concern, while I kept assuring them that they would all be pleased when they reached the top of the hill. As soon as Father Bapst entered the church, the whole expression of his face brightened. Turning towards me, he gave me an approving smile, and shortly afterwards said: "It is a splendid little church. My heart was lifted up the moment I entered it. God must have inspired you; and God must have helped you, for you never could have done all this alone. But I do not see the utility of it: I counted the houses along the way, and I am certain that we did not pass twenty, and you tell me that very few of them are Catholic families. Where is your congregation coming from?" Said I: "Wait until to-morrow morning, and you will see more people coming than can get into the church." He shook his head doubtingly. On leaving the church to return to the house, he said to me, after he had thrown a glance over the hills: "This might please a Benedictine or a Carthusian, but it never would a Jesuit. My child, I am afraid that you will be disappointed, and to-morrow morning you will see very few people here."

I assured him that if I had a priest, the congregation would support him. We then sat down to arrange the programme for the next day. Father Bapst took out a pencil and a piece of paper as though he were going to make a minute. "Now tell me, my child," said he, "how much these good people have aided you; they will expect me to refer to their offerings to-morrow when I address them." "My dear Father," I replied, "that story is very soon told: for no one around here has ever given me a penny. The inhabitants of Connecticut declared that they *could* not help me because they were too poor; and those in New York State declared that they *would* not assist me, because I was across the line." The Father put aside his paper and pencil, with an air as though he was more than ever convinced that this was no place for a Jesuit.

CHAPTER CII.

Morning Sacrifice—Gloria in Excelsis—"The Finger of God"—The Sermons—A Child's Criticism.

THE 21st July, 1872, dawned brightly on my mountain home; and that woodland scene which lies in front of my cottage door appeared to me, that Sunday morning, like a vast altar dressed by the hands of the Creator. Nor was sweet incense wanting for the morning sacrifice: for the shrubs and wild flowers exhaled the dewy fragrance of their hearts to greet the first beams of sunlight, which seemed to my joyous spirit like the smile of God.

I stood looking towards the spot where I had stood years ago, when my guilty heart was moved by a hymn sung by a child, and where my soul for an instant had been enabled to soar above the mists of doubt, and had raised itself to God; and, behold! there was the church that once rose in my mind. It was but a vague fancy then, but now it stood before me a beautiful reality; and

as I gazed upon its spire, and its cross that glittered in the sur,
it appeared to me like a sacred diadem that God Himself had
placed on the brow of that hill.

When I gazed upon the landscape, it seemed as though every
rock, every tree, and every hill-top spoke to me of the past; but
when I would turn to look at the church, its cross seemed to
speak to my soul, and say to it that by Faith it was betrothed,
and by Hope and Charity the spouse of Him to whom all nature
pays homage and adoration.

The long-wished-for hour came, and I began to mount the hill
to the church with a joy that the human heart seldom knows.
For I knew that I was going to receive our Lord, yes, to
receive Him among my beloved hills, which He was about to
sanctify by His presence. I thought as I neared the church how
little did I dream, when a child, that one day our Saviour would
make me—the wicked me—the instrument of bringing Him
among those hills; and I asked my soul: Was it not for this
that He had enkindled in my heart a love for these woodlands?
That love must have been a spark from heaven that descended
into my breast, and it had never been extinguished by the waters
of iniquity through which I had waded for so many years, but
had lived and had drawn me back again to the spot where my
bosom first received it. My soul seemed to answer, Yes, that it
was *for this* that that love for nature had been enkindled in my
heart; that a Divine Providence had ever watched over me, even
from my humble cradle, and that it was now leading me by the
hand to a virgin altar, where I would receive the seal of the alliance that my soul had contracted with God, which secured to it
a title to a glorious Immortality.

Before the hour for the second Mass came, people could be
seen coming from all directions towards the little church. By
nine o'clock every seat was filled, and soon the interior of the
church resounded with the "Gloria in Excelsis." My whole soul
melted into tears as soon as the strains began, for when I had
received our Lord that morning I had asked Him to give me
light and strength to follow it; and, as the strains of music rose,
they seemed to raise the veil that hung before my future, and it
was given to me then to see what was before me, and to appreciate to its full value what I had just accomplished. While I
was building my church I was buoyed up with the illusion that
as soon as it was finished all my trials would be ended; but the
light God gave me then was that my life of sacrifice and suffering had only just begun. My nature shrank from the living
martyrdom, and I wept.

I thanked God that He had never made His will so clearly known to me before; for I felt that that illusion had been necessary for my weakness, but now that my task was done, and I no longer needed it, the illusion vanished, the truth took its place, and I saw that the church was but a grain of mustard-seed that our Lord had bid me plant in the earth, and that I would yet water it with the tears of affliction and disappointment, and would have to shield it against storms of envy and hate, which the devil would raise to blight its blossoms, break its branches, and if possible uproot it. I was then fully satisfied that my imagination, my ambition, and my caprice had had nothing to do with the work, and that I had built that church by the inspiration and the help of God.

At the Canon of the Mass my will was thoroughly resigned to the sacrifice, and I tried to collect all the powers of my soul; for I felt that God would not refuse me anything I asked of Him at that hour.

The bell for the Elevation rung, and for a moment I was lost to the world, for all my faculties were concentrated on this my triple request :—That I might love God with all my heart, that I might ever be faithful to the graces I received, and that my book might be the means of saving souls.

Father Bapst addressed the congregation. He told them, with great force, the importance of improving the present moment to prepare for an eternity which had no end, that unless they sowed now they could not expect to reap hereafter—and without any colouring or disguise he plainly told them that the Catholic Church alone possessed the whole truth, and in a very clear and concise manner proved it to them, which brought smiles of satisfaction to the faces of the Catholics, but made the Protestants wince, for they had never heard anything like it before.

He closed by referring to the little church itself, spoke of its beauty, and complimented my efforts. "But," said he, "that lady never could have done this unless God had been with her. *The finger of God is here*, and every one of you should look upon this little church as a glory of this country place."

The *Amenia Times*, a Protestant paper, published the following notice of the opening :—

"ST. GENEVIEVE'S CHAPEL.

"The beautiful Catholic chapel erected by Mrs. St. John Eckel, in the south part of Sharon (near Amenia Union) was opened for the services of the church on Sunday, the 21st inst. The edifice is placed upon a lofty and commanding eminence, and the prospect to the south and west is of great extent and most striking beauty. The temple itself is a model of good taste and artistic excellence, while the decorations of the interior are unexceptionable, even to the most fastidious criticism. The windows are of the choicest designs and most exquisite workmanship, while the altar-piece, representing the Saviour and St Geneviève, is a painting so charming that the gazer upon its sweet outlines cannot refrain from the thought—

"' A thing of beauty is a joy for ever.'

" The music was given by the celebrated organist and choir from the Sixteenth Street Church, of New York City, and the sublime and thrilling harmonies of the Mass were of course rendered in fullest perfection.

" The sermon was delivered by the Rev. Father Bapst, of the Order of Jesuits, and was a clear and eloquent exposition of the cardinal doctrines of the Catholic Church.

" At five o'clock p.m. the chapel was opened for the beautiful vespers, and again the sweet music peculiar to these evening devotions was given with most charming effect. The service concluded with an excellent sermon by Rev. Father McDonnell, and all who attended both services could not but have been pleased with what they saw and heard of the ritual and the worship."

The next day Father Bapst remarked : " I cannot see the use of a chapel here. But I believed that God inspired you to put it here. All that you have got to do now is to go ahead and write your book, and by your book you will be judged."

I had already given out that my director would preach in the new chapel on Wednesday evening. When he arrived I told him, in the presence of Father Bapst, that I did not wish him to preach a doctrinal sermon. I wanted him to speak on the love of God; for I wished him to please the Protestants, and not send them all away angry, as Father Bapst had done.

" No," said Father Bapst, interrupting me, " he will do nothing of the kind ; the time has come when we must teach the people, when we must proclaim the truth boldly, whether they like it or not. It is only from ignorance that infidelity is making such rapid strides ; and it is our duty to strike at that ignorance whenever we get a chance."

My director preached a long sermon on pure Catholic doctrine. It was to me a most extraordinary sermon. He explained the Catholic doctrine that outside the Church there is no salvation. His explanation was so satisfactory and consoling that both

Catholics and Protestants were equally well pleased. He said
that the Church which Christ established consisted of a body
and a soul. Professing Catholics belong to the body of the
Church, and can, of course, be saved. Those who, through *no
fault of their own*, are outside of the Church, may by the grace
of God belong to the soul of the Church, and may be in very
truth members of the mystic body of Christ and may be saved.
God alone, "the Searcher of hearts," can tell whether they are
in good faith or not, and to His judgment we must leave them.
A man might call himself a member of the Church, and belong
to the body of the Church, yet he might not have Faith, Hope, and
Charity, and if he died without those virtues he would be
damned ; for without Faith, Hope, and Charity, we cannot be
united to Christ, and without that union with Christ no one can
be saved. Therefore those who die having Faith, Hope, and
Charity, do die members of the Church ; no matter how much
they may deny belonging to it, they do belong to it.

I said that everybody was pleased with that sermon. At least
I thought so at the time : but months passed, when one day I
was undeceived, and I found that there was one youthful member of the Catholic Church who was highly displeased, and never
wished to hear another such sermon preached in St. Geneviève's
Church. I was praising that sermon one day, when my little
daughter remarked : "I don't agree with you, mamma, and I
hope he will never be inspired to preach another sermon like
that. I think he encouraged the people a *little too much* to
remain just as they were in their own churches, and not to come
over to ours. I did not like that sermon ; but I like the kind
of sermons that Father Bapst and Father Beaudevin preach,
where it comes out *Bang !*"

CHAPTER CIII.

BROTHER LETIQUE'S STORY.—SUPERNATURAL GUIDANCE.
Consulting the Bible.

ONE evening I was listening to Brother Letique telling me
how pleased he was with his visit, and how it gratified him to
know me better. He confessed that he had been displeased at
seeing me so much at the college taking up so much of the
Father's time, but that now he understood me better, and was
glad to see that I was deserving of the confidence that the
Father had in me. "But," said the Brother, "you know how

it is; we always have to look out for women; there are so many
visionaries among them. When I was in France one of the
Fathers took an interest in a lady whom he believed God had
inspired to found a work. The thing went on for some months,
until one day she sent in some *bills* for our Fathers to pay,
which the door-keeper took to the Rector. The moment the
Rector saw the bills he pronounced the whole work an illusion
of the devil, and that was the last of the work, for the Father
was forbidden to see the woman any more. But she had deluded
him so far that he soon after left the Society, so as to be able to
help the woman in her project; and that is the last that we ever
heard of either of them."

Thought I to myself: " I will take good care not to send you
any bills, unless I wish you to pronounce the whole thing an
illusion."

One morning in the early part of August I awoke so mentally
prostrated, that I had hardly energy enough to raise my head
from my pillow; I was so worn out with spiritual desolation.
My director had promised to come and say Mass in my church
on the Feast of the Assumption.

On the eve before the Vigil of the Feast I took my little Bible,
and kneeling before the statue of the Blessed Virgin, I begged
her to speak to me, and I opened the Bible at the following
verse : (Jer. li.)

" 63. And it shall be, when thou hast made an end of reading
this book, thou shalt bind a stone to it and cast it into the
midst of the Euphrates."

As soon as my director arrived we went up to the church, and
there he handed me a Catholic Bible, which, he said, the Rector
had given him permission to present to me.

The thought occurred to me as I recollected the words I had
opened at in Jeremiah the evening previous: " When thou hast
made an end of reading this book, thou shalt bind a stone to it
and cast it into the midst of the Euphrates," that it might be
God's will that I should no longer consult the Protestant Bible,
but use the little Catholic one which my director had brought
me.

When I told him how I had opened the Bible, and the words
I had read but a few evenings ago, and that I was sure the time
was coming when it was God's pleasure that I should no longer
make use of that little Bible to know His will, he approvingly
replied: " This is the strongest proof yet that God does watch
over you and direct you. I came up here with the full determination to make you stop seeking to know God's will in that

Protestant Bible; and if you had refused, I should have told you to go to someone else in future for direction. This proves to me that it is God's will that I should continue to direct you."

My director had written to Father Bapst, who was then giving a Retreat to the Ladies of the Sacred Heart in Manhattanville to know if I could be received there as a boarder while I was writing my book.

Father Bapst replied that it was impossible for the Ladies of the Sacred Heart to receive me in the convent, because it was against their rules; but that Madame Hardey had said I could have a room in the convent cottage, which was situated on the grounds, and board with the family there.

The day that my church was opened many of the Protestants thought Father Bapst was the Archbishop, as I had given out that His Grace was coming, and they had not heard it contradicted. A few days after the ceremony a Protestant said to me that he never heard such music before, and he guessed that no one else ever did in that part of the country; but he thought the Archbishop laid it down to them pretty strong.

Said I : " That was not the Archbishop—it was Father Bapst, Superior of the Jesuits." " What is a Jesuit?" he asked. I looked to see if he was really in earnest, and his frank and ingenuous look plainly told me that he expected me to anwer him. Said I : " Don't you know what a Jesuit is ?" " No," he replied; " I never heard of them before." " Well," I answered, " it would be hard for me to tell you in a few words what they are ; but you must read my book, and that will tell you all about them. Meanwhile I beg you not to look into the dictionary to know what they are. I will merely say to you that the Jesuits are Roman Catholics, and not Jews, as the resemblance of the name might lead you to suspect."

If my neighbour and others like him will take the trouble to read the next chapter they will learn something of this mysterious Society ; but it will be, however, for many of them at the expense of parting for ever with one of their most cherished bugaboos.

CHAPTER CIV.

WHAT IS A JESUIT?

Dictionary English—What the Master counselled—" The Company of Jesus "—What the Jesuits teach—Their love for their Society.

ASK the dictionaries what is a Jesuit, and they would answer the question by telling us that the primary meaning of this

word is : one of the Society of Jesus so called, founded by
Ignatius Loyola in 1534, a society remarkable for their cunning
in propagating their principles; and that the secondary meaning is: a crafty person—an intriguer. " Jesuitism—the arts,
principles, and practices of the Jesuits. 2. Cunning, deceit,
hypocrisy, prevarication, deceptive practices to effect a purpose."
— *Webster*.

No human being ever had stronger prejudices against the
Jesuits than I had.

Yet after an intimate acquaintance with many of them for
years, and from the testimony of pure and noble souls, both
here and in France, I now protest, from a love of truth and
justice, that the assertion implied in the dictionary definition of
a Jesuit is a monstrous calumny; and while it may be the duty
of the lexicographer to state that such is a common acceptation
of the term, yet the fact of such acceptation is a lamentable proof
of the shameful ignorance and cruel spite of the people and age
that continue to accept it.

I protest, with a full knowledge of what I say, that this definition is precisely of a character with, and presents just about
as much truth as, the definition of the word Christian, which
might appear in some dictionary of the " heathen Chinee," or of
some future free-thinking people : " Christian—a member of the
society founded by Christ; a sneak, a hypocrite, a thief; one
who holds and practises the principle that it is well to cheat
people out of their money and pleasures and comforts in this
world by false promises of some imaginary felicity in the next."

It is far from me to deny anything that may be true of the
imperfections, or shortsightedness, or faults, or follies, or sins, if
you choose, of individual Jesuits, or for that matter the imperfections and incompleteness that must attach to their society,
as to everything human, even at its best. I do not forget that
even the Church of Christ, which is in the highest sense *the
Society of Jesus,* is yet in its merely human side, in its individual members, subject to many miseries, and weaknesses, and
shortcomings, and scandals, beginning with its very head the
Pope, and coming down through the episcopacy, the priesthood,
and the religious orders to the simple laity. If this is true of
the Church, St. Ignatius and his children of the Society of Jesus
should not deny that it may be and is true of their society; and
they ought cheerfully to admit that " *the disciple is not above
his Master.*"

We find in the Gospel that our Lord gave counsels of highest
wisdom and religious perfection, which, He expressly tells us, all

men cannot appreciate, and are not called to practise. Yet we must feel that what is but a counsel for the individual should be like a sacred injunction for the Church. And as a matter of fact, from the apostolic age till now, the Church has ever encouraged and exhorted her most favoured children to practise these *evangelical counsels* of *chastity, poverty*, and *obedience*.

In vowing themselves to the practice of the evangelical counsels, the religious orders, so far from dispensing themselves from the laws of God, profess, beside observing the whole law, to do much that the law of God and the Church would leave them free not to do. By the vow of chastity they renounce the right to marry, and consecrate soul and body to God; by the vow of poverty they renounce, for the good of religion and charity, all right to property and to compensation for their labours; and by the vow of obedience, for the same high ends, they renounce their own will, promising to obey whenever the law of God does not forbid; and so, like true soldiers of Christ, they are ready to go, at a moment's notice, to the ends of the earth to preach the Gospel, and to bear witness to it with their blood, or to some pest-stricken city to bear equally heroic testimony to divine charity.

Such, then, is a perfect Jesuit. He may well be called invincible, for he conquers the world by first conquering himself. The world has no power over a *perfect* Jesuit.

He knows not that fear which makes men cowards in the presence of duty, for he finds God everywhere, in the greatest privations, in sufferings, and in being despised. Death has no terror for him, as it only brings him nearer to the adorable object of his confidence and love.

From my childhood I have heard the Jesuits railed at and abused, and their teachings branded as devilish. What are those teachings that are so much reviled? What do the Jesuits teach? They teach that but one thing is necessary, which is to save our souls in working to know, to love, and to serve God. It is because men study themselves so little that they are lost in pride and led astray by sensual passion. They insist upon the obligation of pardoning injuries, of maintaining the peace, of sacrificing our own interest and self-love to the general good, of being perfectly resigned to the will of God in all things and at all times, and endeavouring to walk as closely as we can in the footsteps of Him who is the " Way, the Truth, and the Life."

They teach that happiness in this world consists in conforming our minds to the truth, our wills to that which is right, our natural activity to the rules of order; and it is this subjection of the whole man to truth, right, and order, which is the central point towards which all their teachings converge.

The Jesuits tell you that if you teach man to believe nothing you cannot expect him to respect anything, because belief is the source of respect. If you teach man to despise the law of God, you cannot expect him to submit to that of the State. They teach that the best way to secure order in the streets is to maintain it first in the conscience of the people. They teach that God should be our only hope, our glory, and our security; that we must not rely upon ourselves, for we cannot without God's aid resist our passions and vanquish the enemies of our soul. They teach that voluntary humiliation leads to glory, for it is God Himself who called it illustrious! and that that which His word has glorified no one can degrade.

The world, to smother its anxieties, says that God is good and He cannot punish for ever; but the Jesuit, replies with as much reason that God is just, and that He will not pardon without end. This is what they teach, and it is for such teachings that they have always been abhorred and persecuted.

But what can despotism do with a society of men of such mould? Why, it can only do what it has always done: either murder them or banish them from its dominions.

Let despotism manifest itself in one man, as in Prince Bismarck of Germany, or in many, as in the French Commune, its conduct is always the same. The Jesuits are murdered in one land, and they are forced to fly from another, yet they ever seek to conquer their enemies by moderation, and adverse fortune by constancy.

Whether they are felled by the executioner's axe, or torn from their labours by a sentence of exile, they die or leave their field of labours without cursing that law of suffering to which we are condemned. Like the martyrs of old, their parting breath is offered up asking forgiveness for their persecutors, whom they invite to meet them on the threshold of eternity.

If any one suspects that the Jesuits will feel flattered at what I have written in regard to them, he is very much mistaken; and whoever thinks so knows very little about the spirit of the order; for the truth is that the Jesuits have such an inordinate love and admiration for their founder and their Society, that if they were listening to the Holy Ghost preaching on either of them, and He should lavish all the praises that it is possible for words to express on St. Ignatius and his order, I verily believe that there is not a Jesuit living but what would feel that the Holy Ghost had fallen short of truth. That is the great defect of the Jesuits; but it springs from their firm belief that their institution is of Divine origin, and that it is all-perfect; and they are so strongly imbued with that belief, that not one of them could be made to believe that there exists anything as good outside of it.

Not having that film over my eyes which seems to grow so naturally over the eyes of every Jesuit, I think I can see a little clearer than they do in that respect; for notwithstanding the great veneration and love and gratitude I now have for the Jesuits, I think I have seen quite as much to venerate and respect in members of other religious orders and of the secular clergy as I have seen in the Society of Jesus.

————

CHAPTER CV.

AN ECHO OF THE PAST—SOLITUDE, SUFFERING, AND RESIGNATION

A Voice from France—In my new Home—My Mistress of Novices—Hunger and Cold.

I CLOSED my house early in September. When I got to the station I found a package for me which had just been brought by the express. It contained a beautiful set of vestments that Mons. de Corcelles had sent from France, and with it came the following letter :—

"NATIONAL ASSEMBLY, VERSAILLES,
"*July 3rd*, 1872.

"MY VERY DEAR MADAM AND FRIEND,

"Tell me, I beg of you, why this painful silence of two years?

"You promised to let us hear from you, yet we have been obliged to send into Germany to the good Princess Sulkowska to learn anything in regard to you, even then we could only obtain the most vague information. My cousin, Madame de Montalembert, alone assures me, with a sort of certainty, that you are building your chapel, and that you live so retired that you do not wish to write to anyone.

"The last time I received a letter from you we were on the eve of the siege of Paris, during which we did not leave the Rue de Grenelle. My young son, nineteen years of age, who enlisted in the Mobiles, took part in several combats, was wounded by a bombshell, and gained the Military Medal. I divided my time between him and the other wounded in the hospitals.

There was one of these at the Sacred Heart, Rue de Varennes.
It was a sad pleasure for me to visit it and the ten others committed to my inspection.

"After the siege we were all dejected, but reunited without
private misfortunes. At the same time one of the largest departments of France—that of the North—named me Deputy,
entirely without my knowledge. I had hardly learned that I
had received these two hundred and six thousand votes, compelling me to take a prominent part in the greatest and saddest
duty that ever could be imposed on a representative assembly,
when I was obliged to go to Bordeaux, and then to Versailles
during the siege of the Commune. It would be too long to tell
you all my grave occupations. The principal ones have for
their object new laws to insure to our poor France a Christian
instruction. They continue to occupy my attention.

"Two months ago I availed myself of an interruption in our
labours, during the Easter festivities, to pay my homage to our
Holy Father, the Pope—my last homage, perhaps; for it was
my seventh journey to Rome. He overwhelmed me with his
sweetness and goodness, and I returned penetrated, more than I
know how to express with the incomparable apostolic beauty of
his soul. Not a thought of self—not a word of bitterness; the
most holy courage united to the most perfect meekness! His
opinions on our trials were full of wisdom and moderation. All
this I had occasion to love and to admire in the several audiences that were granted to me. How I should like to enlarge
upon this subject! You would be touched by it, and then,
perhaps, you will be induced to answer this letter.

"Meanwhile I must inform you that I have happily succeeded in my appeal to the excellent Baroness de l'Espérut, the
wife of one of my colleagues, to obtain from the society to which
she belongs a complete set of vestments for your American
chapel. The Marchioness de Noailles has brought it to America
for you. I join to it a little book of 'Visits to the B. Sacrament,' to recall to your mind the Feast of Easter at Notre Dame
a short time before the catastrophes, the end of which I fear we
have not reached.

"Madame de Corcelles joins me in the expression of her most
affectionate sentiments. Pray for us, and accept my profound
esteem.

"F. DE CORCELLES."*

---

* Mons. de Corcelles has since been sent to Rome as Ambassador of the
French Republic to the Pope.

Mons. de Corcelles's letter was to me like an echo of my past prosperity. It increased the bitterness of my present state. When I arrived at the convent I was received by the Assistant-Superior, who told me that the policeman who watched their grounds resided in the convent cottage, and it was with his family that Madame Hardey had made arrangements for me to board, and I was to pay ten dollars a-week, to all of which I most readily assented. But the moment I laid my eyes on the policeman's wife my heart failed me. She was a short, stout, thick-set woman, with shallow complexion, of a determined and most independent mien.

The first thing she said to me was, that she did not wish to take me, and she had only done so to oblige Madame Hardey, but for no one else would she have done it; if her own mother had come and asked her to board her, she would have refused.

While she was speaking, I thought to myself, "I will make believe that I am making my novitiate and that this woman is the mistress of novices, and that my future work depends on my living peaceably with her;" for I was sure that it would be the easiest thing in the world to get into a quarrel with her. I began to treat her as though she were a queen; which seemed to please her very much; for she smiled when she bade me good-day, although she frowned terribly at me when I came. The next day I took possession of the room. The policeman's wife told me that she did not believe that I would be able to live there; but I knew that I would stay, as there was no other alternative. I knew too, that if I should complain the Jesuits would immediately pronounce to be an illusion my conviction that God had called me to found a work.

Madame Hardey was to sail for Europe on the 11th of September. I saw her the day before she sailed, and promised her that I would do everything I could to give satisfaction, and that she would hear a good report of me when she returned, and that she would never regret having permitted me to come and live at the convent cottage.

October came. I had very little money left. I had long since parted with my diamonds and laces, and most of my finery to raise money to go on with my church.

I never durst intimate a word about my present indigence to my director, because I never forgot Brother Letique's story.

My director, too, became more and more severe. I was not making the spiritual progress that he expected of me. He was disappointed and discouraged, and would frequently tell me that he had feared that all was an illusion. It was seldom that he gave me an encouraging word, and if I ventured to reproach him for never offering me a word of consolation, he would scold me for lamenting over myself.

My room was cold, and there was no possibility of making a fire in it unless I got a stove. I durst not take the little sum of money I had left to buy a stove and some wood. In the meanwhile I had suffered intensely from the cold. The policeman's wife fed me miserably, and once more I knew what the pangs of hunger were, for I durst not spend an extra cent for anything to eat.

The 29th of October was cold and damp. I began to ask myself what I should do and where I should go. If I remained at home I should have had to go to bed to keep warm. The thought struck me that I would go and see my sister. I thought it would be sweet to open my heart to her, for I felt sure that she would sympathise with me. She treated me most cruelly, and refused even to shake hands with me when I left.

CHAPTER CVI.

CHRISTMAS AT THE CONVENT COTTAGE—ST. GENEVIÈVE'S FEAST—FAITH REWARDED.

"Merry Christmas"—St. Geneviève's Day.—A Godsend.

THAT evening, on returning from my sister's to Manhattanville, my pocket was picked in the cars, and I lost all my ready money. The next day I resolved to go and tell my director how I was situated, and thought, if the Jesuits chose to abandon me because I was poor, they might go.

When I told the Father I laid all the whole blame for that distrust on Brother Letique, saying that had it not been for that story I should have opened my heart to him long ago. He was provoked with the Brother, and declared that he did not know what he was talking about.

The Father gave me sufficient money to supply all my immediate wants. He told me that he could do much more for me if I would only give him permission to tell the Rector, but that he could not in conscience do any more for me without his authority. But I repeated to him Brother Letique's story, and told him that I was afraid that his Rector would do as the one had done in France, and I refused to let him make known to him my necessities.

Christmas morning my child came running down to the cot-

tage, swinging one of her stockings in her hand that the Ladies
had filled with candy. I was sad, for I began contrasting the
present festival with that of five years ago at St. Mandé.

I began talking about it to her; but the child preferred the
present Christmas to all the rest, for none of the French nuns
had ever given her a stockingful of candy. She had a large piece
of pink satin. I proposed making her doll a dress. She frankly
expressed to me her doubts that I was capable of making
a doll's dress. But I prevailed upon her to let me try. So I
made it up in real French style, with a gored skirt trimmed
with bows and an overskirt of blonde. When it was finished she
looked at it and examined it with speechless, joyful, surprise.
Then looking me full in the face she exclaimed: "Mamma,
you have not got *one bit* of *common* sense, but you have a
great deal of *extraordinary* sense. You could not keep a
room in order or make a loaf of bread, but you can build a
church and make a doll's dress. You can't do what everybody can do, but you can do what nobody else can do, and
you are just the mamma for me!" At that she sprang into
my arms, and covered my face with kisses. Whenever I recalled the speech I would begin to laugh; and she at last said
to me: "Mamma, I really think that we are *both* happier
here than in France; for I never knew you to laugh like this
on Christmas there." Before the day was ended I concluded
that she was right, and that the happiest Christmas I had ever
known was passed alone with my child in the convent cottage.

The next morning I began a novena to St. Geneviève, whose
Feast falls on the 3rd of January. As my director had promised to celebrate Mass for me on St. Geneviève's day I
determined to assist at it. It was to be in St. Xavier's Church.
The morning of the 3rd of January was blustering, and the rain
fell in torrents. I rose at four o'clock so as to get ready to take
the first down train, that left Harlem at 6 A.M. I put on one
of my best dresses, which was a black velvet suit made at
Worth's, Paris. I wanted to show St. Geneviève all the interior
and exterior devotion that I could, for I was sanguine that she
would not fail to obtain for me some great grace. The wind blew
violently, the ground was flooded with water and very slippery.
I must have fallen at least seven times before I reached the
train. I was dripping wet. My director was so annoyed at my
coming out in such a storm, exposing my health and foolishly
ruining my clothes, that it seemed as though he could think
of nothing else. I assured him that I should not have dared to
remain at home, nor should I have dared to wear my ordinary

clothes. I should have been afraid that God would punish me for my want of faith. For when I was in the world, if I had an engagement to go to a party of pleasure, wind or weather never prevented me from keeping it; and I felt that I ought to try and do as much for God as I used to do for the world. At last he said: "If it is God's work He will take care of it and will provide for you; and it is no use to be anxious, for no one but God can ever make anything out of you. I have given you up long ago. One thing that inclines me to believe that it is God's work is that He often makes use of the refuse of mankind to work with, so that His glory may be the more manifest."

While he was speaking a lay brother came in and handed him a large letter. I noticed how the whole expression of his face changed as he perused it. He asked me: "From whom do you suppose this letter is, and what do you think it contains?" I could not imagine. He handed me the letter. It was from a lady, and contained one thousand and fifty dollars and was addressed to him, but the money was for me.

The Father pronounced it a miracle. Said I: "St. Geneviève inspired it." "Well," said he, "I do believe St. Geneviève does take care of you. But this lady cannot afford to give away such a sum, and I will not permit you to accept it unless you give her your note and bind yourself to pay it back." The lady refused to give it to me as a loan. But the Father would not yield, and in accepting the money, he made me give her my note. The graces I received on St. Geneviève's day were an increase of faith, a clearer insight into the truths of faith, and perfect peace of mind, which I have ever since retained.

———

CHAPTER CVII.

I LEARN THAT I AM NOT TO SEEK TO KNOW GOD'S WILL IN EXTRAORDINARY WAYS.

My New Director.

MY health had been failing, owing, as I thought, to the miserable diet that I had lived upon for months. At the request of my director, as it was against the rules to take any person to board at the convent, Mother Jones began to send my meals to me at the cottage. The next time I saw my director, he said to me, "To-morrow you will go to Father Perron to make your confession; Father Perron is a saint, and I believe that it is God's will that he should take my place."

The next day I made my confession to Father Perron. I found Father Perron like an iron hand that raised my soul to God.

He at once put an end to my presumption, and forbade me ever to seek to know God's will in such extraordinary ways as I had made use of. He told me that I should pray humbly and earnestly to know God's will, but that I should not dare TO SUGGEST TO HIM THE MANNER IN WHICH HE SHOULD MAKE IT KNOWN TO ME, but always hold myself before God in humble submission, and that He would not fail to make His will known to me.

If I approached God with presumption He might allow the devil to deceive me, but approaching Him with humility, never.

God had not permitted me to go astray heretofore on account of my good-will, and because I did not know any better, but now that I was more enlightened He would demand a stricter account of my conduct.

I promised the Father that I would follow his counsels, and have fervently prayed that I might ever have the grace to do so.

CHAPTER CVIII.

HUMILITY.—CHARITY.

False views of Humility—A vision of Lilies—Their perfume is Charity.

ALL the extraordinary favours that it pleased God to shower upon me had not made me a whit more humble. In the latter part of February I made a novena to St. Perpetua and St. Felicitas, who were martyrs in the third century. Their feast falls on the 7th of March. On the night of the 5th of March I had a vision. I was lying down several feet beneath my director's feet, who was suspended in the air over me with his hand raised in a triumphal gesture, as though he were glorying over my abasement and his own superiority. My bosom was filled with the most rapturous delight and joy. When I awoke the vision was distinct on my mind, but all those joyful and rapturous sensations had left me; I only retained the memory of them. The 6th of March being the vigil of the Feast of St. Perpetua and St. Felicitas, I was making a most earnest invocation to those two saints, imploring them to obtain for me the grace that I most stood in need of, when the same vision that I had seen in my sleep arose before me, and instantly my whole soul was filled with the most rapturous delight, the same as I had experienced in my sleep.   "O beloved Jesus," I exclaimed, "what new grace is this that thrills my whole being with delight?"   I heard an interior voice reply : "IT IS HUMILITY."   I shouted with rapture, "O beloved Saviour, if this be humility let me ever be humble."

My heart was now overflowing with peace and joy, and I felt that God had nothing more to give me, that my heart could not contain more.   But these thoughts had hardly time to impress themselves upon my mind when an interior voice replied that there was still a greater grace that God had to bestow upon me, and that was CHARITY.

The next morning as soon as I awoke I recollected what my director had said to me, that humility was a virtue that I knew nothing about.   When he said it to me, however, I felt that I knew more about it than he did; but now I was convinced that he was right; and I asked myself what I had always mistaken humility to be, and I smiled as the truth flashed over my mind. I had always believed that *humility and strong nerves were one and the same thing;* that the depth of a man's humility all depended on the state of his nervous system ; that that man could stand the greatest humiliations who was possessed of the strongest nerves.   For in reading the life of St. Ignatius, when I came to that part where the Saint used to try the patience and resignation of the members of the Society by every species of humiliation, which they would bear with the most angelic humour, I would say to myself, "What tremendously strong nerves that monk must have had!"   I had borne all the humiliations that I had gone through since the 18th of March by the force of my will ; for I was sure that God had called me, and I was determined to persevere, and was willing to suffer anything sooner than to yield.   Whenever I would feel inclined to rebel I would instantly check myself by saying : "This will never do; you must not give up, but keep up your nerve."   For I could not believe that there ever existed such a thing as *a love* for humiliation.   But the moment that God in His mercy showered upon me that inestimable gift, I took pleasure in imagining myself trodden upon and despised.

From that day my life at the convent cottage was like a heaven on earth, for everything that had been to me a cause of humiliation and a cross now became to me a source of delight.

My constant prayer now became "Give me, O Lord, the graces I most require, and above all Charity ; and may I ever be faithful to the grace of Humility."   God in His mercy seemed to grant my request.

One night in my sleep I saw myself arranging an altar, on which stood a statue of the Blessed Virgin. I thought that I had erected this statue in honour of the most chaste mother, " MATER CASTISSIMA."

Everything around me breathed calm and peace.

The altar on which the statue stood was placed on a broad, thick platform. I was cleaning, and dusting, and trying to adorn this altar ; but I had no flowers, and I was turning sadly away to leave the chapel, when the chapel door opened of itself, and a hand most radiant and beautiful passed to me four bunches of lilies. They were transparent and of every size, exquisitely arranged, and emitted a soft light and a most delicious odour. I took the flowers, and the moment I touched them my whole being was filled with joy. The door closed noiselessly, and I hastened back to the altar; but instead of placing the lilies on top of the altar I put them on the platform on which the altar stood. The two larger bunches I placed next to the altar, and the lilies gracefully reclined on the columns that supported it. The two smaller ones I placed on the two outer corners of the platform. As I stood there gazing on these flowers my whole being seemed to inhale the delicious odour that they exhaled. I woke, and instantly I raised my heart to God, and exclaimed : " What a sweet dream ! Always give me such dreams !"

In the morning I opened a little book called " The Voice of the Saints," at the following passage : " O my God ! make me know Thee, and make me know myself."

I had no sooner read those words than the altar, the statue, the platform, the radiant hand, the flowers and their exquisite odour, came back to me, and I exclaimed : " O beloved Jesus ! teach me to know Thee and to know myself. Tell me what new grace is this ?" An inward voice answered :—" *It is order.*"

I asked the Lord what the four bunches of flowers meant. An interior voice replied : " The first bunch was Purity, the second Diligence, the third Simplicity, and the fourth Modesty." " But," I continued, " why did I not place them on the altar instead of the platform ?"

The answer was : " Because those virtues should repose on Humility. The altar is your heart, and the statue that adorned it is Chastity; but your heart to keep chastity must rest on humility, which was the broad, thick platform."

" But," I replied, when these thoughts passed through my mind as though God Himself was speaking to me, " I thought that purity and chastity were the same thing."

The answer was: " You need purity of intention. Purity and diligence, which were the two larger bunches, you placed nearest to your heart, and simplicity and modesty you placed on the two outer corners of the platform, for they should be the most apparent virtues of every chaste and humble soul."

Yet I was not satisfied, and I said, complainingly to our Lord: " But still Thou refusest me that which my heart most longs for. Why dost Thou still refuse me *Charity?* I ask not for those other graces, all I ask for is Charity."

Distinctly then the voice replied: " *The perfume of these virtues is Charity; when you become perfectly humble, chaste, pure, diligent, simple, and modest, then you will have charity. But to ask me for charity without wishing to cultivate those virtues is like asking for a victory without desiring to combat in order to win it.*"

CHAPTER CIX.

CONCLUSION.

WHEN God, in answer to our prayers, grants us such special and sensible graces, they are frequently but the precursors of some new and severe trial, as if He would immediately put our sincerity to the test, and give us an opportunity of making use of those graces which we have so long and ardently besought Him to grant us.

In the spring of 1877 I returned with my daughter to my home among those hills that I loved in my childhood. I found Betsy Dot still playing at her loom. Aunt Huldah was still the pet of her heirs, although she was teaching them patience and resignation. It promised to be a pretty long lesson. Aunt Mercy had died, and her remains lie beside those of my uncle Horace down in the valley.

I was devoting the greater part of my time to the education of my daughter.

We had our allotted hours for study, work, recreation, and prayer.

When the time for recreation came we would climb the steepest hills and scramble through the netted brakes, gathering ferns and wild flowers to decorate St. Geneviève's altar.

The same thoughts would simultaneously arise in our hearts, and we would frequently exclaim, " How sweet it is to be here alone with God !" Every shrub and every hillside breathed to

us His holy name and spoke to us of His goodness. We never
passed the little pond on whose surface we saw reflected St.
Geneviève's chapel, but its tiny waves would seem to whisper to
us, "God is a good Father." At sunset, when we strolled by
the road-side, and listened to the singing birds and the chirping
insects, it was as though all nature joined our hearts in offering
up a hymn of praise to the Creator.

One Sunday we had spent the early hours of morn in the little
chapel, the rest of the day we had passed in the cottage. It
seemed as though we had never appreciated and loved our
mountain home so much before. The very prospect from its
windows was like some enchanted tableau. Our library was
filled with the choicest books, our *salons* with the finest instruments of music, and the whole house was furnished with rare
paintings and articles of *virtu*, precious *souvenirs* many of them
from friends abroad.

My child uncovered the harp, and begged me to play for her
the airs I used to play in France, While my fingers were passing
over the strings I saw a tear roll down her cheek. I instantly
arose, and, kissing the tear away, said to her, "As it makes you
sad, sweet child, I will not play." "No, mamma," she replied,
play on," I am not sad, yet I could not restrain my tears; it
never makes me sad to think of France, because I am happier
here with you." I covered the harp, little thinking that my
fingers were never to draw music from its chords again.

I began to confide in my little daughter, and told her that
I thought I had a vocation to take care of the sick. We
then began to while away the time passing from room to room,
little suspecting that we were taking our last look and bidding
them all a final farewell ! My child began prattling of how
comfortable this or that piece of furniture would be for the sick;
and we began calculating how many sick people the cottage
would accommodate. I had raised it a storey and had added to
it several wings.

Father Bapst once remarked that my home was not intended
for a private house, but that it would make a charming little
convent.

In the evening we promenaded the piazza while gazing on a
most brilliant sunset. After the last shadows of the day had
departed we repaired to a little oratory we had fitted up in our
home to Our Lady of Perpetual Succour. There we said our
evening prayers and were about to retire, when I said to my
child: "Let us kneel again and say our prayers aloud." We
then recommenced our prayers. At the end an impromptu one

came to my lips, which I recited aloud and which my child repeated after me. We then embraced and immediately retired.

I soon fell asleep. At midnight I was awakened by a sense of suffocation from smoke, and the crackling of flames. I sprang to my feet and flew to a door which opened on a verandah. Never can I forget the terrific scene that met my gaze! The trees, rose-bushes, shrubs, and grass in front of my cottage door were on fire, which was leaping and dancing with a sort of savage glee around the cottage.

I rushed to rescue my child, whom I caught in my arms. She was so bewildered that it was several moments before I could make her understand that the house was on fire. I led her down-stairs to the front door and she swiftly made her way in her bare feet and night-dress over the burning grass to give the alarm to our nearest neighbour, who lived over the hill on the other side of the pond. I then tried to save the sacred vessels and the vestments of my church, which for safer keeping I had kept in the house, but I was driven back by the flames. I seized my harp and dragged it to the front door, in trying to open which the knob came off in my hand and dropped on the floor.

My strength then began to fail me, but I managed to drag the harp back again through the corridor into the dining-room; I threw it out of the door and it dropped near the well. Instantly the burning branch of a spruce tree fell upon it and it was consumed before my eyes.

My thought now was to save myself. I enveloped my head in a table cover, and through a back staircase I escaped. The wind, which was blowing from the north, drove the flames quite away from the direction of the Church. I climbed the hill, and kneeling beside the chapel door began calling for my child, that she might know where I was, as it was time for her to return. But I received no answer save the echo of my own words.

I then began to pray. I had no sooner raised my heart to God than my soul was filled with peace and hope, and I felt the futility of placing my heart on baubles which could, in the twinkling of an eye, be thus rudely snatched away. A myriad of consoling thoughts then rushed through my brain. I felt that God did not wish me to begin a work for Him with those luxuries of the past; that He was a jealous God; that it was His will to deprive me of those reminiscences of unhallowed days; and that my heart could never be entirely His until my idols had vanished with them. I said to Him: "Take them all, dearest Lord, but give me Thyself in return." It was more than half-an-hour before the neighbours came. It was then too late to save anything in the house; they could only prevent the flames extending to the fences and spreading over the farm.

When they joined me on the hill they expected to find me weeping and in despair; for they knew that twenty thousand dollars would not cover my loss, and that I was not insured. But I did not shed a tear. I was perfectly resigned. The first thing I inquired for was my child. I was told by a bystander that one of her feet had been slightly burned, and that his wife was attending to her and would not let her come; but I begged them to go and bring her. She soon came, wrapped in a large shawl, and on her feet a pair of women's shoes.

The instant she beheld me she sprang into my arms, and we both began to laugh, for we recollected the castles in the air we had been building for the sick but a few hours before. I was so rejoiced to press her again to my heart that I could not speak! But my child exclaimed: "Who cares for the house and all it contains? You are saved, mamma! I prayed our Lord to protect you, and that He might take all the rest."

The people that surrounded us were amazed, and one old woman sobbed out: "What's the use of crying for them? Why they don't care any more about it than if it were a stack of hay!" A man brought me a statue of St. Joseph; he had burnt his shoes and his fingers in trying to save it. The statue was slightly scorched. I took it in my arms, kissed it and exclaimed: "St. Joseph is the patron of my house." "Well," replied the man, sucking his burnt fingers and drawling out his words, "He didn't take very good care of it, and, if I were you, I would give him away." "The house was not good enough for him," my child answered; "he requires a better one, and may give it to us some day." They all laughed derisively at her words, and simultaneously exclaimed: "Ha! for *that* we'll have to wait many a long day." "But," she retorted, "not so long, perhaps, as you may think!"

The cause of the fire is unknown.

Forty miles from the ruins of our mountain home is a lovely valley, interspersed with rippling streams; around it azured peaks rise dimly in the horizon's verge. In its midst is a charming little convent belonging to the ladies of the congregation of Notre Dame. Shortly after my house was burned, these good religious gave my child a home, and she is with them now. I can scarcely trust myself to speak of all they have done for her. They have spared no pains in endeavouring to endow her with all that the most careful training and the most competent instruction could possess her of. I once heard my daughter say : " What a blessing it was, mamma, that the house did burn, otherwise we might never have known the ladies of the congregation of Notre Dame."

The burning of my house has, I hope, proved to me a blessing in many ways. It has taught me many a valuable lesson. Amongst others how comparatively easy it is to suffer humiliations when we are sustained by sensible grace, by the sympathy of friends, and by their succours ; but if God withdraws His grace, and we are bereft of human sympathy and material aid, then it is that we begin to find out how far we are from that entire *self*-renunciation, and complete abandonment to the will of God, without which the " *Thy will be done* " of the "*Our Father* " is only a lip prayer. The cross with Jesus' loving arm of consolation encircling us is ever pleasant to bear. But alone ! with no other support or encouragement than faith supplies ! no sign of Jesus near us ! it is then we begin to find whether we have any true humility !

But I never cease to pray that I may ever be faithful to the lights and graces that God our Father in His mercy has deigned to bestow upon me ; and to Him with childlike confidence I commit my future life, and all that concerns me for time and for eternity.

And you, dear reader, who have followed me through my wanderings, and communed with my thoughts ; you, for whom I have, not without many a pang, laid bare and dissected my heart, fail not to profit by such light as even from these pages may have been reflected upon your mind by the " Father of Lights," and join me in begging His mercy on me and on yourself.

And now, O God, my Father, do Thou make me and mine entirely Thine. And when the hour will come for me to render back this life to Thee, who gavest it, may I, unworthy as I have been, be worthy of being received by Thee into heaven as a child of Mary and a spouse of Jesus.

www.ingramcontent.com/pod-product-compliance
Lightning Source LLC
Chambersburg PA
CBHW050902130726
47900CB00015B/1705